BODYGUARD OF DECEPTION

A NOVEL OF SUSPENSE

VOLUME ONE OF THE WORLD WAR TWO TRILOGY

FOREWORD
OSS WARTIME RECORDS DECLASSIFIED

On May 2, 2015, precisely seventy years after the Battle of Berlin and German surrender during World War Two, secret documents of the United States Office of Strategic Services, the wartime spy agency and precursor to the Central Intelligence Agency, were quietly released in Washington, DC. The subject matter of the declassified U.S. military and intelligence records, as well as the accompanying previously classified British Enigma intercept documents, was a German espionage operation referred to by the OSS as Operation Cheyenne. The previously unavailable records were filed under OSS Record Group 228, Entries 1 through 88, Records of the Office of Strategic Services, Office of the Director, Microfilm Publication 1642, Reel 108, Templeton, Capt. K. (OSS), von Walburg, Maj. E. (Wehr.) and Comm. W. (Krieg. U-521), and MacGregor, Col. T. (MI5) to Donovan, Gen. W.J. (OSS), 12-14 June 1944, Operation Cheyenne-Double Cross Case Materials. The declassified files in RG 228 had been previously archived under "Source OC-XX-MAY-JUNE1944 Previously Withdrawn Material" in the "Director's Office Microfilm Files" of OSS Director William J. Donovan. The files covering Operation Cheyenne describe in minute detail the espionage activities and pursuit of a German spy and his U-boat-commander brother in their efforts to warn Hitler's High Command about the Allies' greatest military secret, a secret that, if disclosed, could have won the war for Germany in the spring of 1944. This book, *Bodyguard of Deception*, is the story of Operation Cheyenne precisely as it happened during the Second World War and has been concealed for the past seventy years by the U.S. and British governments. In reviewing the declassified documents, I didn't believe the story at first; it seemed too wild and fantastic to be true. But now that I know why it was covered up, and by whom, I know how wrong I was in my initial assessment. This book is the story of what really happened between May 24 and June 6, 1944 when the entire world was at war and Allied victory hung in the balance.
—Samuel Marquis, March 14, 2016

Praise for Bodyguard of Deception

"*Bodyguard of Deception* grabbed my attention right from the beginning and never let go. The character development is excellent. Samuel Marquis has a knack for using historic details and events to create captivating and fun to read tales."
—Roy R. Romer, 39th Governor of Colorado

"Readers looking for an unapologetic historical action book should tear through this volume."
—Kirkus Reviews

"As usual, Marquis's descriptions are vivid, believable, and true to the time period...*Bodyguard of Deception* is an intriguing launch to his new trilogy. Warmly recommended."
—Dr. Wesley Britton, Bookpleasures.com (Crime & Mystery)

"Old-time spy buffs will appreciate the tradecraft and attention to detail, while adventure enthusiasts will enjoy the unique perspective and setting for a WWII story. A combination of *The Great Escape*, *Public Enemies*, a genuine old-time Western, and a John Le Carré novel."
—Blueink Review

"The world hangs in a delicate balance in the heart-pounding *World War Two Trilogy* opener, *Bodyguard of Deception* by Samuel Marquis. Put together with an intricate plot to follow and a commitment to realistic detail, there's a lot going for the read...a wonderfully nail-biting experience with good characters and solid intrigue."
— SP Review – Four-Star Review

"A fast-paced, riveting WWII espionage thriller. *Bodyguard of Deception* is as good as the best of Daniel Silva, Ken Follett, Alan Furst, and David Baldacci and brings back fond memories of the classic movie *The Great Escape* and Silva's finest novel, *The Unlikely Spy*."
—Fred Taylor, President/Co-Founder Northstar Investment Advisors and Espionage Novel Aficionado

"*Bodyguard of Deception* is a unique and ambitious spy thriller complete with historical figures, exciting action, and a dastardly villain. Fans of prison-break plots will enjoy this story of a loyal German struggling to save his homeland."
—Foreword Reviews

Praise for Samuel Marquis

#1 *Denver Post* Bestselling Author
Foreword Reviews' Book of the Year Winner (HM)
Beverly Hills Books Awards Winner
and Award-Winning Finalist
Next Generation Indie Book Awards Winner
and Award-Winning Finalist
USA Best Book Award-Winning Finalist

"*The Coalition* has a lot of good action and suspense, an unusual female assassin, and the potential to be another *The Day After Tomorrow* [the runaway bestseller by Allan Folsom]."
—James Patterson, #1 *New York Times* Bestselling Author

"In his novels *Blind Thrust* and *Cluster of Lies*, Samuel Marquis vividly combines the excitement of the best modern techno-thrillers, an education in geology, and a clarifying reminder that the choices each of us make have a profound impact on our precious planet."
—Ambassador Marc Grossman, Former U.S. Under Secretary of State

"*Blind Thrust* kept me up until 1 a.m. two nights in a row. I could not put it down. An intriguing mystery that intertwined geology, fracking, and places in Colorado that I know well. Great fun."
—Roy R. Romer, 39th Governor of Colorado

"This ambitious thriller starts with a bang, revs up its engines, and never stops until the explosive ending…Perfect for fans of James Patterson, David Baldacci, and Vince Flynn, *The Coalition* is a standout thriller from an up-and-coming writer."
—Foreword Reviews Four-Star Review

"An entertaining thriller about a ruthless political assassination...Marquis has woven a tight plot with genuine suspense."
—Kirkus Reviews (for *The Coalition*)

"This high-energy, rollicking misadventure will change the way you look at the publishing industry forever. The plot is unpredictable…twists and turns and counterturns abound. So, too, does the humor…The dialogue is superb…Marquis laid the groundwork as a thriller writer with *The Slush Pile Brigade* and hopefully his following novels build up a James Patterson-esque empire."
—Foreword Reviews – Five-Star Review

"With *Blind Thrust*, *Cluster of Lies*, and his other works, Samuel Marquis has written true breakout novels that compare favorably with—and even exceed—recent thrillers on the New York Times Bestseller List. [He is] constantly tightening plot, character, and upping the stakes and tension to make sure that they are genuinely great stories."
—Pat LoBrutto, Former Editor for Stephen King and Eric Van Lustbader (Bourne Series)

"*The Coalition* by Samuel Marquis is a riveting novel by an uncommonly gifted writer. This is the stuff from which blockbuster movies are made! Very highly recommended."
—Midwest Book Review - The Mystery/Suspense Shelf

"The science of earthquakes is truly fascinating, and Marquis has captured this science and packaged it into a really fine thriller 'against the clock' style for almost anyone to pick up and enjoy, and readers will no doubt want more from Higheagle and his intrepid grandfather once they have devoured this installment."
—SP Review – Four-Star Review (for *Blind Thrust*)

"*Cluster of Lies* has a twisty plot that grabs hold from the beginning and never lets go. A true page turner! I'm already looking forward to the next Joe Higheagle adventure."
—Robert Bailey, Author of *The Professor* and *Between Black and White*

"Reminiscent of *The Day of the Jackal*…with a high level of authentic detail. Skyler is a convincing sniper, and also a nicely conflicted one."
—Donald Maass, Author of *Writing 21st Century Fiction* (for *The Coalition*)

"*The Slush Pile Brigade*, by Samuel Marquis, is a hilarious and exciting read filled with one crazy turn after another…The author slams on the accelerator early in the story and doesn't let up, forcing the reader to flip the pages frantically. And once it's over, it's still hard to catch one's breath."
—SP Review - 4.5-Star Review

"In *Cluster of Lies*, Samuel Marquis touches all the bases. He starts with a murder and the action doesn't let up until the very last page in this compelling environmental thriller that is often uncomfortably realistic."
—Charles Salzberg, Author of *The Henry Swann Detective Series*

"*Blind Thrust* makes good use of Marquis' background as a professional geologist. It is the novel's characters, however, that really stand out. For suspense fans who enjoy science mixed with their thrills, the novel offers page-turning pleasures."
—BlueInk Review

By Samuel Marquis

THE SLUSH PILE BRIGADE

BLIND THRUST

THE COALITION

BODYGUARD OF DECEPTION

CLUSTER OF LIES

BODYGUARD OF DECEPTION

A NOVEL OF SUSPENSE

VOLUME ONE OF THE WORLD WAR TWO TRILOGY

SAMUEL MARQUIS

MOUNT SOPRIS PUBLISHING

BODYGUARD OF DECEPTION

VOLUME ONE OF THE WORLD WAR TWO TRILOGY

MOUNT SOPRIS PUBLISHING
Trade paper: ISBN 978-1-943593-12-5
Kindle: ISBN 978-1-943593-13-2
ePub: ISBN 978-1-943593-14-9
PDF: ISBN 978-1-943593-15-6

Third Mount Sopris Publishing premium printing: October 2016
Formatting: Rik Hall (www.WildSeasFormatting.com)
Printed in the United States of America

To Order Samuel Marquis Books and Contact Samuel:

Visit Samuel Marquis's website, join his mailing list, learn about his forthcoming novels and book events, and order his books at www.samuelmarquisbooks.com. Please send fan mail to samuelmarquisbooks@gmail.com. Thank you for your support!

ATTENTION: ORGANIZATIONS AND CORPORATIONS
Mount Sopris Publishing books may be purchased for educational, business, or sales promotional use. For information, please email the Special Markets Department at samuelmarquisbooks@gmail.com.

Dedication

For the Allied heroes of World War II—and the many "Decent German" military and political figures like Admiral Wilhelm Canaris, Colonel Claus von Stauffenberg, and lawyer Josef Müller who actively resisted Hitler.

Bodyguard of Deception

VOLUME ONE OF THE WORLD WAR TWO TRILOGY

In wartime, truth is so precious that she should always be attended by a bodyguard of lies.

—Winston Churchill, Tehran Conference, November 1943

Fascism in general and Nazism—the German variety—in particular were viewed by the American people as a blur of swastikas, marching Prussian robots, violent racism, strutting leaders, brown-shirted hooligans, and a veritable sea of hysterical followers...Nazism appeared simply a monstrous and evil political philosophy, the new religion of an apparently incorrigible German Nation. Above all, to Americans it was a philosophy of aggressive militarism...With Nazism and militarism thus interchangeable, the War Department, as well as the American public at large, saw the incoming thousands of German prisoners of war as representative of the detested enemy philosophy of world enslavement. But the assumption that every German soldier was an obdurate Nazi was far from accurate.

—Arnold Krammer, *Nazi Prisoners of War in America*

God, I hate the Germans.

—General Dwight D. Eisenhower, German-American, Supreme Commander of D-Day and Allied Forces in Europe

D-Day stands today as a monumental victory and, with hindsight, historically inevitable. It did not look that way in [1944]...If Hitler had correctly anticipated the site of the D-Day invasion, then the war might have been extended for an additional year, or two, or more, with an incalculable cost in bloodshed and misery. The stakes could not have been higher or the margin for error smaller.

—Ben Macintyre, *Double Cross: The True Story of the D-Day Spies*

DAY 1

WEDNESDAY

MAY 24, 1944

CHAPTER 1

NORTH SEA OFF STONEHAVEN FISHING VILLAGE NORTHEAST COAST OF SCOTLAND

THE U-BOAT signaled three times across the fat, rolling swells of the North Sea. Four miles off the Aberdeenshire coast, rowing a stolen skiff that was battered but seaworthy, Major Erik von Walburg saw the flickering illumination as nothing more than a twinkle against the soot-colored dawn. But for the German that was enough. He immediately set down his oars and began digging through his dry bag for his flashlight to deliver the designated signal.

The sight of the friendly vessel made him feel a great unburdening in his chest. For four months now, in London, he had been living a lie—he had been trained at the esteemed Agent School West in The Hague and it was his job to lie and lie well—but now, finally, thankfully, his double life would come to an end and his country would bear the fruits of his clandestine activities.

He held the secret that would drastically alter—and quite possibly win—the war for his beloved Fatherland.

All that remained was to row the skiff a few hundred yards more, board the awaiting U-boat, and give her five minutes to engage her diesel engines, slip noiselessly below the surface, and steal away like a stealthy shark from the prowling Allied gunships and aircraft bristling to send her to the bottom of the North Sea. Once the U-boat leveled off to snorkel depth, it would transport him south to the Lorient base south of the Cherbourg peninsula. From there, he would be driven north to Chateau La Roche Guyon and report to his father the general and his father's superior officer and mentor, *Generalfeldmarschall* Erwin Rommel. It was here, in a picturesque French chateau built in the 12th century, forty miles north of Paris alongside the Seine River, where Rommel had set up his Army Group B headquarters to counter the much-anticipated Allied invasion of Fortress Europe.

In one fell swoop, Erik would change the outcome of the war.

He flashed his light at the U-boat. Receiving the prearranged response signal, he picked up his splintery oars again and began rowing hard as the torpedo-shaped craft continued to hold at the five-mile offshore marker.

Though he was on the verge of collapse from being hounded by the Tommies for three days running with no sleep, he dipped and stroked his way through the choppy waves like a demon possessed, coaxing the flimsy skiff with the shredded mainsail forward by sheer will alone. Within minutes, there was sufficient daylight and he was close enough to make out the forward deck gun and conning tower of the German Type VII-C attack submarine, as well as the reassuring inscription "U-521" painted in big bold letters. The sleek vessel sat low in the water, rolling gently in the groundswell against a violent backdrop of purple storm clouds, whitecaps, and a flock of soaring seagulls.

He rowed on with the rainy breeze pelting the back of his neck, hard against the prow. Out of long habit, he periodically scanned the shore and overhead, searching both sea and sky for signs of the pursuing enemy. Like a nervous gunfighter in the American dime novels he had enjoyed growing up, he had a nagging fear of being caught and forcibly returned to London: there to be interrogated by MI5, tortured, and hung as a spy. But thankfully, there was no sign of a patrolling enemy corvette or spotter aircraft.

Slowly but steadily, the bobbing U-boat grew bigger and bigger on the horizon, like a mirage becoming real before his eyes. Shivering away the cold, biting North Sea wind, he picked up his pace and really put his shoulders into it. But to his dismay, the seawater felt heavier with each successive stroke. The pushing-and-pulling motion sent shockwaves of agony through his robust, twenty-six-year-old frame that, after four years of war, felt considerably older. He longed to feel the sturdiness of dry land beneath his feet, or at least the solid floor and safety of a German naval vessel. He tried to forget the pain of his despoiled body and thrust the oars mechanically, without thinking, but his limbs felt so damned heavy. They were almost unresponsive to his mind.

And yet, he was so close now, he could almost taste it.

Summoning his last reserve of energy, he gritted his teeth and dug in for the final push. Overhead, a pair of seagulls hung virtually motionless in the stiff wind as speckles of sunlight broke through the cumulous cloud cover. He was fueled by not only a fear of being hunted and a grudging respect for his Allied enemy, but by the sheer magnitude of what he stood poised to reveal to his father and Rommel, who had appealed to his patriotism and cajoled him into his insanely daunting, yet soon-to-be sublimely successful, intelligence mission in the first place.

With a coughing spurt, the U-boat's diesel engines engaged and the vessel nudged its way towards him. The captain must have sensed he was struggling during the closing stretch and ordered his first watch officer to engage the diesels at quarter speed. When he was within hailing distance, a party of seamen decked in *arbeitspäckchen*—working U-boat crew suits of seaman's jumpers, grey-brown denim battle-dress uniforms modified from British uniform stocks abandoned at Dunkirk, and heavy water-resistant oilskins—flittered down from the bridge onto the U-boat's aft deck and threw him a line.

His heart lifted.

He really *was* going to make it out of England with his momentous secret intact! By what strange alchemy, by what higher power, had he been granted the opportunity to save Germany from certain defeat? By what twist of fate would he now be able to ensure that true patriots like his father and the Desert Fox could rescue the Fatherland from the maniac Führer who was destroying the country and its people for his demented Thousand Year Reich? The intelligence that he, at this very moment, carried in his head and had tucked away in his anal cavity would drive the Allied invaders from all of Greater Germany and provide the framework for a negotiated peace on favorable terms, without the intrusion of Hitler and his Nazi stooges. He felt a great upwelling of emotion, a sense of clarity and purpose. All of his hard work, all of his dreams for the future of his country, were about to be realized.

He would save Germany from Hitler.

And all he had to do was get to his father and General Rommel.

CHAPTER 2

NORTH SEA ABOARD U-521

WITH RENEWED ENERGY, he let go of the oars, clasped the line, and pulled himself hand over hand toward the steel nose of the U-boat. One of the seamen latched onto the skiff with a grappling hook and pulled it alongside the vessel. As the line was tied off, Erik stood up unsteadily on his cold, stiff sea legs. Two pairs of sturdy hands reached down to him. Taking them, he was hauled up on the wet steel deck.

"Welcome aboard U-521," said a crusty old tar, a *Kriegsmariner* in a rain-slicked sou'wester, a petty officer. "I hope you like the taste of stale bread and the overpowering smell of rancid farts and diesel."

For a moment, Erik was too frigid, exhausted, and overcome with emotion to even crack a smile let alone speak. Then, shivering, he responded: "*Danke vielmals.*" Many thanks.

"Don't mention it. Come now, Herr Spymaster, we must hurry and get you below deck before you turn into an icicle."

The youthful seamen all gave a hearty laugh through thick tangles of beard and chapped lips before leading him along the walkway of the long, narrow deck of the VII-C. They stepped past the heavy steel cable of the net guard slanting towards the conning tower, over a closed galley hatch and torpedo supply hatch, past the main deck gun, fielding a lethal 8.8-centimeter cannon, and finally to the edge of the bridge with its horseshoe-shaped wind deflector. Here he paused to gawk up at the radio direction finder aerial, gleaming sky observation periscope, and taller attack periscope sprouting up from the conning tower. On the other side of the tower stood the gun platform, and here he feasted his eyes on the two pairs of squat, menacing anti-aircraft guns pointing to stern.

The Type VII-C was the workhorse of the German U-boat force and the most lethal fighting machine of the North Sea theatre of operations. Propelled by two supercharged *Germaniawerft* 6-cylinder, 4-stroke diesels totaling 3,000 horsepower, it was known for its quick diving ability and mobility. But life on a U-boat was a dangerous one, as German *Kriegsmariners* were under constant threat from Allied aircraft, warships, submarines, and sea mines.

From the bridge, a familiar commanding voice suddenly caught him by surprise.

"*Brother*, what the hell are *you* doing on *my* boat?"

He squinted up at a heavily bearded man wearing a distinctive white cap and battered oilskin. It was the captain and he was glaring down at him fiercely.

Wait a second! Did he just call me Brother*?*

He looked closer at the man.

Fucking hell, it can't be him!

But there was no doubt about it as he took a closer look: it was his older brother Wolfgang all right, and the son of a bitch was still the same exquisite specimen of Aryan perfection. Tall, blond, blue-eyed, broad-shouldered, ramrod-straight, he radiated supreme confidence and authority. Erik wanted to say something, but his lips refused to move. How long had it been? Three years? Four? April of '40 so over four years.

My God, that long?

"What's the matter, aren't you happy to see your *own* goddamned brother?"

He felt the eyes of the other *Kriegsmariners* heavily upon him. Ignoring them, he stared intently at his bellicose older sibling, wondering what unfortunate fate had brought him aboard U-521. Suddenly, all of the buried resentment of being ridiculed and bullied, both physically and psychologically, by his older and stronger brother came rushing back to him in a gushing torrent.

"With the beard I didn't…I didn't recognize you, Brother," he spluttered. "Of course, I am glad to see you. It has been far too long."

"Aboard my boat you will address me as *Kapitän zur See*."

He gulped hard and took an invisible deep breath, summoning his courage and recovering his composure. "Very well, captain it is," he fired back, silently vowing to himself never again to be bullied by his older brother as he had when they were teenagers in Berlin. "Or would you prefer I call you 'the scourge of the North Sea' as does Herr Churchill?"

His brother gave a bloodless smile. "That moniker is reserved for that fat cigar-smoker and his enemy Parliament. It is not for you to bandy about, *Brüderlein*—Little Brother."

"It's good to see you haven't changed. You still strike mortal fear in your enemies."

"Are you referring to yourself by chance?"

"Why would I be speaking of myself? You and I are brothers, and blood is thicker than water."

"So it has been said. But do you truly believe it?"

"Of course I do. I put up with your incessant bullying all those years, didn't I?"

"You two are really brothers?" gulped the first watch officer in disbelief.

His brother smiled thinly. "If by that you mean Major von Walburg and I shared the same mother and father over a decade ago, then the answer is yes. But that was a lifetime ago."

"Well, lifetime ago or not, the prodigal brother hath returned," said Erik with a challenging grin, which he punctuated with a smart salute that carried a whiff of insubordination.

But to his surprise, his brother, rather than showing anger, looked vaguely amused. "I can see you haven't changed, either. You're still a pretty Harvard boy and wise ass. Now get your tail up here on the double before we are spotted by a Spitfire."

With help from a crewman, he climbed up the steel ladder to the bridge where he came face to face with his lifelong nemesis. Tall and erect as a Black Forest pine, his older brother had always been a natural leader. But what Erik remembered most about him was his utter fearlessness, meticulous attention to detail, and furiously competitive nature. It was this rare combination of traits that had ensured, at an early age, Wolfgang von Walburg, first born son of a Prussian count, would rise to the top of whatever profession he chose. Looking at him up close, Erik recalled how much he had once idolized his big brother. Then he remembered the terrifying change, the abrupt transformation that had led to the dark years. Shortly after his fourteenth birthday, when Wolfgang was sixteen, his brother had joined the Hitler Youth and turned into an ardent Nazi and brutal brownshirted thug. Over the next three years, the two brothers grew to hate one another and the entire family had been torn apart over their fierce rivalry. Unfortunately, that was how things had been left between them.

He saluted again, this time in earnest. "Thank you for plucking me from the North Sea, Captain *and* Brother. But I must confess my surprise that you are the U-boat commander assigned for the rendezvous."

"And I am equally surprised to see you. I didn't know you were a spy. The last I had heard, you were on Rommel's staff with Father."

"I was reassigned several months ago. And now I carry vital information for the war effort."

"I know you do. That's why we are *both* here."

"Per my orders from General Rommel, I am to be delivered to the Lorient U-boat base and then be driven straight away to Army Group B Headquarters at Chateau La Roche Guyon."

"I am aware of your orders. But you are on my boat and, therefore, I expect a full briefing once you have had a chance to dry off and put on your uniform. Your cover is as my staff medical officer. But of course, I don't expect to be caught by the goddamned Tommies."

"No one ever does. But those British bastards are out there, and caution is, as they say, the better part of valor."

"It would appear that my German brother has transformed into a British Poet Laureate. What are you Lord Fucking Tennyson? All right, you'd better get your half-frozen ass below. I have arranged a bunk for you with all the necessary clothing for your cover."

Erik saluted and started for the hatch, but was brought up short as his brother grabbed him firmly by the arm.

There was a gleam in his eye. "You have surprised me, *Brüderlein.* I would never have thought you capable of being a spy."

"That makes two of us. Father had to actually talk me into it."

"The old man can be very persuasive. But still, you *have* surprised me." The gleam lingered a moment longer before his brother turned away abruptly and snapped out an order to the first watch officer and other seamen. "Clear upper deck to dive!"

"*Jawohl, Kapitän!*"

A series of crisp orders, ringing bells, and coordinated maneuvers swiftly followed: the aft diesels were stopped and disengaged, the air and exhaust vents closed, and the entire group disappeared from the bridge, the last man, the watch officer yelling down "Upper deck cleared for diving!" and cranking shut the hand wheel sealing the conning tower hatch home in its bed.

Once below, Erik watched as his brother barked a series of commands over the crackling loudspeakers of the public address system. In response, the officers and crew frantically yet systematically punched buttons, pulled levers, and checked dials. When the necessary preparations were complete, his brother shouted out, "Prepare to dive! Snorkel depth!"

The U-boat nosed down at a slight angle until, eventually, a last foamy wave broke against the partially submerged bridge and the vessel disappeared just beneath the rippled surface of the North Sea, heading southeast towards the French coast.

When the U-boat leveled off to snorkel depth with the periscope protruding slightly above the surface—the shallow depth allowed the U-boat to move at a faster clip and recharge the batteries to drive the electric motors—the two brothers looked at one another. Everyone else in the control room was holding their breath, watching them with great anticipation.

"Lieutenant Hoffman will show you to your bunk. We will talk in five minutes. Then you will brief me in full on your merry adventures in the land of that corpulent toad Herr Churchill."

He felt himself twinge inside. "I am sorry, Brother, but I am to report only to General Rommel. Those are my orders."

"I have my orders, too. That's why you will tell me *everything*."

"I don't…I don't think that will be possible."

"Oh, yes it will, *Brüderlein*. You are going to tell me all of the Allies' dirty little secrets."

"And if I refuse?"

His brother smiled belligerently. "Then I will launch you through a fucking torpedo tube."

CHAPTER 3

NORTH SEA ABOARD U-521

ERIK'S BRAIN WORKED FEVERISHLY as he was escorted by the lieutenant down the narrow passageway towards the petty officers' quarters. How in the world was he going to fight off his fanatical brother and not give up any information? His orders from Father and General Rommel were clear: he must not divulge either the purpose or findings of his top secret mission, not even to his own comrades-in-arms in the *Wehrmacht*, under any circumstances. And that definitely included his goddamned brother!

As he and Hoffman worked their way through the claustrophobic passageway, they were forced to make themselves small and push and shove their way past seamen scrambling to quarters. Every available nook and cranny was being used to store something: boxes of hand tools, crates of provisions, spare leather clothing, sweaters, oilskin jackets, rescue gear, teapots, sacks of potatoes, chests of spare parts, bulging hammocks filled with loaves of dark bread swinging back and forth like pendulums. Again, he couldn't help but wonder what horrendous fate had brought him to the one *Untersee-boot* captained by his brother, whom he detested more than any other human being on the planet. Could his luck have been any worse?

But at least it was logical. His brother Wolfgang was the top U-boat commander in the North Sea, the Führer himself having awarded him the esteemed Knight's Cross of the Iron Cross with Oak Leaves and Swords. It had been broadcast all over the airwaves by Goebbels himself, and celebrated in Berlin with much fanfare, this past winter. Thinking it through, Erik realized that he shouldn't be surprised. The German High Command would not have selected any old commander to pick him up from the Scottish coast when he possessed military secrets vital to the Reich.

But still, he couldn't help but feel as if he had been singled out for cruel and unusual punishment. Was it God, or perhaps fate, or how about just plain bad luck?

Reaching the U-room, Lieutenant Hoffman pointed him to his bunk. He saw that the uniform of a *marineoberstabsarzt*—staff medical officer—had been laid out on the bunk for him alongside a pair of heavy wool socks, a fur-lined jerkin, a heavy oilskin, and a brown sailcloth bag filled with rescue gear. On the floor next to the bunk lay a pair of heavy U-boat boots with thick cork soles, and resting on the bunk was an official *Kriegsmarine* Medical Advice Manual for U-boat Service, dated May 1944. That was his brother all right: everything had been prepared with Teutonic thoroughness for the new arrival.

"You will bunk here," said Hoffman, ignoring the sleeping seaman snoring in the third bunk, the only other person in the compartment. "And you will mess in the forward wardroom, the officers' mess. There's a working head up there. The other is filled with food stores."

"*Danke, Leutnant,*" he said, but all he felt inside was the oppressive constrictiveness of the confined space and uneasiness over his damned brother. How much time did he have?

"Is everything in order then, Major?"

"Allow me a moment to check."

Momentarily pushing aside his worry, he picked up and examined the Navy blue medical officer's jacket. It contained three gold sleeve stripes and the *Äskulapzeichen* symbol worn by German military physicians, the Rod of Asclepius entwined by a snake stick representing the art of healing and practice of medicine. From his pocket, he removed his *Soldbuch*—the official pocket-sized booklet carried by every enlisted man and officer in the German navy, infantry, and air force—and checked the photograph of himself in uniform on the inside cover against the uniform laid out on the bunk. The Germany Military *Soldbuch* was a condensed personnel file with data such as birth date, height, weight, parental information, vaccinations, eye examinations, but also information about military training, units, transfers, duties, and promotions. The uniform on the bunk and the one in the picture matched perfectly. But there was a catch. Instead of his own name on the inside cover of the booklet, along with his photograph, there was a fake name and signature: Staff Medical Officer Manfred Otto Weiss of Bremen.

Satisfied, he snapped shut his *Kriegsmarine Soldbuch.* "Everything appears to be in order, Lieutenant. My compliments."

"And now, if I may offer a bit of advice."

This was a surprise. "Advice?"

"A word of caution with regard to the *kapitän.*"

"Of course."

"He expects his orders to be obeyed without question."

He smiled indulgently. "That I already know. After all, I grew up with him."

"Your brother is a great sea captain. A finer commander no man could serve under."

"I'm sure that is true too. I can tell that you and the rest of the crew admire him greatly—and are also scared to death of him."

"He has that effect on people, but his record speaks for itself. He has sent more than fifty enemy ships and three submarines to the bottom of the Mediterranean and North Atlantic. No one but Commander Kretschmer himself has sunk more. They are the pride of Germany."

He had heard enough—this wasn't a goddamned political rally. "Very good, Lieutenant, I appreciate the briefing. Now if you'll excuse me, I would like to get out of these wet clothes and put on my masquerade as chief medical officer. *Before* the great sea captain returns to interrogate me."

"*Jawohl, Herr Major*. But don't say I didn't warn you. He has a terrible temper."

"As I said, I grew up with him so I am well aware of his ill temper. You are dismissed, Lieutenant. Thank you for showing me to my quarters."

Hoffman saluted and left. Erik turned his attention to his fresh clothing. In three minutes, he had donned the full medical uniform along with the big, felt-lined boots. Instantly, he felt warmer. With his uniform complete, he picked up the copy of the *Kriegsmarine* Medical Advice Manual for U-boat Service and quietly thumbed through it. By the time he had read to page 7, he heard a sound coming from down the passageway. He looked up to see his brother and another man in a gray SS uniform with a distinctive scar on his cheek marching towards him.

They looked like jackals moving in for the kill.

CHAPTER 4

NORTH SEA ABOARD U-521

WITHOUT INTRODUCING THE MAN WITH THE SCAR, his brother led the two of them to his captain's quarters, where they would have more privacy. Located in the foreship, the commander's compartment was smaller and more spartan than Erik had expected. There was no door, only a thick black curtain with a small swastika flag in the upper right corner. The bunk was no larger than those in the petty officers' mess or seamen's quarters. The only other items in the compartment were a worn, fur-lined leather captain's jacket hanging from a hook, a single metal chair screwed to the floor, a metal map bin, a pair of small lockers, a foldout writing table, and a little nook for writing materials.

His brother took a seat in the chair and motioned him and the other man to the cramped bunk. Then he pulled out a small silver flask, took a sip, and held it out for his brother.

"Care for a drink? It will warm you."

"Don't mind if I do." He took a pull, letting the fiery liquor sit in his mouth before letting it slide down his throat. It was *kirschwasser*, a colorless fruit brandy with a subtle cherry flavor and hint of almond. He felt himself warm up instantly.

"So, *Brüderlein*, you are no doubt wondering who our friend here is."

He looked at the man: shiny bald head, beady blue eyes, face all harsh angles like stacked knife blades, and, finally, the most salient feature of all, the puckered, pink dueling scar that ran from his jaw nearly to his left ear. He wore the uniform of a *Sturmbannführer*—a major in the *Sicherheitsdienst*, or SD, the political intelligence branch of the SS. He was armed with a 1939 Walther PPK Waffen SS 7.65-mm officers' pistol. Apprehensively, Erik noticed that the strap to the Death's Head holster holding the gun was undone.

"Allow me to introduce myself. I am *Sturmbannführer* Prochnow."

"*Sturmbannführer*." They shook hands. "And what, may I ask, is an SS major doing on a U-boat in the middle of the North Sea?"

"I will ask the questions if you don't mind. You see, there have been some changes in the Reich Security Administration since you set foot in the land of our enemy."

"What kind of changes?"

"Changes in leadership and management. Admiral Canaris is no longer in charge of German intelligence. In fact, the *Abwehr* as you know it is no more. It has been absorbed into the SD, though the name has been retained for convenience."

"Who is in charge then?"

"General Schellenberg. He controls all German intelligence now, military as well as, shall we say, political. Which is why I am here. I need to know the details of your mission."

"I'm afraid I cannot discuss my mission with you. That comes from General Rommel himself. I am under strict orders to report directly to him and no one else."

"Yes, the Desert Fox is a beacon of light for all of Germany. But I'm afraid that he does not have the authority to send his own personal agents to foreign countries and put our existing operatives at risk."

"What has happened to Admiral Canaris?"

"He has taken on a new assignment."

"What does that mean?"

"He was awarded the German Cross by Field Marshal Keitel and General Jodl and offered an important post in the new Ministry of Economic Warfare, which he accepted."

"In other words, he's probably been shipped off to a work camp with all the Jews, communists, and gypsies. So what you're, in fact, telling me is that there is no longer an *Abwehr* and Admiral Canaris has been replaced. At this rate, the Allies will no doubt have Berlin by Christmas."

"Mind your tongue, Herr Major. This is not a good time to have your loyalty questioned. What I need from you are not traitorous remarks, but a formal debriefing. I am to report everything to *Brigadeführer* Schellenberg as soon as possible. The Führer is counting on it."

That was a lie, Erik knew. Hitler didn't know anything about him or his mission. Schellenberg just wanted to look good in his new role as head of German intelligence. Now in charge of the Old Fox's myriad agents sprinkled around the world, he must have been desperate for an eye-opening intelligence coup to jump-start his career and justify his promotion as the Führer*'s* top clandestine services officer.

"Before we begin, let me see your papers."

"My papers?"

"Yes, I need to see them."

"If you insist." He pulled his *Soldbuch* from his pocket and started to hand it to the grim-faced SS man.

But Prochnow merely wrinkled his nose and pushed it away. "No, not that. I need to see your British papers."

"There is no reason for you to see those. They are part of my mission."

"Why are you making trouble? Just give them to him!" snapped his brother.

"I take my orders from General Rommel, not the SS. My papers will be delivered to the general, and he can decide what to do with them."

Prochnow's puckered scar quivered ever so slightly, and his eyes narrowed. "Are you refusing the direct orders of two superior officers?"

"You are not my superior officer, Major—we are of equal rank—and my orders are to report to General Rommel, and no one else. Those orders supersede all others, I'm afraid."

His hand reached down slowly and touched the top of his unstrapped Death's

Head holster. "I'm afraid I must insist, Major."

Erik stared at him, unable to believe his eyes. My God, is Prochnow actually threatening to use that thing? But what choice, Erik wondered, did he have but to comply when he was trapped on a U-boat in the middle of the North Sea? Damnit, he should have known the SS's influence would grow while he was spying on British soil the past four months. These brutal, second-rate bastards would ruin Germany, the whole lot of them!

Reluctantly, he pulled out his British government-issue foreign-national-identity card and other carefully forged supporting documents and handed them over.

"Wise decision, Herr Major."

With a supercilious smile, the SS man clasped the identity papers around his bony fingers, withdrew a glass monocle from a jacket pocket, and took what seemed an interminable amount of time to calmly unfold and inspect each and every one of the forged papers. After a moment, Erik looked at his brother, who was closely studying Prochnow. He read his brother's mind: Wolfgang was desperate to know how his younger sibling—a junior officer on Rommel's staff, thanks largely to his father's connections—had managed to become, with the Allies poised to strike Fortress Europe, perhaps the most important spy in all of the German Army. Erik couldn't help but feel satisfaction: he and his brother had competed furiously with one another growing up, and Erik had usually been on the losing end of their many bouts.

After several minutes, the *sturmbannführer* looked up from the identity card and other papers, the artificial light glistening in white splotches off his bald pate. "So you have been posing as a Swedish industrialist named Henrik Carlsson. The name is invented, I presume?"

"No, it is real. I have been living in London and posing as Carlsson for the past four months."

"Lucky you didn't bump into the fellow. Does he work for the British?"

"Yes, he's a spy working for MI6. He passes on information during his routine trips to Stockholm and Lisbon. By a trick of fate, I happen to look like the man."

"And, of course, you speak Swedish. Oh yes, I have reviewed you and your brother's files in precise detail. I know that you both have Swedish ancestry on your grandmother's side and are fluent in the language. But there was no mention, Herr Major, that you were a spy posing as a Swedish industrialist named Henrik Carlsson. Unfortunately, that critical fact was not included in my dossier. I find that troublesome." He paused to flick a nearly invisible fleck of lint from his SS uniform. "What has become of the real Carlsson?"

"With any luck, he has been thrown into a Scottish jail."

"What do you mean?"

"I followed him on the train from London to Aberdeen. The British authorities—agents from MI5, I believe—have been hot on my tail for the past few days. But I managed to lose them north of Stonehaven. On the train, I planted certain evidence on his person that implicates Carlsson as a double agent. That is, once British intelligence is notified from the Scottish authorities and the inevitable turf battle between MI5 and MI6 begins."

"What makes you think there will be a turf war?"

"Because the two competing British intelligence agencies are fierce rivals." His brother was looking at him curiously so he offered further explanation. "MI5 is the domestic branch that runs internal security and double agents inside Britain, while MI6 deals with foreign intelligence. But occasionally their responsibilities overlap and agents being run by MI6 pose internal security risks. That's when the backbiting, interference, and finger-pointing starts."

Prochnow looked suspicious. "How did you come by this information?"

"I have my sources. And they're much better than yours, I can assure you."

The Nazi's jaw clenched and his posture stiffened, but he didn't press the matter further. Instead, he posed another question. "What about this evidence you mentioned?"

"It was a roll of undeveloped film and a murder weapon."

"What kind of murder weapon?"

"A pearl-handled stiletto. It was particularly lethal and a favorite of mine."

His brother was eyeing him skeptically. "You actually killed someone with it?"

"Once—in the performance of my duty and in the name of the Fatherland."

His brother gave an approving nod, reappraising him in a different light. He hadn't thought him capable of such a bold, desperate act.

The SS major, too, regarded him more approvingly now. Again, the puckered scar on his cheek quivered slightly as his jaw tightened reflexively. Erik glanced at the Walther PPK pistol in the unstrapped holster. Would he really shoot me in cold blood for not telling him what he wants to know?

"So, your cover as Carlsson was because you look like him and he has high-level security clearance since he's working for MI6?"

"Yes."

"And with the British authorities hot on your tail, that's why you planted the evidence on Carlsson and fled the country?"

"Correct again."

Once more, Prochnow pressed the monocle to his eye and closely examined the identity card and two other documents. "These papers appear to be perfect forgeries. How did you get copies of Carlsson's identity card?"

"Let's just say that, like many spies, Carlsson enjoys the night life. His papers were stolen from him and forged after a night of drunken debauchery. They were later quietly returned to his hotel room in Stockholm when he was out two days later. He thought that he had lost them and didn't report anything to his control agent."

"What about this roll of undeveloped film you placed on Carlsson? What was on the film?"

"That I can't tell you." He looked at his brother. But Wolfgang merely gave him an admonishing look that said "Don't even think about not telling him what he wants to know!"

"As I told you, my orders are to report to *Brigadeführer* Schellenberg without delay. The Führer is anxiously awaiting news of your successful mission.

It was successful, wasn't it, Herr Major? Otherwise, you wouldn't be here. Now tell me what was on the film and the news you bring to General Rommel right now, or I will have you arrested and imprisoned, with your brother the U-boat captain here acting as my witness."

Erik looked at Wolfgang and could tell that he wasn't about to go out on a limb for him. His brother was not about to intervene in an SS matter that went all the way to the top of the German intelligence hierarchy, not for his sibling that he loathed.

"I have my orders too, Major. I have already told you all you need to know and cannot disclose anything more."

The captain's quarters turned deathly silent, the only sound the background hum of the diesels. He felt a blink of fear cross his face as his bald-headed adversary's hand again touched the Death's Head holster. Would he actually draw his weapon over this?

"You can start off by telling me, Major, what is on that roll of film you planted on Carlsson."

He hesitated. Why should he tell the bastard anything?

"Just do as he says, Brother. We all swore an oath to the Führer, not to Rommel. Please tell the major what he wants to know."

"No, I will tell him nothing more."

"You are aboard my ship, and I am giving you a direct order. Now tell him!"

Several seconds passed. Prochnow's look narrowed; Erik could tell that the bastard wasn't bluffing and really would pull his gun. Was obeying his orders to his father and Rommel really worth dying for?

Slowly, the Nazi's bony fingers started to open the holster.

Erik blinked once, twice, and then he held up his hands.

"All right, all right, I'll tell you, damnit." He shook his head in dismay, glanced at his brother, and took a deep breath to steady his nerves and control his anger. "The film…the film shows pictures of the British coastline."

"The British coastline? Where along the British coastline?"

"Slapton Sands in Devon."

"Slapton Sands in Southern England? I was there in April," exclaimed his brother with surprise. "The Americans and British were conducting a military exercise off the coast."

"*You* were at Slapton Sands?"

"I spotted a convoy of landing craft with a single corvette escort. I sunk one of the LSTs with a direct torpedo broadside and crippled another one with a partial hit. It caught on fire and was abandoned. But what's so important about Slapton Sands? I mean, it was just a training exercise."

Erik remained silent.

But Prochnow was studying him intently. To his dismay, he could see a little light go on in the major's head. The bastard was putting it all together, second-rate though he was like all of the other petty SS goons who strutted about like peacocks, drunk with their newfound power and the fear they instilled in their own countrymen.

"You know where the Allied invasion will take place! That is what your mission was: to determine where and when they will strike! And now, you have discovered the truth!"

"You overestimate my ability, *Sturmbannführer.* I am a German spy not Nostradamus."

"No, I can see by your face that you know the Allies' plans. Now you must tell me everything, or face the possibility of imprisonment for treason," he said with chilling calm.

Erik looked at his brother.

"Don't look at him," snarled Prochnow. "He does not care if I lock you away forever, or shoot you down like a mangy dog. His loyalty—unlike yours—is to our beloved Führer."

Erik continued to stare at his brother. *Is it true? Do you care more about that maniac and his Thousand Year Reich than your own flesh and blood? Would you really not feel any sense of remorse if that Nazi bastard were to lock me up and have me tortured?* Behind his stern gaze, Erik thought he saw a glimmer of sympathy, a hint of brotherly compassion. Despite all the bitterness between them, they were still family after all. Or was he just imagining it?

"Make no mistake I am quite serious, Herr Major. *Brigadeführer* Schellenberg was quite clear that I use all means at my disposal."

He said nothing, staring back defiantly.

His brother reached out and touched his hand. "Just tell him what he wants to know, *Brüderlein.* There is no need for extreme measures."

"My orders are clear. I can tell him nothing."

"Brother, listen to me. The major, too, is under direct orders, from General Schellenberg. You must tell him everything right—"

They were interrupted by a booming voice over the loudspeaker.

"Masthead off the starboard bow!"

Erik looked first at his brother and then at Prochnow. The two blue veins in the SS man's bald temple pulsed and throbbed like a beating heart. He looked ready to explode.

"British destroyer identified, Captain! Alarm!"

His brother leapt to his feet. "This interrogation is finished, Major! I must report to the control room!"

Before the gaping-mouthed Prochnow could utter a word of protest, he pushed through the black curtain bearing the swastika and dashed down the narrow passageway.

The SS *sturmbannführer* glowered after him before turning and glaring flints at Erik.

"Fuck you!" spat Erik, and he got up to leave.

Prochnow gave a bellicose smile and spoke in a chillingly calm voice. "We'll continue this later, Herr Major. And when we do, you'd *better* answer my questions to my complete satisfaction."

"Or else what?"

"Or else I will have you sent off to a French work camp like a prisoner of fucking war."

CHAPTER 5

NORTH SEA ABOARD U-521

DISMISSING THE NAZI BASTARD with an infuriated wave of his hand, Erik darted through the curtain and headed towards the control room before Prochnow could make another threat. En route, he knocked aside a clump of hanging sausages and life vests as he squirmed his way through the narrow cluttered passageway, wondering why SS monsters like Prochnow couldn't be fighting for the British or Americans instead of Germany? How was it possible that the Fatherland had so many bitter, second-rate bureaucrats and brutal thugs in positions of uncontestable power?

When he reached the control room, he peered up through the conning tower hatch. His brother Wolfgang was already up in the tower, astride the attack periscope saddle, his face pressed against the rubber-eyepiece shell and legs set in a wide stance so he could more easily grip the huge shaft. Erik made his way quickly up into the tower, taking up a position two arms' length away from him.

The great U-boat captain was in his element, he saw at once, his concentration nursed to the highest level. Metallic clicking noises filled the air and the periscope motor hummed like a swarm of bees as his brother carefully adjusted the elevation of the attack periscope above the wave-splashed sea, keeping its head above the uneven surface. Finally, after what seemed a long time, he pulled his foot off the periscope peddle and looked directly at Erik, his eyes suffused with excitement like when they were boys.

"The destroyer hasn't spotted us yet. We have an opportunity here to sink her to the bottom of the sea."

"Are you sure that's wise, given our mission?"

"What are you a U-boat commander as well as a spy?"

"The last thing you need is another red pennant, and the last thing Germany needs is for me to be killed or captured. I hold the secret to the whole war, Brother."

"Is that so?"

"Yes, it is. That's why you have to trust me and stand down. You may sink one enemy ship, but I can save all of Germany."

"Are you telling me that prick Prochnow is right? You really do know about the Allied invasion: the time and place, the order of battle, the diversionary strikes?"

"I said no such thing. But I am telling you, here and now, that I hold the key to the whole bloody war. It's the God's honest truth. You must believe me,

Brother—I am not exaggerating."

"What do the Allies have, some special weapon? A superbomb? A rocket? A chemical gas that can kill millions?"

"No, the Allies have something much bigger than that, believe me. That's why I must stop them."

"Damn your stubbornness, why don't you just tell me?"

"You know the reason. I have my orders."

"Well then, fuck you. All I know is I have a destroyer in my sights. If I don't send her to the bottom, and quickly, she may very well sink the next U-boat. Or the one after that. I cannot allow that to happen. Those are our rules of engagement. It is a U-boat captain's responsibility to take out the enemy whenever the opportunity presents itself so that the enemy cannot bring harm to our comrades at sea. That destroyer hasn't spotted us and I intend to sink her."

"It's too risky. The destroyer will radio her position when she's hit."

"This is not your decision to make. I, not you, am the captain of this boat." He leaned down and yelled down into the control room below. "Man battle stations!"

"Brother, you don't need to do this. I hold the key to the whole war, goddamnit!"

"Flood tubes one to four!"

"Don't you understand, just get me to General Rommel and we can win this fucking war—or, at the very least, obtain peace on our terms!"

"If anyone is going to report anything to the High Command, it will be me," declared a new voice, and they turned to see Major Prochnow climbing up into the conning tower. "And you, Captain, will not engage this British destroyer. If your brother carries intelligence with him that will help Germany win the war, it cannot be compromised at any cost."

"Stand down, *Sturmbannführer*. You are aboard my boat and I am commander here." To the control room below, shouting: "Proceed and hold at periscope depth!"

"He's right, Brother, you must not do this."

"Flood stern tube!"

"Listen to your brother, *Herr Kapitän!* You cannot do this. The risk is too great." Prochnow started to withdraw his pistol, but before it had cleared halfway from his Death's Head holster, Erik saw his brother reach out and knock the gun from his hand with a timely blow.

"There is no time for your nonsense, Major. It is my duty to obey our rules of engagement and not leave a Tommy destroyer out there to sink a whole fleet of U-boats. We are attacking!"

Satisfied that the SS man no longer posed a threat, he peered through the periscope again, sighting the target in his crosshairs.

"Open torpedo doors! Direction fifty! Range four thousand feet! Chief, I need you to fire a double, one forward of the bridge and radio mast, the other just behind!"

As the outraged Nazi leaned down to pick up the gun, Erik kicked it through the conning tower hatch down into the control room, making a loud clanking sound. The *sturmbannführer's* head jerked up, his eyes burning with rage.

"You're going to regret this, both of you!"

"Tubes one through four clear and ready to fire, Captain!" came the shout from the first watch officer down in the control room.

Erik decided to make one last, desperate appeal. "Damn your rules of engagement! Don't do this, Wolfgang! We have a chance to end the war!"

But it was too late. His brother had already pulled the firing lever—twice.

CHAPTER 6

NORTH SEA ABOARD U-521

A GEYSER OF SEAWATER and fiery flash of red-orange rose up into the cumulus-laden sky, splashing against the charcoal-colored backdrop like a gigantic fountain as the two torpedoes hit their mark. The first explosion sent a shudder down the keel of U-521, and the second shook the heavy steel floor plates like an earth tremor. The destroyer's shallow draft and swift maneuverability made it a difficult target to bring down, but both torpedoes—one striking fore of the bridge, the other aft—couldn't have been better placed if they had been fired from half the distance of 4,000 feet.

Erik, of course, saw none of this, but he could feel the concussive power of the detonations as the vibrations navigated through his body and every inch of the U-boat. A moment later, he heard the dull groan of the imploding destroyer, the wrenching of metal, as her bulkheads collapsed and she began her lonely descent to the bottom of the North Sea.

Then there was nothing, no sound at all, except the dull thrum of U-521's diesels.

No one said a word: no cheering, no handshakes, no backslapping, no seaman songs of celebration. Nothing.

"She's gone," said his brother quietly, and Erik saw the sadness mingled with admiration for the enemy in his eyes, an unspoken code of honor amongst naval combatants.

The respectful silence persisted for several seconds until it was broken by the giddy Prochnow.

"You have done it, *Herr Kapitän zur See,* as I knew you would! You have sunk the enemy destroyer!"

Erik watched as his brother frowned at the SS man in disgust.

"As long as the major tells me everything I need to know, I am willing to forgive your insubordination and will personally recommend you for the Iron Cross! You are a fortunate man, *Herr Kapitän,* to be on the receiving end of my generosity instead of experiencing my fearsome wrath!"

Erik saw a quiet rage build up in his brother, but Wolfgang held his tongue. In that moment, he realized that although his older brother was a member of the National Socialist Party—a Nazi—he was nothing like Prochnow. While the bombastic SS man was drunk with authority and reveled at the prospect of annihilating the enemy for his beloved Führer, Wolfgang felt genuine remorse at the sinking of an enemy vessel and the taking of human life. Eric couldn't but feel sorry for his brother, knowing how hard it must be to fight on behalf of the

Fatherland when he genuinely admired the enemy—and especially her seafaring combat vessels. He was a true sea captain.

"Clear tower and prepare to dive!"

From the control room, the navigator called out, "Captain, new vessel veering this way, hard on our port beam!"

His brother's contemplative expression abruptly vanished and his battle mask returned. He nestled his eyes into the rubber shell and began quickly working the foot pedal, swiveling the periscope column and sweeping the sea for the enemy. After several seconds, he looked up and gasped in disbelief, "Another destroyer and she's firing at us! Hard a-starboard! Alarm!"

Again, from the control room: "Captain, second destroyer hard on our stern!"

"Clear tower! Prepare to flood!"

Obeying his brother's order, Erik scrambled for the hatch, reaching it just before Prochnow, who in a fit of panic tried to shove him out of the way.

But Erik was having none of it. He drove an elbow into the SS *sturmbannführer's* chest and threw his own leg down into the open hatch, taking first position.

At that precise moment, a massive explosion rocked the U-boat. The conning tower opened up like a tin can, and Prochnow was impaled and driven hard against the wall by an exploding metal fragment of the sky periscope and its stanchion.

Looking up in shock, Erik saw a sudden flash of fiery light. The flash was followed quickly by another explosive burst as the main deck gun was ripped from the U-boat by a second and then a third cannon shot from one of the destroyers bearing down angrily upon them. Struggling to jump into the hatch, he caught one last look at Prochnow, whose chest had opened up in a meaty spray of heart, lung, and tissue around the metal protruding from his chest. He kicked and thrashed, his ruined lungs working frantically to draw in air. Blood frothed with air bubbles as it poured from his gaping chest wound and open mouth. Erik knew there was no use trying to rescue the dumb brute, for the wound was fatal and the Nazi major would not last another minute.

Suddenly, he felt his brother at his side, shoving him down into the hatch. "Go, Brother, go!"

He slipped through the narrow aperture and hit the floor hard, the metal plates ringing in his ears along with the three explosions. As he tried to roll away, he felt his brother's heavy sea boots strike his back. The U-boat commander was only a split second behind him down the tower hatch and already shouting orders to dive before the hatch was closed.

"Flood, Chief, flood!"

Together, they pulled the hatch shut. Two seaman jumped forward to throw the seal as freezing-cold seawater surged over the deck and poured down from the battered conning tower through the partly open hatch, soaking them from head to toe.

"Close torpedo doors! Dive to two hundred and fifty feet—fast! All hands forward!"

To Erik, what happened next seemed like total chaos as the U-boat was flooded to make up for the 6,000-pound weight of the two fired torpedoes and allow her to make a swift downward descent into the deep blue. His brother shouted out orders to the chief, who in turn shouted out orders to the first and second watch officers, navigator, hydrophone operator, and control room mate, who in turn shouted back in confirmation. *Kriegsmariners* rushed forward from the stern of the U-boat, poured into the tilted control room as if it were a chute, and acrobatically flung themselves through the open hatches like swinging chimpanzees, their scuffling and stamping boots thumping against the floor plates. Amid the controlled pandemonium, all eyes in the control room fixed anxiously on the needle of the depth manometer as the crippled, creaking U-boat slipped into deeper waters.

After a few minutes, the commotion died down, the hydroplanes were eased up from their hard-down position, and the bow-heavy vessel began to level off to the horizontal.

That's when the first depth charge exploded.

The floor plates rattled like a wheezy old stevedore, and they were jostled about like crickets in a whirlpool. Erik was thrown across the chart table and smashed his head on a pipe, which let loose a cold, wet spray.

Another monstrous explosion rocked the U-boat to port, followed quickly by another beneath the keel. Two drums at two different depths. If single and double charges didn't work, Erik knew, the Tommies would lay down a carpet of saturation detonations to send them to the bottom.

"Full ahead both! Depth report!" cried the captain.

"Two hundred twenty feet!" answered the chief.

"Take her to three hundred!"

Another depth charge pair rocked the pressure hull from the side and beneath the keel.

His brother cursed violently. With an explosion within five hundred feet of the hull, the pressure wave would open her up like a tin can.

The hydrophone operator's head popped out of the adjacent sound room. "Both destroyers are coming up on us now, Captain! They're moving astern!"

"This is just the opening round! Brace for detonation!"

But there was nothing.

Erik reached out and grabbed a dribbling water pipe for support. He had never felt this vulnerable and exposed in his entire life. Like a sitting duck. Following each explosion, he had heard a great sucking sound, and only now did he realize what it was: the sound of the seawater pouring back into the vacuum generated by the detonation of the depth charges. The sheer power of the explosions was terrifying, magnified as they were from the underwater pressure.

The U-boat was all quiet again. *Too quiet,* he thought.

Anxious seconds ticked off. The only sounds he could hear were the hum of the e-motors, the anxious breathing of the others in the control room, and the steady drip-drip of water from the leaking pipes.

"Start your bilge pumps when they fire next, Chief," whispered his brother.

How can he be so calm when the enemy is bombarding us?

More tense seconds ticked off.

"What the hell are those British bastards up to?" eventually wondered the first watch officer aloud.

"Destroyer bearing one hundred eighty degrees and holding steady," whispered the hydrophone operator. "Slow revs—they've gone silent. I think they're listening."

"Trying to get a fix on our position," murmured the captain. "And the other destroyer?"

"Noise bearing two hundred twenty degrees. Growing fainter."

"Goddamnit, they're both running silent and working together." He looked at the navigator, who was busy making calculations at the chart table, before resting his gaze on the chief. "Slow ahead. Steer two hundred degrees."

"As ordered, *Kapitän*."

Erik felt the tension almost unbearable. Confined in this claustrophobic tin can, he realized that he could never have been a U-boat captain like his brother. It was excruciating. He anxiously watched the needle of the depth manometer as it moved down slowly over the dial another set of divisions. When the manometer read three hundred feet, he felt the hydroplanes ease up and the U-boat trimmed to level.

"Continue motors, slow ahead," his brother whispered. "We're going to try to slip past these damned Tommies."

The U-boat turned deathly silent, again.

But the silence was shattered by a series of tremendous underwater explosions, much closer this time.

CHAPTER 7

NORTH SEA ABOARD U-521

ERIK SAW HIS BROTHER GO DOWN, followed by the chief, the first watch officer, and the control room mate. Then he felt his own knees buckle as he was thrown backwards into the attack periscope. The first explosion was followed by a cluster of detonations. Seawater sprayed in a torrent from a pipe just beyond the open stern hatch. Something sharp dug into his back, and he saw flames licking up from beneath the floor plates. To his surprise, the flames were quickly extinguished by the control room mate.

Again, he heard the monstrous sucking sound of seawater rushing in to fill the vacuum resulting from the explosions. The dull roar mingled with the orders being called out by his brother, the shouts of the other officers and crewmen, and the spraying of water from the leaking pipes in the various compartments.

Six more explosions, close to the stern, in rapid succession.

The floor plates danced; the hull creaked and groaned. To his astonishment, a new array of pipes ruptured. The control room mate bounded around the room with his handy wrench to stop the leaks like the little Dutch boy. But this time there were too many. Then the lights in the control room flickered and dimmed and then went out altogether, and they were shrouded in darkness. He heard curses and fumbling. After a moment, his brother and the chief had flashlights out and were cutting through the misty gloom. The instrument panel smoldered. The acrid smell of burning diesel reached up to his nose along with the briny smell of saltwater.

How the fuck can we survive this and not sink to the bottom?

Another round of furious explosions. Overhead lights flickered and then died. He realized they were being carpet bombed into submission.

Damn the Tommies!

A momentary lull followed. He heard his brother's voice cut through the darkness over the loudspeaker. "Damage report! Damage report!"

"Bow compartment flooding! Torpedo stowage destroyed!" came the reply over the loudspeaker from the forward compartment.

"Permission to engage bilge pumps?" asked the chief as the lights flickered back on.

"Be quick about it! Pump out torpedo cells one and two!"

The U-boat was rocked again by several more explosions, the enemy throwing down another carpet. The lights on the control panels flickered and flashed. Then they went out altogether before coming back on in a weak, sporadic glow. The chief pumped water from the bilge pumps and trimmed the U-boat forward to return the stern-heavy vessel to an even keel. When the control room was quiet again, except for the hum of the motors and hissing leaks, the captain again keyed the loudspeaker.

"Main motor room—report!"

"Motor room here! Two electrical fires, but we're getting them under control!"

"Good. Engine room?"

Nothing.

"Engine room report!"

Still no reply.

"Come in, engine room, goddamnit!"

A crackle of static then, "Engine room here…every…everyone's dead except me and Roemer and he's badly wounded."

"Who is this?"

"Diesel stoker Bomblies."

"What is the damage?"

"Engine room breached. Severe flooding, one diesel out, other badly damaged along with fuel pump and compressed-air cylinder!"

"They're right on top of us, *Kapitän*!" announced the hydrophone operator in a frantic whisper. "Running silent again!"

Erik gasped inwardly as a flurry of sparks erupted from one of the control panels and another pipe began to spray. But the control room mate was there with his extinguisher and pipe wrench and quickly brought the flames and leak under control as if it were nothing at all.

More anxious seconds ticked off. Then the captain ordered the stations to again report.

"Motor room reporting—we're making water now! Both e-motors at three-quarters power and falling rapidly!"

"Engine room, Bomblies here! Pipes are spewing oil and we're already shin-deep in water! We can't stop it—I repeat, we can't stop it!"

Erik looked at his brother, who bore an expression of intense focus, thinking through his options.

How can he possibly be this calm under fire?

"We're taking on a lot of water," said the chief, his expression as solemn as a pallbearer.

"No, Chief. We've taken worse than this before and made it back to base."

"One diesel is down and our motors are at three-quarters and dropping. We couldn't maneuver even if we wanted to. We're going to have to surface—we have no fucking choice."

"No, we can make it. Report depth."

The chief looked at the manometer. "Three hundred thirty. We're sinking, Captain."

Erik saw a stubborn glint in his brother's eye. "Half speed ahead both! Reduce hydroplanes! Steer one hundred eighty degrees!"

The chief closed in on him. "We've got too much leakage! We must surface!"

"No, goddamnit! We will not let these bastards beat—"

His voice was cut off as several bursts rocked the U-boat.

Erik saw his brother driven hard into the periscope stanchion at the same time he himself was thrown to the floor and flames licked up again from beneath the floor plates. As he jumped to his feet to escape the flames, cold seawater flooded in from the stern compartment. The surge picked him up and drove him into the wall. A second searing flame licked up from beneath the floor plates, worse this time. The enemy must have ruptured one of the fuel tanks with the last saturation depth charges.

Black smoke began to fill the control room. Through the haze, he saw men climbing to their feet, scrambling about, screaming commands. In the commotion, he looked around for his brother. He saw him lying on the floor, leaning against a dislodged control panel amid a stack of nautical almanacs and navigational handbooks that had fallen from the chart table. His brother's head was gashed open, and seawater was flowing in through the hatch and soaking his pants. He had been knocked unconscious from the last set of underwater detonations.

With the help of the chief and navigator, Erik picked him up and laid him on top of the chart table. The first watch officer and the chief then conferred. The chief ordered the buoyancy tanks blown. Then the first watch officer stepped into the sound room to confer with the hydrophone operator as a fan turned on and the smoke began to clear. A minute later, he came back out and stepped up to Erik. The depth charges were becoming more distant.

"How is the captain?"

"Unconscious, but he'll live."

"I worship the son of a bitch, but he shouldn't have gone after that damned destroyer," grumbled the chief. "His actions have doomed us."

"I should have tried harder to stop him," said Erik.

"You did your best," said the first watch officer. "He wasn't going to listen to anyone. Your brother always does things by the book, and I am afraid our *Kriegsmarine* rules of engagement supersede your secret mission. But we can't worry about that right now. We have to get this boat to the surface and scuttle her before the Tommies can take a look inside."

Erik nodded in understanding, while silently cursing his bad luck. He had spent the last four months spying in a foreign land, had, by some miracle, stumbled upon a treasure trove of top-secret intelligence information, and now it was all for naught because of his brother, who had put not only his entire crew, but all of Germany, at grave risk by insisting on doing things rigidly by the book and following some unnecessary U-boat protocol. Now the intelligence that Erik carried with him—intelligence that could very well decide the outcome of the war—was worthless unless he could somehow manage to avoid capture, which at this point appeared unlikely.

Damn you, Wolfgang! Damn you and your petty rules of engagement!

"All hands stand by for emergency surface!" shouted the first watch officer over the loudspeaker. Then to the chief, "Report depth!"

"One hundred eighty feet!"

"Bow compartment, set scuttle charges! All hands, prepare escape gear!"

Another series of distant depth charges, this time to stern.

Erik listened to the surge of seawater as it rushed in to fill the void along with the sound of the water pouring in from the stern compartments, the groaning of the bilge pumps, and the hiss of the buoyancy tanks being blown full. Feeling the boat slowly rising beneath his feet, he looked at the depth manometer as it moved backwards over the dial.

"Destroyers bearing one hundred forty and one hundred eighty degrees," announced the hydrophone operator, poking his head out from the sound room again. "Sounds growing faint."

"They've gone silent again," said the chief.

"They think we're done for," said the navigator.

"We are fucking done for," lamented the first watch officer. "Equalize pressure and clear tower." Then again over the loudspeaker: "Bow compartment, we don't have much time—get those scuttle charges set! All hands, all hands! Don rescue gear and prepare to surface!"

He then turned to the chief.

"Chief, give those tanks one last hard blow. Navigator, send a message to base reporting our last known position. Operator, what's the bearing of the enemy?"

"Steady at one forty and one sixty."

"Damn, they're hard on our starboard beam. They must have seen our oil slick."

As more commands were issued, Erik looked at his brother, lying still as a statue on the chart table. His breathing was slow and steady, but he was still out cold. A lump the size of a ripe plum had formed on the side of his head. After a moment, Erik noticed that the others were looking at Wolfgang too. From their expressions, he could see how much they admired—and feared—their aggressive U-boat commander. He recalled that he had felt the same mixed feelings as a boy, before he had grown to hate his brother.

"There's going to be hell to pay when he wakes up," warned the chief. Then a crack of a smile appeared on his weary, raccoon-eyed face. "He must have been a son of a bitch growing up."

Erik gently wiped away some of the blood on his brother's head with the cuff of his medical jacket, silently cursing him and his arrogance. "You have no idea."

"Let's just pray we get to the surface before he does wake up," said the first watch officer. "I fear his wrath a hell of a lot more than I do the damned Tommies."

Two minutes later, U-521 surfaced and the bosun turned the spindle to the tower hatch. Due to U-boat's fast rise to the surface, the hatch still hadn't achieved full pressure equalization and sprang back like a slingshot.

Instantly, the clean, frigid North Sea air poured into the dank, smoky U-boat like a gift from the heavens. With help from the bosun and chief, Erik pushed his brother up through the hatch and assembled with the rest of the crew on the battered deck under the glare of flares and searchlights from the two British destroyers. During the U-boat's ascent to the surface, the Tommies had pinpointed its location and rushed into an intercepting position.

With the searchlights beating down on the crew, Erik watched anxiously as the enemy from the closest destroyer blared out orders in muddled German over a loudspeaker, commanding him and the others to throw up their hands and form up.

Pretending not to understand, the first watch officer ordered a quick count of the survivors and instructed the crew not to disclose any information to the enemy during interrogation except what was in their *Soldbuchs*. There was to be no mention of the passenger they had taken on board only an hour earlier off the Scottish coast. Once the first watch officer had made sure that all survivors—including the dozen wounded and engineering officer assigned to set the scuttling charges—was on deck, he gave orders for the remaining crew of thirty-seven to assemble in the inflatable rubber life rafts so that the U-boat could be scuttled.

As the men pushed out in their rafts from the crippled U-boat, the British blew a shrill whistle. The lead destroyer tied up to the semi-floating junk heap, which was now listing badly to port in the swells. With the damaged U-boat secured, an armed boarding party scrambled onto the vessel just as the scuttling charges went off in the forward compartment.

With his still-unconscious brother in his arms, Erik watched as a fountain of fire exploded from the tip of the U-boat along with a geyser of seawater, spilling the guts of the craft like a disemboweled whale. The long, gray cylinder, already a quarter-filled with water and close to sinking, simply rolled over and disappeared into the sea, gurgling like an old man giving his last gasp as a flurry of stunned British seamen dove over the side to keep from being drowned.

It was then that his brother regained consciousness.

"What the hell…where…where am I?"

Erik peered down at him, relieved that he was alive and kicking. But did he dare answer him?

A walrus-mustached English naval officer in a rain-splashed oilskin yelled down at them from the bridge of the closest destroyer.

Erik felt defeat and resignation wash all over him: he had been so close to success and now this. The British officer cursed some profanity and imperially commanded them to paddle towards him as the first two rafts nosed up alongside the destroyer and tired, wet *Kriegsmariners* began to be plucked from the ocean.

With misgivings, Erik finally answered his brother. "We've scuttled the ship and are about to be taken captive by the enemy."

The great U-boat commander looked at him in muddled disbelief. "We're…we're prisoners of war? Me and my men?"

Erik fixed his older brother with a ferocious glare. "You shouldn't have attacked that destroyer, Wolfgang. You may very well have cost us the whole fucking war!"

DAY 2

SUNDAY

MAY 28, 1944

CHAPTER 8

LEFT HAND RANCH
SOUTHEASTERN COLORADO, USA

WITH THE MID-MORNING BREEZE at her back and her appaloosa tethered nearby, Katherine Templeton—owner of Left Hand Ranch and Colorado Springs' opulent Broadmoor Hotel—stared out at the Great Plains from a rocky knob of Cretaceous limestone. Out riding along the western edge of her ranch, she was comfortable in her wide-brimmed western hat, embroidered leather riding skirt, and hand-tooled riding boots. Spread before her was a monstrous herd of bawling beef cattle, and she couldn't help but picture what the land before her had looked like back in the time of the buffalo—before the cattleman had wrested control of it from the lance-wielding Plains Indian a century earlier.

Imagining a colossal herd of the shaggy, cloven-hoofed beasts, she remembered back to her schoolgirl days reading the exciting Western tales of one of her favorite authors growing up, Karl May. The late nineteenth-century German novelist, prone to literary embellishment but nonetheless wildly popular in his day, had recounted the adventurous exploits of noble chief Winnetou, leader of the Mescalero Apaches, and his scouting partner, blood brother, and loyal friend Old Shatterhand. Katherine took a deep breath of the sage-scented air and felt somehow whole, pure, connected as her mind drifted back a century to the world of the buffalo and wild red men who had hunted them in Karl May's inspiring novels. And then, after a few minutes of quiet reverie, the past slowly metamorphosed once again to the tangible present and she was no longer overlooking a massive herd of buffalo, but a herd of bovines bearing her distinctive brand: LH with an arrow through it. She had named the ranch after the illustrious 1860s Arapaho Peace Chief Niwot, or Chief Left Hand as the southpaw's name was translated into English.

After giving her horse a nugget of salt, she climbed back into the saddle and headed to the ranch house. By the time she had combed him down and was climbing the freshly varnished wooden steps to her house, her top ranch hand, Jack Running Wolf, and three other cow hands rode up with a pair of mounted men with their hands tied to the saddle horns. She had a total of eleven men working for her as ranch hands. Four of them were young Jewish men that she had helped escape from Paris when the SS was rounding up French Jews and deporting them to the Natzweiler-Struthof concentration camp in the Alsace-Lorraine area.

She squinted into the late May sunshine. "Looks like I owe you a dollar, Jack. You caught the rascals."

The Comanche Indian nodded. "Yes, ma'am. They were heading for Wild

Horse."

"Are you sure they are the rustlers?"

"They confessed, ma'am. What do you want me to do with them?"

"I'm not sure. I need time to think."

"Well, while you're doing that, do you mind if we get out of these hot, dusty saddles?"

"Be my guest. In a moment, I will have Kate fetch you all a cool glass of lemonade." She was referring to Jack's half-Kiowa, half-Comanche wife Kate Running Wolf, who was also under her employ, as the ranch cook and domestic. Jack's cousin Henry also worked for her as a doorman at her Broadmoor Hotel in Colorado Springs, which she had inherited from her wealthy late husband, John Percy Templeton III of Tuxedo Park, New York.

She looked the two captured men over as Jack and her other ranch hands slid from their saddles and tied the horses to the hitching post, leaving the two rustlers mounted. They were young men in their early twenties. The tougher-looking of the two, who appeared to be the leader, had obviously put up a fight before surrendering. His left eye was swollen shut and the side of his head had a big gash from some blunt implement. They were gaunt as scarecrows and dressed in dirty jeans, ragged shirts, and workman's boots that had seen better days. Katherine shook her head. She had expected violent desperados straight out of a dime novel to have stolen her cattle, but these miserable wretches were hardly desperado-like. Already she felt pity for them.

"Before we examine your options, gentlemen, would you care to tell me your side of the story?"

To her surprise, it was the gentle-looking one who spoke up, pleading their case: "We ain't cattle thieves, ma'am. Not like you think anyways. We were just frightfully hungry and butchered just the one cow. To be honest, we thought it was a stray and that no one would miss it. We're awful sorry."

She could tell he meant it, but a lot of people in the world were sorry. After all, there was a world war going on killing millions. "Why aren't you men fighting in the army? You look to be the right age."

They exchanged nervous glances. "Uh, they wouldn't take us," said the tougher-looking one, speaking up so quickly that it instantly raised a red flag in Katherine's mind. "I've got a club foot, and Hank here is missing a thumb."

Thus prompted, his partner in crime held up his right hand like it was some sort of badge of honor, and sure enough his thumb was missing—but only half of it.

"I didn't know they kept a man out of the army for missing half a thumb," said Jacob Levinson, one of the four Jewish cow hands that worked for her and that she had helped smuggle out of Occupied France. The other two ranch hands next to him were non-Jewish. "A whole thumb I could understand, but you're only missing half."

"Well, they must have changed the rules before we tried to enlist," replied the gentle one, still trying to be friendly. "I guess that's the way it is in Uncle Sam's Army."

"Half a missing thumb or a club foot—it don't much matter to the army if you're damaged goods," said the tougher-looking one, who she was beginning to realize, wasn't so tough after all. "They're particular, I guess. Hank and I both would like nothing better than to lick the Japs and Krauts, ma'am, if Uncle Sam would only give us a crack at them. But he won't."

Jack Running Wolf looked at Katherine and smiled. She could tell he wasn't buying it.

And neither was she. She had seen the frightened, hunted look before: they had to be army deserters on the run. There were a lot of them knocking around out here in the West.

"What do you fellows do for a living, then?"

"To be honest, ma'am," said the gentle one, "we are what you might call rambling men. We mostly travel about performing odd jobs and such, you know, to help the war effort."

"That's funny," said Jack Running Wolf with a mischievous grin. "Because if I had to guess, I'd say you were either draft dodgers or army deserters. Now which is it, boys?"

They looked anxiously at one another. Katherine just shook her head: these poor fools were about the worst liars she had ever seen.

The Comanche's eyes narrowed hard and lean. "Come clean, or things will go hard for you. Mrs. Templeton, the owner of this here ranch where you have committed your depredations, does not suffer fools."

They looked at one another again before the tougher-looking one gave a rueful sigh. "No use lying about it. We deserted from Fort Gibbons a week ago."

Katherine crossed her arms. "You're a long way from Fort Gibbons. Last time I heard, it was in Texas."

"Hank and I both grew up in Greeley and we were trying to get up to our old haunts and hide out."

The gentle one, Hank, had tears in his eyes, and Katherine couldn't help but feel sorry for the both of them.

"We wanted to fight, ma'am, and that's the God's honest truth. But our drill sergeant, Sergeant Thompkins...well, he's a Lone Star fellow and he didn't take too kindly to us Colorado boys. In fact, he made every day of our training a living hell. He treated us far worse than the other recruits, making us scrub and clean at all hours of the night, run with our packs on twice as much as the other recruits, and hike three times as far. Old Thompkins had it out for us. He's a genuine monster. Why he'd scare the britches off old Adolf Hitler himself. But the truth is we're not very good soldiers, either. We both tried hard, but we could never do enough to satisfy the man. So we deserted. We just couldn't take it anymore. Now the army's looking for us, and we'll be court-martialed and sent to prison at Fort Leavenworth if they catch us."

So that was it then. They had come clean, and now she was left with a dilemma: what to do with the poor rascals? They had to be punished, of that she was certain. But what would be the point of turning them in only to have them locked up in an army stockade or forced to fight when they clearly weren't up to snuff?

"The truth of it, ma'am, is we are a pair of hungry, no-good army deserters who stole one of your cattle. All so's we could have ourselves a nice, big old steak dinner before the army catches up with us and sends us to prison. It was our last supper, ma'am, or at least that's the way we reckoned it."

Jack Running Wolf held up a Colt service pistol. "We found this on them. They shot the damned cow in the head."

Katherine felt a little spasm of anger. What was she to do with them? She remembered back to last fall when she had become owner of both Left Hand Ranch and the Broadmoor Hotel upon the reading of her late husband's will. Back then, a predatory horde of bankers, lawyers, shady businessmen, and unscrupulous cattlemen had swooped in to take advantage of, and outright steal from, her. In response, she had fought back fiercely and dealt with those who had tried to bamboozle her harshly, wanting to make sure to set a firm example so that in the future people would know that she was not easy pickings just because she was a woman. But these men looked pathetic, and there was a great world war on where millions were dying and where harsh discipline and barbaric cruelty were the order of the day and she had no inclination to be severe with these poor miserable wretches and send them back to be locked away in a military prison or to be shipped off to the front to be slaughtered when they were not equipped to be soldiers.

Despite the outrage she felt at the killing of her poor cow, she couldn't help but sympathize with their plight.

"Put them to work cleaning the stable, Jack. But first they're going to wash up and change their clothes."

The Comanche did a double take. "Are you sure, ma'am? I mean, these men could be dangerous."

"Do they look dangerous to you, Jack?"

"Well, not particularly, ma'am, but you never know with this kind. They are good-for-nothing deserters."

"Well, like it or not, I'm going to give them a second chance."

"Are you sure that's a good idea, ma'am?" said the Jewish hand Jacob Levinson, who along with the other two non-Jewish ranch hands was looking uneasy.

"Yes, I'm sure." She looked sternly at the two rustlers. "You two are working for me today and tomorrow. You owe me two good days of hard labor for that cow. If you do a good job, I will send you on your way and that will be the end of it. If you don't, I will be contacting the military authorities and you will complete your sentence at Fort Leavenworth. Do you agree to my terms?"

Jack Running Wolf laughed. "You're far too generous, ma'am. Those thieving skunks don't deserve such fair-minded treatment, and you know it."

"Jack's right," said Jacob Levinson. "I say we turn 'em in and let the army handle—"

"That's enough, you two," she cut them off. "I've made up my mind. Bring them inside."

At that moment, Jack Running Wolf's Indian wife Kate stepped out the front door. "Well, well, look what the cat dragged in? Who are these scoundrels?"

"Two desperate, cattle-rustling army deserters. Now see to it that they're properly showered, fed, and clothed and then your good husband Jack here is going to put them to work in the show barn. Aren't you, Jack?"

"Yes, ma'am."

His wife Kate Running Wolf frowned. "You think that's a good—?"

"Probably not, but I'm going to do it anyway." She looked at the two rustlers. "You'd better get inside, gentlemen, before I change my mind. It appears everyone but me wants to see you strung up from a tree."

"Thank you, ma'am!" they cried with relief in unison.

Once the two men were untied and escorted inside, she dismissed everyone but Jack. They each took a seat in the oversized rocking chairs on the spacious wooden porch. For a moment, they just sat there in silence, staring out at the green, rolling hills and leafy cottonwoods flanking the cool-watered creek. Jack Running Wolf and his wife Kate had always been her most trusted employees on the ranch. Since her husband John Templeton had died and her nineteen-year-old son Max had joined the Rangers and been shipped off a year ago to North Africa to fight the Germans, they were also her favorites to pass the time with on the front porch.

"I'm sorry, ma'am," said Jack Running Wolf. "I shouldn't have questioned you like that in front of the men. But those two skunks are lowly deserters."

"Oh, it's all right. I've grown used to your stubborn ways."

"Yes, ma'am, I know you have, and I want you to know I appreciate it. But I'm still sorry for crossing the line. It's just that…"

"Spit it out, Jack."

"It's just that…well, it just seems unfair that Max is overseas fighting in Italy while these two jokers have skipped out of the army and are stealing cattle. It just doesn't seem fair."

"I was thinking the same thing. But I am not sure I would want those two fighting alongside my son even if they could. By their own admission, they are poor soldiers and the army is probably better off without them."

"I still think you're being too generous."

"I suppose it's in my nature to see the best in people."

"Yes, ma'am, it is."

"Since John died and Max went off to war, I haven't had a stubborn, knot-headed man in the house to argue with, have I?"

"No, ma'am, you haven't."

"Except you, Jack Running Wolf. I do believe you have filled that role quite nicely."

"I don't know if I should take that as a compliment."

"Oh, it's a compliment all right. I know you're just looking out for me."

"Thank you, ma'am. You've always done right by me and the missus. We would do anything for you."

"I know you would. That's why I also know that you will put those men to hard work for the next two days and then send them on their way with a hundred dollars in their pockets and never say another word about it to me again."

"Yes, ma'am, I do believe we have an understanding in this matter."

They fell into a reflective silence. Beyond her front porch, the Plains lay nestled like a lumbering giant, coming to life with the chatter of birds and prairie dogs. She felt the late May wind warm on her face as she took in the fragrant smell of sagebrush. The sun's golden glow touched the tops of the mountains to the west, which stood gray and jagged against the clear blue sky. High along the rocky slopes, the snow lay in dwindling patches. God, did she love this country. It made a person feel small and big at the same time, rolling onward to infinity like the sea.

But she also felt lonely. Something about this vast, lonesome flatland tugged at her soul and made her feel sad. Her house was empty, save for her staff. Her husband was dead, and her son Max had trundled off to war. Of course, as owner of a large cattle ranch and the illustrious Broadmoor Hotel, she was a millionaire ten times over, but what good was money if you didn't have someone to enjoy it with? All she did was work and support the war effort. When would this damn conflagration end? When would she feel the gentle touch of a caring man? When would her strapping son Max return from the European theatre and marry a sweet young girl?

"Someone's coming," said Jack. He pointed to a cloud of dust along the dirt-road driveway that linked up with the main road.

They watched as the dust cloud turned into a hazy vehicle, and then the hazy vehicle turned into a dull-green military jeep with two men, a driver and an officer in a neat cap, inside. She and Jack looked at one another as the jeep came to a halt and the officer riding shotgun stepped from the vehicle, carrying a letter in his hand.

"Well now, that was quick," said Jack. "Looks like our two deserter friends have got a date at Fort Leavenworth after all."

But Katherine wasn't listening. She had stood up from her chair and was staring at the white envelope in the officer's hand.

"Mrs. Templeton?"

She nodded, feeling a horrible clutch in her chest.

The officer withdrew his cap and looked at her grimly.

"Dear God, no!" she gasped as he came to a stop at the foot of the porch stairs. "Not my Max—please, not my beloved Max!"

He held out the envelope. "I'm sorry, ma'am. He was killed at Anzio. He died in honor for his country."

CHAPTER 9

CAMP 020 INTERROGATION CENTER
SOUTHWEST LONDON, ENGLAND

LIEUTENANT COLONEL TIMOTHY ABERNATHY MACGREGOR—chief of the B1A counterintelligence section of British Military Intelligence Section 5—gazed up through the drizzling rain at the forbidding Victorian mansion known as Latchmere House in Ham Common. He felt uneasy. Though he was well-versed in interrogation techniques and was adept at catching German spies, turning them, and running them as British double agents, he loathed coming here.

It was the combination of the dreadful silence and knowledge of what went on behind the closed doors that unnerved him. Britain's top secret incarceration and interrogation center for suspected spies, subversives, and enemy aliens was as quiet as a mausoleum; yet, what lurked behind her secluded walls, surrounded by three rows of barbed-wire fencing, was a world that would make even the most Blitz-hardened British citizen howl in protest. For here, in the secret MI5 interrogation center code-named 020, where British officers from the First World War had once convalesced to overcome shell shock, was a torture chamber that rivaled the Tower of London.

The difference was the torture was primarily psychological.

Within the sprawling mansion were 92 block cells with hidden microphones, a punishment room known chillingly as Cell 13, and interrogation rooms where wartime enemies of His Majesty the King were mercilessly grilled until "broken" into telling the truth by any and all means necessary, short of outright physical torture. The prisoners were isolated in solitary confinement and were not allowed to speak to one another. Guards wore lightweight tennis shoes to muffle the sound of their footsteps. Pipes were buried within masonry to prevent prisoners from tapping Morse code to one another. Food was kept bland, and cigarettes were not allowed. Sleep deprivation and the hooding of inmates were commonly used tactics, particularly in the first few days of incarceration when the enemy was most vulnerable to breaking down and confessing.

Once broken, those precious few who were high-placed enough within the *Abwehr*—the German intelligence service—to warrant special consideration and showed a willingness to spy for England were not sent to the gallows or imprisoned. Instead, these fortunate few were "turned" and subsequently used as double agents by MacGregor to feed false intelligence to the Germans through the MI5 Double Cross system he had created in 1940. For the past four years, MacGregor's clever double-agent system had been deceiving Hitler about Allied intentions in the battlegrounds of North Africa, Sicily, Italy, Greece, and the

Balkans, as well as in the occupied countries of Europe and neutral Spain, Portugal, Switzerland, and Sweden.

Colonel MacGregor—or Tam as he was affectionately called on account of his initials—felt all his senses on high alert as he walked through the front entrance of Latchmere House. He wore his trademark Glengarry cap and McKenzie tartan trews of the Seaforth Highlanders, or "Passion Pants" as his colleagues at MI5 jokingly referred to them. These same colleagues unanimously agreed that such attire was curiously conspicuous for a man running one of the most secret intelligence operations in a world at war. After signing in at the front desk, he was escorted down the hallway by a young officer to the office of Lieutenant Colonel Robin Stephens, the commandant of Camp 020. Tendrils of silence reached out to him as he stepped down the bland-white corridor, lending a sepulchral aura to the cavernous, insane asylum-like compound.

The escort knocked timidly on the door.

"Come in!"

The voice boomed like a cannon. Tam smiled at the young man. "I'll take it from here, Lieutenant."

The lad looked relieved. "Good luck, Colonel."

CHAPTER 10

CAMP 020 INTERROGATION CENTER

TURNING THE KNOB, he opened the door and came face to face with the legendary Robin "Tin Eye" Stephens. So nicknamed because of the steel-rimmed monocle screwed into his right eye, which reportedly he wore even when he slept and made him as terrifying as the fiercest Nazi interrogator. He sat behind his stately desk, shuffling through paperwork. When he looked up, Tam could feel the air in the room thicken. He took in the vigilant, ruddy face, the neatly creased Nepalese Gurkha military uniform, the gleaming monocle.

My God, does he really sleep with the bloody thing?

"Greetings, Colonel. Please sit down," said Tin Eye.

"Thank you." He smiled easily, closed the door, and walked to the chair in front of his desk. As he sat down, his eyes passed over three of the leather-bound titles in the bookcase: Sigmund Freud's *"Introduction to Psychoanalysis"* and *"An Outline of Psychoanalysis"* perched next to Carl Jung's *"Psychological Types."* Tin Eye was not only a first-class military interrogator, but something of an amateur psychologist.

"So, Colonel Stephens, what can you tell me about our spy?"

"I'm afraid the jury's still out. I've narrowed it down to three of the bloody Huns, but I'm afraid I don't know which one is our man. That's why I wanted you to have a look at them, maybe take a run at them yourself."

"I'm honored, Colonel. But my skills at interrogation are no match for yours. What can you tell me about the three men? For starters, who are they?"

"U-521's second watch officer, chief engineer, and chief medical officer. One of them is our German spy, I'm sure of it. But I'm afraid I'm going to need more time to uncover the clever devil."

"How much more time?"

"Two more days—at least."

"We don't have two more days. The invasion is coming any day now. Look, Colonel, everyone in B branch—especially me—values the tremendous work you do here. But we need our spy to confess and we need it to happen *today*."

He paused to clear his throat for effect.

"The day of reckoning is upon us, Colonel Stephens, and our time is swiftly running out. We need to know if our invasion plan is blown. We need a verifiable confession from our man."

"And Double Cross?"

"Of course, we need to know if Garbo, Tricycle, and our other double agents are blown too. I don't think I need to remind you that the bloody fate of the whole damned war hinges on this. But there's also another reason."

Tin Eye peered at him through his glinting monocle.

"Whoever our spy is, he is a highly valued German asset. If you can break him and turn him quickly, we can use him to full effect to deceive Hitler and his generals in the coming weeks—before, during, and after the invasion."

"You're getting ahead of yourself, Tam. I've just only this morning narrowed it down to three."

"But you are sure it's *one* of them?"

"Yes, but which one?"

"Have any of those you've interrogated admitted that they took aboard a passenger?"

"Six crewmen have given confirmation, but they said they never saw his face."

"Do you believe them?"

"Yes."

"What about the officers?"

"One claims they did not take anyone aboard, and three maintain that they did. But they say that the new passenger was killed during the battle because they never saw him again on deck when they surrendered."

"So you have conflicting accounts. What about the U-boat captain, Commander von Walburg? What is his account?"

"We've gone after him bloody hard. At first, he said that he took no passengers on board. Then, early this morning, he changed his story and confessed that he picked up a man in a rowboat off the Aberdeen coast, but that the man was killed during the ensuing action and he didn't get a chance to speak to him. He said that the subject was questioned by an SS *sturmbannführer* named Prochnow and the two were killed during the attack by our destroyer."

"But you think Walburg is lying, or at least covering up?"

"Most definitely. Look, these U-boat men are a tough bunch, and I've had more than thirty of them to question personally. I'll break every damned one of them—I just need more time."

"Unfortunately, Colonel, time is the one precious commodity we don't have."

They fell silent. Tam felt the tension in the room rise a notch as Tin Eye's already ruddy-complexioned face turned a shade redder. He found the man utterly captivating: larger-than-life yet also a living, breathing dichotomy. As commandant of Camp 020, Stephens hated any and all things German with religious-like fervor, and yet, he was half-German himself. The object of interrogation, he routinely instructed his staff of officers, was simple: "Truth in the shortest possible time." And yet, he stood steadfast in his mantra—drilled into all of his officers—to never inflict physical pain on his charges, and he had a superb record of breaking down even the most hardened Nazi spies without raising so much as a finger. He spoke seven different languages fluently and had commanded a regiment of Ghurkas, the elite Nepalese troops of the British Army, yet he was a raging xenophobe and stodgy imperialist. A frustrated writer, he was outspoken and cruel in his criticism of others, yet he had a natural, comical way with prose and could actually be quite charming when far removed from an interrogation cell. Yes, Robin "Tin Eye" Stephens was certainly a man of many contrasts.

"If time's in short supply, we'd better get at it then," pronounced the legendary commandant. "I have the medical officer standing by right now with Captains Short and Goodacre. He goes by the name Weiss—Manfred Weiss."

"So he's your prime suspect?"

"That is correct. But I've sent for the captain as well. I'd like to interrogate them together."

"Commander Wolfgang von Walburg—'the scourge of the North Sea' as Churchill likes to call him—in the flesh? Well now, I guess this truly is my lucky day. What are you up to, Colonel?"

"I want to see how they react to questioning when the other subject is in the room."

"Is there some connection between them that I'm missing?"

"Nothing from the interrogations. It's just a gut feeling I have."

"No offense, Colonel, but I've never thought of you as a man who put much stock in *gut feelings*."

"I'm aware of that, sir. But in the present case, I could swear that these two captured Boche are actual brothers."

"Brothers, you say? Do they look alike?"

"Not particularly. They have features in common, of course, but it's not their appearance that vexes me."

"Then what is it?"

"Their mannerisms. The way they stand, the way they compose themselves, the way they move when they walk down the hall."

"And how exactly do they move?"

"They walk on the balls of their feet like a bloody panther."

"Could they be cousins? Or perhaps half-brothers?"

"Both are possibilities, but I think they are closer than that."

"What about their *Soldbuchs*?"

"We only have one for the medical officer, Weiss. We've studied it closely and questioned him thoroughly on everything in the book."

"And?"

"We've come up dry. Either he knows the history of Manfred Weiss of Bremen frontwards and backwards—or he's telling the truth and he really is the chap. And that's not all. Dr. Deardon has questioned him extensively on medical matters and seems confident that he is the genuine article. The bastard may or may not be a certified physician as he claims, but he definitely knows his medicine."

Dr. Harold Deardon was the resident psychiatrist at camp 020 who dreamed up creative regimes of psychological torment and sensory deprivation in order to quickly break the will of the inmates. If this Weiss fellow could fool a trained expert in the medical profession, wondered Tam, what chance did they have of breaking and turning him? This was shaping up to be a most intriguing case, indeed.

"As you can see, sir, the situation is complicated."

"Two brothers—one of them a top U-boat captain, the other a cutthroat spy—keeping their brotherhood a secret. Now you truly have piqued my interest, Colonel."

"There's something else. According to MI6, the captain's father is General Robert Graf von Walburg, Prussian count and right-hand man to Field Marshal Rommel in France."

"If that's the case, it should be easy to find out if this Weiss fellow is the general's son. Does this Count von Walburg have any other sons besides Wolfgang?"

"Two, but their whereabouts are unknown. We have an extensive file on Wolfgang, obviously, given his prominence in the *Kriegsmarine*. But for the other two we have nothing. They could be stationed in any unit from the eastern front to Italy or Norway. Or they could be MIA. I've put in a request for more information on the general's sons from MI6, but I'm not holding my breath."

Tam was inclined to agree. Due to the fierce competition between the two rival intelligence agencies, MI5 was treated no better than a homeless tramp by its sister service, often having to wait for weeks for information that should have been handed over within twenty-four hours.

"Very well, then. Let's start the interrogation."

"Blow hot, blow cold to start?" asked Tin Eye, referring to the "good constable-bad constable" technique he often employed in his interrogations of particularly recalcitrant inmates.

"That will be fine. I'm hot, you're cold?"

"I'm always cold. You know that, Tam."

"Yes, you most certainly are, Colonel."

Tin Eye stood up from his chair, puffed out his chest, and took a deep breath as if preparing for a rugby match. His face glittered with savage delight. In that instant, Tam realized that there would be no holding back, no mercy, no sympathy for the two German captives. It would be all-out psychological warfare. Whatever was required to break them, short of pulling out their fingernails or crushing their arms and legs in a vise, would be performed in the next few hours. Then, when it was all done, if he and Tin Eye so desired, they would put the two terrified Huns back together again, piece by piece, and turn them into British double agents.

CHAPTER 11

CAMP 020 INTERROGATION CENTER

ERIK VON WALBURG—onetime Harvard pre-med student now posing as U-521 Staff Medical Officer Manfred Otto Weiss of Bremen—felt the hairs on the back of his neck bristle as the fierce-looking officer with the monocle, his two subordinates, and a new, fourth man stepped into Interrogation Room 3. The newcomer had a dashing, well-bred manner about him. He wore a fancy Scottish cap and pair of striking, neatly-pressed tartan trousers that seemed the antithesis of an intelligence operative. The four men quietly took their seats without saying a word, leaving him and his brother to continue standing against the wall even though they were both on the verge of collapse. The question was did their captors know how perilously close they were to being broken?

"No chivalry, no gossip, no cigarettes. Your life as you know it is over," the man with the monocle had chillingly greeted him and the other U-boat prisoners *auf Deutsch* upon their arrival on Friday. He was the camp commandant, and Erik had overheard one of the staff officers in the hallway refer to him in a hushed whisper as "Tin Eye." Since his arrival, Erik had been strip-searched twice, poked and probed by a man purporting to be a doctor, photographed, savagely and relentlessly interrogated, and fed barely edible food. He had also not been allowed even a wink of sleep or any interaction with the other prisoners. His British captors were trying to impress upon him, his brother Wolfgang, and the rest of their German comrades the hopelessness of their position—and they were succeeding.

Tin Eye looked them over with a scornful expression on his face. "So, how does it feel for the two brothers to be reunited?" he asked in ragged but serviceable German.

Erik and his brother looked at one another with exaggerated surprise. "Brothers? We are not brothers," replied Wolfgang. "Dr. Weiss is my medical officer."

"Come now, do you really expect me to believe that? What do you take me for, a bloody fool?"

"It is the truth."

"And what do you Jerries know about truth? Why your own Führer is the biggest liar of all. He has been deceiving you and your people for the past decade. Why Berlin is in shambles from Allied bombing and you probably didn't even know it."

The two brothers said nothing. The less they volunteered the better.

"Do you really expect me to believe that you are not brothers?"

"But we aren't," said Erik, composing himself in the most honest expression he could muster despite his terrible fatigue.

But Tin Eye was having none of it. "I'm going to ignore your insolence, at least for the time being. Now tell me what you were doing in the conning tower when the SS *sturmbannführer*—what was his name again, Major Prochnow?—was blown to bits. It doesn't make any sense."

"I was there to offer medical services," answered Erik.

"But you were already there. What were you doing in the tower in the first place? The British destroyer had not fired upon the vessel yet."

"The captain summoned me. The explosion went off as soon as I arrived."

"I ordered him to the tower in case of attack," explained Wolfgang. "I always have a medical officer standing by when the enemy is spotted."

Tin Eye glared at him. "You're lying again. Will there be no end to your treachery, Captain? Very well, if you are going to be defiant, please keep in mind that you are only delaying the inevitable. We will get back to this unanswered family matter in due time. Of course, you two must realize that you could be here for months, if necessary."

Erik felt himself twitch. *Months! Did the tin-eyed bastard just say they would be imprisoned here for months!* He wasn't sure he could last another week with barely any food and not a minute of sleep!

"I'm not saying this in any sense of a threat, but you must remember that you are in a British Secret Service prison and it's our job in wartime to make sure that we get the whole story from you. So, do you two really want to be here for months, because this will go on like this until we have the answers we seek?"

For the first time, the new man in the tartan cap and trousers spoke. The officer appeared to be Tin Eye's superior. He had an easygoing, ruling class manner about him, like the Prussian aristocrats Erik and his family had rubbed elbows with their whole lives.

"I don't think we need to terrorize these gentlemen," he gently chided Tin Eye in a mild Scottish brogue. "While I'm certain they are enjoying our accommodations, I don't believe they would like to extend their holiday too long. Am I correct, gentlemen?"

Erik looked at Wolfgang. What could they possibly say to that? The Scotsman gave a little chuckle. It was then Erik realized that beneath the man's upper-crust affability lurked a more cold-hearted, ruthless streak.

Tin Eye was leaning across the table, squinting at them sourly through his glass monocle.

"You're not even a real doctor, are you, von Walburg?"

He tried to look affronted despite his exhaustion. "My name is not von Walburg. I told you I am Manfred Weiss."

"Yes, yes, Manfred Weiss of Bremen. And how many hours were you aboard U-521 before she was attacked by the British destroyer?"

"I told you, I am a medical officer, not a spy. I was commissioned in Brest and have been with the boat since the war began. Except for the four months I was interned in Berlin for my wounds."

"And to that I say you're a bloody liar."

"Enough!" protested Wolfgang, holding up his hands. "Do I need to remind you again that you are in flagrant violation of Geneva Convention Articles 5 and 6 that protect military prisoners of war from precisely this kind of abuse? We are required to give our true name and rank, but you are not allowed to torture us into giving more information."

"You have not been tortured, sir, and I resent any implication to that effect in my camp. Figuratively speaking, a prisoner in war should be at the point of a bayonet, but that, of course, is figuratively speaking. Because in my camp, Captain von Walburg, violence is taboo, for not only does it produce answers to please, it lowers the standard of information. That's why, unlike your murderous Gestapo, we never strike a man. In the first place, it is an act of cowardice. In the second, it reeks of stupidity. A beaten prisoner will lie to avoid further physical punishment and everything he says thereafter will be based on a false premise. So I say to you, sir, there is not—and never will be—a shred of violence against any prisoner in my camp. So kindly watch your tongue!"

Erik saw that, despite Tin Eye's forceful tone, his brother was undaunted. "You have deprived me and my men of sleep for two days running, and that is a violation of the Geneva Convention," pointed out Wolfgang in a deliberate yet passionate voice. "We are not spies—we are prisoners of war—and you *will* abide by the Geneva Convention. You are required to report our capture to our War Office within the shortest period possible, and the Red Cross is allowed to visit us and see that we are being properly treated. You are in direct violation by holding us here and subjecting us to this abuse. We prisoners have rights."

"Not in my camp you don't," growled Tin Eye.

"Now, now, gentlemen," said the chivalrous-looking Scotsman, stepping in as referee. He looked sympathetically at the two Germans. "I concur wholeheartedly that the Geneva articles are of the utmost importance for men at arms. But I'm afraid they don't cover spies."

"We are not spies," bristled Wolfgang.

"You see, that's the problem, old boy. That remains to be proven. Until we have accounted for each and every crew member and have determined, with one hundred percent certainty, that there are no spies among you, I'm afraid the Geneva Convention articles do not apply."

"That is preposterous!"

"Unfortunately for you, it is anything but. So you had better start answering the commandant's questions. Continued lies will only bring you and your men misery, I can assure you. So tell us, Captain von Walburg, which of your crew members is the spy? Once you come clean, this will all be over."

"I have nothing to say to you."

"Well then," said Tin Eye, "we'll just have to march you and your men out into the courtyard, line you all up, and bring you upstairs one by one. In exchange for a nice warm bed and a good hot meal, heavy on the sausage and potatoes of course, I can guarantee that at least two or three of your men will tell us what we need to know."

"I already told you, the spy is dead. He was killed during the attack."

Erik looked at his brother with surprise. Because he had been isolated from the other prisoners, including his brother, he hadn't known that any of the crew had admitted that there even was a spy. But how did the British know that the U-boat was rendezvousing with a spy if they didn't have the ability to read enemy wireless transmissions? That was the question he should be asking Tin Eye, if for no other reason than to get a reaction. It was then he noticed the bellicose commandant staring at him, as if reading his mind.

My God, the clever bastard doesn't miss a thing, does he?

"How did you steal the rowboat at Stonehaven when there was a posted guard?"

"I don't know what you're talking about. I haven't been to Stonehaven."

"Yes, you have. It's the small fishing village a few miles south of Aberdeen. You stole a rowboat from there five days ago."

"I did no such thing."

"We have had enough of these questions!" interrupted Wolfgang. "Under the Geneva Convention, this must stop! We are seamen not spies! The spy was killed and his body is in the North Sea!"

"Now, isn't that convenient?" said Captain Goodacre, one of the other interrogators. "We've told you several times now that when you lie to us, you are just making things more difficult for you and your men."

"We are not lying," protested Erik. But even as he said it, he wondered how much longer he and his brother could possibly hold out. He was so damned tired!

Tin Eye was up and on his feet. "I have had enough of this balderdash. Captain Short," he ordered the officer to his right, "please assemble the crew in the yard for inspection. We'll have our spy in ten minutes time."

"My pleasure, Colonel," said the pudgy captain, and he started for the door.

Erik saw a look of panic take hold of his brother's face. "This is preposterous!" Wolfgang roared back, but already Erik had a sick feeling that the game was up. His father, General Rommel, and the German High Command would never know the great military secret he possessed, a secret that would tip the balance of the war in his beloved Fatherland's favor and perhaps even lead to ultimate victory. In that instant, he realized that his life as he knew it was over. As a spy, he would be hung or shot before a firing squad.

"There's nothing preposterous about it in the least," countered Tin Eye. "We are at war and you have been lying to us!"

"We have not been lying! We are *Kriegsmarine* officers and crewmen!"

"No, sir, you have been lying to us, and doing a rather poor job of it, I might add!"

"I'm afraid he's right, gentlemen," said the Scotsman as the captain turned the door handle. "The game is up."

"But you can't do this! We are protected under the Geneva Convention!"

Tin Eye shook his head. "Not as bloody spies you're not!" He looked hard at the two brothers, his face a study in controlled intensity. "I'm giving you one last chance. Is there something you want to tell us?"

A tense silence gripped Interrogation Room 3. To Erik, time seemed to stand still. He felt a rivulet of sweat roll down his temple. A part of him wanted to tell them what they wanted to know so he could go back to his cell and sleep for a week. He was so fucking tired!

Anxious seconds ticked off. He glanced at the captain at the door, whose chubby hand was still paused on the handle. His brother and the stubborn Tin Eye just glared at one another, as if waiting for the other to blink.

Suddenly, a booming, official-sounding voice piped up outside the interrogation room in the hallway.

"No, we will see the colonel right now, damn you!"

Everyone looked up in startlement as a tall, high-ranking officer with a neatly-trimmed mustache shoved his way into the room. He was trailed by another senior officer, who was, in turn, followed by a terrified-looking junior lieutenant.

The Scotsman and Tin Eye both stood up with alarm from their chairs. "Sir Frederick!" exclaimed the Scotsman.

"Colonel MacGregor, Colonel Stephens"—he tipped his head to them—"my humble apologies, but this interrogation is finished."

Tin Eye stiffened. "But General Morgan, they were just about to—"

"Not another word, Colonel. We've got our man and we're taking these prisoners off your hands."

Despite his physical exhaustion, Erik watched with a sense of relief and renewed interest as the Scotsman named MacGregor stepped forward to plead his case. "But Sir Frederick—"

"No buts, Colonel. My orders come straight from the top. Now if you'll please follow me, I'll explain."

CHAPTER 12

CAMP 020 INTERROGATION CENTER

THEY WENT TO A SPARE CONFERENCE ROOM, took seats around a battered oak table, and conducted a gentlemanly military briefing in the fine British tradition. Towards the end, Tam MacGregor looked at Lieutenant General Sir Frederick Edgeworth Morgan, Deputy Chief of Staff at Supreme Headquarters Allied Expeditionary Force, or SHAEF, and couldn't believe what the bloody hell the general was asking of him. Seated beside Morgan was Major Sir John Cecil Masterman, distinguished Oxford don and chairman of the Double Cross Committee that ran and controlled German double agents living in England. Tin Eye Stephens and his two subordinate officers, Captains Short and Goodacre, had been dismissed from the proceedings. Unlike Tam and his cohorts, they were not BIGOTs—members of the Allied intelligence inner circle with the highest security clearance for the BRITISH INVASION OF GERMAN OCCUPIED TERRITORY—whose job it was to deceive the Germans into concluding that the invasion of Occupied France was to take place in the Pas de Calais rather than Normandy.

Tam knew better than anyone else in British intelligence how to spot a lie, and therefore how to sell one. But his biggest operation thus far, Operation Fortitude, was damn near impossible: to fool the German High Command over the location of the landing of the Allied Invasion Force while, at the same time, keeping a secret of the actual invasion location at Normandy. It was a monumental undertaking, one that required meticulous attention to detail and impeccable teamwork. He had deftly handled a widely disparate collection of Double Cross agents among them playboys, criminals, and drunks with inspired code names like Zigzag, Tricycle, and Garbo—to bring spectacular military successes to the Allied cause. But the outcome of the war depended, ultimately, on the success of Fortitude—and right now Sir Frederick was putting the massive covert operation at serious risk.

When the general was finished with his oration, Tam cleared his throat irritably before summarizing: "So what you're telling me is this Swede Henrik Carlsson is our spy, and your boss Eisenhower wants these U-boat men shipped off to America immediately so they have no chance to escape and bugger up the invasion? Is that what you're telling me?"

"It's out of my hands, Tam. Ike's made his decision. It's all part of the new policy in preparation for D-Day. All German POWs apprehended in the northern theatre of European operations are to be sent to the U.S. as soon as possible after they are rounded up. There's too much risk that one of them could escape and muck up our deception plans for the invasion."

"General Eisenhower and his staff remember only too well what happened with Summer and Jeff—and they don't want to risk a repeat performance," said Masterman, referring to the two British-controlled double agents that had almost blown Double Cross wide open to the enemy. "You know the problem we face, Tam. No intelligence service, no matter how good, can maintain a bluff indefinitely. Sooner or later, a blunder or sheer mischance will give it away. If the Germans gain knowledge of even one of our doubles, they will inevitably become suspicious of all the other agents under our control. Then they'll examine every agent's case record in minute detail and end up piecing together the truth about them all."

Sir Frederick nodded and added his thoughts. "You know what that would mean for Fortitude. It would be a disaster, six months of planning down the tubes. Ike can't abide that. He wants all newly captured German POWs from the northern theatre shipped as far away from the war zone as possible—just to be safe."

Tam could appreciate the need to ensure absolute secrecy, but he was still livid that the two prisoners in Interrogation Room 3 were to be released. "But what makes you so certain that this Carlsson is the spy?"

"Inspector Jenkins has incontrovertible evidence. He's standing by at Aberdeen police headquarters interrogating Carlsson as we speak." Jenkins was the Scotland Yard detective who had been coordinating with MI5 during the last two weeks to hunt down the spy, who was linked to the murder of a British intelligence officer in Hyde Park in London. The murder was what had precipitated the manhunt over half of England and Scotland.

"What evidence?"

"They found the murder weapon on him, Tam—a stiletto," said Major Masterman.

"The same one used on poor Jamison? But how do they know?"

"The stiletto has a pearl handle on it that was partially broken during the attack," explained Masterman. "Jenkins managed to retrieve a pearl fragment at the crime scene. It's an exact match to the fragment missing from the stiletto found on Carlsson. But that's not all."

Though perturbed, Tam felt an excitement building inside him. But everything seemed to be happening too fast, as if sand was shifting beneath his feet.

"Carlsson had a roll of film on him as well."

"Film? Has it been developed?

"Indeed it has."

"What does it show?"

"We still need final confirmation, but the preliminary analysis is that the photographs are of the southern coastline and our training exercises in and around Slapton Sands."

"Slapton Sands? That was a bloody disaster. Are you suggesting that this Carlsson knows of our Fortitude South deception plan?"

"We don't know, but we have to prepare for the worst," said Sir Frederick, thoughtfully stroking his mustache. "The pictures look exactly like the beaches at

Normandy. That's why we chose Slapton Sands for our training exercises in the first place."

"What do we know of this Carlsson?"

"Born and raised in Stockholm, prominent industrialist, ball bearings and machine parts mostly," said Masterman. "He's an engineer by training. He travels on routine business between Stockholm, Lisbon, London, and Scotland. He's been on our watch list since the outbreak of the war, but nothing has come up."

"So he's not one of ours. What do our brethren at MI6 have to say?"

"They deny all knowledge of the Swede," said Masterman. "He's not spying for them."

"Or, they're not telling us."

"Come now, Tam. We're on the same side as those chaps."

He thought: *I'll believe that when I see it. If this Carlsson fellow is doubling for us and the Jerries, we bloody well should have been informed about it from MI6. But the bastards always keep things from us.*

In fact, since the war had begun, the collaboration—or lack thereof—between the two rival British intelligence services had always been a cause for consternation for both sides. While the task of MI5 was to control counterespionage in the United Kingdom and throughout the British Empire, and MI6's charter was to operate in all areas outside British territory, in actuality the intelligence gathering and dissemination activities of the two agencies often overlapped, causing inevitable friction. It was in these circumstances that relations between the two competing British intelligence services were most strained. The men who ran the internal espionage branch did not appreciate their rivals from the external security branch that ran overseas operatives encroaching on their patch—and vice versa.

"What about Carlsson's security clearance?"

"He has government-issued, top-level security clearance. He is allowed even in our restricted areas for Fortitude North and South."

"Good heavens! We might as well just give Hitler and his henchmen the keys to Whitehall!"

"Yes, well, the main thing is our spy has been apprehended," said Sir Frederick. "Jenkins is bringing him down here by train tomorrow from Aberdeen."

"Tin Eye will be rather pleased to have a go at him, I should expect," said Masterman, the paternalistic, cricket-obsessed Oxford don with a dry grin. "He'll be delivered straight here to Latchmere House."

Tam felt a vexing prickle of doubt about the whole situation. Only five minutes ago, during the interrogation, he had felt as though the two prisoners were about to break down and confess everything; and if not, that Tin Eye's clever ploy to assemble the entire U-boat crew in the common, pull out the seamen one by one, and give them the opportunity to anonymously identify the spy would have sealed the spy's fate. But now, they had this Swedish fellow Carlsson, who had been apprehended with the Hyde Park murder weapon on his person and a roll of film of the Slapton Sands training area, which would have tipped off even the most dim-witted *Abwehr* officer that the true Allied invasion would occur at Normandy. Was it possible that there were two spies?

Sir Frederick was looking at him. "What is it Tam? What's bothering you?"

"My problem with all this is I believe our man got on board that U-boat. Otherwise, who stole the skiff at Stonehaven?"

"It could have been anybody."

"No, it was our man. Look, we lost him north of Aberdeen, and the skiff was reported missing a stone's throw away in Stonehaven. We had a late-breaking decrypt of the radio transmission telling us the precise time and place of the rendezvous off the coast of the fishing village. We showed up there, but we were too late. All the same, we were able to re-vector and we got our U-boat. There is no question it was headed south, presumably to the Lorient base. So why the devil do we then conveniently catch a Swedish industrialist along the coast the very next day with enough evidence on him to hang himself like Captain Kidd? I'll tell you why. Because that's what our real spy wants us to believe. It's too neat and tidy, and I don't like it. In fact, I don't like it one damned bit."

"Well, like it or not, Act One is over," said Sir Frederick, looking like a man who would brook no further opposition. "As I've made abundantly clear, it's out of our hands."

"I understand you have to watch Ike's back, sir. But I would be remiss if I didn't point out one very important thing."

"I'm listening, Colonel."

"At the very least, those two Jerries we were interrogating only moments ago know a hell of a lot more than they're letting on. That, I can guarantee."

"I've no doubt you're right, but we have our orders, Tam," said Masterman, flexing his owlish brows upward in that professorial way of his when he wanted one of his peers to stand down.

"Tin Eye is going to have bad case of indigestion over this."

"You let me deal with Colonel Stephens."

He tried to put aside his doubts, but the whole situation still nagged him. Everything was happening too damned fast. If only he had time to think. But unfortunately, his time had run out.

He turned back to Sir Frederick. "All right, so what is the plan for Captain von Walburg and his seamen?"

"They are to be delivered to the Bristol airfield by 0200 this afternoon."

"Bristol? If you don't mind my asking, Sir Frederick, where are they headed?"

"To Camp Shanks, New York. Or so I am told."

Tam had a bad feeling of déjà vu. The last time he had dealt with the bloody Yanks—specifically that imbecile J. Edgar Hoover and his FBI—they had almost blown the cover of his best double agent, the Yugoslavian playboy Dusko Popov, code-named Tricycle.

"How soon will the Americans be here?" he asked.

"The transports will be here within the hour."

"From this point on, the Americans are running the show," said Masterman, without much reassurance. Like Tam, he was only too familiar with the ineptitude of Hoover and his G-Men, as well as the inherent dangers of working closely with the American intelligence community. But slowly yet assuredly, the inexperienced

Yanks were improving in espionage, particularly in South America.

"They're General Marshall's problem now—not ours," echoed Sir Frederick. "We're getting those U-boat men the hell *out of here* and *back over there* as quick as we can, and that order comes straight from the top. So, gentlemen, now that this matter has been resolved, I will now leave you to liaise with the Americans. And please be sure to keep the British end up."

Tam saluted smartly. "Yes, sir, we most assuredly will."

"I also want to wish you good luck."

"Thank you, Sir Frederick."

"No not you, Colonel MacGregor. I was talking to Major Masterman. After all, he's the one who has to break the news to bloody Tin Eye."

CHAPTER 13

CAMP PERSHING
GERMAN PRISONER OF WAR INTERNMENT CAMP
SOUTHEASTERN COLORADO, USA

COLONEL JACK MORRISON—Commandant of Camp Pershing—stared out his office window at the mounted patrol along the west fence line, and thought back to the time he had chased the wily Pancho Villa across Northern Mexico.

The year was 1915. He was a second lieutenant fresh out of West Point, commanding a troop of black cavalry—the famed Buffalo Soldiers of E Troop, 9th Cavalry Regiment. It came back to him like it happened yesterday: a mad charge down a hillside in pursuit of a band of swift-riding *Mexicanos*, rawhide quirts slapping muscled rumps, heads bobbing in the saddle, the wild screaming of the men on both sides, the crackle of gunfire, and, best of all, the warm camaraderie and drinking of mescal at night with the boys after a hard day's fight.

War had seemed such a romantic undertaking back then—before the trenches and mustard gas of the First Great War, and before the blitzkrieg tank battles and massive aerial bombs of the Second. By God, he had even been awarded the Mexican Service Medal during the campaign from his hero General "Black Jack" Pershing, who was, ironically, the namesake of the internment camp where he was now languishing as commandant. The world had seemed so full of promise and adventure in those youthful glory days. As he stared out the window and compared it to his miserable present, he couldn't help but feel old and tired, like a spent warhorse.

To think that he had sunk so low as to be banished to a wretched German POW camp five-thousand miles removed from the closest combat.

He took a stiff drink of Wild Turkey from his silver flask to steady his nerves and ease the pain of the shrapnel still lodged in his leg, a present from Rommel's Africa Corps in Tunisia. Beyond the mounted patrol loomed a barren western country bereft of trees, flat as a billiard table, an expanse so vast that Morrison lost himself staring off into it, the sensation of smallness magnified by the endless, dusky-pink sky and his own feelings of impotence.

Damnit, he thought miserably. *How have I let it come to this?*

His thoughts were interrupted by a ringing phone. He glanced at his desk, thought a moment about not answering it before deciding to. He picked up before the fourth ring.

"Colonel Morrison here."

"Colonel, this is General Bryan." The voice on the other end didn't need to say that it belonged to the Assistant Provost Marshal General.

"Hello, General. What can I do for you?"

"Well, Colonel, we've got ourselves a problem. It's been brought to my attention that you're impeding the POW Labor Program by conducting a little social experiment with the Krauts at your camp."

A little social experiment? Morrison felt like he had been sucker punched in the gut. "You're talking about my proposal to separate the Nazis from the non-Nazis here at Camp Pershing?"

"It's causing problems here in Washington, Colonel. Since word of your proposed program leaked out to your prisoners, more than three hundred POWs, who just last week were happily employed, are now refusing to work because of this new segregation policy of yours. We don't like work strikes, Colonel. We're not going to tell you how to run your camp, as long as the Hun bastards are working. But right now, they're not and that's a problem."

"I'll get them back to work, sir. But it's going to take some time."

"We don't have time, Colonel. It's already been a week and we want those damned Krauts back to work."

"I'm going to need another week."

"That's unacceptable. Adolf Hitler himself has issued a directive that he wants all German POWs to take part in the Labor Program to keep up morale and retain their physical fitness—and yet you have more than three hundred men on strike because word leaked out of your planned social experiment. It's an embarrassing situation for the army, and it needs to stop."

"I've already brought charges against the officer responsible."

"I don't care about the goddamned inside leak. I care about the Labor Program. I don't care how you do it, but you need to get those Krauts back in the fields—and I mean pronto. I have strict orders from the very top to make sure that the POW Labor Program is operating at peak efficiency."

"If you'll excuse me, General Bryan, I think there's more at stake than the profitability of the Labor Program."

"Are you lecturing me, Colonel?"

"No, sir, I'm just trying to say that prisoners' safety—in fact, their very lives—are on the line here. Colonel Kepler and his gang will beat up, and maybe even kill, some of these men if I put them back in the main camp. He's already had his thugs beat the crap out of more than a dozen enlisted men, as well as two officers. And those are just the ones we know about."

"I'm aware of the situation with the Africa Corps commander. But Kepler is not the bogeyman. You've got to get your camp under control, Colonel, or we'll bring in someone else who will."

"Believe me, I'm trying, General. But they take their orders from Kepler and no one else. They threaten anyone who's a non-believer or sympathetic to us Americans."

"Non-believer. What do you mean non-believer?"

"Anyone who's not a Nazi fanatic. Which means any prisoner who's not a hard-line National Socialist. They threaten them by telling them that they'll harm their families back in Germany if they don't comply. Even worse, they control all of the important positions here at the camp: the hospital, library, canteen, sports teams. They even control the movies the prisoners watch as well as the newspapers they read. It all started with Major Tatum—"

"Now there's no reason to bring the former camp commandant into this. He was relieved of duty."

"Yeah, and now I'm cleaning up his mess. You are aware that he was drinking with Kepler and two of his officers until two o'clock in the morning on the very night that a prisoner was killed."

"The death of the Austrian was a regrettable matter. But you don't know that Colonel Kepler was behind it. And besides, it was ruled a suicide."

"It was no suicide. It was a coerced murder orchestrated by Kepler and his crew. They locked Private Faymann in a closet with a rope and wouldn't let him out until he had hung himself. It wasn't a suicide—it was cold-blooded murder. And it's not going to happen again, not on my watch!"

"There's no need to raise your voice with me, Colonel. Now I understand you've got to maintain control of your camp, but you've made the mistake of letting this become personal between you and Kepler. The top priority is to get these Krauts back to work. Most of those on strike were working just fine in the Labor Program before you came up with your hare-brained scheme to segregate the prisoners into Nazi and non-Nazi barracks. And then, you screwed up royally by discussing your proposed policy change with your officers, who let word of it leak out to the damned prisoners. You should never have made the *unilateral decision* to segregate the camp into Nazis and non-Nazis, and you should never have let word of your plans leak out. Do you understand me, Colonel? That's where you went wrong."

"Unilateral decision? You're saying I made a unilateral decision?"

"You know damned well it is not the official policy of the War Department to segregate Nazis from non-Nazis. What's next, separating out the commies?"

"Communists don't beat up, torture, and kill people like the Nazis. At least, not in my camp. Look, General, if I don't separate out the damned Nazis from the non-Germans and the German anti-Nazis, more men will get hurt and the POW work program will suffer even more from a lack of volunteers."

"What do you mean the non-Germans? You mean the Austrians?"

"I don't just have Austrians, General: I've got Poles, Czechs, Hungarians, Ukrainians, and even a pair of Mongolians captured on the Eastern Front and forced to fight for Hitler. These men are no more Nazi than you or I—and Kepler and his gang make them pay for it every damned day. I'm not going to allow these bastards to make the lives of the other prisoners a living hell."

"I'm afraid the War Department doesn't see it that way, Colonel. Nazis get things done. They're very efficient, and they know how to obey orders."

"So you're telling me to just turn my camp over to Kepler and his goons?"

"No, I'm telling you that the Labor Program is the top priority and you'd better get your damned camp in order, or you won't even be commanding a troop of Cub Scouts. I am also informing you that the War Department is growing tired of fielding complaints from the Swiss Legation. It takes up valuable time that could be spent on more important matters."

"There was another complaint?"

"Dr. Fischer of the Swiss Legation has notified us of a fifth complaint against you for your treatment of the German POWs at Camp Pershing."

The charge was ludicrous, but he said nothing. His German prisoners—in fact, all POWs interned in America—were treated better than POWs in any other country, including the United Kingdom. It was true that he had imposed reduced privileges and a restricted diet upon Kepler for one week for his intransigence, but all of the German POWs in his camp were treated in strict accordance with the Geneva Convention, and were actually better fed and had more free time to pursue hobbies and play sports than most hard-working, war-weary Americans.

"Don't tell me. It was Kepler who lodged the complaint against me, right?"

"He has it out for you."

"May I ask the basis of the colonel's complaint this time?"

"It's not just your proposed segregation policy. He says that you are openly discriminating against him and other German officers for their political beliefs."

"You know that's a lie."

"Is it? You do seem to be punishing them for their ideology."

Morrison didn't like Bryan's accusing tone; it made him feel as if he was the stubborn, narrow-minded one, not Kepler and his fucking Nazi thugs. "I have not punished anyone. All I did was come up with a plan to separate the hardened Nazis from the non-Nazis for safety reasons, that's all. I discussed it with my officers and one of them spilled the beans for two packs of smokes. Kepler's only angry because I have undermined his authority."

"The colonel also says that you're trying to indoctrinate him and his men with the films you show."

"So I stopped the gangster movies. That's all Kepler would allow the POWs to see: movies that showed American gangsters, and Negroes being treated badly. He doesn't want any of his men to see the good, democratic side of America. So I put a stop to it."

"But the Swiss Legation—"

"The Swiss are in bed with Hitler and we all know it. They just do it behind the scenes."

"You've got to solve this problem, Colonel. We need those Krauts back to work. Why don't you just send Colonel Kepler to Alva? The camp will take its first prisoners next month." He was referring to the high-security POW camp in Alva, Oklahoma. It was being specially built for the internship of the most disruptive, obdurate Nazi prisoners.

"I'll take that into consideration," said Morrison, though he had no intention of doing any such thing. He wasn't about to take the easy way out. He was going to deal with Kepler head on and force him to terminate his bullying. He wasn't going to take the path of least resistance and remove one bad apple just to achieve a smooth running operation. In his view, true democracy and fair play were messy things and not to be subverted just to grease the wheels of profit.

"I'm going to say it one last time, Colonel. Get your goddamned camp in order, or I'll have you stripped of command!"

And then he was gone.

CHAPTER 14

CAMP PERSHING

MORRISON SLAMMED DOWN THE PHONE, feeling even more agitated than before. He reached for his flask and swigged back another shot of Wild Turkey. Sourmash whiskey would be the death of him, he knew, but he needed a drink badly right now. And a walk to clear his head. He didn't want his staff to see him in this angry state, so he slipped quietly out the back door of his office and headed towards a little knoll in the west corner of the compound, facing the mountains.

It was his one little sanctuary.

He looked out at green plains in the foreground, crinkled like an old man's jowls. They were still and peaceful. To the west, the plains rose to meet the distant snow-covered mountains, and to the north, they gave way to a smattering of rolling hills covered with scrub brush, crumbling pinnacles of cream-colored chalk, and finger-like coulees scarred by wind and rain. With the towering Rockies forming a majestic backdrop, what spread before him was a magnificent, awe-inspiring sight.

It reminded him of how much he had always wanted to be a soldier. But now, just look at him. Now he wasn't even a soldier—he was a goddamned babysitter for violent German POWs!

How had it come to this?

Angrily, he remembered back to his demotion. It had been a crushing blow. After the fiasco at Meknassy Heights during last spring's Tunisian campaign, he had begged Patton to give him a second chance. Gotten down on his knees and actually begged the man. But Old Blood and Guts would have none of it. The thing about the incident was that the initial night assault he had led on the stubbornly defended knolls, in front of the 1st Armored's lines, had been a resounding success. But then he had been struck in the leg by an exploding shell, the enemy had dug in and counterattacked, and before he knew it March had turned to April and the American offensive that had begun at El Guettar had bogged down against stiffened Axis resistance. He had received a Purple Heart, a Silver Star, the Distinguished Service Cross—and a bad limp for the rest of his life. But worst of all, he had to suffer the crushing embarrassment of being relieved of duty.

Patton had thought him too timid in battle.

He was shipped stateside and quietly given command of the new Camp Pershing in Colorado. That in itself was bad enough, but then disaster struck again. That same month, his wife was killed by a hit-and-run driver near their home in Chicago. Stricken with grief, he started drinking like never before.

He still hadn't let up.

Sometimes, he wondered what was the point of living?

He watched as a small group of German POWs stepped out from the main compound to watch the sunset. The prisoners had spent their Sunday afternoon relaxing and playing soccer, and these fellows were still kicking a ball around. After a few minutes of horseplay, they locked arms and began to sing. The faint strains of *Lili Marlene* rose up on the plains wind, and Morrison couldn't help but smile.

As he listened to the Germans singing, he realized that he didn't hate them. With the exception of Colonel Kepler and a handful of the other most hardened Nazis, he bore no animosity towards his German charges. In his view, a soldier who fought in the name of hate and did not respect his enemies was not worthy of the uniform.

But Kepler and his Nazi gang posed a serious, festering problem. It had turned into a battle of wills, and he was going to have to deal harshly with them.

He looked again at the singing prisoners.

The song about a lovesick German soldier drifted up and hung there in the sage-scented air. Morrison felt the great lonesomeness inside. *Lili Marlene* made him think of his late wife. He remembered the warmth of her body, her womanly scent, the soothing femininity of her voice. That was the thing about a woman. Whether they had passed from this earth or lay beside you, once you had been touched by one, they could reach down and tug at your soul like nothing else in the world, make you feel all muddled and yearning for an entire lifetime.

He looked up at the sky. The ball of sun was leaning into the hazy blue mountain peaks in a brilliant blaze of purplish-pink. The scenery fairly took his breath away. Even though the anger hadn't completely vanished inside him, he couldn't help but feel the power of the land, the infinity of it all and the feeling of oneness inside. The land was a reassuring presence, like an old friend.

The land itself was eternal. The West was eternal.

He bent down and picked up a clump of loamy soil, sifting it through his fingers, watching the flour-like dust blow off in the crisp breeze. He would always remember this small moment: the lonesome tug he felt inside as he gazed out at the sweeping western landscape and took in the homesick voices of the Germans singing about the loved ones they had left behind.

But then, when the sun went down, the dark thoughts seeped once again into his mind.

What the hell am I going to do about Kepler and his violent gang?

DAY 3

THURSDAY

JUNE 1, 1944

CHAPTER 15

PULLMAN COACH PASSENGER TRAIN
EN ROUTE TO CAMP PERSHING, USA

ERIK VON WALBURG—known to his U.S. captors as Manfred Weiss and, since his processing at Camp Shanks, New York, Prisoner 7WG-27341—stared out the window of the finely-appointed Pullman coach. America was even more of a land of plenty than when he had attended Harvard four years ago. The growth of the nation was unbelievable: automobiles were ubiquitous; the cities seemed bigger than he remembered and were bustling with industry; the sheer monstrosity of the skyscrapers staggered the imagination; and the land itself seemed endless. Even the music was new and catchy, upbeat and rife with freedom. Outside the train station before they had boarded, swinging jazz saxophones and trumpets blared up and down the street, as if to announce to any and all newcomers to the New World that this truly was a land of opportunity and unbridled optimism.

The Americans seemed to have it all.

He and the other U-boat prisoners had been flown from Bristol to New York on a Douglas C-54 Skymaster. Upon their arrival, they were transported to Camp Shanks to be examined by medical staff and processed as U.S. Army Prisoners of War. First, they were given net sacks with two brass tokens, stripped, searched, marched into showers, and forced to scrub every inch of themselves and submit to being sprayed with delousing powder while their clothes were disinfected with DDT. Once they and their belongings were clean, they were inspected for skin and venereal diseases, weighed, measured, and given a brief medical examination. Next, they were herded into another large room where another doctor stuck a huge needle into their buttocks. Then they had to fill out a three-page form covering their name, military rank and unit, personal and medical history, fingerprints, serial numbers, and personal effects. At this point, they were now official prisoners of war and copies of their records were forwarded to the International Red Cross so that their families could be informed about their fates. Once processed, they were delivered to Grand Central Station, searched again, and then loaded on a westbound train.

Now, as Erik stared out the window, he had to admit that even though he had lived in the United States before the war and knew what to expect, he was surprised at the generosity of his American captors. Though the processing at Camp Shanks had been an annoyance, thus far on their journey he and his German comrades-in-arms had been treated with courtesy and even occasional warmth by not only the guards but American civilians. They had been supplied with cigarettes, writing paper, and books for both their flight and train ride. The

Americans' generosity made him resent the brutality and paranoia of the Nazi Germany Hitler had created all the more.

A Negro porter in a cap and white jacket came by and politely offered coffee and sandwiches. He and his brother each plucked a ham sandwich off the silver tray and took another cup of coffee rich with cream and sugar.

"So what do you think, Brother?" he whispered in a low voice so the other officers couldn't hear him. "Would you not say that the Americans treat us better than even our own army and navy?"

His brother scowled at him. "I think you and I need to escape as soon as possible and report to the Führer. Have you forgotten about your sacred duty to the Fatherland?"

"No, of course not. But that doesn't mean I can't marvel at all this around us. That is what a spy does, you know. He must take in every detail, because he never knows what one day might day save his life. Or keep him from getting caught."

"This is all for show. They are taking us only through the cities that have not been bombed into rubble by our *Luftwaffe*."

Erik cackled with laughter. "That is all Goebbels propaganda, Brother. Not a single American city has been attacked by a German air raid. What you and I have been fed is nothing but lies."

"It doesn't matter. The Americans are our sworn enemies, and you sure as hell shouldn't be praising them."

"Are you saying that it makes me a traitor to marvel at their skyscrapers? Or their handsome automobiles, first-class Pullman coaches, or wonderful jazz music?"

"Yes, that is exactly what I am saying. You lived in America too damned long, Harvard boy. It has clouded your thinking."

"Perhaps, Brother, perhaps. But as I recall, you used to like jazz music just as much as Father and I did, and you never lived here a day in your life. This place is liberating in the same way that Dizzy Gillespie's music is liberating. I am just willing to admit it is all. Why even the military police have been nice to us."

"I admit that, compared to Bolshevik Russia, this place is paradise. But if you think these people are doing anything but tolerating us, you are sorely mistaken. At the train station, did you not see the pair of women in uniform who made a sign cutting our throats as we boarded?"

"Yes, I saw them. They were just horsing around."

"You are kidding yourself. These people hate us just as much as they hate the slant-eyed Japanese-Americans they have imprisoned in their internment camps. Or the lowly Negroes they lynch from trees down in Mississippi and Alabama. But we do not need to concern ourselves with that now. We must develop a plan of escape."

Erik glanced down the aisle at the two armed guards assigned to their coach, rifles draped across their laps. "Well, it's safe to say we won't be doing any escaping on this train." He tipped his head towards the guards.

His brother eyed them closely before nodding his head in concurrence and leaning in close. "At Camp Shanks, I overheard two MPs talking. They said the POW camps are lightly guarded. I heard them say that it's actually quite easy to escape if you can get on one of the work details. That is the Americans' Achilles heel. They are lazy and too trusting. We will escape when the lazy guards are napping and then we will save Germany."

"I'm sure it will not be that easy. And if anyone is going to save Germany, it's me, Brother. I am the spy, not you, remember?"

"I am your commanding officer and you will obey what I say. We will be making our report together to the Führer himself—or I will be making it alone after you have debriefed me—but under no circumstances are you to report without me present."

"I am not going to report anything to the Führer, or even Schellenberg for that matter. My orders are to report directly to General Rommel, as I've told you several times."

"I am giving you new orders."

"Oh, so you're going to try and control me just like Prochnow. I'm not sure that's a good idea. Look what happened to him."

"You'd better worry more about what's going to happen to you."

"Are you threatening me, Brother?"

"I am your commanding officer and you *will* obey me, whether you like it or not."

He knew that his brother wasn't bluffing. The great sea captain wanted in on his hard-earned intelligence coup, so he could take the credit for himself by reporting directly to Hitler himself. But how could they even pull off an escape if they did make a try? The Americans may have been lax when it came to guarding POWs in their gigantic country, but there was still no guarantee that he and his brother could escape from whatever camp they were sent to, seize a radio, and send a detailed message back to Germany or Occupied France. Then again, maybe they didn't even need to escape. After all, there might be a short-wave radio at the camp that they could use.

But which POW camp were they being sent to? As of yet, there had been no word.

He took a bite from his ham sandwich, washed it down with some hot coffee. "Maybe we can transmit a message from the camp and don't even need to escape. Have you thought of that, *Herr Kapitän?*"

"As a matter of fact, I have. That will be our first option."

"And if that isn't possible and we do escape and are caught, they could hang us and then we will have no chance to save Germany. Have you also thought of that?"

"There is always a risk. That is why you should tell me right now what secret intelligence you discovered in England, and let me take care of it upon our arrival to the camp. You can just sit back in this so-called *New World* that you admire so much and listen to jazz music. Meanwhile, I will get the message to the High Command. What do you say?"

Though the voice was casual, he saw in his brother's eyes how desperately he wanted to be the one to break the news to his beloved Führer and, thus, receive all the glory. My God, was he truly that greedy for another Iron Cross? Or was he trying to redeem his honor for having gotten his entire U-boat crew captured? Erik suspected that he was doing it for both reasons.

"You should just tell me, Brother. It will be so much better for everyone if you do."

"I'm not telling you a damned thing. When the time comes, I will be the one to send the message, because I was the one to gather the intelligence in the first place. My God, I had to kill a British spycatcher to get it. Do you think I wanted to do something like that?"

His brother scoffed as he stuffed the last bit of ham sandwich into his mouth. "This country has made you soft. Now it has your head spinning and questioning your own Fatherland. You, Brother, are a defeatist. I can see it in your damned eyes."

"That is a lie. I am as loyal a German as you. I risked my life and killed a man with a knife to help my country win the war."

"That may be, but your motives are questionable. You don't believe we can actually win the war. You want Germany to capitulate on favorable terms and overthrow our own Führer. Why even thinking such thoughts is treason. Don't forget, Harvard boy, I know your true nature. That's why I know you don't deserve to report to Rommel or the Führer. It should be me!"

For the first time, Erik noticed that some of the other soldiers—both U-boat men and regular army—were looking at them. But he didn't care. He would say whatever the hell he wanted to his damned brother. He felt a deeply buried, but familiar, anger resurface, a reawakening of the furiously competitive and toxic sibling rivalry that he had known all too well growing up, but had not experienced in years.

"Don't talk to me about absolute loyalty, Wolfgang. You have doubts too. I can see it in your eyes. You are taken in by America's might just as much as me and our comrades on this train. Where before there was blind loyalty to our cause, absolute certainty, there is now a hint of doubt. You, too, should remember that I am your brother. I know you."

"No, you don't. Not anymore. You and I ceased to be family a long time ago."

"I can't argue with that. But I do still know you."

What came next was spoken in a chilling murmur, so low that even the eavesdropping soldiers in the nearby plush Pullman seats could not hear. "It has been many years since you felt my wrath, Brother. But when I get through with you this time, you will wish that you had been left behind with that British bastard Tin Eye."

He stuck out his chin defiantly. "You're welcome to try. But just remember, I am not *der Schwächling*—the little weakling—you used to bully back in Berlin."

"That may be, *Brüderlein*. But I, not you, will be the one to report to the Führer. That is the *one thing* you can count on."

CHAPTER 16

BROADMOOR HOTEL
COLORADO SPRINGS, USA

WHILE WARTIME AUSTERITY had taken some of the luster off Katherine Templeton's world renowned Broadmoor Hotel & Spa, for connoisseurs of luxury it still rivaled the best that Saratoga Springs and Palm Beach had to offer. Built in an Italian Renaissance style at the foot of Cheyenne Mountain, the resort had an alpine European feel with its soft pastel colors, soaring towers, and immense facades set against a rugged backdrop of Precambrian granite. Vacation home to the world's elite, the resort had always had one rule and one rule only: guests were to be coddled endlessly, never to see a dull moment, for the duration of their stay.

But with the war against Hitler's Nazi Germany and Tojo's Imperialist Japan in full swing, Katherine had changed the resort's mission to aid the war effort and conform to the new reality of fifty-hour work weeks, as well as gasoline, meat, sugar, shoe, and liquor rationing. To this end, she now offered elegant dining, shopping, golf, polo, bathing, hiking, an animal zoo, and fly fishing, previously only available to her rich and famous clientele, to local U.S. military officers and their families at steeply reduced rates. In addition, Katherine housed officers who were unable to secure rooms at nearby, overcrowded Camp Carson at minimal cost, though they were still required to meet a semi-formal dress code to maintain the Broadmoor's exclusive ambiance.

In support of the war effort, tonight Katherine was hosting a fundraising party to raise war bonds for Uncle Sam. The gala was being held in the Jungle Room—the hotel's Hawaiian village-style nightclub and the guest list included Colorado Springs leading citizens, as well as the officers from Camp Pershing and Camp Carson. Up on the stage, the evening's entertainment—Woody Herman and his talented band the First Herd—were belting out a lively bebop tune to a packed dance floor. Woody and his band mates had been joined by special guest Count Basie, who was banging away at his piano with a cheery smile on his face. The room was swinging with a steady, brassy sound and shuffling rhythm, broken occasionally by the rapturous screams of the officers and leading citizens of Colorado Springs up on the sweaty dance floor.

After saying a few words to the mayor and his wife, Katherine stepped into the kitchen. Chef Stratta and his staff were wrapping up for the night with the last of the coffee and deserts and making final preparations for tomorrow's breakfast. She congratulated the Italian master chef and his staff on a job well done and then headed outside to the patio overlooking the lake to mingle with guests who had taken a break from dancing. Along the way, she was intercepted by her concierge

Jurgen Krupp, a fellow German who had emigrated to the U.S. a decade before her. He quickly informed her that a pair of drunken army officers had gotten into a brawl out front of the hotel.

She hoped it would be the only blemish on the thus far successful evening. "Should I be worried, Mr. Krupp?"

"No, I have taken care of it. I called security and had both men driven back to Camp Carson. Luckily, they are not guests at the hotel."

"Thank you for handling the matter discretely. By the way, what were they fighting about?"

"I believe it was over a woman, Madame."

"Isn't it always?" she said, and with that she winked conspiratorially, left him, and stepped out onto the patio.

The last rays of sunlight trickled over Cheyenne Mountain to the west and slanted down upon the lake. She remembered standing at this exact spot on the flagstone patio with Charles Lindbergh and Viscount de Stroelbergh, during her first visit to the hotel with her family a decade and a half earlier in the Roaring Twenties. War had been the last thing on anyone's mind back then, and she recalled how wonderful domestic life in Germany had been. For a moment, she lost herself in the past, thinking back to the idyllic times before Hitler and his Nazi henchmen had come into power and her world had been turned upside down.

"Great party," she heard a vaguely familiar voice say, pulling her from her musing.

She looked up to see Colonel Jack Morrison, the Commandant of Camp Pershing. His tie was loose, he clutched a fresh martini in his hand, and a cigarette dangled lazily from his mouth like a Hollywood movie star. His complexion was ruddy from dancing, and she realized that he was a handsome devil in his dashing military dress uniform. She didn't know him well; they had only met on three separate occasions prior to tonight. She employed a number of his German inmates from Camp Pershing at her Left Hand Ranch as part of the U.S. Army POW Labor Program. She thought back to the last time she had seen him: it had been two and a half weeks ago, when she had taken him on a horseback tour of her ranch.

She stepped forward to greet him. "Well thank you, Colonel. You certainly look like you've been enjoying yourself."

"Been dancing up a storm. Woody and Count Basie together—it sure beats the heck out of playing wet nurse to Hitler's finest all day long."

She detected an edge to his voice. "Are your German prisoners giving you problems, Colonel?"

"That's putting it mildly, ma'am. But it's all part of the job."

He winked, took a long pull from his drink, and smiled devilishly at her. She felt a little tingle, and she realized that she found him both attractive and funny. And having grown up in Germany, she had always been interested to know what life was really like inside the barbed wire at Camp Pershing.

"So Hitler's finest, as you call them, are making life difficult for you, eh?"

"Yes, ma'am. The truth is I've got a problem, a big problem: the Nazis have taken over my camp, and that's the God's honest truth. It happened before I assumed command, but now it's fallen on my shoulders to turn the miserable situation around."

"Taken over your camp? How so?"

"Most of them are from the vaunted Africa Corps, and they are a hard bunch. They terrorize the other POWs they don't believe to be ideologically pure."

"Terrorize how?"

"They ostracize them, calling them cowards and defeatists, and sometimes they beat them up. Badly. Several of their victims have been put in the hospital, and one private was actually killed. They especially like to pick on the Austrians. It's the natural order of things with these hard-core National Socialist brutes. They have to dominate others with their ideology—or they can't survive."

"But there must be some way to control them."

"I'm not a prison warden. I'm a combat soldier, and it's harder than you think. The idea that I came up with is based on the British and Canadian model."

"And how does that work?"

"It involves separating out the hardened Nazis from the non-Nazis. I figured if I could do that, I would have a smooth running camp where nobody gets hurt and everybody is more or less equal within their military rank. So I presented my plan to my officers to see if they had any ideas or concerns, but one of them leaked it to the Germans for two packs of smokes. And now the bastards are refusing to work."

"So they're on strike."

"Yes, ma'am, they're on strike—a Nazi strike."

"If they're on strike, how come I have had more than a dozen prisoners out working at my place this week?"

"Because they like working for you. You are *very* popular with the Germans."

"I remind them of home, is that it?"

"They do call you *the countess* for a reason. So do my officers and enlisted men, to be honest."

"Perhaps I should consider it an honor."

"We Americans like royalty too—we just pretend not to. And here in America one does not get to meet a countess every day."

"Perhaps you've forgotten, Colonel, that I am an American citizen."

"Yes, ma'am, I didn't mean to imply—"

"Need I remind you that it has been nearly a decade since I lived in Germany. I am as American as Babe Ruth, who, as you may not be aware, is also of German ancestry. I love baseball, apple pie, and Clark Gable—and I buy war bonds every chance I get. Is that American enough for you?"

"I meant no offense." He grinned good-naturedly and took a big pull from his cigarette. "You want to know the real reason my POWs like working for you so much?"

"Do I have a choice?"

"It's because you treat them so darned well. That's why they prefer to work on your spread instead of the other ranches in the area."

"Are you saying, Colonel, that I treat them *too* well?"

"No, ma'am. I didn't mean—"

"That's good because I believe workers should be treated well, whether they are prisoners of war or not. By the way, you must call me Katherine."

"Okay, as long as you call me Jack."

"Jack—I've always liked that name."

"Then it's my lucky day." He smiled bashfully. "For a second there, I thought you were sore with me."

"Indeed I was. You have to understand, Colonel, I truly hate what Germany has become. That's why I take offense when people try to paint me as German. I am an American citizen and damned proud of it, though, of course, I still fondly retain certain aspects of my original culture."

"Yes, ma'am. I understand how you feel and promise not to bring it up ever again."

"Oh, but you will, Colonel. You won't mean to, of course, but you will."

They fidgeted uncomfortably for a moment. Then he took off his hat, held it formally in his arm, and licked his lips anxiously. She could tell that he had something important to say.

"There's a reason I came out here to talk to you, Katherine. I wanted to tell you that I'm sorry about your son Max. General Shedd told me. I'm awfully sorry."

His look was sincere, and she felt guilty for being overly sensitive and brusque with him. She felt the usual sadness rise up in her throat, but with an effort she fought it back. She had spent the last two days crying over her lost son, and didn't want to break down again.

"That's kind of you to say," she said softly. "The supreme irony is that he was born in Germany, yet he died as an American soldier killed by the Germans. I miss him terribly."

She felt a tear tumble down her cheek and swiped it away. *Damn this war,* she thought miserably.

"You are a brave woman." He reached out and took her hand in his, his eyes reaching out sympathetically. "I mean it. You are a damned brave woman. I can't imagine losing a child. I think I would call it quits."

"I am just stubborn, I suppose. Or perhaps I am inured to tragedy. But I think you are forgetting that I also lost my husband."

"Yes, you told me on our horseback ride. We are both widowers, it seems. But now you have lost your son, too, and it just seems like God is piling it on. In fact, stuff like that makes me question whether there really is a God."

"It makes me question that too."

They stood there a moment in somber silence. A part of her wanted to reach out and hug him, but she didn't know him that well and didn't want to embarrass herself by being overly emotional. She let out a little sigh and stared off at Cheyenne Mountain, as the sun tucked itself behind the piney treetops and dusk began to fall. A part of her didn't want to admit that her dear Max was truly gone.

"I'm sorry, ma'am. I've ruined the festive atmosphere."

She touched his hand. "No, I appreciate what you said. It has been hard for me, but I would rather hear your heartfelt words than no words at all."

"When I lost my Elizabeth, I thought I would never recover. But that must pale in comparison to what you're going through right now. If you ever want someone…someone to talk to, please call on me. We could go for a ride again."

She felt herself brighten. There was a playful innocence about him that she liked. "That was fun the last time. You are quite the horseman, Colonel Morrison."

"Well, when I was a young buck fresh out of West Point, I chased after Pancho Villa south of the border. I believe that wily Mexican bandito unintentionally made a cavalryman out of me."

She was intrigued. "You've always been a soldier, then?"

"Yes, ma'am. I'm what you call a *lifer*."

"Well, perhaps these stubborn Nazis in your camp would not meddle with you if they knew you had gone toe to toe with the legendary Pancho Villa."

"You know, I hadn't thought of that."

He gave her a wink and they laughed. She wiped the last trace of a tear away.

"It's funny that the German prisoners cause you so many problems, Colonel. The young men you send to my ranch are such hard workers and proper gentlemen that it is almost hard to think of them as the enemy."

"I can change that up tomorrow if you'd like. I'm getting in a fresh batch of veteran U-boat men."

"Are they as fierce as the infantrymen from Rommel's Africa Corps that you have mending my fences and haying my fields?"

"These U-boat fellows, I believe, are harder cases."

"Well then, you'll have to send me a few of them. I'll break them with a rawhide quirt and a pair of jagged spurs just like I do my horses."

He looked skeptical. "Nah, you wouldn't do that."

"Are you saying that I'm too soft and mushy to discipline your unruly POWs?"

"No, I just think you've gotten mostly the good ones. I mean, they actually like working for you. So much so that I have to rotate them to different ranches, since they all want to work for you."

"My, my, I didn't know I was *that* popular."

"Well, when you started feeding them potato pancakes, the best apple strudel any of them has ever tasted, and genuine German beer, what did you expect?"

"Can you blame me for having a reward system that works? A little strudel and lager is known to ensure very high productivity from Germans, whether here or in the Fatherland."

"Maybe I should try that on my recalcitrant Nazis."

"Maybe you should. Maybe you should at that."

He smiled and bowed cordially. "You are a most remarkable woman. Would you please allow me the honor of the next dance?"

She gave an exaggerated curtsy. "Why of course, Colonel. And by the way, Mr. Herman and his band are saving *Woodchopper's Ball* for my personal request."

"Well then, we'd better get out there on that dance floor. I've always wanted to jitterbug the *Woodchopper's Ball* with a beautiful countess."

DAY 4

FRIDAY

JUNE 2, 1944

CHAPTER 17

CAMP PERSHING
SOUTHEASTERN COLORADO

ERIK LOOKED UP at the sign with large block letters above the gate that read *CAMP PERSHING* and then at the bronze-faced German POWs standing inside the compound, wearing the distinctive desert caps and insignia of the vaunted *Afrika Korps*. He felt like he was back in Libya or Tunisia with his father and the Desert Fox. The prisoners were tough-looking, battle-hardened veterans, and he couldn't help but sense a trace of disdain in the way they looked at him and the other new arrivals. But perhaps he was misreading their faces and what he was actually seeing was merely the competitive rivalry endemic to the different service branches within the *Wehrmacht*. After all, most of the 150 or so newcomers in his group were pasty-faced U-boat men from the North Sea, while the sun-burnished desert rats with their noses pressed against the wire had fought in North Africa under the legendary Rommel.

It had taken three days for him and his brother to traverse the country by passenger train from Camp Shanks, New York, to Camp Pershing. They had traveled the last leg of their journey today from Topeka, Kansas, to Wild Horse, Colorado; and from there, they had been packed into army trucks and driven the final twenty miles to the camp. Though the plush Pullman coaches and train victuals were far better than what was available to the average German soldier in Occupied France or the Russian front, Erik was still tired and cranky from being pent up on a clattering train for three days and nights.

As he stepped through the main gate, he looked at Wolfgang, trying to gauge his brother's reaction to their new surroundings. The U-boat commander wore his usual stoic expression, but underneath the cool exterior Erik saw that he was closely scrutinizing the camp, the guards, and their soon-to-be Africa Corps comrades with the studied precision of a police detective.

The camp was divided into four separate compounds, each consisting of several rows of barracks as well as a mess hall, workshop, canteen, infirmary, administrative building, and what looked to Erik like some sort of recreation hall. Dirt walkways and gravel roads traversed the camp, and a wide flat area in the foreground of the compound buildings served as a combination inspection ground, processing center, and soccer field. In the distance, he could make out what looked like a small infirmary, a chapel, and a showering area.

All in all, his first impression was that the place wasn't too bad as far as internment camps went—and far better than the harsh, isolating environment at Camp 020 in London under the stern hand of Tin Eye. But as the guards lined him and the other newcomers up, counted them, and searched them like petty criminals, while their Africa Corps counterparts looked on disdainfully, he reminded himself that the place was still nothing but a prison.

He and his brother continued to scan the camp as they were patted down and their names checked off by the guards. Two chain link fences, each ten feet high and eight feet apart, surrounded the entire facility. The double-graduated fence and eight guard watchtowers made Erik feel claustrophobic in spite of the open plains all around them. Each tower was manned by one or two guards and sported a menacing-looking machine gun, a pair of sirens, and an array of search lights. No trees, shrubs, or tall grasses grew between the compound buildings or around the perimeter patrol road, ensuring that any escape attempt would be in full view from at least one guard tower. He could not see any guard dogs or kennels, but he did see a horse stable to the west and a pair of guards patrolling the perimeter of the camp on horseback.

It would be no small task to escape from this heavily-guarded place. But he might not have to. There might be a radio that he could use to transmit his urgent message to Rommel, by bouncing the signal from station to station until it made its way to Army Group B Headquarters at Chateau La Roche Guyon. But what if a radio transmission was not possible? Then the best way to do it, he and his brother had been told at Camp Shanks, was to quietly slip away from one of the work details. The guards on the details were said to be lazy and careless, but he would have to verify with the camp spokesman which work detail would be the preferred choice to escape from. Time was critical: the long-anticipated Allied attack on Fortress Europe could come any day now.

Once they were searched and checked in, he and the other prisoners were led to a spacious dining hall where they were fed a surprisingly sumptuous noon meal of sauerkraut, mashed potatoes, and mutton chops. Afterwards, they were given International Red Cross cards to sign to inform their families of their whereabouts: *"I have been taken prisoner and am fine. My new address is Camp Pershing/Colorado, Box 20, New York, New York."* Once the signed cards were collected, the American guards left the dining hall and the German camp spokesperson stepped up to the microphone to welcome them.

Erik's jaw instantly dropped.

"What is it?" asked his brother, seeing his surprise.

For a moment, he was too stunned to reply. "I know that bastard," he said finally.

"The senior camp officer? Well, who the hell is he?"

"Colonel Franz Kepler." He couldn't believe his bad luck. *Of all the POW camps, I had to be sent fucking here?* But then he realized it made complete sense. The Americans and British had been in such a hurry to get them overseas out of the war zone that they had had no choice but to send them to a camp that could accept a large number of German prisoners on short notice. And Camp Pershing way out on the desolate plains of Colorado was an internment camp that obviously fit the bill. *Just my goddamn luck,* he thought bitterly.

"How do you know him?" asked his brother.

"I fought with him and Father in North Africa. He commanded the 21st

Panzers. The man is a fanatic."

"Come now, everyone who wears a German uniform is a fanatic to you."

"No, this one is different. He'll try to kill me, I swear."

"Kill you? Why would he try to kill you?"

"For a lot of reasons, but one big one."

"What the hell did you do to him?"

"Nothing, not a goddamned thing. I told you he's a fanatic. There is no way to reason with the man. We had better both steer clear of him."

"He is an *oberst*—a full colonel, the same as me. He couldn't have risen to such a high rank if he wasn't a good soldier."

"Oh, he's a good soldier, all right. But he's still as dangerous as a viper. Just you wait and see."

They fell silent. His brother closely studied the Africa Corps commander. Erik just shook his head in disbelief. *Mein Gott, what did I do to deserve this?* Feeling a jittery feeling in his stomach, he made himself small in his seat, hoping like hell that Kepler couldn't make him out among the sea of new faces, though he knew he was merely delaying the inevitable. As if on cue, the tall, brawny specimen—a study in Aryan perfection—smiled down at the crowd, cleared his throat at the microphone, and ran a practiced hand over his silvery goatee. He took a moment to survey his audience, his piercing blue eyes the color of a tropical sea, taking everything in like a man who was truly in charge.

Erik wished then that he was invisible.

CHAPTER 18

CAMP PERSHING

"GREETINGS *KAMERADS*! My name is Colonel Kepler of Army Group Africa. As the senior ranking officer of this camp, I am the camp spokesman. I offer you a most hearty welcome in the name of the Fatherland. I am here to introduce myself and tell you what you can expect here as official prisoners of war at Camp Pershing. The Americans—despite the fact that they are our sworn enemies and most of them are gangsters—are not horrible hosts. That is why they have allowed us to talk in private before your formal processing, so that I may give you an overview of life here on the plains of the western state of Colorado. From here, you will move on to finish your paperwork, complete your medical checkup, and settle into your various compounds.

"Judging by your appearance, I have a good idea of what lies behind you. But you can be sure that, inside this barbed wire, everything will be done to make your heavy burden lighter—as long as you toe the line with your commanding officers. Per the Geneva Convention, the ranks of the *Wehrmacht* apply here just as they did in the battlefields of Europe and North Africa. So you must obey your officers. Of course, you are among your comrades once again, and can speak and act freely. But we still have order and discipline here. After all, we are German soldiers, the finest fighting force on the face of the earth."

This was met with a round of cheers and head bobs of agreement. When the audience had quieted down, he continued in a crisp, commanding voice.

"Presently, there are three thousand prisoners here. With the addition of you men, we will be near the camp capacity. The local townspeople think we are treated too well here. They refer to Camp Pershing scornfully as the 'Fritz Ritz.' But you will learn quickly that life out here in the Great American Desert is no picnic, regardless of what the local farmers and ranchers say. And yet, having said that, I think you all will come to enjoy your stay here. You will be kept busy, but you will also have time for relaxation. However, I want to inform you that not all of you will be staying at Camp Pershing. Only this morning, I was informed by the commandant, Colonel Morrison, that all noncommissioned officers and enlisted men who elect not to work will be transferred to another camp starting tomorrow. This is the new gangster American policy to force us to perform slave labor whether we want to or not."

Now Erik saw looks of worry and confusion navigate through the dining room. Having just arrived here, the prisoners were struggling to adjust to their new circumstances, only to be told that they might be shipped off somewhere else if they did not agree to work.

"Work is an important thing, but we must be treated fairly too. As some of you may have heard, many of the men in this camp have been on labor strike. That is because the American commandant has unfairly broken us up into two groups: Nazis and anti-Nazis. But there is no such distinction. We are all just German soldiers—nothing more and nothing less. We have all sworn an oath to our Führer and are, therefore, bound to perform our duty as men at arms, whether on the battlefield or in captivity, whether we are members of the National Socialist Party or not. The Führer has made it clear that he wants us to work. But when the commandant tries to pigeonhole us into one group or the other based on his own ill-informed impressions, I think it is your decision whether or not to work. For we are not simply Nazis and anti-Nazis: we are German soldiers—as I said, the best soldiers in the world!"

At this, another cheer went up from the crowd. Looking around at the faces, Erik saw that Kepler was inspiring the newcomers through their fraternal bond as members of the *Wehrmacht*.

"I will tell you that, if you do work, the days will pass more quickly and you can earn twenty dollars per month. Which, in terms of purchasing power, is the same as twenty *Reichsmarks*. Otherwise, if you elect not to work, you will only earn five dollars a day and will be denied the right to purchase tobacco. Whether you choose to work or not, you should be of as little use to the Americans as possible. Your job as a prisoner of war is to disrupt, confuse, and aggravate our American captors, so that they have to devote considerable manpower and resources to keep us in captivity, or to hunt us down if we escape. I can assure you that the Allied prisoners in the *stalags* in Germany are doing the same thing at this very moment."

He held up a pamphlet. "I hold in my hand a 'Memorandum Addressed to German Soldiers.' A copy of this document will be given to all of you as guaranteed by your rights under the Geneva Convention. Let me tell you briefly what it says. You are to reminded to keep physically fit, to make yourselves fully familiar with your rights as captured German soldiers, and, most importantly, to take every opportunity to escape! That is a direct order from your Führer!"

Erik looked around. There were many nodding in agreement, but others looked less enthused. After enduring years of hardship in the war, many were skeptical of high-ranking officers, especially martinets, puffed-up elitists, or those they viewed as overzealous.

"With regard to the work details, all newly arrived non-commissioned officers are to report immediately to the American orderly room to prove your rank. If you do not have your *Soldbuch*, or other paperwork, to prove your rank, you will need to request verification of your rank from the International Red Cross in Geneva. A list will be compiled and sent to them. In the meantime, the Americans will require you to work and assign you to work groups.

"You must remember that, although you are in captivity, you are still a loyal German soldier. There will be no tolerance for traitors or defeatists in this camp. Reprisals for such misconduct will be taken against your relatives back home, or against you yourself following your repatriation to Germany. I must remind you that, when sick or wounded POWs are exchanged with the Allies, lists of the names of 'disloyal Germans' are smuggled out of the United States and presented to the SS headed by Himmler himself. So remember to be a good soldier and loyal to your Führer at all times; otherwise, you will be putting not only your relatives in jeopardy, but your very own existence when you return to Germany to be confronted with your record as a prisoner of war."

Here, Kepler paused and asked if there were any questions. Erik looked around at the faces that only moments ago had been filled with pride and patriotism. While a few hard cases were nodding, most of the men looked terrified out of their wits. After all, the colonel was talking about reprisals against them and their families if they didn't toe the line!

"Now that you have been fed and introduced to camp life, it is time for you to be processed. You will spend the next few hours filling out registration forms, undergoing examination by doctors, and being photographed and fingerprinted. In closing, I would like to say that you will all soon adjust to your new surroundings and carry out your solemn duties as soldiers of the Third Reich. You will, once again, return to the military discipline you knew before your capture. You must learn to make the best of a difficult situation and obey your camp leaders. At the same time, it is your duty as German soldiers to exploit the weaknesses of our American captors wherever possible and to make a nuisance for them, so that they have to devote significant manpower to watch over you. Go now to finish your processing!"

He clicked his heels together and raised his right hand to the rim of his colonel's cap in the formal *Wehrmacht* salute. "To German victory!"

Half the newcomers stood up on their feet. "To German victory!" they shouted back, throwing up the standard military salute, while a few diehards shouted "Heil Hitler!" and gave the official, right-handed Führer salute. Then the dining room doors opened up, the American guards tromped back in, and the prisoners began to be escorted to the infirmary.

Erik tried to slip out the rear door before Kepler, who was making his way out into the crowd, spotted him. But to his chagrin, his brother reached out and grabbed him by the arm, holding him up.

"Why are you in such a hurry?"

"You know why." He nodded towards the front of the dining room, where Kepler was shaking hands. "The man is fucking trouble."

"He seems like a good commander and loyal German soldier to me. But I don't expect these Africa corpsmen to take too kindly to us U-boat fellows."

"He's a damned fanatic and will cause us both no small amount of grief."

"I wouldn't be so negative. After all, we are going to need this man's help. He is the senior officer in this camp."

"You are as senior as he is."

"That is true, but he was here first and is the one currently in charge. I am not going to challenge his authority—not yet anyway."

"You don't know him. I'm telling you the man is fucking dangerous. He is the last person who will help us."

"You can't just run away. You're going to have to come face to face with Kepler sooner or later."

"Your friend has a good point, Herr von Walburg—why are you running away from me?"

Erik looked up to see the *Afrika Korps oberst* smiling belligerently. His heart literally skipped a beat and, for a moment, he was breathless. How did the clever bastard move through the crowd so quickly?

"I can see the cat has got your tongue. Funny, the last time I saw you, you were running away too."

His brother gave him an admonishing look. "Running away? Running away from what?"

Kepler stepped forward, his smile widening with malice. "Why from the enemy, of course. You see, this little Prussian shit abandoned his comrades in the North African desert!"

CHAPTER 19

CAMP 020 INTERROGATION CENTER
SOUTHWEST LONDON

THE STRAIN AND TERROR of the last two days of relentless interrogation showed on Henrik Carlsson. The Swede appeared unusually gaunt and fragile as he stood against the wall of Interrogation Room 3, like a condemned man facing a firing squad. Dark circles ringed his eyes. His mannerisms were halting and nervous. A heavy Dunhill smoker, he had been begging for a cigarette for the past hour, but his pleas fell on deaf ears. Commandant Robin "Tin Eye" Stephens didn't allow tobacco of any kind at Camp 020.

Carlsson claimed to be working on behalf of MI6 as a spy. The only problem with that, in the mind of Lieutenant Colonel Tam MacGregor of MI5, who had been closely watching the interrogation for the past hour, was that rival MI6 insisted vehemently that he wasn't one of theirs. Which meant one of two things: the Swede was lying through his teeth, or he had somehow managed to cross, or implicate, MI6 and the agency was refusing to vouch for him. In either case, it was the job of Tin Eye and his two veteran interrogators, Captains Short and Goodacre, to grill the prisoner until there was no question of whether or not he was a spy. Depending on the outcome, Carlsson would then be hanged from his neck until dead, locked away in prison, or turned into a double agent.

He would under no circumstances be released from prison as a free man until the war was over.

But, even as good as Tin Eye and his interrogation team were at extracting vital information, Tam had the feeling that they hadn't gotten the whole truth out of Carlsson yet. He suspected that the Swede was withholding something critical, for what purpose he wasn't sure. He also had the nagging feeling that Carlsson might actually be telling the bloody truth about being a spy for MI6. But then why would the agency deny all knowledge of him? Even if he had crossed them in some way, surely they wouldn't leave him out in the cold and refuse to claim him.

Or would they?

"What are you not telling us, Henrik?" asked Tam, taking over the questioning for a moment from Tin Eye. "I know you're not telling us the full story."

"I *have* told you the truth. I am a Swedish citizen and I work for British intelligence. My code name is Tango."

"So you've told us a dozen times. Inspired choice, I must say, if it is in fact true." He smiled graciously. "Now look here, Henrik. I do not doubt that you are a Swedish national, or that you have some connection to our intelligence services, however tenuous. But I still believe you are withholding information from us, and I'd like you to tell us what that information is. We'll get it from you sooner or later anyway, mind you, but for obvious reasons I would like it to be sooner."

"I am not withholding anything. I am a spy for your government."

"Yes, yes, we've been through this a dozen times before," interrupted Tin Eye, taking over again. "You work for MI6, your code name is Tango, and your case officer's name is Percival—another inspired choice I might add, if it were only true. But the problem is that it is not true. In fact, everything you've been telling us is a stack of bloody lies."

"I'm telling the truth. Now, may I please have a cigarette?"

"No, you may not. Now, Henrik, do you truly expect us to believe these Brothers Grimm fairy tales you've been foisting upon us?

"It's the truth."

"Truth? You don't know the first thing about truth. You're a damned Nazi spy."

"I am not. I am a British agent…I mean, I'm a Swedish citizen working for British intelligence. I told you my code name is Tango."

Tin Eye calmly rose from his seat, walked over to Carlsson, and began pacing in front of him, studying him as if he were a zoo animal in a cage. Without warning, he drew close in a sudden aggressive movement and shouted in his ear. "So you work for British intelligence, eh? That must be why you killed one of our operatives in Hyde Park last week, because you are a loyal spy for His Majesty the bloody King!"

Carlsson raised his hands as if to protect himself from a flying fist, but Tin Eye did nothing more than breath on him, his fiery, monocle-ringed eye mere inches away.

"I didn't kill anyone. You have the wrong man!"

"We found the knife you used to commit the murder on your person! You actually expect us to believe that it was planted on you?"

"I don't know how it happened! But I tell you I'm innocent!"

"But you were positively identified at the murder scene!" Tin Eye darted to the table, picked up the police artist's sketch, and shoved it into Carlsson's trembling hands. "Take another good look at that sketch, Mr. Tango, and tell me that isn't you!"

"Please, I want a cigarette!"

"I've told you a dozen times, Henrik, there's no smoking allowed. Now just look at the damned sketch."

"I've already looked at it a dozen times, and I tell you it isn't me! I'll admit that the person in the drawing does look somewhat like me, but it still isn't me. The nose is too sharp and the eyes too wide. Your artist has drawn the wrong man!"

"No, no, it's you Henrik. You're lying again."

"I told you I am not lying! I didn't kill anyone, and I am not a Nazi spy!"

"And I'm the King of bloody Sweden! I've never heard so much poppycock. Are all Swedes this dim-witted?"

"I tell you, I'm not lying! I want a cigarette! Give me one, please!"

"Of course you're lying, Henrik, and you're also hiding something. You know how I know that? When you tell a lie, your pupils contract and you fidget with your hands."

"You must contact my case officer, Percival! He'll tell you that I am not a Nazi spy! I work for your government!"

"Come now, there is no Tango and there is no Percival. They're both nothing more than names you've made up."

"They are not made up!"

"You're a liar, Henrik, and not a very good one at that."

"I am not! You must track down Percival! He will vouch for me!"

"I already told you—we've already spoken to MI6 and they say they don't know you. In fact, they have no record of you whatsoever."

"It is MI6 that is lying!"

"No, Henrik, the only liar in this whole sordid affair is you." Tin Eye returned to his seat and squinted through his monocle. "Look here, do you really want to continue this charade, because we can keep on doing this for the next month if we have to? It makes no difference to me or my officers." He nodded towards Captains Short and Goodacre. "You see, I have handpicked these men because they have the specific qualities I seek: an implacable hatred of the enemy, an innate aggressiveness, a disinclination to believe, and, above all, a fierce determination to break down a spy, however hopeless the odds, however many the difficulties, however long the process may take. It's your choice, Henrik. But mark my words, these gentlemen and I will not let up until we have the information we seek from you."

At that moment, a rap was heard on the door.

"Yes, what is it?" snapped Tin Eye.

An officer poked his head in. "Your visitor has arrived, gentlemen."

Tam looked at his watch. "Already? Well, we're off then."

Tin Eye motioned to Captains Short and Goodacre. "Please continue. We'll return momentarily."

"Yes, sir," said Short. The captain was known to be very skillful at playing good copper to Tin Eye's bad copper and extracting vital information from feigning simple kindness once his boss left the interrogation room.

As he got up to leave, Tam glanced at Carlsson, who looked relieved to be rid of him and the unrelenting Tin Eye, if only for a few minutes. He still had the nagging feeling the Swede was withholding something. But what could it be?

"Carry on, then," said Tin Eye, and he and Tam left the room. The lieutenant escorted them to a waiting room where their invited guest, Constable Richards, was waiting. The constable was the sole witness to the Hyde Park murder. He had observed the spy fleeing the crime scene and had given the killer's description to the police artist for the sketch. He was a spare man in his late thirties, with a walrus-mustache and neatly pressed navy-blue policeman's uniform. From the waiting room, they went to a special room with a two-way mirror that looked onto Interrogation Room 3. Captains Short and Goodacre were talking in soft, sympathetic voices and treating Carlsson with kid gloves in an attempt to extract information. From behind the glass, Tam and the others could see the prisoner, but

Carlsson could not see them.

"Thank you for coming, Constable Richards," said Tam, as they took a moment to acclimate themselves to the darkened room and the two-way mirror. "We've called you here to identify the prisoner. We already have the police artist's sketch. But I thought it would be worthwhile to obtain direct visual confirmation from you since you are the only eyewitness who actually saw the spy's—or, I suppose I should say, the murderer's—face close-up. We're just being thorough. It's really just a formality."

"Yes, Colonel. I'm happy to be of service."

Tam pointed through the two-way mirror at Carlsson as Tin Eye looked on impatiently. Interrogation Room 3 was bugged with two separate microphones. They could hear the voices of Carlsson and Captains Short and Goodacre coming over the overhead speakers in the room. In a separate room at Camp 020, a rotating team of expertly trained stenographers was recording every word of the interrogation. It was standard operating procedure to prepare a final transcript of each and every session.

"Tell me, Constable, is that the man you saw last week standing over Lieutenant Jamison's body and fleeing from Hyde Park?"

Richards stepped closer to the glass and peered closely at the prisoner. Tam noted that he didn't wear glasses.

"Please take your time, Constable. And remember, he can't see you." He gave his most reassuring smile.

"Thank you, sir. But I can tell you right now that it's not him," pronounced Richards.

Tam was taken aback. "Excuse me?"

"It's not him, Colonel. I'm positive of it."

Out of the corner of his eye, he saw Tin Eye give a skeptical look. "What about his voice? Do you recognize it?"

"No, sir, but it doesn't matter. The man in that room is *not* the man I saw."

Tam held up his hands to Richards in a gesture of mollification, not wanting him to be too hasty. "Please, have another look, Constable. And take as much time as you need. We're in no hurry."

"But I don't need any more time, sir. That's not the man from Hyde Park. It looks like him, but it's not him. His nose is too sharp and his eyes are too widely spaced."

Good Lord, that's just what Carlsson said! Tam looked at Tin Eye, who looked perturbed more than anything else.

"That fellow's also a shade taller than the murderer. I'll admit they do look quite a bit alike, and they resemble the police sketch. But they're still two different blokes."

"But are you certain?"

"Yes, I've seen enough. That's not our man, Colonel."

"Well, just to be certain, have another look at him compared to the police artist's sketch." He pulled a copy of the sketch from his pocket and handed it to him.

Richards looked back and forth between the sketch and Carlsson several times before shaking his head. "As I said, the nose is too sharp and his eyes are too far apart. You've got the wrong bloke."

Tin Eye reached up and turned a control knob, turning off the volume on the overhead speaker. "I don't want to hear that blubbering Swede for a few minutes. He rubs me the wrong way. Damnit, man, how did this all get buggered up?"

"I believe FUBAR is the word the Yanks use."

"Yes, well, I'm not waving the white flag yet. That dim-witted Swede might not be our spy, but he is definitely lying through his teeth. I'm not letting him out of that room until I bloody well find out what he's hiding from us."

"I agree with you that he is definitely covering up something. But that doesn't change the fact that Constable Richards here is right: the man in that room is not our spy."

"Then who is?" asked the constable.

Tam looked at Tin Eye. "You do recall our friend Manfred Weiss, Chief Medical Officer of U-521?"

"How could I forget? I tried to tell you that the clever bastard was our man last week."

"Indeed, you did."

"We shouldn't have let him go. I told you that he was a bad egg."

"I didn't want him shipped overseas either, Colonel. But what's done is done. If Weiss is indeed our man, we're going to need confirmation. Irrefutable confirmation."

Tin Eye turned to his lieutenant standing by, his ruddy expression one of renewed vigor, like a fox hunter taking to the chase. "Lieutenant Murchison, I want the complete file on our mysterious Manfred Weiss of Bremen back here in the next five minutes."

"Yes, sir." He started for the door.

"And another thing, Lieutenant. Don't forget the photographs and transcripts of all of the interrogations. Every single one of them."

"Yes, sir!" and he was off.

CHAPTER 20

CAMP 020 INTERROGATION CENTER

WHEN THE LIEUTENANT WAS GONE, Tam again peered through the two-way window. Inside the interrogation room, Carlsson appeared to be spilling his heart to Captains Short and Goodacre. He was talking to them and nodding animatedly. Somehow, the situation had changed and he appeared to be voluntarily opening up. The blow hot, blow cold approach seemed to be working after all. The two interrogators were listening intently, asking questions, and jotting down notes.

Tam wanted to kick himself. If Weiss truly was their man, it would make no difference that he and Tin Eye had been ordered by their superiors to give the spy up to the Yanks. They would be blamed for the security disaster by one of their second-guessing superiors, their rivals at MI6, or even Churchill himself, who was always meddling in intelligence matters whenever he was briefed on Double Cross and the Ultra radio intercepts referred to officially as "Most Secret Sources."

But far worse was that the spy could still pose a monumental threat to the war effort even from across the Atlantic. All he had to do was get his hands on a bloody radio and relay a message to his contacts in German intelligence. Tam cursed under his breath at the staggering prospect.

Suddenly, Carlsson stopped talking. The two interrogators put down their pens, conferred for a moment, and then Goodacre nodded, rose from his chair, and stepped outside the room. Seconds later, a light knock was heard on the door to the observation room and Goodacre appeared.

"Yes, what is it, Captain?" demanded Tin Eye brusquely.

"You mean you haven't been listening, sir."

"No, we turned the speakers off. I was growing tired of that insolent Swede's voice." He reached up and turned the volume back on.

"Well, we've just had a breakthrough, sir. I think you should come back inside."

"A breakthrough? What kind of breakthrough?"

"My apologies, sir, but I believe you're going to want to hear it straight from the horse's mouth."

CHAPTER 21

CAMP 020 INTERROGATION CENTER

THEY MADE THEIR WAY quickly back to the interrogation room and returned to their seats at the table. At the sight of Tin Eye, Carlsson tensed like a frightened dog. He was still standing against the wall, but now he was wiping tears from his eyes. Yet, despite the tears, he somehow looked relieved, as if a heavy burden had just been lifted from his shoulders.

Seated at the table, Captain Short looked at Tam and Tin Eye. "Mr. Carlsson has something to say to you, gentlemen."

"I'm pleased that you have come to your senses, Henrik," said Tin Eye in a tone that was unusually sympathetic for him. "You may proceed."

Without further preamble, Carlsson began to explain his situation. "It is true that I am a spy for MI6. But it also true that I have given top secret military information to the enemy for…for reasons of a sexual nature."

Tin Eye squinted through his monocle. "Reasons of a sexual nature? Do come to the point, Henrik."

"What I mean to say is that I am a married man, but I also like..."

"Also like what?"

"I also like…men."

Tin Eye gave a look of unconcealed disgust. "So you like to dip the dipstick, eh? Is that what you're telling us?"

"Yes." Tam noted a trace of shame in Carlsson's voice, or perhaps it was just a deep, abiding fear of Tin Eye, who continued to scowl like a martinet.

"So, you're a bloody experimental sodomite. I should have known it would be something unseemly like this."

Tin Eye's voice dripped with open contempt, and Tam couldn't help but feel badly for poor Carlsson, who didn't seem like a bad fellow, even though he was this very moment confessing to being both a double agent and a queer, both of which were regarded as criminal violations in the stodgy British intelligence service. The prisoner withdrew half a step, and another flicker of shame passed across his face.

"I love my wife, truly I do. But I also like male companionship. At least…at least on occasion."

Tam quickly jumped in, keeping his tone sympathetic. "Are you telling us, Henrik, that you disclosed sensitive information to the SS in return for sexual favors?"

"No, I'm informing you that the Gestapo blackmailed me, the bastards. I had no choice but to comply or they would have killed me."

"How did they blackmail you?"

"They took secret pictures of me with two of my male lovers, and they threatened to show them to my wife if I didn't provide them with certain military information."

"What did you give them?"

"The design specifications for the Miles M.52."

"The bloody what?" snorted Tin Eye.

"The Miles M.52. It's a turbojet powered supersonic research aircraft. My company makes the shock cone and some of the other components of the plane."

"These male lovers...how did you meet them?" asked Tam, wanting to keep Carlsson talking and not badger him like Tin Eye now that he had opened up.

"One was a young Swede, the other a Dane. I met them in a club on different occasions. The Gestapo presumably had files on them both and had them initiate contact."

"So these young men were the initiators?"

"Yes, they—or the Gestapo—must have known that I was...vulnerable...and that's why they lured me in. The SS used these young men to get to me, and once they had the dirt they needed, they blackmailed me into giving information by threatening to send explicit pictures to my wife. That's what they threatened to do to me if I didn't comply. The Swede and the Dane were working for the Nazis—probably under threat of deportment to a labor camp."

"The honey trap, but in reverse. Did the SS know you were spying for MI6?"

"No."

"Did they ask you?"

"Yes. But I told them that I was decidedly neutral, like my country."

"So they detained you for questioning?"

"On two occasions. But I told them nothing. It was only later that they blackmailed me. That's when I handed over the design specifications for the Miles M.52 turbojet."

Tin Eye frowned. "You are a far more complicated man than I would have taken you for, Henrik. Here I thought you were just a simple *Abwehr* agent, but you are actually an experimental sodomite betraying not only the very country you are supposed to be spying for, but your own wife and children. And yet, at the same time, you still have not offered any concrete proof that you actually work for MI—"

"That's because it's classified," declared a new voice.

Tam jerked his neck to see Claude Dansey, deputy chief of MI6, and a junior intelligence officer he didn't recognize barge into the room. They were trailed by Murchison, the young lieutenant who had been sent off to retrieve the Weiss file.

The lieutenant quickly stepped in front of them, an exasperated look on his face. "My apologies, Colonel Stephens, but Colonel Dansey insisted on seeing you immediately."

Tam rose from his seat abruptly, unable to conceal his mortification and contempt. "Colonel Dansey, this is most unusual." He detested the bespectacled, ferret-faced deputy chief of rival MI6, considering him a dishonest trouble-maker, incessant meddler, and constant fly in the ointment of MI5's internal security and counterespionage program.

"Yes, I'll admit it is a bit unusual," said the diminutive intelligence chief, taking a seat at the table without asking. "But now we have independent confirmation from you chaps that our Swedish friend here has turned on us. He's one of ours—his code name is Tango—but I'm sure he told you that already." He gestured to the officer with him. "Lieutenant MacIntyre here is his case officer. His code name is Percival, as I'm certain you are also aware."

Tin Eye looked about ready to explode. "So this was all a bloody sham?"

"Oh, I wouldn't say that. You have confirmed what we have suspected for some time now," said Dansey, arrogantly touching his bristly white mustache. "Namely, that Tango is a double agent and has been compromised by the Germans."

"I am not a double agent!" protested Carlsson. "I was blackmailed!"

"Tell that to the firing squad, Old Chum," said Dansey, nicknamed "Colonel Z" in British intelligence circles on account of his low cunning.

"We don't know anything for certain, yet," said Tam. "We need to verify his confession."

"Oh, we've already done that. We just needed the confession from an independent party. And you gentlemen have done that quite nicely. The word gift-wrapped comes to mind."

Tin Eye's face turned crimson, but he said nothing. Tam suppressed a gulp: they had been played like a fiddle by their rivals at MI6. Though Dansey should have had plenty to do overseeing his own vast network of spies and counterspies scattered across the globe outside Britain, he was such a fiercely competitive, vindictive bastard that he seldom passed up an opportunity to provoke and upstage his brethren in the domestic branch of the Secret Intelligence Service.

The room settled into an uncomfortable silence as Tin Eye and Dansey scowled at one another like enraged pit bulls. Suddenly, the young lieutenant, Murchison, stepped forward and handed Tin Eye the file he had requested. "Sir, I believe this will put a different spin on the present situation."

He gave him a knowing glance.

"Yes, let's have a look." With exaggerated nonchalance, Tin Eye took the file and examined it for a long moment before handing it to Tam, who looked over the three photographs in the folder closely. Smiling subversively, Tam sat down, instructed Carlsson to take a seat at the table too, and pushed the photographs towards him.

"What the devil are you doing, MacGregor?" demanded Dansey, irked at being left out and potentially upstaged.

Tam didn't answer. "Henrik, have you ever seen the man in the photographs before?"

The Swede examined the head shot first, followed by the side profile, and finally the full figure picture of a man in his late twenties, wearing the same flannel prison trousers and prison jacket with the six-inch white-diamond shape sewn in the back that he was wearing. After examining all three photographs a second time, a look of comprehension came over his face. He nodded his head.

"Yes, I see now. It was him. Damnit, I should have known."

"Who are you referring to?" asked Tam.

"The man on the train."

"You mean the train from London to Aberdeen?"

Carlsson was still closely examining the pictures. "Yes, that's him. That's the man on the train. The man I thought was following me. He's the one that did it, the clever bastard."

"Did what?" demanded Dansey, confusion evident on his ferret face.

"Planted the knife and film on me."

"How do you think he did it?" asked Tam.

"I left my jacket in my compartment when I went to the dining car. That's when he must have pulled it off. I thought he was a railroad detective or military policeman."

"When did you first notice him?"

"Just before Edinburgh. I knew he was watching me, but I thought he was an official of some sort. And yet, I was also struck by how closely he resembled me, at least superficially." He pointed to the photographs. "That's him all right. That's the real spy, the one you're all looking for. He's the one who killed your agent and took the photographs. It damn well wasn't me!"

"Bloody hell. I knew Manfred Otto Weiss from Bremen was a bad egg," chafed Tin Eye.

Dansey wiped his spectacles with a smug look on his face and sniffed, "So what you're saying, gentlemen, is that you've assisted in the capture of one spy, but in the process you've lost another, more important one. I should think the PM won't be too happy about that."

But Tam wasn't listening. His mind was racing forward, all of his focus now on how to catch the real spy.

"We know what he looks like, but we still don't know who he is," Tin Eye said to him, also ignoring Dansey. "Ten to one says he's Captain von Walburg's brother, but we still haven't received the files from MI6."

He then delivered a frosty glare to the deputy chief, knowing that Dansey was most likely the one responsible for the delay.

Tam shot the deputy chief a sharp look too as he grabbed his coat and hat. "Claude, you small-minded little prick. You're going to send the complete MI6 file on the von Walburg brothers, and their father the general and right-hand man to Rommel, to my office within the next hour—or John Masterman and myself will bring court-martial charges against you. You'll be lucky to get a posting in bloody Reykjavík. Is that clear? Now I must be going."

Dansey gave a rare look of befuddlement. "What, you're leaving? Where are you going?"

"I'm catching the first transport plane to New York. Our man is over there, somewhere."

"But you don't even know where," sniffed the MI6 deputy chief. "You're looking for a bloody needle in a haystack."

"That may be, *Old Chum*. But I'm still going to find him—before he costs us the bloody fucking war!"

CHAPTER 22

CAMP PERSHING

AFTER A HEARTY DINNER of roast beef, steamed spinach, roasted potatoes, and fig pudding, Erik and Wolfgang headed back to their newly assigned officer's barracks, where a runner informed them that Colonel Kepler wanted to see them. At first, Erik sharply refused. But his brother pulled him aside and, after a heated discussion, convinced him that it was his duty as a soldier to put aside his personal feelings towards the colonel. After all, if there was any prisoner in the camp who could arrange for them to send a message to the *Oberkommando der Wehrmacht*—the Supreme Command of the German Armed Forces, or OKW—it was Kepler.

They were quickly escorted to the *Afrika Korps* officers' compound. As the ranking officer of the camp, Kepler had his own private room. Though it was small, Erik was surprised at how well-appointed and amply stocked it was, even for a full colonel. He doubted that captured British or American officers imprisoned in Germany lived in such comfortable quarters. But then again he was in America, the land of the free, and not in Occupied Europe, or God forbid, Bolshevik Russia. All the same, he realized that this was precisely the kind of country club living that made the local farmers and ranchers sarcastically refer to Camp Pershing as the Fritz Ritz.

The colonel sat at a table in the center of the room, wearing a blue khaki uniform with the printed letters P.W. for Prisoner of War on it. He was busy writing something in a notebook. On the table next to his notebook was a copy of *Nue Volkszeitung*, a German language newspaper published in New York that was generally critical of American policies, as well as a copy of *Deutsche Stimme*, The German Voice, the local POW paper mimeographed on the camp printing machine. The room contained a cast iron stove, a wooden dresser, a bunk bed with the top bunk packed with neatly arranged toilet articles, underwear, socks, wooden sandals, and hand towels, and, finally, a nightstand with a lamp and a pair of black-and-white photographs. One picture showed Kepler posing in his immaculate dress uniform with none other than Adolf Hitler and a corpulent Hermann Göring; the other displayed the colonel with his stunning wife and exquisitely Aryan children posing somewhere in the Alps. A small swastika flag hung over the head of his bed, and at its foot was an open footlocker overflowing with tins of food, bottles of liquor, chocolate bars, pens and stationary, and German magazines.

Erik's eyes scanned the bookcase against the wall. It contained fresh, leatherbound copies of *Mein Kampf* and Hans Grimm's *People Without Space*, as well as other works by state-approved, pro-Nazi writers such as Werner

Bumelburg, Gottfried Benn, Agnes Miegel, Rudolf Binding, and Börries von Münchhausen. He recalled the line in Grimm's book that had been co-opted by the Nazis when they came into power: "The Germans: the cleanest, most honest people, most efficient and most industrious."

Erik was surprised at how laissez-faire the Americans were with regard to POW belongings; with liquor, chocolate, and a copy of *Mein Kampf* on prominent display in the colonel's quarters, there were obviously lax restrictions on what a German prisoner could have in his possession at Camp Pershing. But perhaps such democratic courtesies only extended to high-ranking officers like Kepler, though somehow Erik doubted it. Judging by the colonel's room, the Americans seemed to allow great personal freedom, which contrasted with how he remembered things back home in state-controlled Nazi Germany under Hitler during his last visit six months ago.

"You wanted to see us, Colonel?" said Wolfgang.

Kepler continued to write for several seconds before looking up. With a quick snap of his wrist, he closed his notebook and extended his hand towards the two empty chairs across the table from him, assuming the look of a gracious host.

"Please be seated." Then to the runner. "Lieutenant, that will be all."

The young officer saluted and was gone.

The two brothers took their seats. Erik had an uneasy feeling and looked warily at Kepler.

"How are you two settling into your new quarters?"

"Just fine," answered Wolfgang in an eager voice, and Erik realized that his brother, too, was tense and anxious. "But this heat will take some getting used to."

"In two weeks, you will be used to the climate."

"At least it is dry," said Erik, trying to act casual.

"Dry and dusty. We are in the land of the cowboys and Indians."

"It brings back fond memories of Karl May," said Wolfgang.

"It does, doesn't it? As you know, Karl May is a favorite of the Führer."

"I didn't know that," said Wolfgang.

"I didn't either," said Erik, wishing it weren't true. Somehow, it didn't seem right that Hitler was a fan of the legendary German writer of Westerns, whose wild and exotic stories Erik had cherished growing up. He drew a mental image of buckskin-clad Old Shatterhand and his blood brother Chief Winnetou roaming the Southern Plains on horseback. It made him angry to think that the Western adventure stories he had so loved as a child were also cherished by the fanatical Führer who was destroying his country, and most of Europe.

Kepler's face turned more serious now, signaling that the preliminaries were over. "No doubt you are wondering why I have sent for you." He paused and looked directly at Erik. "I want you to know that your secret is safe with me."

Erik pretended not to know what he was talking about. "Secret? What secret?"

"Why your true identity, of course."

"My identity?"

"Please don't play me for a fool. Obviously, you are a spy. I already know you are Erik von Walburg: son of General von Walburg of Rommel's staff and brother of U-boat Commander Wolfgang von Walburg standing beside you. I did enjoy your *Soldbuch* though. Chief Medical Officer Manfred Weiss of Bremen. Very creative."

"But how did you…?"

"I have eyes and ears all over this camp, and the Americans give us a lot of freedom and are asleep at the wheel, half the time anyway. For these reasons, I am nearly as well informed as the commandant himself. That's why I also know that you are, in fact, a spy."

Erik remained still and quiet. Every instinct told him not to respond, or to trust Kepler at all. And yet, as his brother had so assiduously pointed out, he would need the colonel's help if he was to have any chance of transmitting his urgent message to his father and Rommel as quickly as possible.

"You must tell him, *Brüderlein*," said Wolfgang in that demanding, brotherly tone that Erik had always resented. "Tell him, or I will."

Now Kepler's face bore a look of curiosity mingled with amusement. "Tell me what?"

Erik remained quiet, but inside he cursed his brother.

"Please indulge me, Major von Walburg. I am all ears."

Still, he gave no response.

Kepler frowned. "Major, you are going to have to learn to trust me. I am the senior officer of this camp, and nothing takes place without my approval."

To his chagrin, Erik realized there was no way out—he had to submit. "I suppose, as senior officer, you have a right to know."

"Indeed, I do," said Kepler sternly. "When it comes to the SO, there are no secrets."

"Very well, it is true that I am a spy. I lived in London for four months and gathered vital intelligence on the Allies' plans and methods."

"Vital intelligence?"

"Top secret."

"Top secret? You surprise me, Major. Here I thought you were nothing more than the spoiled son of a Prussian aristocrat. Yet you are, in fact, a high-level spy."

"You might want to treat my brother with a little more respect, Colonel," said Wolfgang firmly, but without a trace of anger. "What he knows could very well win us the war. That's why we need your help—we haven't much time."

"Win the war? Are you sure you two aren't exaggerating?"

"It is not an exaggeration. Right, Brother?"

"That is correct. The intelligence I have in my possession could change the outcome of the war."

"Well then, as your senior commanding officer here at Camp Pershing, I am naturally going to have to be fully briefed."

He felt himself stiffen. "I'm afraid, Colonel, that that is out of the question."

"Is it now?"

"My orders are to report directly to General Rommel and no one else."

"Ah, the Desert Fox himself. The man who—along with you and your father—abandoned me and my 21st Panzer Division in Tunisia. How ironic?"

Erik felt himself crimsoning with embarrassment, but forced himself to remain calm and composed. "We were recalled to Berlin along with General Rommel by the Führer himself," he replied, knowing that his explanation sounded like nothing more than a pathetic excuse, even though it was the absolute truth.

"Well, that was certainly convenient for you all, wasn't it?"

"Look, we don't have time for this, Colonel," interjected Wolfgang. "We need a radio. We have to get a message to the High Command."

"High Command? Don't you mean General Rommel?"

"It doesn't matter who—what matters is when. We need to notify *someone* in a position to act on this intelligence as soon as possible. Can we count on your support, Colonel? It was our understanding that you might have a shortwave radio we might be able to use to transmit a message from right here inside the camp."

"I'm afraid that will not be possible."

"And why the hell not?" demanded Erik.

"Because Colonel Morrison has confiscated all of our radios. At this moment, we can't even listen to Jack Benny, let alone Axis Sally."

"So how can I alert General Rommel?"

"For that, you will need to escape and then steal, or gain access to, a high frequency radio transmitter."

He looked at his brother. Wolfgang frowned.

"Don't worry, it is not as difficult as it seems. Many Americans have sophisticated wirelesses. Even the ranchers and farmers out here in the middle of Old Shatterhand's vast American desert have them. Once you have got your hands on a two-way shortwave, all you have to do is send your message. Every radio intelligence post between here and Berlin will be listening in. They will descramble and transmit the information to the High Command almost instantly. It could be Lisbon or Madrid, or maybe South America. Or perhaps your message will be picked up by one of our stations in Occupied France, Italy, or the Netherlands. It doesn't matter. Someone will be listening in and will descramble your message in minutes. But the first thing you must do is escape."

"And what is the best way to do that?" asked Wolfgang.

"You gentlemen are jumping ahead of yourselves. You don't know the first thing about escape—either one of you. And besides, all escapes must be approved by the Escape Committee. Of course, I am the head of the Committee with full veto power."

"Surely, the fact that I have top secret military information on our enemies will expedite the process?" said Erik, trying to stem back his anger at Kepler's bureaucratic insolence.

"That depends on the quality of the intelligence."

"All right, assuming I did obtain approval by the Committee, what is the best way to escape?"

"Why a work detail, of course. But it normally takes weeks of planning for an escape. There are forged documents, supplies, clothing, money, and many other things to consider."

Erik could stand it no more. "We have to go by tomorrow, Colonel!" he said urgently. "The fate of our beloved Fatherland hangs in the balance!"

Kepler laughed mockingly. "I'm afraid that is impossible. But I do appreciate your spirit."

"You don't understand, Colonel. This intelligence will determine the outcome of the whole damned war!"

"My brother is not exaggerating! It is absolutely critical that we get to a working radio as soon as possible!"

"I can see that you are quite serious and, for that, I must commend you. If the future of the Reich is truly at stake, I suppose I could get you and your brother on a work detail tomorrow morning. But I will not be able to have even rudimentary papers for you until the next day. So the soonest you would be able to escape is June 5, the day after tomorrow."

Erik felt a wave of jubilant relief. "Thank you, Colonel. You won't regret this, I promise you. And in time, all of Germany will thank you as well."

"Before you thank me, you should know my conditions. They are—as the gangster Americans like to say—non-negotiable."

Erik shook his head emphatically. "I already told you that I cannot disclose any information. My orders are to report only to General Rommel, and if that is not possible, to send a special transmission that his listening post can pick up. I have an authentication sign so they will be able to verify that it was sent from me."

"I'm afraid that is not good enough, Herr von Walburg. I am going to need to know everything. Then I will decide how best to proceed."

He started to protest, but the colonel cut him off with an abrupt chop of his hand. He looked to his brother the fearsome U-boat commander for help, but all he got was a shake of the head. *Verdammt!* Every instinct told him not to tell Kepler a fucking thing, but how then could he save his country? If he disclosed his vital intelligence to the colonel, he would be striking a devil's bargain. But did he have any other choice if he wanted to do the right thing for Germany? He decided that if he told him anything, it would only be a small portion of the truth, enough to whet his appetite. He could not tell Kepler the whole story of what he knew, or he risked the whole intelligence gambit blowing up in his face. Then where would his beloved Fatherland be?

"Suppose I agree to tell you what I know," he said to bring the colonel into his confidence, while at the same time distracting him and changing the topic. "Which ranch or farm would be the easiest to escape from?"

Kepler gave a knowing, devious smile, and Erik could tell at once that he was up to some clever trick. "That is easy—the one that belongs to the countess."

"The countess?"

"Yes, the Countess von Walburg. She is very popular in this camp, though she now goes by the American name Katherine Templeton. She sings songs to my men and cooks them up fine German food."

Erik wasn't sure he had heard correctly. He looked at his brother, who had gone suddenly pale, and then he knew that he had heard it right the first time. "Countess von Walburg? You mean my…my…?"

"Yes, your mother. Or, I should say, the mother of *you both*!"

DAY 5

SATURDAY

JUNE 3, 1944

CHAPTER 23

LEFT HAND RANCH

KATHERINE TEMPLETON stared out at the POWs in the distant field—cheerfully singing their work songs as they tilled the soil, mended fences, cut weeds, and dug irrigation ditches—and was reminded of her glorious youth growing up in Posen, Prussia, and, after the Great War, her early married years living in Berlin. She remembered back fondly to long summer days spent walking through the woods, playing the piano, and riding her auburn mare, Minna, through lush grassy fields that stretched endlessly like the ones she stared out at now. Life had been so splendidly simple back then.

Born four years before the turn of the century, Katherine Gräfin von Stroheim was the daughter of two noble families with considerable land holdings and royal lineage going back more than two centuries. Her marriage just before the Great War to a handsome, young captain and count named Robert Graf von Walburg further ensured a life of opulent aristocracy. It also produced three fine young sons named Wolfgang, Erik, and Maximilian, and brought her bountiful happiness until her late thirties, when von Hindenburg died, Hitler consolidated his power by taking over as both Führer and chancellor, and she was embarrassed to be a German citizen. In the fall of 1934, she fled to America with her two youngest sons—sixteen-year-old Erik and nine-year-old Max—leaving her husband Robert and oldest son Wolfgang, both newfound ardent supporters of Hitler and his brown-shirted hooligans, behind in Germany.

Although she was now an American in heart and soul, she had fond memories of the romantic land of Goethe and Beethoven she had treasured as a young woman. She supposed that was why she enjoyed having German POWs working around her ranch. When she heard them talking *auf Deutsch* as they labored in her green pastures and dined at her picnic table on the front lawn, she was reminded of her homeland during nobler, gentler times. The familiar sound of their German work songs, joking voices, and pleasant stories of the Fatherland, as they swung their scythes back and forth, lopping away at the thistle that proliferated along her network of irrigation ditches, brought back sweet memories of the old country. Before Hitler had sent it into a downward spiral of death and destruction that had literally torn her family, and all of Europe, apart.

Katherine's thoughts were interrupted by the sound of Kate Running Wolf's voice. "Lunch will be ready in ten minutes, ma'am. Should I go ahead and ring the bell?"

"Please do." She looked out at the POWs laboring in the far field. "They have been working hard all morning. They will be very hungry."

"Yes, ma'am. But if you don't mind my saying so, I think you are too kind to them darned Germans."

Katherine felt amusement tug at the corners of her mouth. "Am I now?"

"Yes, ma'am, you are. After all, they are the same Nazi scamps that killed your poor Max in Italy. You don't owe them a darned thing except to work them as hard as a plough horse."

"My wife's right," chimed in Jack Running Wolf, the Comanche's plaits swaying across his broad shoulders as he swung around the edge of the house. "You do treat the sons of bitches better than they deserve."

"Those German boys work hard for me, Jack, and the war is over for them. They've laid down their arms, and deserve to be treated fairly."

"They get paid for their labor."

"Eighty cents a day. I make a handsome profit off those boys—and you know it. The least I can do is feed them lunch."

"Yes, ma'am, but they don't need no Broadmoor-style vittles. I know it's because you were born and bred over there, but you *are* too nice to them young bucks. After what that jack-booted thug Hitler has done to you and your family, I would think you would be out for a little bit of vengeance. That's how we Comanche did it back in the day—and I think you ought to try it. You've been moping around since you heard the news about Max. It might do you some good to kick a little Kraut ass."

"You know very well, Jack, that that would solve nothing. That's why I came to this country in the first place: to get away from dictators and violence."

"There's always going to be dictators and violence in the world. The only thing that matters is whether you're on the right side of the fight or not. And in this war, ma'am, we happen to be on the right side. And them damned Nazis ain't."

"Now that's something you and I can both agree on."

"The missus and I aren't trying to upset you. It's just that we…well, we miss Max. And don't forget, German soldiers just like those ones out in those fields yonder are the ones that killed him."

Katherine felt a clump in her throat. *I miss him too, damn you! He was my son!* she wanted to scream. But she kept her voice calm. "Taking out our anger on those POWs out there won't bring Max back and you know it, Jack."

"I know it won't, ma'am. But it would make me feel better if you didn't treat them so damned nice. They don't deserve it. Now Kate and I have said our piece. We won't bring it up again."

"I would hope not." She turned to Kate. "Please ring the lunch bell," she said tartly. "Let's see if we can't at least eat like civilized human beings."

"Yes, ma'am." She cast a guilty glance at her husband, before turning on a heel, walking to the edge of the porch, and ringing the lunch bell.

Jack Running Wolf took his hat in his hands and bowed his head. "I'm sorry, ma'am," he said with feeling. "We didn't mean to upset you. Kate and I just loved that boy is all. We're both torn up about it. We can't have children of our own, and Max was the son we never had."

"I know you loved him, Jack," she said, and she touched him gently on the arm. "But you've got to stop telling me how to run my ranch."

"Yes, ma'am." He bowed his head apologetically and stepped into the house, leaving her standing on the front porch feeling raw and wounded inside.

She thought of how much she missed her Maxey. Of her three sons—including her two oldest, Wolfgang and Erik, who were no longer a part of her life and fighting for Germany—he had looked the most like his father, her first husband General Robert Graf von Walburg. Max had been a handsome, brilliant, cheerful young man. She remembered how strapping and full of promise he had looked when she had watched him board a Liberty ship bound for North Africa. That had been over a year ago in May, 1943. She hoped that he had not suffered too badly when he had lost his life on the beachhead at Anzio.

Kate stopped ringing the lunch bell and went inside to finish the lunch preparations. Katherine turned and watched as the Germans began walking in from the fields and assembling next to the military truck that would transport them in for lunch. A part of her knew that Jack was right: she was awfully kind to them, considering that only a short time ago they had been slaughtering American GI's just like Max all over Northern Africa, Sicily, and Italy. But when she saw them out working peacefully in her fields, singing their songs, and smiling at her as she fed them their noonday meal, it was hard to think of them as the enemy. After all, they were just homesick boys like her beloved Maxey.

She thought of her other two sons: her oldest, Wolfgang, and second-born, Erik. She realized that, with Max gone, a part of her longed to see them again. She hadn't seen Wolfgang since she had left Germany a decade earlier. Back then, he had been a brown-shirted Hitler Youth that she had come to detest. But a part of her longed to see him now in the hopes that he had somehow changed. Erik, on the other hand, she missed terribly. The most like her, he had always been her secret favorite.

Erik and Max had lived with her in America when she had left her husband and Wolfgang behind in Berlin in the fall of '34. She had pretended to be taking her two youngest on a tour of the U.S., but it had really been a way to smuggle them out of Germany. She didn't want them to turn into incorrigible Nazis like their father and oldest brother. Once in America, she hired a powerful New York lawyer and filed for divorce, giving up Wolfgang but retaining custody of Erik and Max. Less than a year after the divorce, she became romantically involved with a wealthy, recently widowed American businessman named John Templeton, whom she and her husband had been acquainted with from their American vacations and through their friendship with the well-connected Charles Lindbergh. She and her two boys soon took up residence in Tuxedo Park near where Templeton lived, though she and the Wall Street titan did not marry. But Erik grew restless. Even though he loathed his older brother and Nazism, he was always torn between staying in America and returning to his homeland. And then, on the eve of the *blitzkrieg* invasion of Belgium, he was coerced by his father—the great General von Walburg, that paragon of Prussian nobility and bellicosity—to drop out of Harvard, return to the Fatherland, and join him on Rommel's staff in the *Wehrmacht*, leaving her and Max alone in America.

Katherine bowed her head in silent reflection, thinking back to when her original family was still together living in Berlin. She had been so content with her husband the count and their three young boys back then. The family's prodigious wealth had insulated them from the squalor and ravages of the 1920's post-war German world wrought by the one-sided Treaty of Versailles. And then, as the 1930s were ushered in, Hitler and his brownshirts cajoled and savagely beat their way into power and everything changed. The Nazis ended up ruining her family—and now they were ruining Germany.

But she was as much to blame for the disintegration of her family, she realized sadly. She had taken Erik and Max away to make a fresh start in America, and now her youngest son was dead and her ex-husband and two oldest sons were either fighting against her country, or dead themselves, from a brutal war that was killing millions. She felt diminished, a hostage to the painful decision she had made ten years ago: to leave her husband and oldest son behind, and forge a new life with her two youngest in a land of opportunity and democracy, a land without the fiendish brutality and paranoia she had experienced under Nazi rule. Now, with her second husband and Maxey gone, all she had now was a world of emptiness, a world with no family at all.

And it broke her heart.

CHAPTER 24

LEFT HAND RANCH

THE ARMY TRUCK PULLED UP, parked next to the barn. Out of the driver's seat tumbled Corporal Grayson, a gangly twenty-year-old from Minnesota. After tipping his hat up to her, he unlatched the rear door of the truck to let the German prisoners out. The western sky was bright and blue, though dark storm clouds appeared to be gathering force far to the east along the edge of the horizon. The POWs, dressed in sweat-soaked blue khaki uniforms with the printed letters P.W. on the back, piled out of the truck. At Grayson's squeaky-voiced command, they started marching across the grassy lawn over to the picnic tables.

Katherine made a count of the men. There were seventeen total. They were guarded only by Corporal Grayson, who was armed with a single-shot, bolt-action rifle. Most of the POWs were regulars who worked on her ranch, but there appeared to be two or three new faces as well. These must have been the captured U-boat men Colonel Morrison had told her were being transferred to the camp. One of them had a dirt-smudged face and wore a seaman's cap pulled down low on his head. He had a shy, introspective quality about him, and she was thinking that he looked vaguely familiar when a shout came up from the head of the little column.

"*Guten Tag*, Countess!" a burly sergeant she knew as Becker greeted her in gravelly German as the group shuffled its way towards the table where Kate was serving lunch. "Another fine day in paradise!"

"Yes, it most certainly is," she replied in her native tongue, peering down from her shaded porch.

"Paradise, yes, yes," agreed another German POW in broken English, smiling up at her. "Thank you for hosting us for lunch yet again!"

"We have a deal, gentlemen. You perform the work, I provide the lunch."

A third soldier waved. "Hello, Countess, how are you today?"

"Just fine, Corporal Romer, thank you. Enjoy your meal."

"If I may be so bold as to ask, Countess," said Sergeant Becker, "what is on the menu today?"

"Fried chicken, mashed potatoes, green beans, and dark bread."

He beamed. "Fine dark German bread—wonderful. Like I said, another day in paradise. Will you be joining us?" There was a hopeful note in his voice.

"Not today, Sergeant, thank you. I have a call to make."

"Ah, we shall miss you," he responded cheerfully.

There were head nods all around and a chorus of thanks echoed down the line. Corporal Grayson tipped his hat towards her in acknowledgement and then assembled the prisoners into the food line. They were all in their late teens to early thirties, the pride of the Fatherland. How could she be cruel to these German farm boys who earned less than a dollar a day for eight hours of hard work and took the utmost pleasure in a simple picnic lunch?

She went inside her office to make her business call and attend to some ranch paperwork. A few minutes later, Kate came in with a plate of food for her. Katherine thanked her, sent her away, and ate her lunch alone. Through the open window, she heard the soldiers talking and joking animatedly. Every so often, a tremendous peal of laughter would rise up from the picnic table and she found herself smiling.

Then she thought of poor Max and tears came to her eyes.

He had been all that she had left of her original family, and now he, too, was gone. For a moment, she imagined that she had it all back: her husband the charming count; her three adorable sons; and the Fatherland that she had cherished, back when anything and everything seemed possible. She loved her job as the manager of a large cattle ranch and as owner of the illustrious Broadmoor Hotel. But a fulfilling career was not enough when you had lost your entire family and no longer had a loving husband with whom to share your hopes and dreams.

Her reverie came to an end as she heard noises outside. The soldiers had finished their lunch and were making their way to the truck to return to the fields. She quickly made her way to the front door to see them go, as sometimes Corporal Grayson liked to have a parting word with her. As she stepped out onto the front porch, she saw that one of the soldiers was standing at the foot of the stairs, his back turned towards her. It was the shy one whose seaman's cap had been pulled down low over his forehead. The soldier turned, pulled off his cap, and started coming up the stairs. As before, there was something vaguely familiar about the way he—

"Hello, Mother, I wanted to thank you for the wonderful meal," he said in flawless English with the slightest trace of a British accent.

Her mouth fell open. "Oh my God!"

He raised his finger to his mouth. "Please, don't raise an alarm. I just wanted to talk to you before I go back to work."

"You…you're a prisoner of war at Camp Pershing?"

"As you Americans like to say, it's a small world."

She felt suddenly lightheaded, as if about to faint. But with an effort she was able to steady herself. Was it really her Erik? He looked so much bigger and stronger than she remembered him, and also more mature and deeply lined in his face. And yet, with his cap pulled away, he was as familiar to her as if she had seen him only the week before.

He gave a beguilingly innocent smile, and she realized that he had been anticipating this moment and had prepared himself for it. He wore the same bland prisoner-of-war uniform as the other inmates, but he somehow filled it with a more commanding flair than the other men.

His shyness had obviously been an act as his face was now calm, composed, and watchful. He carried himself with a manly confidence that far exceeded his years. She wanted to say something in reply, but her lips wouldn't move. It had been how long…over four years?

Corporal Grayson was motioning from the back of the truck. "Let's go, Weiss! Time to get back to work!"

"Yes, just one second! I was just thanking our host!" He turned back to her. "Mother, I have to hurry. When can we talk?"

She was still tongue-tied. She felt her heart thumping against her chest, the eyes of the other POWs shifting towards the two of them. They sensed that something unusual was happening. My God, she still couldn't believe her son Erik was here in America!

Her mind filled with a torrent of thoughts. All of the wonderful memories of his childhood—and their last terrible argument—came flooding back to her. It had been mid-April 1940 when they had fought bitterly over his decision to drop out of Harvard and return to Germany to join his father in the *Wehrmacht*, and three days later he did just that. But was her son Erik truly standing before her this very moment, or was she only dreaming? It seemed impossible. And yet, there he stood in the flesh on her front porch. It had to be some sort of miracle. Max was gone…and suddenly in his place appeared her longstanding favorite child, the middle one Erik, who possessed the finest qualities she saw in herself and was the most like her.

"Come on Weiss, let's go! *Schnell! Schnell!*"

"Just a second! The countess was telling me something!"

"Ma'am, is he harassing you?"

Her son turned angrily and she saw that now, at twenty-six, he had a physical power about him that he had not possessed four years ago as a mere college boy. "I'm not harassing anyone, Corporal! We're just talking!" He turned and whispered urgently. "Please, Mother, tell him!"

She hesitated.

"Tell him, Mother—please! But don't let him know that I am your son!"

"Why not?"

"Because…because I don't want anyone to know. Back at camp, some of the officers are hardened Nazis, and they don't take kindly to those of us with American ties, or who associate freely with Americans. Please, mother, you've got to listen to me! And my name is Weiss…I'm a medical officer! I don't have time to explain!"

She looked into his pleading eyes. Inside, she felt a jumble of mixed emotions. The old motherly affection came rushing back, but there were other feelings too: anger, pain, thwarted love, fear, a sense of betrayal, and dread. But her strongest emotion was the instinctive pleasure at being reunited with her long lost son, whom she had given up all hope of ever seeing again.

Corporal Grayson had crossed the lawn and was climbing up the stairs, looking none too pleased at this delay in the work schedule. Meanwhile, the POWs that had assembled at the back of the truck were staring up at them now with great interest.

Katherine quickly decided how best to diffuse the situation.

"Corporal Grayson, would it be possible for POW Weiss to assist me this afternoon here at my home rather than in the fields? I have several heavy objects that need moving and items that need fixing inside the house. Of course, I will be paying at the prevailing rate. You can pick him up at the end of the work day."

The pimply-faced corporal looked resistant at first, but after thinking about it for what seemed like a full minute without coming up with an actual objection, he relented. "I suppose that would be fine, ma'am. I'll pick him up out front here at five."

She looked at her son. "Any objections, Medical Officer Weiss?"

"No, ma'am," he said with a knowing grin. "As you say in America, I am all yours."

"Very well, then." She turned back to Grayson. "Thank you, Corporal. I'll hand him back over to you at five o'clock—sharp!"

CHAPTER 25

LEFT HAND RANCH

AT THE FRONT DOOR, Erik paused before stepping inside to run his hand along the wood, feeling the smoothness of the grain. The craftsmanship was superb, and the door frame still carried a fresh piney scent. Both the exterior and interior of the ranch house were straight out of a Western novel. He remembered that his mother, too, had been a big fan of Karl May, and had always dreamed of building a beautiful Western ranch-style house that looked out onto pristine mountains and plains. She had read May's adventure stories to him and Wolfgang when they were little boys, and it was through their mother that they had come to worship the mythical Old West of Chief Winnetou and his Mescalero Apache warriors.

She led him to a sitting room with a large window that looked out upon the massive Rocky Mountains. On the wall opposite the window loomed a giant grizzly bear mounted on its hind legs, a U.S. Army Model 1864 Springfield rifle, and a pair of hand-woven Navaho rugs, all of which Erik guessed must be worth a small fortune. The bear was set in a fierce pose, with fangs bared and clawed arms outstretched. Off to the right stood a burgundy leather couch, an engraved Spanish table, and a pair of upholstered chairs. Above the couch hung several framed black-and-white photographs of the historic Broadmoor Hotel from its grand opening in 1918 to the present day.

Erik had been to the illustrious, European-style resort several times before: three times with his father, mother, and two brothers when his family had lived in Germany; and five times later on when his family had broken up and he had lived with his mother and younger brother in Tuxedo Park, New York. This was after she had divorced his father and was courting the wealthy American businessman John Templeton. It was only later—when he had returned to fight for Germany—that he had learned that she had married Templeton, whom he had always liked and with whom she had not had any children. That was the last he had heard about his mother.

"Why don't we sit over here?" she said in English, pointing to the handsomely furnished couch and chairs.

He noticed that she had lived in America so long now that she had almost no German accent. "Don't I have to get to work?"

"Not yet," she said. "We need to talk first."

"Of course," he said obediently, feeling strange to be in the presence of his mother as an authority figure again.

He took a moment to study her. Though time had taken its inevitable toll on her, she was still a sublimely beautiful woman. Her jaw line was smooth yet well defined, her nose sharp and aristocratic, her figure in fine form from a combination of sheer hereditary luck, vigorous outdoor activity, and disciplined eating habits. Her blue eyes sparkled with vitality, and her delicate skin had a healthy quality when she gave her luminous smile. Though a trace of webbing had taken root around her eyes and a few strands of gray had appeared at her temples, these changes only added to her gracefulness and feminine majesty. She was as he had imagined her and still looked every inch a countess. But somehow, despite her well-maintained beauty and regal bearing, there was a trace of melancholy in her eyes, like someone accustomed to hearing bad news and eternally fearful of receiving more. He couldn't help but feel that she must be a tad lonely despite her prodigious wealth and small army of ranch hands and servants.

"So, you have been captured and are pretending to be a medical officer," she began by stating the obvious. "Why? Does that ensure better treatment?"

"Let's just say it allows me to move around more freely among both my German comrades and my American captors."

"Fair enough. Were you with your father when you were captured?"

"No."

"But I thought you were on General Rommel's staff in France with him."

He tried to conceal his surprise. "Now how would you know something like that?"

"A mother has her ways," she said cryptically, and he wondered if she was trying to hint at something more.

"It is true that I am on Rommel's staff in Western France with father. But that is not where I was captured. I was on a U-boat taken by the British. That's how I came to be here."

"You were on a U-boat?"

"Yes. As it happens, one captained by your oldest son."

Her hand went to her mouth. "Wolfgang?"

"So you remember his name. How magnanimous of you." He paused a moment, letting his sweetly acidic barb resonate. "He was captured as well and is here with me at Camp Pershing."

She looked as if she didn't believe him. "Wolfgang is at the camp, too?"

"Yes, and as you might expect, he still makes a lousy conversationalist. He's so damned serious."

She couldn't help a little smile. "That's how the oldest always are."

He saw that, whatever ill feelings she had once felt towards her eldest son, she was at least relieved that he was alive. Somehow, it was reassuring to know that, after all of the misery experienced before, during, and shortly after the family breakup and subsequent divorce, his mother still cared for him and Wolfgang. Of all her sons, her firstborn was the one who had enraged and disappointed her the most, Erik knew from growing up in the same house with them both. Their savage arguments during Erik's last two years in Germany, when Wolfgang was a member of the Hitler Youth, had been terrifying to behold.

"Where is the master of the house?" he asked, looking around the room.

"You mean John? He died last fall."

"I'm sorry to hear that." A reflective pause. "You know, I always liked him.

He never bossed Max and I around and always lavished us with ridiculously expensive and exotic gifts."

"He understood young boys because he was a boy himself at heart."

"Well, I'm sorry he's gone. I know you loved him."

"Thank you," she said quietly, and he saw how fragile she was.

An awkward silence passed between them. He looked around the room again, this time committing everything in it to memory. For he now agreed with Kepler that his mother and this cattle ranch of hers represented, far and away, his best chance to escape. He took a moment to study the locked gun rack bearing a wide assortment of pistols and rifles that he knew had been the pride and joy of her late husband, an avid gun collector. Of course, today was not the day to make his escape; today was the day to reconnoiter and ingratiate himself with his mother, in case she might be willing to help him, in some small way. With all of the necessary preparations made, tomorrow was the day to make his move, or at least that was the plan according to Kepler. He continued to study the guns in the case. One of them might come in handy tomorrow, and he wondered where he might be able to find the key to unlock the case. *How about the desk in the study?*

"When did you move out west?" he asked her.

"Shortly after you left for Germany. That's when John and I were married."

"Yes, father told me. It was early on in the war when we were in France. Right after Dunkirk. There was a notice in the *New York Times*."

"The wedding was at the Broadmoor."

"I should have known you would settle out here...with John owning the Broadmoor and your love of the wild, wild West."

"It was Karl May that opened my heart up to it all...the same as you and your brother." She waved her hand expansively out the window towards the towering, majestic mountains in the distance. "When I used to read those books to you boys, I dreamed of a life out here in the American West. It was a fantasy of mine, just as it was for you boys. And now look at me. I am the owner of a big cattle ranch and the Broadmoor Hotel. Who would have thought?"

"You are Frau Shatterhand."

"Yes, I suppose I am." She smiled dreamily, and then after a moment her face hardened. "And you are a captured German soldier with a country on the brink of defeat. How do you feel about that?"

"Germany is your country, too."

"Not anymore it isn't. The country where I was born and raised, the country that I once loved, is gone. It vanished the day that maniac Hitler took power."

"Let's not argue over politics, Mother. What's done is done. Let's talk about you."

"Me?"

"Yes, you look tired. Have you been working too hard?"

"No, it...it is Max. He is gone."

"Gone?"

"He was killed at Anzio. In Italy."

The words were delivered in a mere whisper, and suddenly she was fighting back tears. He felt for her, felt powerfully for his mother, this suddenly fragile woman that, deep down, he had always loved unconditionally, even after he had dropped out of Harvard and returned to Germany. So that was why she seemed so tired and troubled. He nodded his head sympathetically. He had adored his baby brother, and had often wondered what had happened to Max after he had returned to the Fatherland to join the *Wehrmacht*. Now he knew: his little brother was dead.

"I still can't believe he's gone," she said sadly. "I found out only a few days ago."

She was crying now, and as he saw the tears rolling down her cheeks, he wanted to cry too. But he held back. He tried to picture what Max had looked like in his American G.I. uniform before he had died. That his kid brother was no more was a tragedy that shook him deeply. He couldn't believe that he would never see the rosy-cheeked baby that he had shuttled around in a carriage at the Tiergarten for his mother; or the smiling partner-in-crime with whom he had lit off firecrackers, gone cliff jumping, and horsed around in Tuxedo Park as an adolescent when he had lived in America. Somehow, it seemed pointedly unfair that his little brother, the baby of the family that everyone had adored, should be the first to die.

He reached out and touched her hand. "I'm sorry about Max. I loved him more than you know."

She wiped away the tears from her eyes. "Is that why you went off to fight for Hitler?"

"I said let's not argue, Mother. It is a miracle we are together again, and we should not be at each other's throats."

"Yes, of course." She gave a weary sigh, crossed her arms, and proceeded to change the subject. "So how is your father? I hear he is quite busy on General Rommel's staff building up the Atlantic Wall?"

Again, how in the hell did she know that? Was she, on account of her wealth and prestige, somehow privy to classified intelligence information? Or was the fact that his father—her former husband—was the Desert Fox's top general common knowledge here in America?

"You know I cannot discuss military matters with you, Mother. Our countries are at war."

"Very well. Then tell me something else about him. Is he still so stubborn that he thinks Germany can actually win?"

"You're getting into politics, again."

"There's no way around it when a deranged dictator has been turned loose on the world."

He forced himself to stem back his growing exasperation with her. He looked around the room again, taking it all in. Then he peered outside the room to the far end of the hallway. That was the study where Kepler said a radio was tucked away. Who knows, maybe he didn't even need to escape tomorrow. If he could work at the ranch house again, he might be able to slip into the study and transmit a quick message to Rommel, especially if his mother was busy in another part of the house. There would be no reason to escape if he could do that. Perhaps his mother might even be willing to help him if she knew how many German lives would be saved. If he could just explain to her that he and Father both detested

Hitler and were only doing what was best for her once-sacred homeland, maybe she would allow him to use the radio. But could he reason with her? Would she even listen to him? More importantly, could she be trusted?

"If you want to know the truth, Mother—Father and I *both* hate Hitler. The war has changed both our minds about a lot of things."

"Isn't it a little late to be changing sides?"

"I am not changing sides. My loyalty is to Germany—and so is Father's."

"If you were assigned to General Rommel's staff in Western France with your father, what were you doing on a U-boat with your brother?"

My God is she sharp, and nosy too! "You know I cannot tell you that."

"I think you are a spy. That's why you are posing as a medical officer, because you are a damned Nazi spy!"

"Watch your tongue, Mother. I am not a spy. I am merely a captured soldier in a strange, new land who is trying to protect himself."

"From what?"

"From my own German comrades, and the Americans. Truthfully, I fear them both in equal measure."

"I don't believe you. Why do you have a British accent?"

He feigned a look of disbelief. *My God, she's as clever as Tin Eye!* "I don't have a British accent."

"Yes, you do. It's subtle, but it's still there. Do you really think you can fool your own mother?"

He abruptly rose from his chair. "I am not trying to fool anyone. I am a prisoner of war five thousand miles from his home. I am struggling to adjust to a new situation in a strange foreign land."

She studied him coolly. "What is my middle son not telling me? You know you cannot fool me, Erik."

What? Does my face look guilty? "I am not trying to fool anyone, least of all you. I just wanted to talk." He gave his most innocent smile. "Come now, Mother, let's not play these cat-and-mouse games. It has been too long since we have seen each other. Why don't you show me around your wonderful house?"

"You want to see my house?"

"Yes, of course I do. Let's start with your study. I want to see where Frau Shatterhand conducts her important business."

She crossed her arms. "You think you can fool me, don't you? You think that, because you were once my favorite, you can pull the wool over my eyes with your charm?"

He felt transparent. "I told you I am not trying to fool anyone."

"Yes, you are. You are up to some sort of trick. That's why you didn't want me to see you until after you had finished lunch and were going back to work."

"Mother, how can you say that?"

"Don't call me Mother, you Nazi brute."

"Damn you, I told you I am not a Nazi. And neither is Father—or for that matter Wolfgang."

"Wolfgang not a Nazi? That will be the day."

"You haven't seen him. He has changed. He is still a bull-headed son of a bitch, but where before he was a Hitler stooge and never questioned authority, now there is at least uncertainty. You should have seen his face when we saw the giant skyscrapers. He is in awe of America's power. Though, of course, he would never admit it."

"If he has changed so much, why didn't he come here today? Like you, he must have known I was here."

"Yes, we both found out last night. But he couldn't come. Like me, he volunteered for labor duty, but the camp commandant wouldn't allow it. To be perfectly honest, I think Colonel Morrison spent the day interrogating him."

"Why didn't he interrogate you?"

"I am just a harmless medical officer, not an important U-boat captain. Churchill himself refers to Wolfgang as 'the scourge of the North Sea'. For me, anonymity has had its benefits."

"Is that what my eldest son has turned into, a scourge?"

"You haven't heard about his exploits? He has sunk more tonnage than all but one U-boat commander. I would think that your open, democratic American newspapers would have given him the same coverage as your General Patton who likes to slap around shell-shocked privates in field hospitals."

"Don't try and twist around what you and your brother are. You are the enemy."

"That may be, but you should know that I'm telling the truth about Wolfgang. He has changed since you last saw him. The war, and being a prisoner here in America, have both changed him."

"The war has changed us all."

"True, it has made you into a red-blooded American. Have you been buying your war bonds?"

"Of course. And the war has turned you into a dangerous spy."

"Those are just empty words. You don't know how to tell if someone is a spy or not."

"Ah, but I do. I may not be a spycatcher, but I am a mother. And right now, my mother's intuition tells me you are spying on me because you want something. The question is what is it?"

My God, it's like she has a sixth sense! He rolled his eyes and gave a look of bemusement, hoping to diffuse her suspicion. "Right now, all I want is to quietly sit out the rest of the war. Is that too much to ask?"

"You were always a good liar, because you were so charming, but you cannot fool me. Even after many years, a mother never forgets her own son."

"I'm sorry to disappoint you, Mother, but there is no skullduggery going on."

"I know you are hiding something. Why don't you just tell me what it is?"

"Don't you have any work for me? If not, I will return to the fields."

She studied him closely. He felt her maternal eyes boring into him like a steel auger. He shook his head with consternation, rose from his seat, and started from the room, feeling anger bleeding into his mind. He could feel his control of the situation slipping away. How could she possibly read his thoughts when she hadn't seen him in over four years?

Her stern voice brought him up short. "I'll find out, you know. I'll find out what you are hiding, and also what you want from me."

He turned and glared at her. "No you won't, Mother. Because there is nothing to find out!"

CHAPTER 26

CAMP PERSHING

COLONEL JACK MORRISON stared expectantly at the telephone on his desk, waiting for it to ring. But of course it didn't. Feeling restless, he tugged at his collar and looked at his watch for the tenth time. The call was scheduled for 1600 hours, yet it was already 1608. He knew the call was important because it was coming in from London via Washington, using a special military radio-telephone link and trans-Atlantic speech-scrambling device. The latest in wartime technology provided for secure Allied communications and offered encrypted protection from eavesdropping Axis code breakers. It was housed in the Pentagon and carefully overseen by the 805th Signal Service of the U.S. Army Signal Corps, which referred to the device by its abbreviated name: SIGSALY.

He had been told to be ready waiting at his desk for the call. Why the hell some high-level army brass would want to communicate with him all the way from London, England, was anyone's guess? Secretly, he held out the vague hope that it might be one of General Eisenhower's aides asking him to return to active command for the upcoming Allied invasion of Western Europe.

He looked at the phone. Damnit, why didn't it ring?

And then suddenly it did.

He nearly jumped up from his chair, like a kid scared on Halloween night. To settle his nerves, he cleared his throat before picking up. He wanted to sound official yet nonchalant, as if he took scrambled radio-telephone calls from London, England, every damned day of the week.

"Colonel Morrison here."

"Hello, Colonel?" The voice was scratchy but audible. "This is Colonel MacGregor of the British Intelligence Service."

"Good day, Colonel."

"Good day. I'm radioing from the Supreme Headquarters Allied Expeditionary Force HQ in London. It seems we have a bit of a bugger-up that I believe you can help us out with. This is a top priority with a critical timeline and comes straight from the very top. I am under direct orders from General Eisenhower and his deputy chief of staff here at SHAEF, General Morgan."

He held his breath. *Was this his chance to get back in the game with a field command for the big invasion?* "How can I be of service, Colonel?"

"Well, it's rather simple. It seems that you have two Jerries in your camp out there in Colorado that we need to have a little chat with."

He felt his heart sink. He wasn't being offered a field command at all. The Brits just needed to talk to a couple of damned Krauts. He shouldn't have gotten his hopes up.

"Have a chat with, Colonel? You mean like a fireside chat?"

"Fireside chat, yes…American humor, I see…jolly good. No, actually we were thinking of something a little…different."

"Different. Interesting word choice, Colonel. So who are these *Jerries* that you are so interested in?"

"They're actually related. One is a U-boat commander named Wolfgang von Walburg, and the other is his younger brother, Major Erik von Walburg. They were delivered to your camp just yesterday."

Morrison sifted through his paperwork and quickly found the list of the most recently interned POWs, sorted by branch of military service and rank. "I've got a Commander Wolfgang von Walburg, Colonel, but I don't see any brother. I personally interviewed all officers, with the exception of the medical officers, yesterday and today. There is no Major Erik von Walburg on my list."

"He isn't on your list. And you didn't interview him, because he is posing as Chief Medical Officer Manfred Weiss, late of the attack submarine U-521 sunk in the North Sea. But this man you know as Weiss is no medical officer. He is a German spy who, up until recently, was living in London. He also happens to be a very young and promising major in the *Wehrmacht* and aide-de-camp to a high-ranking German general."

"And who would that be?"

"His father. General Robert Graf von Walburg is on Rommel's staff in Occupied France. He's the Desert Fox's top general as well as his closest confidant and advisor."

"So, you're telling me I have a Nazi spy posing as a medical officer in my camp, whose father happens to be an important general close to Rommel? I thought all you guys were supposed to be sending me were ordinary German soldiers from the *Wehrmacht*?"

"That *is* the normal procedure. But, unfortunately, this one slipped through our fingers."

"He obviously has important intelligence in his possession. Otherwise, you wouldn't be calling me all the way from London. Are you at liberty to tell me what that intel might be, Colonel?"

"No, I am not."

"But I can guess. It obviously has to do with the planned Allied invasion of Western Europe."

"I can tell you, Colonel, that it is far bigger than that. But that is just between you and me. The one thing I can disclose is that both of these men pose a grave military threat and are to be regarded as extremely dangerous. Especially the younger one, who as I said before, is a most clever yet unassuming spy."

"Actually, you didn't tell me that before. But thank you, that does paint a more accurate picture. So what do you need from me?"

"I need you to place them both in solitary confinement as soon as we get off this call, and hold them until I get there."

"You're coming to America?"

"I will be boarding a military transport plane in the next hour. I will meet with you and General Shedd, commander of the U.S. Army's 7th Service Command, at Camp Carson tomorrow morning. The general's staff is making the arrangements and will contact you with the details. The plan is for me to interrogate them at length along with two G-2 chaps, as well as your senior intelligence officer, Captain Avery. When I have the information I need, I will report directly to Supreme Allied Commander Eisenhower and Field Marshal Sir Alan Brooke, Chief of the Imperial Staff, take the two prisoners into custody, and return them to England to be imprisoned for the duration of the war. May I ask where they are now?"

"The older one, the U-boat commander, is in camp. As I said, I interviewed him this morning."

"And the other?"

"Just a moment, I have to check." Morrison felt his fingers fumbling as he scanned through today's POW labor roster. God, did he need a stiff drink? "Ah, here it is. He has been detailed to labor at a local ranch. He is due back within the hour."

"Good heavens, he's outside the bloody camp?"

"Yes, but he's scheduled to be back any minute now. I can either take him into immediate custody upon his return—or radio the officer responsible for the work detail and instruct him to return to camp at once. There's a radio in his truck."

"Please radio him at once, Colonel. And I must remind you that the information in the possession of this spy von Walburg—and probably by now his brother, too—could cost us the bloody war. It is imperative that you quickly locate them and place them in solitary confinement. As I said, this goes all the way to the top to Ike. We cannot afford to fail."

"You have nothing to worry about, Colonel MacGregor. I'll take care of it."

"Yes, I'm sure you will," said the Englishman, but Morrison could tell he didn't really believe it. "Oh, and there's one more thing."

"Yes, Colonel?"

"We've received a tip on another unusual bit of information. It seems that the mother of these two bad eggs has moved into your neck of the woods."

"You mean out here in Colorado, near Camp Pershing?"

"That is correct. Her German name was Katherine Gräfin von Walburg. She was a countess of some distinction. She immigrated to America a decade ago and married a wealthy New Yorker. A man by the name of John Templeton, a Wall Street big wig and owner of the Broadmoor Hotel in Colorado Springs. I have been advised to warn you that, if one or both of these von Walburg brothers escapes, he or they may try to contact her for help. Katherine Templeton is American, of course, but you never know how a mother might react in a situation like this."

For a startled moment, Morrison couldn't believe his ears. It seemed like something out of a movie like *Casablanca* or *Above Suspicion*. Katherine was actually the mother of these two prisoners? He looked down at his POW labor duty roster for the name Manfred Weiss to see where he had been assigned to work today.

His heart leapt from his chest.

Left Hand Ranch!

It couldn't possibly be a coincidence. Somehow, the clever son of a bitch must have gotten himself assigned there. And then he remembered back to late last night: Kepler! The goddamned colonel was the one who had arranged it! They had met late, at 2100 hours, and at the time Morrison had wondered why the Africa Corps commander was suddenly being so cooperative. During the meeting, Kepler had informed him that, starting tomorrow, all non-commissioned officers and enlisted men would no longer be on strike and would take part in the POW labor program. He went on to say that, to set an example, several officers would be volunteering for work detail even though, under the Geneva Convention, officers were not required to participate in the labor program. At the time, Morrison had gladly welcomed Kepler's change of heart. But now, he realized that the Nazi son of a bitch had played him like a fiddle. He had greased the wheels for Erik von Walburg, probably to set him up for escape!

"Is something wrong, Colonel?"

"I need to contact Corporal Grayson, the guard on the work detail, and secure the prisoners."

"Yes, of course. I will call you by telephone when I reach New York and give you a more precise estimate of my arrival time tomorrow morning."

"I'll talk to you then, Colonel. Goodbye."

CHAPTER 27

CAMP PERSHING

HANGING UP, he lunged for the bottle of Wild Turkey in his drawer. His fingers trembled like a tuning fork as he tried to unscrew the cap. Finally, he had it off and tossed back a shot of the fiery brown liquid. It was like a jolt of electricity, and he felt better instantly. He took one more blast for good measure before putting the bottle away.

He jumped up from his chair, popped open the door to his office, and called out to his aide.

"Lieutenant Marks, I want Corporal Grayson and his work detail ordered back to camp immediately. Radio him right now. Is that understood?"

"Yes, sir. What's going on? Is it the tornado?"

"Tornado? What tornado?"

"There are tornado warnings for Kit Carson, Kiowa, and Cheyenne Counties. And all along the Kansas border. It just came up on the radio a few minutes ago. It's some kind of meteorological anomaly. It started in western Kansas this morning and is heading this way."

Morrison rushed to the window. The sky was silvery gray to the east, darkening to charcoal gray with a few visible, purple-rimmed storm clouds, but that was it. He didn't see anything resembling a black funnel shape. The branches of the cottonwoods were waving in the wind, but that was common out here on the exposed plains. And he didn't hear the usual high-pitched howling or rattling at the windows that signaled a particularly fearsome wind whipping through the area.

"It's windy out there, but I don't see anything that looks like a tornado."

"It hasn't made its way this far west yet, but it's coming all right."

"All the more reason to get Grayson and his crew back here. Radio the corporal on the double. In fact, recall all of the labor crews!"

"Yes, sir!"

He stepped back in his office and dialed Katherine Templeton at Left Hand Ranch. After being connected by the telephone operator, he was able to get her after two rings.

"Hello?"

"Katherine, this is Colonel Morrison at Camp Pershing."

"Yes, Colonel. I wanted to tell you that I had a wonderful time dancing with you the other night. I haven't seen anyone jitterbug quite like that before."

It pleased him that she remembered the evening; she was right, it had been wonderful. "I had a great time too. That was quite a shindig."

"You'll have to come out to the ranch again. We could go riding."

"I would like that very much." He cleared his throat officially. "My apologies, ma'am, but I'm afraid I'm calling about some urgent business. I wanted to inform you that your…your two oldest sons are being held in my camp. Were you aware of that, ma'am?"

The phone was silent for several seconds before she responded. "Yes, I found out a couple of hours ago, Colonel. I visited with my son Erik."

"You talked to him?"

"Yes, he was assigned to work at my ranch. We spoke after lunch and I put him to work."

"You spoke after lunch and then you put him to work in your fields?"

"No, I had him clean out my barn. It was a filthy mess."

"When was the last time you saw him? Before today, I mean?"

"It has been more than four years. He returned to Germany and joined the army in the spring of 1940 just before the *blitzkrieg*."

"Where is he now?"

"They are loading up in the truck to return to camp. Why, do you want to talk to him?"

"Can you tell me, is he in the truck?"

"Let me check." A moment's pause. "As a matter of fact he is, and it's pulling away now."

"You're sure he's on the truck, ma'am?"

"Yes, Colonel. Is there something wrong? Why are you asking me all these questions?"

He felt torn. On the one hand, he wanted to be honest with her, but on the other, he had to be cautious and treat her as if she might potentially aid and abet the enemy. "It's routine, ma'am."

"That's funny, it doesn't sound routine. In fact, you sound distinctly worried. Maybe it's because you've said the word *ma'am* to me three times already, when you know perfectly well that my name is Katherine."

"You are a former German citizen, and he is a German POW as well as your son. Naturally, there are going to be questions—and trust me, the FBI would be asking them a lot less sympathetically than me."

"So let me get this straight. You think I would actually help a German soldier escape after everything I've done to promote the war effort? My God, Jack, I'm putting up half the officers at Camp Carson at my hotel."

He couldn't help but feel sympathy for her defensiveness. "I'm not accusing you of anything. It's just that…well, your son is apparently a Nazi spy."

"My son Erik is not a damned Nazi. He may very well be a spy, but he is no Nazi."

"Well, he has been identified as an important enemy officer and a serious security threat. In wartime, that makes people jumpy."

"So you're looking out for my welfare, is that it?"

"You don't need to be sarcastic. I'm on your side."

"It sure as hell doesn't sound like it to me."

"Katherine, look I didn't mean to—"

"Do you have any more questions for me, Colonel?"

Jesus, was she stubborn! Beautiful and stubborn. "Just one: did he ask about or try to gain access to a radio?"

"No, Colonel, he did not. He was too busy scooping up horse droppings from my barn. Will that be all then?"

"I didn't mean to make you angry. I just needed to know what happened between you two. Your son represents a serious security risk."

"This may sound unduly harsh and un-motherly, Colonel, but I do not care what happens to my two remaining sons. The son I cared the most about—my one and only true son, Max—was killed at Anzio fighting against Nazi Germany. The other two have not been part of my family for some time now. You can lock them up or you can hang them; it doesn't matter to me. They made their choice to fight for that madman Hitler, and they will have to, as you true red-blooded Americans like to say, reap what they sow."

"I know you don't really mean that."

"Oh, I don't, do I? Are you telling me what I'm supposed to think now, Colonel?"

"No, but deep down, as a mother, you've probably never stopped loving those boys. After all, they are your own flesh and blood, regardless of how much you disagree with their politics. They may have chosen to fight for the Reich, but they are still your sons."

"Not any more, they aren't. They chose to fight for Nazi Germany and are not part of my family. My family died the day Max was killed at Anzio. Those two strangers are your prisoners now. You do with them as you wish."

"Surely, you don't mean that."

"I most certainly do."

"Look, Katherine, I didn't mean to insult—"

"It's too late, Colonel, you already have." And she hung up.

CHAPTER 28

CAMP PERSHING

AS SOON AS THE TRUCK pulled up to the outer gate, Erik could tell that something was wrong. Standing there waiting with his brother Wolfgang was the camp commandant, Colonel Morrison, and a detail of armed guards; while fifty yards beyond, Colonel Kepler and two dozen POWs stared out intently from behind the barbed wire of the internment camp. Erik was overcome with a feeling of dread. He had suspected that something was going on when Corporal Grayson had received a radio call just before the work detail had boarded the truck to return to camp. After taking the call, the young guard had looked at him nervously, ordered him into the back of the truck, rushed the other POWs on board, and then drove back to camp at breakneck speed.

When the truck passed through the gate, it pulled up in front of the commandant and his armed guards, whose uniforms were flapping in the stiff breeze that had picked up in the last half-hour. The guards stepped quickly to the back of the truck where Erik was sitting to take him into custody. A beefy, bullet-headed sergeant pointed his rifle at him, motioning for him to climb out. He looked to his brother for some explanation of what was going on, but Wolfgang didn't seem to know any more than he did and just shook his head.

Colonel Morrison stepped forward and spoke over the sound of the whipping wind. "Major von Walburg, if you and your brother would be kind enough to follow me."

Erik pretended not to understand. "There must be some mistake. My name is Manfred Weiss. I am not a major, and this man is most definitely not my brother."

Morrison smiled with amusement. "And I'm Joseph Goebbels, and these men pointing the guns at you are the Three Stooges. Please don't insult my intelligence any further, Major, and follow me. We need to get out of this blasted wind."

Erik hesitated. In response, he felt a rifle jab into his back.

"Come on, Fritz, you heard the colonel," said the beefy sergeant with a malevolent smile. "Giddyup now, Little Doggy, and no more fucking lying to the colonel."

Erik looked at his brother, who scowled at the guard with unconcealed disdain. If Wolfgang could have ripped the throat out of the dumb-looking American with his bare hands and get away with it, Erik had no doubt that he would do it. They followed in behind the colonel and headed towards the front door of the camp administration building.

To the west, Erik saw Kepler and the other POWS still looking on with keen interest from behind the barbed wire, a few of them booing in protest at their

American captors. But there was nothing that could be done, the spy knew. Morrison was about to give him and his brother the third degree, just as that bastard Tin Eye had done back in London.

Damnit! Someone must have contacted the commandant and informed him of my true identity. Or, at least warned him to keep a close eye on me.

Just before stepping inside, he took one last look at the growing thunderhead along the eastern horizon. It appeared powerful and threatening, but was a long way off. And yet, having been out west to Colorado several times before, Erik knew how quickly a stiff wind and a few storm clouds could turn into a lethal force of nature. Out here on the open plains, seemingly routine foul weather could escalate to extremely dangerous conditions within minutes, wreaking death and destruction across a broad swath.

He noticed that Morrison had paused to study the ominous-looking storm clouds, too. One of his officers said something to him and they took a moment to confer with another officer. As if on cue, a flash of lightning lit the blackened sky, and Erik could tell it was going to be a bad storm.

When they were finished conferring, Morrison said, "Keep me posted, Lieutenant."

"Yes, Colonel." He saluted smartly.

Morrison led them inside the building to his small office, stationing two guards outside his door, and offered them each a seat in front of his desk. Once they were seated, he sat down behind his desk and pulled out a bottle of Glenlivet single malt Scotch whiskey and three glasses. Scanning the titles of the books in the bookcase, Erik saw that Morrison was something of a military historian. Gracing the shelves were such diverse military treatises as Sun Tzu's *The Art of War*, Von Clausewitz's *On War*, Sir William F.P. Napier's six-volume study of Wellington's campaign in Portugal and Spain, *History of the War in the Peninsula*, and General Heinz Guderian's *Achtung - Panzer!* and Rommel's *Infantry Attacks*.

Morrison then said, "You both speak my native tongue as well as Lord Hah-Hah, so if you don't mind we'll converse in English." Smiling pleasantly, he waved a courteous hand towards the bottle. "Before we begin, would either of you care for a drink?"

"Not me," sniffed Wolfgang, his chin sticking out stubbornly and face slightly reddened with barely suppressed defiance. Erik wondered how long his brother had been detained before his arrival. He seemed testy.

Morrison then turned towards Erik, as a gust of wind rose up and the branches of a cottonwood scratched against the office window. He and Wolfgang looked uneasily at the window, but Morrison seemed unfazed.

"What about you, Major? Would you like a drink?"

He tried to appear polite but official. "As I told you before, I am not a major. My name is Manfred Weiss, Chief Medical Officer aboard U-521, as it states in my *Soldbuch*."

Morrison continued to smile with amusement. "The Brits are right, you are a first-rate liar. I think it's because you have a pleasant quality about you that lures people into mistakenly thinking that they can actually trust you. I'll bet you got it from your mother the countess."

"I don't know what you're talking about."

"Of course, you do. You met with her this afternoon at Left Hand Ranch. Your mother has remarried and goes by the name of Katherine Templeton. Corporal Grayson told me all about your afternoon with her. It must have been quite a reunion after all these years. Would you like a drink?"

Erik felt his brother staring intently at him, but forced himself to keep his face studiously neutral. The game was up, but he wasn't going to admit anything to Morrison. "I suppose so. After digging ditches and scooping up manure all day, a libation is certainly warranted. Wouldn't you agree, Colonel?"

"I certainly would." He poured three fingers into a glass and handed it to him. Erik raised the glass to his brother, who looked about ready to burst, and took a hearty swig, letting it sit a moment in his mouth before allowing it to trickle down his throat.

"Glenlivet. Now that is good Scotch. I thought it was banned."

"Only in England. Where you were, as I understand it, recently an enemy spy of some repute."

"I can see you have a sense of humor, Colonel. That must be why you don't seem too upset about having been assigned to this dead-end backwater of an internment camp, instead of the front lines where the real war is taking place."

If Morrison was offended, he didn't show it; his expression remained one of vague amusement. "I admit I would rather be killing Nazis than watching them scarf down potatoes, play soccer, and build model airplanes all day. But as the French, who will soon *own* your country, like to say, *c'est la vie*."

His smile widened as he brought his Scotch once again to his lips, again seemingly oblivious to the window shaking violently behind him. My God, did they have crazy weather like this all the time out here? Was that why the colonel didn't seem the least bit fazed? Erik also realized that, although Morrison seemed a somewhat easygoing fellow with a sense of humor, he was not one to be rattled or pushed around. He was unconventional, and a cleverer and more formidable opponent than first appeared.

Erik took another sip of the velvety smooth Glenlivet. "You can try to get me drunk so I will talk, Colonel, but you are just wasting your time. I have nothing to tell you."

"And neither do I," echoed Wolfgang harshly.

"Oh, come now, gentlemen, we're just having a friendly drink. Of course, I would appreciate it if you would open up and talk. But if you don't, it's not as if I will torture you like your Gestapo."

"We have nothing to do with the Gestapo," bristled Wolfgang. "We are German soldiers."

"You may be, but your brother Erik here is most certainly not. In fact, he is a spy, and a rather clever one, I am told."

"That is not true. I am a navy medical officer."

"No, your name is Major Erik von Walburg—though personally, I think you look too young to be a major—and you were most recently a spy in London. Your father is General Robert Graf von Walburg, Rommel's right-hand man in France. And your mother, whom as I noted earlier you met today, is Katherine Templeton, formerly the Countess von Walburg."

Erik said nothing. The wind continued to whistle dangerously outside the window. He and his brother exchanged nervous glances. That bastard Tin Eye, or the silky smooth Scotsman in the tartan trousers, must have figured everything out and contacted Morrison. Which meant that Erik had to find a way out of the camp and to a radio transmitter as quickly as possible. But what about the coming storm? Was it turning into a tornado?

"So, what did you find out in London?" asked Morrison. "Do you know where and when the Allied invasion is going to take place, because I would really like to know myself?"

"I was never in London. I was on a U-boat in the North Sea."

"What about your mother? Wasn't it good to see her?"

He didn't respond. He noticed that Wolfgang was hanging on every word. His brother's urge to know what had happened between Erik and his mother during today's visit filled the room with an air of tension, made even worse by the wind howling outside like a wailing demon. Suddenly, another gust of air blasted into the glass, making it shudder so violently that Erik thought it would shatter. The direction of the conversation and the fierce weather made him feel frantically uneasy. He looked again at his brother, whose face had visibly whitened as he sat on the edge of his seat.

"I'm sure you two had a lot to talk about," Morrison went on as if nothing was happening. "The funny thing is your mother and I happen to be good friends. Why as a matter of fact, we were out dancing together just the other night at the Broadmoor. Your mom…she just loves to dance, especially with handsome American officers like myself. Of course, she hates Nazis more than anything else in the world, so she probably won't want to see you two ever again."

"That's enough!" snapped Wolfgang, and he was up and on his feet, the combination of Morrison's incisively probing manner, the howling wind, and rattling windows pushing him to the brink.

"Oh, Commander von Walburg, I can see you are agitated. Did you change your mind about that drink after all?"

"Shut up, damn you! I've heard enough of your insolence!"

An abrupt knock was heard at the door, cutting through the sound of the screaming wind and shaking window.

An officer poked his head in. Morrison shot him a look.

"What is it, Lieutenant?"

"I've just received another report. The tornado's going to hit us after all. And it's not just one tornado, it's a tornado swarm. That's what they're calling it, sir: a doggone tornado swarm!"

"Don't get too excited, Lieutenant. You might upset our German guests." He looked pleasantly at Wolfgang. "You don't get tornado swarms in the Fatherland, do you? I didn't think so. Well then, this ought to be a new and exciting experience for you both."

"I'm not joking, Colonel," said the lieutenant, looking as jittery as the two Germans. "They're saying it's an EF-4."

"What the hell is an EF-4?"

"I don't know, but they say that we can expect sustained winds of up to one hundred eighty-five miles per hour and severe damage. Apparently the tornado's changed course and is headed straight this way."

"Very well, we need to secure the camp. Lieutenant, please form a detail and personally escort my two new German friends here to the stockade, on the double."

"Stockade?" spat Wolfgang. "You're putting us in a prison cell?"

"You should consider yourselves lucky. The stockade is built out of concrete and is located below ground. It's the safest place in camp to be right now."

"You have no right to lock us up. We have not done anything to warrant this treatment, and you can rest assured I will be reporting this to the Swiss Legation."

"Report all you want, Commander, but my orders stand. Get them out of here, Lieutenant. I'm done with them for now."

"Yes, sir, on the double!"

He winked at them. "We'll be speaking again soon, boys. Very soon."

CHAPTER 29

CAMP PERSHING

AS THEY were escorted outside by four armed guards, Erik couldn't believe how quickly the sky had changed. It had turned from a black smudge against the distant horizon to several distinct funnel-shaped clouds. The whole scene had a terrifying, dream-like quality reminiscent of the strangely hypnotic American film *The Wizard of Oz*, which he had seen before the war during the fall of his senior year at Harvard. The branches of the cottonwoods around the perimeter of the building swayed dangerously, and sand grains pelted his face. All around, tumbleweeds rumbled past along with smaller objects like newspapers, tin cans, and trash that seemed to have appeared out of nowhere.

"Hurry up, let's go!" shouted one of the guards, his voice drowned out by the roar of the wind.

They started west towards the main compound with the wind at their backs, pushing them along. Through the curtain of dust, Erik saw Colonel Kepler staring at him and his brother intently from the entrance of one of the buildings. He wondered why the colonel seemed to have focused his attention on them; it was peculiar given the furious storm sweeping in from the east. Most everyone had already gone inside, but there were still groups of prisoners making their way to the various barracks and guards coming down from the towers. The weather had gone from bad to worse in the blink of an eye, taking the camp by surprise. Behind Kepler, a team of prisoners stopped unloading the food truck that had pulled up next to the dining hall. Erik saw the driver step down from the cab and take refuge inside the dining hall along with the German POWs. There was no tornado shelter so everyone was taking cover as swiftly as possible out of harm's way.

By the time they reached the inner gate, Erik couldn't see more than twenty feet ahead and the roar of the wind was deafening, assaulting his ears like a Sherman tank. The dusty haze parted in spurts as the guards directed them towards the camp stockade. It took all of their effort to keep their knees from buckling and from being knocked down as they fought against the stiff gale, but eventually they made it to the concrete-bunker-like building.

After being led down damp concrete steps, they were placed in separate cells with steel bars. As his door was clanked shut and locked, Erik felt two powerful, conflicting emotions. The first was relief. He was inside, out of the fierce wind, and hopefully safe as he was below ground in a shelter of sorts, though it was in fact a prison cell. The second emotion was a feeling of grim uncertainty about the future. With his true identity discovered, he would have to undergo an extensive interrogation once again. But would they keep him here in Colorado or ship him back to England? It didn't matter, he realized, for they now knew who he was and it was only a matter of time before they extracted the information they sought. He could not hold out indefinitely. His goal of helping attain German victory, or at least helping put an end to the war and ensuring dignified terms for his people, was out of the question. Regrettably, he would now have no impact on the outcome of the war.

The guards went away, leaving him and his brother alone in their steel-barred jail cells. They fell into silence as they struggled to adjust to their new situation. The only sound was the rush of the wind as it butted and battered the stockade building. As soldiers, they had long ago learned how to adapt; and, as a spy, Erik was always calculating his next move, trying to determine how he could control the world around him, gauging how best to avoid discovery. But right now, locked away behind bars in a damp subterranean stockade, he felt hopeless and powerless.

After a few minutes, the walls began to shake uncontrollably. The concrete cell block was below ground and protected, but Erik could still hear the steady wind roaring like a Spitfire and the crackle of thunder overhead. The storm was moving in quickly, and he wondered if he and his brother were truly safe after all.

"She's not going to hold," said Wolfgang, peering at him through the bars of the adjacent cell.

"What's not going to hold?"

"The roof. She's going to be torn open like a tin can any second now. The concrete walls are strong, but the roof and ceiling aren't."

"How can you be so sure?"

"Because I've spent the last decade beneath the sea in a U-boat, and I know what it feels like when a tin can's about to open up. There's too much pressure built up out there."

"That's reassuring."

"Don't blame me, *Brüderlein*. You are the one who got us into this mess."

"That may be, but you heard the colonel. This is the safest place in the whole camp."

His brother shook his head. "No place is safe, not today."

Erik shook the bars. "Damnit, I don't know why they had to—"

Suddenly, the metal door to the stockade banged open and Erik heard shuffling boots on the concrete stairs, barely audible over the roar of the wind but still distinct. Had the guards returned? The feet pattered down the walkway in front of the prison cells, moving quickly. A figure appeared.

"It's your lucky day. We're getting the hell out of here," said a voice.

Erik stared with stupefaction at Kepler, who had somehow managed to change into civilian clothing since he and Wolfgang had seen him watching them from the building entrance a half hour earlier. So that's what he had been doing: planning an escape under the cover of the storm. The colonel jammed an iron key into the lock and opened Erik's cell, then did the same with his brother's cell.

"But how did you get a key?" asked Wolfgang.

"The guards hide a key inside a little metal box outside the jail. This is where they come to sneak a drink and trade for liquor, cigarettes, and the like. I told you the Americans are lazy, incompetent fools. Come on, follow me. With this storm, we will never have a better chance to escape than this."

Erik was stunned. "Escape? In this weather?"

"This is the fucking best opportunity to escape. There hasn't been anything like this since last spring when I first arrived at Camp Pershing. You and the Führer can thank fickle Colorado weather for this great opportunity to save the Reich. Now we must go."

"Go where?"

"Away in the food truck. It is parked outside, if we can get to it without being spotted. Dust is everywhere and you can't even see ten feet in front of you. Follow me."

They dashed down the hallway. Kepler flung open the stockade door. It crashed open with a loud clanging sound and suddenly they were literally sucked into a vortex of dusty air. The subterranean darkness turned to a swirling, chaotic brightness with objects flying past at lethal speed. To his startlement, Erik could see an actual funnel-shaped cloud raging towards the front camp entrance and the administrative building where Colonel Morrison had interrogated them.

"Here, one of you grab the other in front of you by the belt and the second in line grab my belt," said Kepler. "I will take the lead."

They started through the haze in the direction of the food truck and dining hall with Kepler in the front, Wolfgang in the second position, and Erik behind him, each clinging to the waist belt of the man in front of him. Erik felt a tremendous pulling sensation and tightened his grip on his brother's belt as they stumbled forward into the maw. The power and fury of Mother Nature was mindboggling, the rumbling sound of the wind on the cusp of ear-splitting. The visibility was so poor that he could see no more than a few feet in front of his face.

"Stay with me and don't let go!" commanded Kepler. "This is our chance! There will never be a better one than this!"

Erik shook the cobwebs from his dazed head. *Chance? What kind of chance could we possibly have in a fucking tornado? This isn't* The Wizard of Oz.

"Keep moving! Keep moving!"

Erik still couldn't see more than a short distance in front of him. With strenuous effort, he fought his way forward before the force of the gale knocked both him and his brother flat onto the ground.

Kepler called out to them to again take hold of each other's belts and keep moving.

They stumbled to their feet and pressed onward, following the *Afrika Korps* commander. A brief gap appeared in the curtain of dust and Erik saw one of the prisoner barracks and the officers' mess literally devoured by a pair of merging twisters. Then the dust consumed his field of vision again and the twisters disappeared.

"Jesus Christ!" he cried, scarcely able to comprehend the powerful earth forces on display. "We've got to get the hell out of here or we're done for!"

"Just hold on! We're almost there!"

He forced himself to hold on to his wits and keep moving forward, clutching hard at his brother's belt. They clamored around a pile of debris dislodged from the eviscerated first floor of the officer's mess and the next thing Erik knew, a pair of hands reached through the curtain of dust and pulled him forward.

"We've made it!"

They stumbled up to the large vehicle which only a half hour earlier was being unloaded by prisoners. Luckily, the tornado had missed the truck and the main dining hall.

"Hurry! Get in!"

They climbed up into the cab. Kepler grabbed the work cap and jacket on the seat and put them on.

"Where are we going?" asked Wolfgang as Kepler turned the key in the ignition, engaged the gears, and the truck lurched forward.

"The plan is in motion—we are escaping. Like I said, you can thank Mother Nature."

"I can't believe we're actually going to escape from this place and transmit our message," said Erik. "It's a miracle."

"No, it is the power of our Führer. What is at work here is true providence. It is our destiny to save the Reich and win the war for our fearless leader. Everything that has happened has brought us all to this moment in history. We *will* save the Fatherland."

Erik didn't agree that Hitler had anything to do with it and he certainly wasn't risking his life to keep the madman in power, but he held his tongue. He did, however, concur that some kind of destiny, an ineffable but powerful providential force, was at work as Kepler swung the truck around and raced for the inner gate. How else to explain their unusual good fortune? Through the curtain of dust, Erik saw two more black funnels knifing in from the east. The big vehicle swayed and bucked, rattled and groaned as it clattered along the road, but by some miracle it stayed upright in the furious wind. To the south, lightning shot down in angry bolts and thunder exploded with a fury that shook the ground, roaring like an artillery barrage.

The truck drove on. Both the inner and outer gates and sentry posts had been decimated by the tornado and abandoned by the guards. But there were still a pair of American officers and an enlisted man peering out the windows of the administrative building, which had been only partly demolished. Kepler commanded the two brothers to duck down. Then he pulled the collar of the truck driver's jacket up and the workman's cap down low over his eyes and raced through the opening, waving a little signal as he passed, as if to inform the Americans at the window that he was getting the hell out of here and they should too.

A moment later, a quarter mile down the road, Erik looked back over his shoulder to see if anyone was following them.

He couldn't believe his eyes when no one was.

CHAPTER 30

CAMP PERSHING

MORRISON SAW SAND CLOSING IN ALL AROUND HIM.

He knew where he was. He was near Meknassy Heights, a series of stubbornly defended knolls in front of the 1st Armored's lines in the Tunisian desert. A German 88-mm, high-velocity anti-tank gun had just fired into his position, blasting out a hole the size of a railroad car and caving in a wall of loose dune sand down upon him. To his shock and disbelief, he had been buried alive. He gasped for air and struggled to make room around his supine body, pushing away the heavy eolian sand, wriggling and clawing desperately to free himself from what suddenly seemed like a coffin. The oppressive weight of the collapsed sand dune, coupled with the claustrophobic darkness, sense of doomed isolation, and lack of air circulation stirred an insane panic inside him, like something out of Edgar Allen Poe.

He felt crushed and utterly helpless.

"Colonel, can you hear me?"

The disembodied voice came from right next to him. But how could someone talk up close when he was buried by a slumping dune of sand?

"Colonel, are you okay? Can you hear me?"

Again, he gasped for air and this time it came in a huge gulp. Wait a second…where the hell was he? It couldn't be the Tunisian desert. It must be some other hellhole.

But where?

Then he remembered. He was not fighting in North Africa at all, but rather had been banished to a job as a lowly baby-sitter for recalcitrant German POWs in Camp Pershing, Colorado, which might as well have been fucking Purgatory.

He heard multiple voices now. Men seemed to be scrambling towards him. A moment later, he felt pressure relieved as several heavy objects were pulled off his body. As he shifted his position, a pair of strong arms reached down and helped him to his feet. He blinked several times as the face behind the voice he had been hearing swung in close to his, but the face was still a blur.

"Colonel Morrison, sir, it's me, Lieutenant Marks. Can you see me now?"

He squinted, blinked, shook his head back and forth several times, struggling to return his vision to normal. Slowly, the face came into focus. He felt the back of his head: a welt the size of a golf ball was growing just above the hairline, and it hurt like a son of a bitch. He wondered if he had a concussion. No, he decided, he was seeing too clearly for that. All the same, he took another minute to shake away the cobwebs and gather his wits before speaking.

"Lieutenant Marks, it's good to see you. How long have I been out?"

"Fifteen, maybe twenty minutes. It took a while for us to find you beneath the roof."

"What's the damage report?"

"I don't have all the details yet, sir, but I can tell you it's bad."

"How bad?"

"Two of the prisoner barracks have been leveled. Another has completely disappeared. And the officer's mess, two of the guard towers, and both of the south gates have all been wiped out. The phone lines are down so we can't call in or out. There's also extensive damage to the motor pool, prisoner's canteen, theater, and stockade."

"The stockade?"

"Yes, sir. Part of the roof was blown off, but all of the cells are still intact. The only problem is the prisoners aren't in there."

"You're telling me the Walburg brothers are gone?"

"Someone must have let them out because the cells were unlocked when we checked. We don't know if they're alive or not. Bodies have been blown all over the place. They could be among the dead."

Somehow Morrison doubted that, which meant that he was most likely in deep shit. "Assemble all of the prisoners on the double, Lieutenant! I want every single one of them accounted for as either dead, alive, or missing. We need to find those Walburg brothers!"

"Yes, sir!"

"I don't think I need to remind you that the very fate of the war may depend on it!"

"I copy, yes, sir!" and he was gone.

Morrison waded through the fallen timbers, rubble, smashed and overturned furniture until he came to what was left of the front entrance of the administrative building. The sky was a boiling purplish-black welt to the west, a hazy pastel gray to all other points of the compass, but to his relief there were no black funnels anywhere in sight. The camp itself appeared serene and desolate, as if some great battle had just passed, and Morrison couldn't help but be reminded of the gutted, burning tanks on both the American and German sides after Kasserine Pass and Meknassy Heights.

He ignored the pain in his gimpy, shrapnel-filled leg and started walking towards the center of the internment camp. A half-dozen barracks, two guard towers, and a handful of other buildings stood untouched, but every other camp structure had either been completely obliterated or seriously damaged. Everyday objects like pictures, mementos, and clothing were scattered to the wind. Fences had been ripped apart, furniture destroyed, windows shattered and broken, jeeps and trucks lifted off the ground and overturned. The larger cottonwoods left standing had been debarked like a skinned cat. Where the eastern prisoner barracks had once proudly stood, now all that remained were four ragged piles of battered wood planks, ravaged bunks, and strewn POW clothing and furnishings on slabs of desiccated concrete.

He went over to the stockade. The west side of the roof had been completely blown off, and he could see down into the individual cells. It was like peering into an open-topped dollhouse. The cells were empty. He wondered what had become of the two brothers. Had one of the guards opened their cells and moved them to safety after the first tornado hit? Or had the two brothers been removed and then been sucked up into a vortex? Or had they by some miracle managed to pick the cell locks and escape the swarm of twisters? After all, they were exceedingly clever bastards.

He looked to the west and saw a pair of bodies lying face down in the grass. He walked over and rolled each of them over with his foot. He recognized one of the men as Sergeant Schmidt, a particularly rabid Nazi and well-known enforcer under Kepler, but he didn't recognize the other man. The sergeant's neck appeared to be broken, while the other POW had been struck in the head by some heavy object that had crushed his skull.

But he couldn't worry about all the dead and wounded right now. He had to find those two damned missing Krauts!

He went quickly to the officers' barracks to find Kepler. He would need the cooperation of his foremost rival to put the camp back together again. The tornado had been their common enemy, claiming both German and American lives, and now they would have to pull together, at least for the short term, if they were to make the camp safe and inhabitable again. As he approached, he saw immediately that the colonel's barracks had been completely obliterated. POWs and American officers were working side by side, pulling men from the debris. But there was no sign of Kepler, or more importantly, Erik and Wolfgang von Walburg.

Damnit!

Twenty minutes later, Lieutenant Marks and the officers had assembled the inmates and taken a preliminary count. Of the 3,146 prisoners at the camp, sixty-seven were still not accounted for. They could be killed, missing, or wounded. Unfortunately, those still unaccounted for included Kepler and the two brothers.

When the count was complete, Morrison made an announcement that there would be another roll call in one hour and that every able-bodied man was to search for their comrades. Before both sides set off to conduct a second, more comprehensive search, the colonel pulled his officers and enlisted men aside. He reminded them of the importance of quickly finding the missing brothers, as well as the shifty Kepler. Then he questioned them about whether any vehicles or army personnel had been seen leaving the camp.

"Well, I saw Jim Grant leaving in his food truck," said Lieutenant Bearman. "It was right when the roof blew off of the admin building."

"I saw him too," said Corporal McCall. "He signaled to us that he was getting the hell out."

Morrison did a double take. "Why in the hell didn't you say something earlier?"

Bearman licked his lips nervously. "We were in the middle of a tornado swarm, sir. I figured Jim was just trying to get to safety."

"And you said he signaled you?"

"Yes, sir," said Corporal McCall. "Lieutenant Bearman and I both saw it. He waved to us right after the front window shattered."

"And you got a good look at his face?"

"Well, the dust was everywhere and the visibility wasn't too good. But I...I'm sure it was him. He was wearing his blue cap and work jacket and everything."

"Was there anyone else in the truck?"

"No, sir. Not that I saw."

"So what you're telling me is while we were being hit by a tornado that destroyed half of our camp, you and Lieutenant Bearman here saw Jim Grant driving off in his food truck, waving at you like a circus clown with a big old smile on his face? Doesn't that seem a bit odd to you, Corporal? That he would take the time to wave at you, as he was driving off in his food truck and struggling to escape a tornado swarm?"

Bearman stepped forward. "But it was him, Colonel. You know he has that silver goatee, sir...and he was wearing his blue cap and jacket like he always does. I know it was him...I...I saw him with my own two eyes."

"What you saw and what you think you saw are not necessarily one and the same. You yourself said the visibility was poor."

"Sir?"

"A lot of goddamned people have silver goatees, Lieutenant! Colonel Kepler, for instance!"

"Colonel Kepler?"

"The man you saw wearing the silver goatee and the blue cap and jacket could just as easily have been Colonel Kepler posing as Jim Grant! Good lord, man, don't you see?"

"I guess it could have been..."

"Could have been? Goddamnit, I tell you it was! Lieutenant Bearman, I want two working transports and six men equipped with sidearms and M-1s here in the next five minutes. We're going to pay someone a visit."

"Who, sir?"

"Why the Countess von Walburg, of course!"

CHAPTER 31

LEFT HAND RANCH

KATHERINE STARED OUT at the storm from her covered front porch. In the far pasture, the horses pressed against one another, their braying protests swallowed by the crash of thunder. The rain that had been pouring down from a cloudburst for the past several minutes swiftly turned to flecks of hail as the temperature dropped precipitously. The flecks then turned to cold, wet bullets that rattled and clattered against the house, barn, and outbuildings. The radio had warned of twisters further to the east possibly veering her way, but thus far she hadn't spotted any dangerous funnel-shaped clouds. All the same, with the hailstones pelting her roof like machine-gun fire, she felt like a soldier under attack.

Saturday was her staff's night off to go into town, and she felt vulnerable being all alone at the ranch. She had seen late spring storms like this for years, and they were seldom a surprise, but this one was particularly fierce and unrelenting. And yet there was a pristine beauty to it, like watching a handsome horse run at a full gallop across a grassy meadow. The hailstones continued to pound against the rooftop, and the wind howled and shrieked like a tormented ghost. But to her relief, after a few minutes the rattling dissipated, the horses stopped tossing their heads, and a pleasant tranquility returned to Left Hand Ranch.

It was amazing how quickly the weather could turn out here on the high plains.

As she started back inside, she heard the sound of an engine and turned to see a truck coming up her road. It was bigger than a mail truck, but smaller than a moving van, and it was heading straight towards her and moving fast. She remembered back to the army officer who had driven out here last week to deliver the terrible news of Max's death. A feeling of dread worked its way into her mind. Something about the vehicle—was it how fast it was moving or the single-minded intensity, noticeable even from a distance, of its driver?—didn't seem quite right. She pulled up the collar of her rain jacket against the cold, wet breeze.

When the truck turned the corner into her drive, she could make out two of the faces. The driver with the workman's cap she didn't recognize, but the sight of Erik and Wolfgang made her heart leap with a mixture of surprise, instinctive joy, panic, and long-simmering bitterness. She realized that it had been a decade since she had last set eyes on her oldest son. When she had left him and his father behind in Germany for her new life in America with Erik and Max, she had detested him. But, to her surprise, she found herself curious to see him again now that he had arrived in the New World.

But first, what in God's name were they doing here? The man driving the truck didn't appear to be a guard, and the work detail was finished for the day, so what was going on? Colonel Morrison couldn't have possibly authorized them to leave the camp, especially not when Erik had been discovered as a spy.

A tug of fear gripped her as the three men stepped from the truck.

"Hello, Mother," said Erik cheerfully as he and Wolfgang approached the porch, wearing blue prison uniforms and excessively charming smiles that instantly sent an alarm bell to her brain. They were also moving quickly towards her—too quickly, like animals stalking prey—along with the older, stern-faced driver in the blue cap and jacket, whose whole personae she found discordant.

"What are you doing here?" she demanded, trying to hide her fear behind an expression of matriarchal sternness.

The driver suddenly bounded forward ahead of Erik and Wolfgang, as if to give explanation. "Ah, Frau…I mean Countess von Walburg, it is a pleasure to meet you at last. I am Colonel Kepler, the senior camp officer. I was able to secure permission for your two sons to visit you, but unfortunately this terrible storm hit. That is Colorado weather for you."

She knew about Kepler from Colonel Morrison and the POWs who worked at her ranch, but she had never met him in person. The Austrians were especially fearful of him. She saw at once that he was a living model of Teutonic perfection: strong nose and chin, eyes the color of blue winter ice, a thin smile that signaled a love of engineer-like order and efficiency but not a hint of artistry or mirth. He had a strong German accent and, as he ascended the third stair, he extended his hand with the false courtesy she remembered so vividly from the Gestapo back in '33 and '34.

All Katherine could think was, *Damnit, I've been had!*

"You are lying to me, Colonel Kepler," she said to him flatly, a stubborn look on her face. "You shouldn't be here, any of you. You must leave at once."

He smiled wolfishly. "Ah, but Countess von Walburg, after all these years you and your two fine boys must have so much to talk about." In a fluid motion, he bounded up the last stair onto the porch, withdrew a pistol from his waistband, and pointed it at her face. "Who is here with you?"

"Wait, don't hurt her!" she heard Erik cry, and in the next instant he and Wolfgang were up on the porch, waving Kepler off.

The colonel wheeled on them. "You two shut up and obey my orders—or I will put a bullet in all three of you!"

"All right, all right, just don't harm her!" said Wolfgang, holding both palms up.

She scowled at him. "Don't try that chivalrous act with me. You're just as much of a cold-blooded bastard as the colonel."

To her surprise, instead of anger, his face bore a wounded look. In that instant, she realized that Erik had been right: Wolfgang did appear to have softened since she had last seen him as a Hitler Youth. But he still looked dangerous and desperate in his prison uniform, and she could not allow her maternal feelings to cloud her judgment with any of these men. They were the enemy, plain and simple, and they had obviously escaped from Camp Pershing and wanted her help.

"I will ask you one more time," said Kepler. "Who else is in the house?"

"No one. Saturday is my staff's night off and everyone went into town."

"You'd better not be lying to me."

"You can check for yourself. My foreman and his wife live in the guest house, and my ranch hands all reside in the bunk house." She pointed to the two wooden buildings fifty yards away. "You won't find anyone over there."

He waved the gun at her. "All right, get inside."

"What for?"

"Just do as he says, Mother," said Erik. "We will be out of here in five minutes and no one will be harmed. We need to use your radio."

"My radio?"

Kepler nudged her toward the door. "Oh, don't play so innocent, Countess. I know all about your hidden radio."

"I don't know what you're talking about."

"Come now, your son Erik here had to get his spying talents from somewhere. Now get inside!"

He pointed the gun at her again.

"What the hell is he talking about?" asked Wolfgang.

"Oh, you'll see soon enough," said Kepler with a knowing smile, and he took Katherine firmly by the elbow and led her inside. "Follow me, we need to hurry!"

He quickly led them to the study and shut the door behind them. Katherine watched as Erik and Wolfgang cast questioning glances at one another. Then they looked sternly at her, and she felt another prickle of dread. The situation, she knew, was about to change dramatically.

"There it is, Major," Kepler said to Erik, and he pointed to the open wooden panel upon which stood a large, specially-adapted version of an RCA SSTR-4 short-wave receiving and transmitting radio, the type used exclusively by American spies in "Wild Bill" Donovan's Office of Strategic Services, or OSS as it was better known. "Impressive, isn't it? Now get ready to transmit."

But Erik just stood there, gawking at the radio. "What is going on, Mother?"

"Yes, what the hell is happening, Mother?" echoed Wolfgang, equally surprised by the highly sophisticated military radio.

Kepler snickered. "I was looking so forward to this—and now I know why. A little family drama certainly spices things up." Mockingly, he looked at Katherine. "Are you going to tell them, or shall I?"

She hesitated. A mixture of guilt, rage, and resignation cluttered her throat. She felt her sons' eyes boring into her, and suddenly she found herself too embarrassed to speak. The truth was too painful and complex to acknowledge.

"What's the matter, cat got your tongue?"

Still, she was unable to speak.

"Can't say I didn't give you a chance, Countess." He turned to Erik and Wolfgang. "Boys, I know this will come as a shock, but your estranged mother is a spy for the Allies."

"What?" gasped Erik.

"I don't believe this!" spluttered Wolfgang.

"Well, you'd better start. She transmits and receives messages from an agent named Otto Renault—a French-German Jew from Alsace, who is very much sought after by the Reich, I might add. He is acting head of the Brotherhood of Our Lady Resistance network in France—or the *Confrérie de Notre Dame* as it is better known. They provide the Allies with photographs of key German officers, personnel, and collaborators as well as detailed maps and information on our defenses and training centers in France, especially the Atlantic Wall. That's where your mother comes in: she is one of Renault's primary contacts. She documents the names and compiles cross-checked lists of German collaborators living in Occupied France. It seems she is obsessed with these people."

"Mother, is this true?" said Erik. "Is that why you have this special radio?"

Kepler looked at her triumphantly. "Why don't you tell them how you and Renault met? I'm sure they would be interested to hear that family yarn as well."

Again, Katherine was unable to utter one word, either to offer an explanation or to argue in her own defense. She felt boxed in, or even worse, as if the entire life she had created in this new land of freedom was slipping away. How could it have all come down to this? By what strange alchemy, by what unfortunate twist of fate, had her sons that had long ago disappeared from her life reemerged after all these years to confront her about her checkered past?

"Very well, since your mother has again become tongue-tied, I will tell you this one last thing, Herr Major, and then you will transmit—"

"Shut up, damn you! I'll tell them myself!"

"Ah, the countess has awoken."

"Damn you, Colonel! Have you no sense of decency?"

"Ah my dear, dear Countess, I must say you are truly lovely when your cheeks are flushed. Why, you don't even need a dash of French rouge?"

"Mother, what the hell is he talking about?" demanded Erik.

Feeling her head spinning, she sat down in a chair to steady herself. It was several seconds before she spoke.

As painful as it was, she decided to tell them everything.

CHAPTER 32

LEFT HAND RANCH

"I HAD AN AFFAIR WITH RENAULT. It happened before the war."

"Before the war?" gasped Wolfgang. "You mean before you left for America?"

"It was *the reason* I left for America."

Erik looked not just bewildered, but crestfallen. "My God, Mother. You dragged me and Max over here because you were running away from an affair?"

His accusatory tone made her feel like a horrible person, and even worse, a failure as a mother. "I didn't run away from anything. I was forced to leave."

"Forced? Forced how?"

"The chief of the Gestapo, Rudolph Diels, knew I was having an affair with a Jew, and he warned me that I would be sent to a labor camp if I did not leave the country. Diels was a monster, but he knew that we had been an important family in Germany for many generations and he gave me a way out. But what he didn't know—and what I never told either of you or your father—is that I had arranged for not just myself, but two of my sons to come to America to live as permanent residents. In return, I agreed that when the time was right, I would spy for the Americans. And who could be a better contact than the head of the Brotherhood of Our Lady Resistance network in France? In fact, Otto insisted on having direct radio contact with me over here. That way the Germans would not be able to compromise me or eavesdrop on his reports. I was someone he trusted."

"But that's where you were wrong, Countess," said Kepler. "Our agents have known about you for some time now."

"Agents? There are German agents here in America?"

"Come now, Countess, you know the answer to that question. And surely, you must realize that there are those of us in the POW camps who are active spies as well. With the virtually unlimited freedom you Americans give us, there are always flies on the wall. Good heavens, even your own newspapers divulge more intelligence information in a week than Berlin gets from radio intercepts over the course of an entire year."

"If you know all this, why do you need my radio?"

Kepler laughed derisively. "My dear Countess, this isn't about you! This is about winning the war!"

She stared at him. "You don't actually believe Germany can win?"

"Of course, we are going to win." He beamed at Erik, his liquid-blue eyes filled with a fanatic's gleam. "In the next few minutes, the military secrets stored in your son's brain are going to change the very outcome of this conflict and assure the continued splendor of the Thousand Year Reich! I know that, deep down, you must be very proud of him!"

"What secrets, Erik? What is he talking about?"

Kepler waved her off dismissively. "You will hear for yourself soon enough. Now we have had enough chit-chat, as you Americans like to say. Major, it is time to transmit the message to the Führer."

But he wasn't listening. "Is it true, Mother? Is the story about Renault and how you left Europe true?"

The look of shock mixed with disappointment on his face made her want to crawl into a hole and die. Then she looked at Wolfgang: he appeared ready to explode with rage. In his eyes, she was a traitor. He would never forgive her for her transgressions against his father and the entire family.

Kepler lifted the pistol. "Major, I am not going to tell you again. Get that radio working and start your call sign. Colonel Morrison is no fool, and we have wasted enough time already. He will be coming soon." He looked at Wolfgang. "You, Commander, go with your mother and bring back weapons. We may have to make a stand here."

"I do not have any weapons."

"Oh, yes you do, Countess. Your late husband John Templeton was an avid gun collector. My men—that would be your innocent little German POW workers—have reconnoitered every inch of this house. How do you think we learned about the radio? What did you think they were doing every time you sat them down for lunch at your picnic table and allowed them to use your toilet? Under my orders, they were collecting intelligence for a day such as this."

You bastard! Choking back her anger, Katherine suddenly realized that she had to do something. Whatever message her son was about to transmit to the High Command was obviously of vital importance to the German war effort. Which meant she had to stop it at all costs!

But what could she do?

Suddenly it came to her: she could destroy the radio.

But how?

She had an idea. "Come with me, Wolfgang," she said. "I will get you food, weapons, and rope."

"Rope? For what?"

"To tie me up. I will not have the authorities thinking that I helped you in any way. You are the enemy—never forget that."

"And you, Countess," hissed Kepler, "are a traitor to your husband, your family, and your country. Never forget *that!*"

Seeing the shock and pain on her sons' faces, Katherine wanted to cry. But her underlying anger gave her a steely resolve. They left the room as Erik and Kepler started adjusting the frequency settings and other control knobs on the radio transmitter. She led Wolfgang into the sitting room, unlocked the gun case, and, crossing her arms, stood off to the side as he began to rummage through the weapons.

After a moment, she said, "Take what you want. I am going to get some rope from the kitchen."

"No, you stay here."

"No, I will go where I please in my own house. And if you have a shred of decency left in you, you will grant me this one request."

He was torn, she saw instantly.

"I don't have time for this. You do as you wish," she said, and she stepped from the room and quickly made her way down the hallway towards the kitchen. She heard him hurriedly clamoring through the gun case to select suitable weapons and ammunition. As she turned the corner into the kitchen, she quickly grabbed a length of thin rope from one of the drawers and then reached for the loaded Colt .45 snub-nosed service pistol she kept in the drawer next to the sink. She slipped it into the pocket of her rain jacket, which, in all of the excitement, she still hadn't taken off. As she turned to leave, Wolfgang strode into the room carrying a handful of rifles, pistols, and cartridge boxes.

He scrutinized her closely.

"What are you up to, Mother?"

She held up the rope. "I am not up to a damned thing." She slipped quickly past him. "We'd better hurry before your master gets suspicious and decides to shoot you, or your brother."

"Colonel Kepler is not my master."

"Oh, yes he is. He is your own personal Führer, you bastard."

They returned to the study. Kepler was looking over Erik's shoulder as he prepared to transmit the first coded message. She didn't have much time. Her son had already set up the call sign, adjusted the transmission frequencies, checked signal strength, and completed all of the various steps to ensure direct communication between her radio—in effect, her very own spy station on U.S. soil for communicating with the French underground—and the designated radio station listening post, which she deduced was most likely not far from Rommel's headquarters at Chateau La Roche Guyon in Occupied France. Wherever it was, they were using call sign SWEDE on 14,320 kilocycles to transmit the message. She wondered at the significance of the code name SWEDE.

"How many messages are you going to send?" Kepler asked Erik as Wolfgang set the weapons down on the table.

"Three. I'm going to respond 'all' and then send the first. Here we go." At that moment, he looked up at his mother. "This will help end the war faster and on our terms. You've got to believe me, Mother. I am doing what is best for Germany."

"Why you talk like a damned defeatist!" snarled Kepler. "The best thing for Germany is to win the goddamned war and ensure our Thousand Year Reich!"

Katherine just stared at him, sickened. "You're a madman."

"I may be slightly mad, yes, but at least it is for a good cause. But you, you are something far worse. You are a woman who cheated on her husband, lied to her sons, and abandoned her country."

Wolfgang stepped forward aggressively. "Now wait a second. You can't talk to my mother like that."

"And who is going to stop me?" He jerked his pistol up and pointed it at him.

But to Katherine's surprise, her son was quicker than Kepler. Though the colonel drew his gun before him, Wolfgang had a pistol of his own, and its nose was pointed directly at the colonel's face only a split second later, making it effectively a standoff.

"I am!" he cried.

"And so am I!" echoed Erik, turning around from the radio with a small butcher's knife she recognized as belonging to her. My God, he must have stolen it from her kitchen earlier today and concealed it on his person before returning to camp.

"You traitors, you don't know what you are doing!"

"Oh, yes we do," said Katherine, feeling a sudden burst of patriotism for her adopted country and a pride in her sons for standing up for her. "Damn you and Hitler both to hell!"

Yanking out her Colt, she unloaded three quick rounds into the radio transmitter and then surrendered the weapon by tossing it onto the floor.

For a moment, they all just stood there in shock watching the sparks fly and the radio smolder. Then, recovering from his stupefaction, Kepler cursed vehemently, snatched a needlepoint pillow from the couch, and scrambled to put out the electronic fire.

That was when Katherine heard the low rumble of a car engine coming from behind the house.

CHAPTER 33

LEFT HAND RANCH

THE SINGLE MOST IMPORTANT LESSON that young Lieutenant Jack Morrison had learned from chasing Pancho Villa across Northern Mexico, and from slogging away in the bloody trenches during the Great War, was to never make a frontal assault on an enemy position with a clear field of fire. He had seen thousands upon thousands of America's finest shredded to bits that way, and the one thing he knew, the prickly thing that stuck in his mind above all else, was that he didn't want himself or his men to meet their Creator in such a wasteful manner. So, he had long favored flanking maneuvers and hit-and-run attacks over conventional frontal assaults, recognizing that Sun-Tzu's maxim about maintaining the element of surprise truly was the field tactician's most trusted ally when the bullets were flying.

After slipping quietly from the lead jeep with his M1 Thompson .45-caliber submachine gun—whose inventor, General John T. Thompson, had ironically created the first hand-held machine gun *to end* the First World War that had led to the mass carnage of the Second—Morrison gathered his men. He had heard the gunshots when they had pulled up in the trees, and his first instinct was to storm the house to make sure that Katherine hadn't been harmed. But then, his soldierly experience came into play, and he thought better of it. No doubt, speed and surprise would be critical in taking the three escaped Germans, but he had to regroup a moment to plan out an attack. He wanted these bastards something fierce. But he also knew that he was dealing with the most unpredictable of all human enterprises—war—and he had to have a sound strategy if he was going to recapture the three prisoners.

He thought of what the British Admiral Lord Nelson had once said: "Five minutes make the difference between victory and defeat." In this case, it was five minutes of planning that would make the difference.

"Lieutenant Marks, you and your team will maneuver around the north side of the house and come in from the front. Lieutenant Bearman, you and your men will come with me and attack from the rear. Lieutenant Marks and I have the two Tommy guns. Once my team enters the house and locates the enemy, I will give them one—I repeat, one—chance to throw down their weapons and surrender. If they do not, Lieutenant Marks and I will provide heavy sustaining fire, while the rest of you locate and engage the targets, keeping them from escaping and ensuring the safety of Mrs. Templeton. Hopefully, if we bring enough firepower to bear, they will give themselves up."

The men looked at him with beady eyes in the not-quite darkness, their faces an odd palette of blood red and soot black in the fading sunset. Cooped up in an interminably dull POW camp for the past year, they looked like they were itching for a chance at real combat.

He continued: "It is critical that we take them alive, if at all possible. G-2 and British Intel need to know what they know and how and when they came to know it. This is it, men. Stay low, keep moving, maintain a hot suppressing fire, and, no matter how bad it gets, don't be pulled into a goddamned cross-fire. When you hear me kick in the rear door, we will hit them from both sides."

Here he paused. "Any questions?"

No one spoke.

"All right, let's move!"

They dashed through the trees, Morrison using every ounce of effort to keep up with the younger men on his 51-year-old, shrapnel-perforated right leg. Upon reaching the open lawn of the back yard, they broke up into the two designated teams. At the rear door, Morrison and his team paused and waited. The ranch house was uncannily still; not a sound, not even a creak could be heard. He ticked off thirty seconds in his head before shouldering his way through the back door and darting into a laundry room.

The world all around him instantly exploded with gunfire.

To hell with politely requesting them to surrender!

He flattened himself down onto the floor, rolled, and let loose with answering fire. The bullets hurled into the walls with terrifying force, causing great destruction. The lethal burst came from deep in the interior of the house. He could tell instantly by the sound that a .45-caliber Tommy gun just like his, a Browning rifle, and a Colt pistol were in play.

He quickly changed the fire-control lever on his Thompson from single-shot back to rapid automatic-fire. Then, from a kneeling position, he delivered a fierce suppressing fire as his team charged into the room behind him, while Lieutenant Marks and his team hit the enemy from the other side of the house. Bullets continued to whine and snarl overhead, dislodging shards of jagged wood, lathe, plaster, metal, nails, and insulation material.

He slid to his right. The storm of lead continued.

He let loose with another blast of cover fire as Marks and his men did the same, pushing in from the front door. The air quickly turned thick with gun smoke.

"*Sie sind hier!*" he heard Kepler shouting out orders. "*Schnell!*"

He let fly with a burst from his Thompson, which felt supple and reassuring in his hands. He was answered by a blast of enemy fire. His team fell back towards him, crouching and firing as they retreated, crab-like.

The shooting slackened for a moment on both sides. Listening closely, he could hear the sound of shuffling feet, Kepler yelling and shouting orders in guttural German. Were they retreating or moving into offensive position?

He took the opportunity to call out to the colonel to surrender, but the only response was a series of obscene, defiant curses.

He let loose with another round of suppressing fire, leapt to his feet, and charged. Once again on the offensive, he and his men quickly drove their way down the hallway that led from the laundry room to the main part of the house.

When they reached a large dining room, they fanned out.

Another ear-rattling exchange of gunfire between the two parties. And then quiet again. In the lull, he ducked into an adjoining hallway and took a moment to assess the damage.

He saw Lieutenant Marks and his men pinned down by fire from Kepler and his comrades. Sprawled along the far wall with part of his head blown off and blood pooling up around him was Corporal Ross, and next to him an upright but seriously wounded Lieutenant Bearman.

Shaking his head in dismay, Morrison signaled Marks that his team would maneuver into position and come in at the enemy from the opposite direction. The lieutenant nodded in understanding. Morrison crept down the hallway, regrouped his men, and repeated the instructions to them.

Suddenly, he heard a muffled noise coming from down the hallway. He took Corporal McCall with him to investigate and sent the other two enlisted men to support Marks. He moved quietly down the hallway with his Tommy at the ready, pausing to listen every so often until he was sure which room the sound was coming from.

They halted outside the door and listened.

There it was again. It sounded like moaning. Was someone injured?

He signaled McCall to go on three. He counted down with his fingers, reached for the handle, swung open the door, and flew into the room.

There lay Katherine, gagged and bound on the floor. He kneeled down next to her and quietly slipped off her gag.

"I was able to destroy the radio!" she cried, tipping her head towards the smoldering mass of metal in the cabinet. "They weren't able to send their message! But they've managed to escape so we must hurry!"

He wondered what she was doing with such sophisticated radio equipment. "Who escaped?"

"Wolfgang and Erik—they're together. They tricked Kepler into making a stand in the other room so they could leave him behind. They backtracked and escaped through the window."

She nodded towards the open window. He went to it and peered out, but he saw nothing. He turned back towards her, once again noting the elaborate radio equipment.

"You're telling me they double-crossed Kepler."

"Yes, that's exactly what I'm telling you. They are trying to break free of him."

"Is that what they told you?"

"Yes, but they didn't need to tell me. Their actions speak for themselves. Quick, if you hurry, you can catch—"

But her voice was cut off by the *rat-tat-tat* of semiautomatic weapons fire. Morrison quickly untied her hands and leapt to his feet. As he made it to the doorway to see what the commotion was about, he and Corporal McCall were practically bowled over by three soldiers retreating towards them under heavy fire.

"We're empty, and Kepler's coming this way! Kill him, Colonel! Kill him!"

Morrison ducked a whistling bullet and heard the sound of crashing furniture down the hallway. He stepped past the retreating troopers and let loose with a burst of cover fire. A moment later, to his surprise Lieutenant Marks, not Kepler, materialized from the smoke. He was making a desperate escape, firing back at the German colonel with his Tommy gun while lugging a wounded private over his shoulder.

"I'll cover you, Lieutenant. Come on, you can make it!" cried Morrison as the three retreating soldiers took position behind him and McCall and began reloading their weapons.

He took three steps forward, flicked the fire-control lever on his Thompson back to single-shot mode, crouched down in a kneeling position, and calmly waited until Kepler appeared at the end of the hallway beyond the scrambling Marks.

The colonel came on like a raging demon.

Morrison aimed for the chest, but ended up striking his target in the arm and shoulder with two consecutive shots, as the lieutenant squeezed past him and delivered the wounded corporal safely into the hands of McCall and the others.

Kepler stumbled and fell. The Thompson in his hand skittered across the carpet and landed near Morrison's feet as Marks came up from behind to offer support.

"I've got him! Hold your fire, Lieutenant!"

He dashed forward, kicked aside the Tommy, and trained his weapon on Kepler, who was pressing his hand against his shoulder wound to staunch the flow of blood.

"You and Private Mercer attend to him, Lieutenant. I want this son of a bitch alive! I repeat, alive! Corporal McCall, you and the others come with me. We're going to get those damned brothers. Let's go!"

CHAPTER 34

LEFT HAND RANCH

AS SOON AS THEY REACHED the front porch, Morrison could tell something was wrong.

But what was it?

And then he saw it: the front tires of both the stolen food truck parked out front and Katherine's sleek, 320-horsepower Duesenberg SJ had been slashed. The two German brothers had come this way all right, but only to make it impossible for Morrison to follow them in pursuit.

"Damnit, they've gone for the jeeps! Quick, to the back of the house!"

As they turned the corner for the back yard, he saw his personal jeep burst through the trees like a Roman chariot and charge towards the gravel road. For a brief instant, the gunning vehicle was framed beautifully against the blood-red sunset. Crouched down low to evade enemy fire, the two daring German brothers looked like Dillinger and his gang making a getaway.

Yelling with rage, Morrison let loose with a blast from his Thompson. But he saw instantly that they were too far out of range and he hadn't hit a damned thing.

Running to the other two vehicles parked in the trees, he saw that their front tires too had been slashed by the clever bastards. Cursing under his breath, he heard the patter of feet and turned to see Katherine dashing across the lawn towards him. *My God, she moves like a gazelle.* Part of him was overcome with relief that she was safe and sound; the other part was angry at her for being the mother of the two sons of bitches who were causing him so much grief and who, because of the intelligence in their possession, posed a serious threat to the United States.

She came to a stop, looked over the slashed tires on the two vehicles, and shook her head in amazement.

"Looks like those boys of yours have gotten away," he said bitterly.

"What did you expect, Colonel? They are well-trained German soldiers, and they are both very clever and resourceful."

"You sound as if you're proud of them."

"Don't take your frustration out on me, Colonel. I am telling you right now that both of their IQs are off the charts, so you are going to have your hands full trying to apprehend them. I don't know what intelligence information they have in their possession, but I know that it is vital. That is exactly why it is imperative that we find them and stop them before they attempt another radio transmission."

"Don't worry, I'm certainly not going to make the mistake of underestimating them a second time." He turned to his two men. "Corporal

McCall, you and your men change out those flat tires on the double so we can commence our pursuit."

"Yes, sir!"

He turned back to Katherine. "So, you're telling me that you're going to help me catch your own sons."

"Of course I am, Colonel. As an OSS agent, it is my job to catch enemy spies."

"Look, I'm in no mood for jesting."

"I am not joking, Colonel. I really am with the OSS."

"The Office of Strategic Services? Wild Bill Donovan's outfit?"

"The only reason I'm telling you is because you'll find out sooner or later."

He scrutinized her closely. "You really expect me to believe that you're an OSS agent?"

"Would you prefer Marlene Dietrich?"

"No, it's just that…" He scratched his head, leaving the words unfinished.

"You shouldn't be so surprised. Many women work for the OSS. General Donovan and President Roosevelt both happen to think women make exceptional spies. At least, that's what they told me when they hired me."

He continued to study her. "I can see you're telling the truth. Now I understand why you have a fancy two-way quartz crystal radio and military headset. So your son Erik is just a chip off the old block, is that it?"

"Apparently so. But at least I destroyed the radio. It was the only way to stop them."

"You know the FBI and G-2 are both going to want to talk to you. They are not going to be pleased when they find out that those boys of yours have escaped and are poised to start blowing up airfields, dams, trains, and bus stations."

"Please, Colonel, my sons would never sink so low as to be saboteurs."

"Tell that to J. Edgar Hoover and his G-Men. They think there's a Nazi saboteur hiding out behind every drawn curtain."

"I'll be sure to tell Director Hoover that in person tomorrow night when I see him."

"J. Edgar Hoover? Tomorrow night? I don't believe you."

"Well, you'd better start, Colonel. The director and his assistant, Mr. Tolson, will be staying at my humble little Colorado Springs hotel at the foot of Cheyenne Mountain for the entire week. It seems they're on their early summer vacation together."

"J. Edgar Hoover is coming to the Broadmoor? Why you're just full of surprises, Countess."

"It's the truth, Jack."

"Good Lord, that's just what you and I both need right now, the FBI breathing down our necks."

"Personally, I can handle myself."

"That's what Mata Hari said. In fact, those were her last words before she faced the firing squad."

"I'm not a German spy. I'm an American spy so that is an incorrect analogy."

"I don't give a damn if it is or not. What I'm doing is warning you that J.

Edgar is going to want those boys of yours twice as badly as he wanted Baby Face Nelson. And that doesn't bode well for you, or for me and my fellow officers in Uncle Sam's armed forces. He's going to trample over the rights of a lot of civilians, military personnel, and policemen in his quest to hunt them down. All so he can get his name in the papers."

"I know all about Director Hoover and his publicity antics. But I suppose I should thank you for warning me."

"You'd better wait until you're free and clear before you thank me. By the way, did Director Hoover and Mr. Tolson book separate rooms?"

"Very funny, Colonel. Even if I did know the answer, I couldn't divulge anything. My phones are probably tapped and my house bugged. After all, I am of foreign birth, and you know how much the director hates foreigners."

"I wouldn't take it personally, ma'am. He hates anybody who doesn't work for the Bureau. Now I've got to notify Command."

"What will you do with Colonel Kepler?"

"He'll go to the hospital at Camp Carson with Lieutenant Bearman and Corporal Grayson. Unfortunately, Corporal Ross is dead." He shook his head in dismay. Jesus, was he exhausted all of a sudden or what? "I need to radio Command," he reminded her again.

She touched him gently on the hand. "I really do want to catch my sons, Colonel. Before they do something to hurt this great country I love."

He sensed there was something more. "But…?"

"But I don't want them to be killed. In fact, I don't want them to be harmed in any way. You know perfectly well that they tied me up and drew Kepler away from me into the other room precisely because they didn't want me to get hurt. They are not like him. What they do, they do for their country, not their purported Führer. Just as Robert E. Lee fought for his state of Virginia—and not Jefferson Davis. But Kepler is different: he has sworn an oath to fight for the maniac who has destroyed my former homeland. He is the monster, Colonel, not them."

"I don't doubt your loyalty, ma'am, and I can appreciate the fact that you don't want any harm to come to your boys. But I'm not sure what you want me to do about it."

"For one thing, you can stop calling me *ma'am*."

"Only if you stop calling me *colonel*."

"Very well, Jack, I want you to give me your word, as an officer and gentleman, that if I help you, no harm will come to my sons."

"You know I can't guarantee that."

"But you can try. That's all I'm asking. I will help you find them, but I need your word that no harm will come to them from you or your men."

"The FBI will be the ones leading the manhunt. I'll be involved, but I won't be making the decisions. J. Edgar Hoover and his G-Men will."

"But you will be closely involved since they escaped from your camp, correct?"

"Most likely. But I've got to warn you that as far as my men go…well, let's just say that they're not going to treat those sons of yours with kid gloves. Not when I have one man headed to the morgue and two badly wounded going to the hospital. I'm telling you, this situation is totally FUBAR."

"That may be, but it doesn't change the fact that you and I are going to have to work together to find my sons and bring them in. And if we're going to work together, we're going to have to have an understanding. We do have an understanding, don't we, Jack?"

"Not yet, we don't. So listen up. When push comes to shove and you are forced to make a choice, your loyalty had better be to Uncle Sam and not your sons. Your job is to help me catch them, not to protect them. Protecting them once they're caught, that will be my job. Now do we have an understanding, Katherine?"

"Yes, Colonel. I believe we understand each other perfectly."

"Good, then we shouldn't have any problems."

CHAPTER 35

EN ROUTE TO CAMP CARSON MILITARY HOSPITAL COLORADO SPRINGS

STRAPPED INTO AN AMBULANCE GURNEY, Colonel Franz Kepler was so angry that he momentarily forgot about his throbbing shoulder. He thought of how much pleasure he would take in hunting down and killing Wolfgang and Erik von Walburg. The clever bastards had betrayed him! They had tricked him into setting up a defensive perimeter in the main living room, and then they had left him behind to fight and die—and, for that, he wanted revenge. Then he remembered an old saying by Confucius: "Before you embark on a journey of revenge, dig two graves." Well so be it, then. He would rather die a thousand deaths than let those two traitors be the ones to notify the German High Command. After all, it should be an *Übermensch*—an Aryan Superman—like himself, not a soft-headed defeatist-aristocrat like Erik von Walburg, who should make the public announcement to the Führer and receive the thanks of a grateful Fatherland.

But to make it happen, he had to pull off a Houdini-like escape. He had done quite a bit of acting growing up in Hamburg, so he had some ability in that area. But he was still strapped into a gurney, and guarded by two armed soldiers, in the back of a military ambulance.

So how could he escape when the odds were so heavily against him? The answer came to him surprisingly quickly: he needed to create a diversion.

But with what?

He felt a sudden burning pain in his gunshot arm and more seriously injured shoulder. They had given him a heavy dose of morphine before loading him into the ambulance. But the pain came and went like the ebb and flow of an armored tank battle in the North African desert. It took all of his effort not to cry out and continue to keep his eyes closed, pretending to be unconscious.

The same question came back to him over and over: how could he create a diversion and escape when he was so grievously wounded?

And then he was struck with a realization: his wound was his most valuable asset.

Right now, they thought he was too weak from blood loss to escape. He had been pretending to be out cold since the two military ambulances had arrived from Camp Carson, one for him, the other for the wounded Americans. But though he was in agony and had lost a great deal of blood, he was still plenty alert, strong, and motivated to pose a serious threat to his captors. The only thing keeping him from attacking the guards and taking control of the vehicle from the driver and medic up front was the single strap across his lower ribcage and the one across his shins. Because his wounds were in both his arm and shoulder and he was heavily bandaged, the medics had left his hands and arms free and bound him into the ambulance gurney only from the midriff down. If he could somehow lure one of the guards in close and seize his pistol before the other guard could draw his own weapon, then he could escape.

It seemed possible in his morphine-hazed mind. But could he actually pull it off?

There was only one way to find out.

He went over it mentally in his head a half-dozen more times until finally he thought he had worked out a plausible scenario. The ambulance bearing the two wounded Americans had been the priority, and it had gone on ahead to Camp Carson. So if he could somehow seize control of this ambulance, he would be all alone with no one to report in or chase after him. The dark of night had descended, and they were on an isolated country road far from any city.

He surreptitiously opened his eyes a crack to study the two guards. They were quietly smoking and talking at his feet, expecting no trouble from a wounded German POW who lay heavily sedated, unconscious, and strapped into a gurney. By the looks of them, they were young, inexperienced, and hadn't seen any action beyond basic training. They were certainly no match for a veteran of two world wars—and an *Übermensch* to boot!

It was time to make his move.

He bit down on his tongue as hard as he could until he could taste blood. Then he worked his gums until he had generated a mouthful of bloody, foamy saliva. Next, he contorted his face into a rictus of agony, grabbed his wounded left arm with his right, and started to scream in a fit of shock and pain.

"*Herzinfarkt! Herzinfarkt!*"

The two guards jerked up instantly, as did the medic sitting up front in the passenger seat. He shrieked louder, clutched at his chest and arm, and let the bloody froth drool from his mouth.

"*Ich habe einen herzinfarkt!*"

"What the fuck is he saying?" cried one of the guards.

"I think he's having a heart attack!" said the medic, crawling into the back next to the gurney to attend to him.

Kepler continued howling out in agony, clutching desperately at his chest, frothing and foaming from his bloodied mouth.

"Heart attack? Are you having a heart attack?" asked the young medic.

"*Ja, herzinfarkt! Ich brauche medizin!*" *Yes, heart attack! I need medicine!*

"Jesus Christ, he is having a heart attack! Do something, Doc!" muttered one of the guards in disbelief.

"Yeah, hurry, hurry!" yelled the other, looking as panicky as his comrade. To Kepler's delight, they were taken in completely by his charade. They rose to their feet to come to his aid, leaning in close to the gurney along with the medic.

Were all Americans this stupid and trusting?

"*Mein herz! Mein herz!*" he moaned, frantically rubbing his heart.

"Okay, okay, just relax!" cautioned the young medic, but with all the commotion he, too, was in a state of panic.

Kepler grabbed his arm. "*Ihr ist schmerz in meinem arm!*"

"Yes, yes, I know, you have pain in your arm because you're having a heart attack! But you have to stay calm!"

Kepler gasped in panic, frothed again at the mouth, repeatedly clutched at his chest and arm, and rolled his eyes as if he had lost all control over his body. The young medic had turned away and was rummaging through his medical supplies on the shelf of the ambulance. Kepler could see that, despite his ample emergency training, he was completely flustered; nothing could possibly have prepared him for this. The two guards were leaning in close to the gurney, but their Colt .45 automatic service pistols were still out of reach.

He needed one of the guards to lean in closer.

"Jesus Christ, Doc, he's fucking dying! Hurry, do something!"

"Would you please calm down and stop acting nuts! This is bad enough as it is, and you're just making it worse!"

Kepler gave a spasm and let loose with a spume of bloody drool.

"Don't you have any goddamned medicine, Doc. The Kraut's fucking dying here!"

"I'm trying to find it if you would just shut up!"

Now he pretended to go into convulsions, waving his arms while moaning over and over again in German, "*Hilf mir! Ich will sterben! Hilf mir! Ich will sterben!*"

"What the hell is he saying, Doc! My God, he's turning white!"

"I think he's saying 'Help me, I'm dying,'" said the other guard.

"Jesus Christ, Doc, help him! We can't let the son of a bitch die like this, even if he is a fucking Kraut!"

"Just shut up! I'm trying!"

"Well, try harder! The son of a bitch is dying!"

Kepler flailed his arms and made a gargling sound, as if he was choking.

"Here, I've got it!" declared the medic, twisting around with a glass bottle of Bayer aspirin in his hand.

"Aspirin? That's all you've got is fucking aspirin?"

"What, you think I carry around nitroglycerin! This is all I've got!"

He took two tablets and tried to cram them into his mouth, but Kepler spit them out in a feigned seizure. The closest guard's .45 was still out of range; he needed him to lean in closer.

"Jesus Christ, what are you doing, you dumb Kraut! The Doc here is trying to save your ass!"

"Hold him down! Hold him down!" cried the medic.

Kepler slid his good arm to the side of the gurney, so that when the time came, he would be ready to use it. With his other hand, he pretended to grab his throat, as if he was suffocating. The medic grabbed two more pills from his bottle as the two guards leaned down to restrain him.

Now was his chance.

As the closest guard reached down to subdue him, he spit bloody froth in his face. The guard, predictably, jerked back his head in disgust.

Kepler snatched the .45 from the man's russet-leather belt holster, snicked off the safety, and pointed the gun at him and his cohort, covering them both with the weapon.

In the blink of an eye, the roles had been reversed.

The two guards and medic started to back away, a combination of mortification and stupefaction registering on their faces.

"Don't move, or I'll let you have it," he said in heavily German-accented English, remembering the line from a James Cagney gangster movie he had watched recently at Camp Pershing.

But the guard that was still armed panicked and reached for his gun.

Kepler dropped him with a single shot between the eyes.

The medic screamed as the other guard, now weaponless, leapt at Kepler with both hands out in an attempt to strangle him.

Kepler unleashed two shots into the burly man's chest. He fell back in a spangle of blood.

Now, there was just the medic and the driver.

He pointed the gun at the medic. "Unstrap me and I will let you live!"

The young man stood paralyzed with fear, unable to move or speak.

"I said unstrap me and you will live! Do it now, or die!"

"Don't do it! He'll kill you!" cried the driver, and he brought the ambulance to a screeching halt along the country road, jumped out, and started running into a field.

Kepler looked at the medic, who was still frozen with panic.

"Now just remain calm. I am not going to kill you. As long as you unstrap me and get me some morphine, I will let you live. As an officer and a gentleman, I give you my word."

The medic complied. Kepler shot him twice in the chest anyway. Suddenly, the adrenaline rush of the kill and the morphine combined to make him feel strong and invincible, as if he had never been wounded back at the ranch. Now, with renewed vigor and single-minded purpose, he carefully slipped off the gurney, snatched two fresh magazines from each of the guard's leather magazine hip pouches, reloaded his weapon, climbed behind the wheel, and swiftly chased down the escaping driver.

He was an older man, in poor shape, and he had only managed to scramble halfway across the open field by the time Kepler closed in on him with his bright headlights. A single shot to the buttocks brought the fleeing man to the ground. The man cried out in agony and burbled like a baby.

Kepler halted the ambulance and stepped from the vehicle to finish him off. The headlights provided a halo of illumination around the wounded driver as he bleated for help, crawling along a loamy furrow like a snail.

The German walked calmly up to him and turned him over onto his back.

The man pleaded for his life, but Kepler cut him off with an abrupt wave of his hand. Then he gave an angelic smile.

"Please remain calm, my American friend. As long as you give me the information I need, I am not going to hurt you. Are you, my good man, perhaps familiar with the meaning of the word *schadenfreude*?"

The man was an emotional and physical wreck and could barely speak.

"What?"

"*Schadenfreude*. It is a German word. It means taking a morbid pleasure in the misfortune of others."

"Yes, I have heard the word…but I don't…"

Kepler smiled reassuringly. "You and your comrades took pleasure in my being shot and captured alive, didn't you? You actually relished the fact that I would be hung as an escaped POW murderer. Isn't that true?"

"No, I didn't take any pleasure in that, I swear."

"Yes, you did. You enjoyed seeing me suffer and the knowledge that I would die. I heard you talking to the medic about me. I heard what you said. And now, just look at you. The roles have changed considerably, haven't they?"

"I'm just…I'm just the driver…I even have German blood just like you."

"Oh, you are a pure Aryan, are you? How fortunate for you." He waited for the man to show visible relief before adding, "But I'm afraid I can't allow you to live."

The driver's expression suddenly hardened, showing his true colors. "You Kraut piece of shit! You fucking Nazi scum! Why I'm staring at the face of the devil himself!"

Kepler allowed himself another pleasant smile, drawing out the moment. These Americans were so fun to toy with; tormenting and thwarting Colonel Morrison and his officers this past month had been a most gratifying experience. But this…this was pure heaven.

"No, Mr. Yankee Ambulance Driver," he responded with icy sangfroid. "You are staring at the face of a true *Übermensch.*"

"A what?"

"Here in your country, he is known as Superman."

"Superman? You?"

"Of course me, you decadent American swine!"

And with that, he shot him three times in the face. Then he stole back into the ambulance and started the long drive to Denver, where there was a man who would patch him up and help him.

A fellow German spy named Carl Weaver.

CHAPTER 36

CAMP CARSON
COLORADO SPRINGS

MORRISON stared across the conference room table at the knife-edged face of his old friend, General William H. Shedd, commander of the U.S. Army's 7th Service Command, headquartered at Camp Carson and encompassing Colorado and a goodly portion of the western United States. Sitting there in his rumpled uniform with a fat, soggy cigar in his mouth, the general looked as though he had a bad case of indigestion.

"Right now, I don't know how the situation could be any worse, Jack," he said in a funereal tone.

"I know, sir, it's a tough one."

"I mean it's bad for you, Jack. The tornado that's left your camp in ruins…well that's nothing more than an act of God, a force of nature, and as you said, it is being dealt with by you and your second-in-command. But what I find unacceptable is these two escaped Kraut brothers. I mean, here you are telling me that these fellows are in possession of vital intel that could change the outcome of the war—and yet you allowed them to escape. That is just a disaster, Jack, a bona fide disaster."

"Sir, I think if we—"

"Now, don't get me wrong, Jack. I'm glad you got Kepler back. From what you've told me, that son of a bitch is a major thorn in your side, and bully for you for recapturing him so quickly. But these two brothers are another matter. My God, to think the Hun bastards have intel that could cost us the goddamned war, and that Katherine Templeton is their goddamned mother? I've known Katherine since before Pearl Harbor—hell, she houses thirty-five of my officers at her hotel and throws us parties every month. Why I saw you out there dancing with her just the other night. But I had no idea that she was an OSS agent working for that reckless cowboy Wild Bill Donovan. Or that she had two German-POW sons at Camp Pershing. You know what this means, don't you? You can talk now, Jack."

"No, General, I'm not sure what you're—"

"It means things are getting complicated, Jack. And you know I don't like complicated. Complicated gets loyal soldiers like us relieved of command, or thrown in the brig. That's what complicated does."

Here he paused to take a puff from his fat, soggy cigar.

"This situation is already FUBAR, but I have a feeling it's going to get a hell of a lot worse. There's only one way to stave off disaster. You need to catch those Krauts pronto—or you could very well be looking at a court-marshal. Making use of the limited resources given to you, do what you have to do, but find them and get them back behind the wire quickly. Do you understand me? The longer this thing drags out, the worse it's going to be and the more heads are going to roll. Starting with yours, Jack."

"But surely the situation is manageable, sir?"

"Manageable? What are you a goddamned accountant?"

"Of course not. I was just—"

"Shut up, Jack. How long have you and I known each other?"

"I think…uh…around twenty years."

"It's twenty-two years, Jack. You and I have known each other for twenty-two fucking years. And in all of that time, have I ever bullshitted you?"

Probably at least a dozen times. "I don't recall you ever having done so, sir."

"That's a lawyer's answer, Jack, and you know how much I hate lawyers. You also know how much it irritates me when an officer doesn't recognize when the shit is about to hit the fan. Blindness in the face of adversity is a serious character flaw, Jack."

"Yes, sir. I understand, sir."

"No, you don't, Jack. So let me tell me where you stand. You are the Commanding Officer of Camp Pershing, Colorado. It's a dunghole, Jack. The end of the line. The last stop on the westbound train. The place where they send the discarded corps commanders that they don't know what to do with or give a shit about. Let's face it, Jack, you can't get any lower as a colonel in the United States Army than you are right now."

Jesus, was it that bad? Had he truly hit rock bottom?

"After that fiasco in Tunisia, you know you're never going to see a combat command again, so why do you want to screw up your last chance? You can't screw up a last chance, Jack, because there aren't any more chances after that. That's why they call it a *last chance*. There are no more chances after the last one. You follow?"

"Yes, sir, I screwed up. But I can make it right."

"Can you, Jack? Can you make it right?"

"Yes, I can. I know I can."

"Are you hitting the hooch again, Jack? Is that what's happened?"

"No, sir, my drinking…it's…it's under control."

"That's not what I hear, Jack, and you know I hear everything. There are no secrets when it comes to the officers under my command. We're a family, Jack, you see?"

God, do I want a fucking drink right now! Just one lousy, goddamned drink! "Yes, sir, I understand. We're a family and…and members of a family support one another. That's why you've got to let me make this right. I can catch them quickly, sir, if you give me a chance."

"I've already decided to give you a chance, Jack. For the simple reason that you are a desperate man—and desperate men perform amazing feats. I've seen it time and again. So I'm not doing this out of any altruistic spirit, Jack. I'm doing it because I can count on you being motivated. That was why you almost got those bastards in the first place out at the ranch. After the twister, you moved in quickly, decisively, and you almost got them. *All-Fucking-Most!* Of course, almost doesn't mean jack shit, and the next time you'd better wait and call in the big boys, but it was still an admirable, quick-thinking show on your part. I know you're smart, Jack—now you'll be smart *and* motivated. I also need someone on the inside I can trust to keep me in the loop on developments, because I sure as hell can't trust Hoover or our military intelligence counterparts at G-2. I also know that you are probably the only person Katherine Templeton will trust, and I believe that she could prove to be of value in tracking down those pain-in-the-ass sons of hers. She's waiting outside to talk to me as we speak. The main question in my mind is can we trust her? She's their mother, Jack, their own flesh and blood."

"She's also an OSS agent and a fervent anti-Nazi."

"Yes, but can we trust her?"

"I believe so, sir, and I agree with you that she can help. She knows them better than anybody. She knows where they might go, what they might do, who they might contact. She raised them for crying out loud. And when the time comes, she might even be able to help convince them to give themselves up. Talk them down from the ledge so to speak."

"But is she one-hundred percent loyal, Jack? When push comes to shove, will she act like an American or a fucking Kraut, an OSS agent or a mother bear protecting her cubs? Will she be willing to do whatever it takes to hunt them down, or will she let her emotional attachment to the little Hun bastards dictate how she handles the situation?"

Since the skirmish at the ranch, he had been pondering that very question himself, over and over. And he still wasn't sure how Katherine would ultimately respond if forced to make a choice. "I believe she'll do all she can to help capture them, sir, as long as they are taken alive," he said, mostly giving her the benefit of the doubt.

"What the hell is that supposed to mean? Is she with us or not?"

"She just doesn't want them shot on sight. In any case, I promise to keep a close eye on her."

"The FBI's not going to like her being involved, Jack, and neither is G-2. Not only are those two escaped POWs her very own sons, she's a German by birth, an OSS agent, and a woman in a man's profession. That's four strikes against her, by my count."

Though he disagreed, he said nothing, not wanting to stir up the outspoken general any more than he already was. He decided to change the subject. "When are we meeting with Director Hoover and G-2?"

"First thing tomorrow morning. Along with Colonel MacGregor of British Intelligence. You'll be working closely with Katherine Templeton, Major Hawkins of G-2, and MacGregor, whom you've spoken to on the phone. Hawkins is the intelligence liaison between the Brits and us. You are to keep him informed of all new developments. He's a bureaucratic pissant so watch your step."

"Where is the meeting?"

"At the Broadmoor. Director Hoover, Colonel MacGregor, and Hawkins are all staying at the hotel."

"Why the Broadmoor for the meeting?"

"Because that bull-headed son of a bitch Hoover wouldn't agree to have the meeting here at Camp Carson. And this equally stubborn son of a bitch sitting in front of you wouldn't agree to have the meeting at the FBI field office. So we had to compromise."

"Wait a second. If you already knew all this, you must have spoken to Katherine Templeton."

"As a matter of fact, I did. She graciously offered us one of her large meeting rooms for our conference. I put it to the director and he agreed."

"So all that talk about her loyalty…you…you were just toying with me?"

"I needed to know where you really stood, Jack."

"So you're not worried about her?"

"Of course not. As you said, she's OSS and hates the Nazis with a bitter passion. She told me all about her radio work with the French underground. I'm more worried about that ruthless bastard Hoover. She's been a secret spy for the Allies for the past three years based on her work with Renault, but the director will be angry that he's been kept out of the loop. He considers all espionage, foreign and domestic, to be the exclusive province of the FBI."

There was a knock on the door. An officer poked his head in.

"What is it, Captain?"

"Sir, I have some new information."

"New information?"

"Yes, sir, and believe me you're going to want to hear it."

Shedd chomped and puffed irritably on his cigar. "All right, Captain Gleason, what is it?"

"Colonel Kepler has escaped."

"Fuck Jack Benny!"

Morrison couldn't believe his ears. "How did it happen?"

"He killed a pair of medics and two guards and stole their ambulance. They found the bodies along a dirt road eight miles east of Colorado Springs."

The general shook his head. "Jesus Christ, Jack, we're running out of time here." He rose from his seat. "You'd better get your ass down to the FBI field office. Take Katherine Templeton with you and fill them in on everything you two know. She's waiting outside. They already have the three escaped POWs' files and *Soldbuchs*, but you'd better get them whatever else they need: physical descriptions for the sketch artists, what they were wearing, any distinguishing marks, what type of weapons they're carrying. Be careful not to ruffle any feathers. I want Hoover to be as happy as a clam tomorrow morning when we meet with him."

"I'll do my best, Bill."

"No, you're going to have to do better than that. I'm giving you one last chance, Jack. If you screw up again, you'll be lucky to get a janitorial position in Swinging Dick, Alabama."

"I copy, General. I take it I'm dismissed?"

"Yeah, Jack, you're dismissed. And remember…"

"I got it, Bill. Don't fucking screw up!"

CHAPTER 37

BROADMOOR HOTEL
COLORADO SPRINGS

ERIK FELT A SHUDDER of animal fear as he and Wolfgang stepped to the edge of the trees and peered up at the towering spires of the Broadmoor. The grand, soaring hotel was quiet as a tomb: no one out walking, no one peering out the window. Behind them, on the road, not a single automobile. Best of all, there were no dogs barking into the night. All the same, he had the uncanny feeling that the enemy was lurking somewhere in the shadows, waiting to pounce on him and his brother and send them to the gallows.

From the darkness came Wolfgang's voice. "Do you think he still lives here?" he whispered.

"I don't know. It's been five years."

"Well, can he help us?"

"I don't know that either. With the war, everything has changed."

"I don't know what the hell we're doing here if we're unsure about Krupp's loyalty."

"We are strangers in a strange land, and he is the only person we know. I don't know of anyone else who might help us, do you?"

"No, but running around the Broadmoor Hotel is not exactly keeping a low profile."

"They house many American officers here. If we can get army uniforms, we can blend in."

"Maybe, but it seems an unnecessary risk."

"No, it's perfect. It is the last place they would expect us to come. Krupp is the concierge. He can get us food, lodging, officer's uniforms from the laundry, and whatever else we need to blend in. He fought in the Great War—he was wounded at the Battle of the Marne and at the Somme. He will be sympathetic to our cause and may even have access to a radio. He is our best chance."

A faint crackling sound cut through the stillness of the night. They stiffened and pricked an ear towards the woods behind them. Erik had the strange feeling that they were being watched. He made eye contact with his brother, who shushed him with his finger and stepped to the edge of the trees.

Erik moved to the right to have a look. After listening a moment, he thought he heard another sound behind them, to the left. He looked back and saw his brother's silhouette in the dark shadows of the forest and moved towards him, bumping into an unseen sapling and fighting the panic as he almost went down.

"What the hell is it?" he asked as he came stumbling up, his heart racing wildly.

"Someone's out there," whispered Wolfgang.

"It could be just a squirrel or rabbit."

"I don't think so."

Again, they strained for sound and scanned the woods, but there were no further sounds and no unusual movement. Erik took a deep breath to steel his nerves, fighting back a faint miasma of fear. Even though he was a trained spy, he could never suppress his fertile imagination when in enemy territory.

He still had the feeling they were being watched.

After a tense moment, they turned and started towards Krupp's Broadmoor apartment, or at least where Erik remembered it being five years earlier during his last visit to the world-renowned hotel. But before they had gone three paces, Erik heard the noise again and halted his brother in his tracks.

Whatever it was, it didn't sound like a small animal.

"Hello?" he called out in perfect English, his voice coming out unnaturally loud in the quiet, confined woods. "Who is it?"

There was no answer.

"Somebody there?"

They peered into the stand of pine and spruce, blanketed in dark shadow. There was nothing more than faint smears of light coming through the roof of the forest. They paused to carefully listen. Again, Erik's instinct told him they were being watched.

"I feel like we're in the Black Forest with the Brothers Grimm," he said. "We should get the hell out of here."

To get to Krupp's apartment, they had to cross an open lawn and make their way through another stand of trees. They started along the edge of the forest, this time at a brisk pace. They walked ten feet, twenty feet, thirty feet without incident and then, quite distinctly, Erik heard a crackling sound behind them, the snapping of a twig.

This time there was no mistaking: they were footsteps. But were they animal or human?

He stopped abruptly and wheeled around, at the same time bringing his brother to a halt. The woods stretched empty behind them, bathed in a pool of faint, eerie moonlight. Was it some kind of mugger stalking them? After all, it was war time. A time of uncertainty and rationing, with most able-bodied American men overseas fighting. Who knows, maybe there was a thief preying on hotel patrons?

"Who's there?" he demanded, his voice louder this time and carrying a note of anger.

Again, there was no response.

They waited, but there was nothing except the sound of the wind whispering through the gently swaying trees. Still, Erik couldn't rid himself of the nagging feeling they were being stalked. It was as if someone was deliberately masking the sound of his own footsteps by keeping in rhythm with theirs.

And then, suddenly, his worst fears were realized. Not more than fifty feet behind them, a dark form poked out from behind a tree and then shrank back from the light into the oblivion of the forest.

He looked at his brother and saw that he had seen it too.

"We have to take the bastard," whispered Wolfgang.

He quietly cocked his pistol. Erik did the same with his own, feeling his heart thumping at the prospect of danger. They made eye contact and backtracked towards the figure, fanning out until they were about fifteen feet apart.

They walked stealthily through the woods, closing in on their mark. As Erik moved past a knotty pine, he saw the partially concealed figure again.

It was a man.

He stood very still, looking intently at Erik, his upper face in shadow. The sight of him sent a chill down the spy's spine. He could feel his hair standing on end.

Suddenly, Wolfgang congealed out of the darkness, his tall, strong frame an outline against the faint smudges of light trickling in from where the woods ended and the open lawn began. He swung in quickly behind the unsuspecting man and pointed the muzzle of his American-made Colt pistol into his neck. Erik closed the distance quickly, moving into a support position.

The man raised both hands in surrender. "Please, don't shoot me!"

"Why are you following us?" whispered Wolfgang harshly, digging his Colt into the man's neck.

"I saw you from my apartment window. I was told you might come."

It was him, Erik suddenly realized, recognizing the massive head, thickly brilliantined hair, protruding chin, square shoulders, and hulking stature as well as the distinctive voice that still carried a trace of working-class Berlin. "Herr Krupp? Is that really you?"

"It is I, boys, your old friend Jurgen."

"What the hell are you doing out here, old man?" demanded Wolfgang.

"I have come to bring you important news. Do you mind pointing that gun away from me?"

Wolfgang kept the pistol at his neck. "I believe I will keep it where it is until you answer our questions."

"What news do you have for us, Herr Krupp?" asked Erik.

"News from your mother. She warned me you might come here. She also advised me not to help you in any way and to instruct you to turn yourselves in immediately."

"She is not my mother," said Wolfgang. "She abandoned me a decade ago, along with my father."

Krupp's voice was sympathetic. "Yes, I know what happened. But despite what you think, your mother has always loved you both, and she has never stopped thinking about you, Wolfgang."

"That's a lie. She doesn't give a damn about us. In fact, she wants us dead. Especially me."

"No, she doesn't. But she does want you both to turn yourselves in so you don't get hurt."

Erik stepped up close enough to smell the roast beef and schnapps on Jurgen Krupp's breath. "Turn ourselves in? But we just escaped."

"The intelligence information we have in our possession could win us the war," said Wolfgang, bristling with intensity. "Doesn't that mean anything to you, Herr Krupp? The Fatherland was your country once, was it not?"

"Whatever I was before, I am an American now. The only reason I am here now is because I have fond memories of you two boys running around and making mischief at this hotel. By the way, I am going to ask you again, can you please show me the courtesy of removing the gun? It is making me most nervous."

"How can we be sure to trust you? As you said yourself, you are an American now."

"Very well then, I give you my word as a former German soldier and your friend."

"I say we give him the benefit of the doubt, Brother."

"All right, but if you make one false move, I will blow your fucking head off."

Slowly, he removed the pistol from Krupp's neck. The middle-aged Berliner blew out a heavy sigh of relief, unruffled his dark concierge jacket, and resumed speaking in a low, lightly-accented voice.

"Your mother also told me to tell you that Colonel Kepler has escaped and may come looking for you so you must be careful. She said that he likely knows about me and the other German staff here at the hotel: Otto Franks, Eva Niedecker, and Ellen Churchman. There are Nazi spies here in Colorado that maintain tabs on German-Americans through the Bund, and she believes that these spies may be in radio communication with German officers inside Camp Pershing. One of these men is a man from Denver who calls himself Weaver. He has come by here snooping around, questioning us about our loyalties. That is why, on your mother's behalf, I have made arrangements for your protection for the night. She said that this Kepler is a dangerous man and is to be avoided at all costs."

"Protection? What do you mean protection?" asked Erik.

"I keep a spare room here at the Broadmoor that is only used by me and my staff at my discretion. You can hide out there and catch some sleep for the night."

"Is it safe?" asked Wolfgang.

"Yes, of course it is safe."

"What is the number?"

"Room 126, north wing. Where you used to stay." He withdrew something from his pocket and handed it to Erik. "Here is the key, but you must be careful. There are military officers from Camp Carson in the south wing and the south part of the north wing. Your mother has rented out half the hotel to army officers, and throws huge parties for them and the other military brass once a month. There are both officers' and civilian clothes in the closet, and a little money in the dresser drawer. You can stay in the room for the night."

Erik wondered: Did he dare trust Krupp, a close family friend and current employee of his mother? Was the man planning on double-crossing him and his brother and calling the police? He hadn't seen him in five years, and for Wolfgang it had been a full decade, so how could they possibly know whether or not to trust him? Or was this all a trap laid by his mother?

"What about tomorrow?" asked Wolfgang. "What happens then?"

"Tomorrow you must leave."

"Why tomorrow?"

"Because that is when you must turn yourselves in to the authorities. It will be light then, and you can go to Camp Carson. If you try to go tonight in the dark, they may shoot you."

"We're just supposed to drive up and turn ourselves in, is that it?"

"That's what your mother told me to tell you. She said if you don't turn yourselves in by tomorrow, they will probably shoot you on sight."

"Shoot us on sight? For escaping?"

"No, for the vital information you have in your possession, and for the five dead Americans and two seriously wounded soldiers you have left in your wake."

"Wait a second. We didn't kill anyone."

"A soldier was killed during the original escape and shootout at your mother's ranch, and two others were badly—"

"I only wounded one at the ranch, and it was in the leg," protested Wolfgang. "I didn't kill anyone. That much I know."

"Neither did I, but not for lack of trying," admitted Erik. "They were shooting at us. What were we supposed to do, not return fire?"

"I can assure you that the authorities are not interested in such fine distinctions when five people are dead and two seriously wounded."

Erik saw the logic in what Krupp was saying. "So it was Kepler who did the killing, but how did he kill so many?"

"After the shootout at the ranch, he killed two guards and two medics when he escaped from an ambulance. He was wounded in the gunfight and they were taking him to the hospital at Camp Carson."

"My God, Kepler will stop at nothing. He will be coming for us, Brother. You know that. The bastard wants another cross of iron and to be recognized by the Führer personally."

"Well, he won't find us, goddamnit. And besides, we are every bit as determined as him," proclaimed Wolfgang stubbornly. He then looked at Krupp. "We intend to save our Fatherland. We will not surrender."

"You will kill innocent people like this Colonel Kepler?"

"If they try to stop me, yes. Herr Krupp, my brother and I knew you when we were young boys running around this grand hotel. We always looked up to you, respected you for being a soldier in the Great War. Now you must show the same respect for us as soldiers. If you were a young man again and could change the outcome of the war for Germany, would you not do the same as us? Even that fanatic Kepler is only doing what he thinks is right for his country. No, Herr Krupp, our old friend, we must hide out here tonight then find a radio and transmit to the High Command tomorrow. The fate of our country hangs in the balance."

With sudden clarity, Erik realized that his brother was right. They could not possibly surrender, not when they were so close to turning the tide of the war. He and his brother were officers in the *Wehrmacht*, and it was their solemn duty to fight the Allies whenever and wherever the opportunity presented itself. Fuck the Führer. What they were doing now, they were doing for Germany, whether the ultimate goal was to win the war outright or secure an honorable peace.

"I don't just know the Allies' battle plans," said Erik to their old friend. "I know about their most secret and most powerful weapon, the very thing that gives them their edge in this war. So I'm afraid my brother is right. We cannot surrender."

"Your mother will be very disappointed to hear that. But I doubt she'll be surprised. That is why she told me to tell you one more thing."

"What is that?"

"Starting tomorrow, she will hunt you down herself. She is working with the authorities, and she told me to tell you that, after tonight, she will give you no quarter. She will do anything in her power to stop you, and that includes killing you both."

"She will fail," snorted Wolfgang belligerently.

"I wouldn't count on that, my friends. Your mother is a very determined person."

"So are we," said Erik. "So are her two remaining sons."

DAY 6

SUNDAY

JUNE 4, 1944

CHAPTER 38

BROADMOOR HOTEL

WEARING HIS TRADEMARK GLENGARRY CAP with tartan facing, and the trousers of his beloved Seaforth Highlanders, Lieutenant Colonel Tam MacGregor stared across the conference table at the humorless pug-face of the illustrious J. Edgar Hoover. He prayed that today would not turn into an unmitigated disaster like his last spy case with the FBI director, the Dusko Popov case. Unfortunately, with the three escaped Germans on the loose and Hoover himself taking an active role in the manhunt, disaster was beginning to look inevitable.

The conference table was packed with an eclectic group of men in addition to Tam and "the director," as the dictatorial, dynamic, and nattily dressed czar of Uncle Sam's foremost domestic intelligence agency insisted on being called. They included FBI Assistant Director Clyde Tolson, Hoover's protégé, longtime companion, and second-in-command; Colonel Morrison, the Camp Pershing commandant; General Shedd, commander of the U.S. Army's 7th Service Command at Camp Carson that included the POW camp; Major Albert Hawkins of the U.S. Army G-2 Intelligence Branch; FBI Special-Agent-in-Charge William Tolliver of the Denver Field Office; and several more junior army and FBI personnel, including a military stenographer. Tolliver was just finishing up bringing the group up to date on the latest developments in the case, specifically what was being done to hunt down the three German fugitives still at large.

When Tolliver concluded his presentation, Tam watched as Hoover cast a supercilious glance around the table. He was well aware of the FBI director's paranoia towards any outside agency that competed with his beloved Bureau. Most notable among them were his chief American rivals, the OSS and U.S. Army, but also the British Secret Intelligence Service, which Hoover loathed and distrusted in equal measure. Judging from the anxious expressions around the table, the recent escape seemed to have had the effect of increasing tensions between the FBI and the army. No doubt these two powerful forces existed in an uneasy truce even in the best of times. At this very moment, Tam surmised that both sides were jockeying behind the scenes to set themselves up to take the credit for recapturing the three escaped POWs and to garner banner headlines.

"I have one main question," declared Hoover, scanning his audience before fixing his gaze directly on Tam. "What is so damned important about these two brothers that you had to travel nearly five thousand miles to interrogate them?"

The Scot gathered his thoughts before answering. "Why, Director Hoover, the answer to that is simple. The motivating factor is the very strong possibility that Erik von Walburg, and his brother, could drastically alter the course of the war if their intelligence gets into the wrong hands."

The director remained unimpressed. "If they were so important, why did you let them get away in the first place?"

He smiled pleasantly, trying not to become defensive and pretending that they were all part of a team trying to solve a common goal. "Let's just say that mistakes were made, and I'm here to rectify them."

Hoover continued to look on with sour skepticism. "I'm going to need to know what information these spies have in their possession, how they got it, and why I wasn't alerted about their escape until 11:28 p.m. last night."

"They're not all spies, Mr. Director. Only Erik von Walburg is, actually."

"Don't parse words with me, Colonel MacGregor. What intelligence information do these German subversives have in their possession?"

"I'm afraid that's classified."

Hoover looked as though he had bitten into a rotten apple. "Classified?"

"Yes, Mr. Director."

"Nothing is *classified* when it comes to the Bureau. We are the very seat of the U.S. government. Now I'm going to ask you again: what intelligence information does this spy Walburg have in his possession?"

"As I told you before, that's classified."

General Shedd cleared his throat to speak. "Actually, Colonel, that's not the case. You'd better take a look at this Telex I received from Washington just before the meeting."

Handing over a neatly typed telegram with a U.S. War Department logo on the cover sheet to both Tam and Hoover, he proceeded to read aloud to the group from his copy.

"The telegram is from Sir William Stephenson, head of British Security Coordination in New York City, and it's been endorsed by Julius Amberg, special assistant to Secretary of War Stimson, and Sir Frederick Edgeworth Morgan, Deputy Chief of Staff at Supreme Headquarters Allied Expeditionary Force in London. As you can see, it authorizes you, Colonel MacGregor, to disclose the classified information to which you refer to Director Hoover, Assistant Director Tolson, Colonel Morrison, Major Hawkins at G-2, and myself to aid in the apprehension of the escaped POWs. It says it right there in the second and third paragraphs. It also states that what you tell us is top secret and not to be repeated outside this room."

Tam didn't like people pulling rank on him, but he had learned to deal with it repeatedly since the war began. Over here on the Yanks' turf, Sir William Stephenson was his superior officer whom he had to obey absolutely. He read over the Telex a second time to see if the order allowed for any wiggle room. Seeing that it didn't, he gave approval of its contents with a nod of assent. He would just have to keep his fingers crossed that Hoover wouldn't be as much of a bloody fool as he had been in the Dusko Popov case.

General Shedd ordered all non-authorized staff to leave the room. While it was being cleared, Tam watched discretely as Hoover handed the Telex to his tall partner and second-in-command Clyde Tolson, who smiled at him invitingly as their hands gently brushed. The FBI director returned the smile. For a flicker of an instant, the legendary man who struck fear in presidents, Nazi saboteurs, and Tommy-gun-toting Public Enemies with equal ferocity wasn't a ruthless, paranoid bureaucrat, but an actual human being with feelings. Then, within an instant, the tender expression vanished and his dark-complexioned face returned to its dour, prototypical law-and-order appearance so familiar to the American public.

"Proceed, Colonel MacGregor," he commanded.

"Very well, gentlemen, you are about to become BIGOT-ed."

Hoover frowned. "Excuse me?"

"BIGOT—it's the super-secret classification of those with knowledge of the forthcoming Allied invasion of German-occupied Western Europe. Needless to say, it is an exclusive club of a few hundred military officers and high-level government officials privy to the innermost secrets of the invasion, including the time and place, deception plans, and order of battle. The name comes from a military stamp "TO GIB" imprinted on the papers of officers traveling to Gibraltar for the invasion of North Africa in November 1942. To confuse the Germans, we simply reversed the letters. TO GIB—To Gibraltar—became BIGOT—or the BRITISH INVASION OF GERMAN OCCUPIED TERRITORY."

"What does this have to do with the German spy?"

"Erik von Walburg was able to compromise one of our BIGOTs and learn the time and place of the planned invasion."

"Good lord!" exclaimed General Shedd.

"Yes, that's exactly what General Eisenhower and Prime Minister Churchill said. The code name for the invasion is Overlord, and the main strike is to occur at the beaches of Normandy. We believe Walburg knows the general details of not only the planned main strike at Normandy, but our deception plans to confuse the Germans into thinking that Normandy is secondary to the Pas de Calais and Norway."

"How did he get his damned hands on this top secret information?" demanded Hoover.

"Unfortunately, he was posing as a Swedish industrialist who was working for British Intelligence and had top-level security clearance. With his unassailable cover, he was able to do two very clever things. One, he was able to pirate at least a partial copy of one of the official stamped SHAEF invasion plan packets."

"What's SHAEF?"

"It stands for the Supreme Headquarters Allied Expeditionary Force. This is the group responsible for planning of the main invasion at Normandy and accompanying deceptions at the Pas de Calais, Vichy-controlled Southern France, Norway, and elsewhere."

"And the second?" asked Assistant Director Tolson.

"He was able to penetrate one of our training exercise beaches at Slapton Sands, as well as a military compound southwest of Dover. We've confirmed that he took photographs at both places."

"What is the importance of those two places?" asked Colonel Morrison, his manner and bearing more reserved, polite, and military than the imperious FBI director, Tam noted.

"Slapton Sands, along the southern coast, was chosen because it closely resembles one of the attack beaches at Normandy—code-named Utah Beach—in terms of physical properties, tides, and the like. We've confirmed that Walburg was there during the second day of practice assaults. Early on the morning of April 28, when a convoy of troops was attacked by a German submarine wolf pack in Lyme Bay. Not only did he witness the German attack, but he took photographs of everything: the beaches, the training exercises, and the German penetration. A review of the photographs by German intelligence—coupled with everything else Walburg knows and the report by the wolf pack commander—would swiftly tip off the enemy that Normandy is the main thrust of the invasion."

"What about the military compound near Dover?" asked Hoover.

"It's not a real compound. What von Walburg stumbled upon is part of FUSAG, a phantom Army Group we've set up in southeastern England. Its purpose is to draw Hitler and his generals off the trail of other invasion plans which have been set in motion as part of Overlord."

"What's FUSAG?"

"It stands for 'First United States Army Group.' The decoy army's supposed commander is none other than General George S. Patton. The goal of the fictitious FUSAG is to deceive Jerry into thinking that our crack troops will land in the Pas de Calais for the major invasion of Europe instead of Normandy."

"Why?"

"So Jerry will hold back twenty or more divisions from Normandy, until, of course, it's too late."

The room went silent a moment as the men around the table mulled over what they had been told thus far. It was a *ruse de guerre* unprecedented in the history of warfare, and Tam knew its greatest weakness hinged on its reliance on total and absolute secrecy.

"But if FUSAG is not a real army," said Colonel Morrison, "how can such a deception be pulled off?"

"Because we've set up a dummy camp that looks and acts just like a real one. In essence, we've built a vast movie set and employed the use of German double agents and fake radio traffic to keep the deception alive. Inflatable and wooden tanks, fake trucks and landing craft, and troop camp facades constructed from scaffolding and canvas have been built all along the southeastern coast as part of the deception. Believe it or not, we even allow the Luftwaffe to photograph the camps. Only above thirty-thousand feet, of course, so they can't make out the details. It's all part of Bodyguard, the code name for all strategic cover and deception operations for the planned invasion."

"Bodyguard?" Assistant FBI Director Tolson wondered aloud. "Interesting name."

"It comes from an inspired quote Churchill whispered to Stalin at the Tehran Conference last November. He said, 'In wartime, truth is so precious that she should always be attended by a bodyguard of lies.'"

"So what you British chaps have developed is a...*bodyguard of deception*...that, in effect, controls German thinking," observed Morrison with a nod of approval. "My compliments, Colonel MacGregor. That is quite an intelligence coup."

"Thank you, Colonel Morrison. Now you can see why we want these bloody brothers so badly. They pose a very real threat to the whole invasion."

The fussy Hoover was still unimpressed with his rivals from across the Atlantic. "So your point in all this is that von Walburg, and most likely his brother too, know the time and place of the main invasion? Which is why you, General Shedd, and you, Colonel Morrison, are relying on the FBI to bail you out and catch these subversives as quickly as possible? Correct?"

Shedd's eyes narrowed. "Damn you, J. Edgar, we are not in competition here. We are a team with the common goal of catching these Krauts as quickly as possible. And once that objective is accomplished, they are to be turned over immediately to myself and Colonel MacGregor for interrogation."

"Do not call me J. Edgar. You may refer to me as 'Mr. Director.'"

"All right, *Mr. Director* it is. But you and your Bureau's orders are clear: you are to hunt down and take these escaped Germans into custody, and hand them over immediately to military authorities. That is me, Mr. Director. Working with Colonel MacGregor and our British allies, the 7th Army Command will then handle the interrogation and incarceration of the escaped POWs. If the FBI would like to be present for the interrogation, that's fine, but under no circumstances are you to interrogate these Krauts without the United States Army and Colonel MacGregor present. Those are the orders, and they come straight from the top. Is that understood?"

Hoover said nothing, just sat there like a hunk of granite. For Tam, it was déjà vu of the most nightmarish kind. Once again, before him was the same intractable, turf-protecting, glory-seeking bureaucrat that he remembered only too well when he had handed Dusko Popov, code-named Tricycle, over to the Americans in 1941 to work with them as a double agent in rooting out German spies on U.S. soil.

Oh no, not again. What in bloody hell have I gotten myself into?

Could Hoover possibly be as inept and intransigent as he had in the Tricycle debacle? Shockingly, the man had taken the Allies' most productive and indispensable double agent and nearly blown his cover and had him killed off by the Gestapo. Hadn't the bloody Yank learned anything about the subtle and creative art of intelligence-gathering in the last two years?

"Excuse me, gentlemen," Tam broke in politely, "but I'm afraid we've only scratched the surface here. The information that Erik von Walburg possesses extends beyond mere troop deployments and the order of battle for Overlord."

"What are you saying?" asked General Shedd.

"I'm saying that this bloody Jerry—this one elusive, determined young man who has managed to escape from under both of our noses—knows about *all* of our double agents. Which means that he doesn't just know of our true invasion and deception plans, he knows that all of the German agents in England have been turned. In short, gentlemen, he knows about Double Cross—the code name of MI5's anti-espionage and deception operation for all of its turned German agents. Up until now, every German agent in Britain has been under our control in our Double Cross system. But now, Erik von Walburg has learned the truth. Though, thankfully, he hasn't yet had the opportunity to report it to his superiors."

"So that's why you want them so badly," observed Morrison. "This isn't just about protecting the invasion—it's about preventing *all* of your double agents working in Britain from being blown for this and *future* operations."

"Precisely, Colonel. It is my turn to say compliments to you."

Hoover looked skeptical. "How do you know that all of the German agents are under your control?"

"Because we can read all German radio traffic through Most Secret Sources, also known as Ultra. In a nutshell, we've cracked their code from a captured Enigma cipher machine. We know what the Jerries are thinking and doing at all times because we listen in and see how they take the bait when we send them false or meaningless information. They value their field agents above all else."

"What about Walburg?" asked General Shedd. "Do they value him?"

"He's something of a mystery. There is no radio traffic on him. We think it's because he wasn't sent by the *Abwehr* or the SS. He was sent by someone in the *Wehrmacht*."

"Who?" asked Hoover.

His eyes darted between the director and Tolson. "We're not sure. But Walburg's father, General Robert von Walburg, is Field Marshal Rommel's closest and most trusted general, so we think he is under orders from either his father or Rommel, or perhaps both. The Desert Fox has little faith in the *Abwehr* or the SS for intelligence. We believe he may have sent in his own trusted man to uncover the Allies' plans."

"That sounds like Rommel," said Morrison. "I fought against the wily son of a bitch in North Africa and nearly lost a leg doing so. If I were in his shoes, I would want reliable intelligence, and the only way to do that is to send in someone you trust absolutely."

"Yes, I quite agree," said Tam, liking the reasonable Morrison more and more by the minute. "So now that you know the full story, gentlemen, how do you plan to catch this most dangerous man and his associates?"

"Of course, we're handling the manhunt," said Hoover with an official, pompous air. "Wanted posters have already been printed up. We've sent them to major U.S. Post Offices, as well as to every single post office in Colorado and all bordering states. Photographs, police artist's sketches, and a physical description of all three of these men have been sent to every police station between here and the Mexican border. The suspects have been placed on the FBI's "ten most wanted fugitives" list. Due to the importance of the case, a $10,000 reward is being offered to anyone with information leading to the capture of the suspects. Now that these men are on all of the law enforcement watch lists, every Bureau agent, cop, passport control officer, and border security personnel in the west will be checking for him. So if you military boys can see fit to just stay out of our way, we'll get these subversive Huns. The Bureau never fails."

General Shedd rolled his eyes at the FBI director's braggadocio. Tam noted that Hoover and Tolson both missed it as Tolson again gently touched his boss's hand in a gesture of support, distracting them both for a moment.

"What about the Countess von Walburg, Katherine Templeton?" inquired Tam. "Are you going to question her, or can I speak with her?"

"She's all yours," said Hoover with a rare, helpful-looking smile. "I already interrogated her personally this morning. I've gotten everything I need from her."

The helpful smile instantly raised a red flag. But what caused Tam even greater consternation was that Hoover made no mention of her being an OSS agent, when it was well known that Hoover loathed her boss, Wild Bill Donovan, and his upstart intelligence outfit more than anything else in the world, even communists. So why wasn't he trying to make Katherine Templeton's life miserable? Claude Dansey's belated MI6 intelligence report revealed that she was an OSS operative working with the French Resistance, as well as the mother of Erik and Wolfgang. Why was Hoover letting her off the hook so easily? Did the FBI director not know that she was OSS?

His musings were interrupted by a knock on the door. An army captain poked his head in and motioned towards General Shedd, who waved him forward. The captain leaned in close and whispered in the general's ear as Tam and the others looked on anxiously, longing to know what they were saying. When they were finished, the captain saluted and left the room. The general shook his head in disbelief and took a moment to look over his audience, his expression one of shock mingled with serious concern.

"What is it, General?" asked Hoover. "You look like you've seen a ghost."

"Our job just got ten times harder, gentlemen. You're not going to believe this, but it seems there's been a mass POW escape from Camp Pershing."

Colonel Morrison jumped to his feet. "What? How many?"

"More than fifty POWs. Which means that we don't just have three German prisoners on the loose—we've got an entire goddamned army!"

CHAPTER 39

BROADMOOR HOTEL

ERIK STARED UP at the huge radio tower on top of Cheyenne Mountain. That was where he and Wolfgang needed to get in order to send the message to Field Marshal Rommel and the High Command. They would be able to broadcast all the way to Berlin from way up there. It might not even be guarded, at least not yet, which meant that if they hurried they could transmit by mid-morning. All they had to do was drive up the mountain in their army jeep and, if the tower was unguarded, seize control of the radio room from a defenseless radio operator or two, make their announcement to the world, and thereby change history. Only by driving the Allies back into the sea would Germany have a chance to either win the war, or get the humiliated Roosevelt and Churchill to agree to sit down at the bargaining table on behalf of their war-weary nations and negotiate an honorable peace. The Allies claimed they would only accept an unconditional surrender, but they would change their minds once their massive invasion force was slaughtered on the beaches of Normandy and driven back into the English Channel.

Changing history was within their grasp!

Feeling a little wave of exhilaration at the paradigm-shifting possibility, he turned his gaze away from the giant radio tower and towards Cheyenne Lake. The lake was stocked with mountain rainbow trout swimming tantalizingly close by the bank, peering up at him with pouty fish lips, their colorful rainbow streaks shimmering in the refracted sunlight. On the west and south sides of the lake, guest-anglers cast their lines into the still water, hoping to reel in a rainbow, which the hotel kitchen staff would roll in corn meal and lemon pepper and cook up for their personal dinners.

Staring out at the lake, Erik remembered back to the glorious summers he and his brother had spent at the luxurious western resort: hiking, fishing, swimming, horseback riding, hunting, playing tennis and golf, and touring up Pikes Peak in his father's plush Mercedes that he shipped overseas every summer by steamer.

Now, they were enemy combatants on the run. If caught, they would be executed as spies.

His brother pulled him from his reverie. "The radio tower. That's the place we need to transmit from." He pointed a long, bony finger towards the top of Cheyenne Mountain.

Erik again studied the massive radio antennae. "Yes, I know. I was thinking the very same thing. We will get a clear shortwave transmission in the next few hours. It is daylight here and in Germany. Every listening post between here and

Berlin will hear us loud and clear."

"The whole world will hear us, brother. This is a momentous occasion."

It is indeed, he thought, suddenly feeling a flicker of euphoria being back here with his brother at one of the memorable places of their youth. He felt a powerful sense of brotherhood and shared history, and a deep connection that now, in adulthood, they stood poised to change history. They would save their beloved Fatherland.

"Good lord, what in the hell are you two still doing here?"

The voice came seemingly out of nowhere. Erik and his brother turned towards the stand of trees and saw Jurgen Krupp walking angrily towards them.

"We need to get up there," said Wolfgang, ignoring Krupp's anger and pointing up at the radio tower. "What do you think is the best way?"

"Quiet, you don't want to draw attention to yourselves."

"Don't worry, we are blending in just fine," said Erik, and it was true. With their American chewing gum and cigarettes, lazy manner, Erik's flawless American accent, and the U.S. Army captains' uniforms Krupp had managed to pilfer for them from the Broadmoor laundry, they came off as no different than the real American officers and civilian hotel guests relaxing about the grounds on a Sunday morning.

But Krupp was not impressed. "This isn't a goddamn game!" he chided them. "Your mother is here, and so is FBI Director Hoover himself! You need to leave at once!"

Wolfgang again pointed up at the radio tower perched on Cheyenne Mountain. "I told you we need to get to that tower. Do you think it's guarded?"

"Of course, it's guarded. Everyone is out looking for you. Walter Winchell's already calling it the biggest manhunt in FBI history."

"Who the hell is Walter Winchell?" sniffed Wolfgang.

"Only the biggest radio and news man in the country. Seriously, what in the world are you two still doing here? I thought I told you to leave at first light."

"This is the last place they expect us to be. We just need to get to that radio tower up there. It has a transmitter that will carry all the way to Berlin."

"You two are crazy! You must leave here at once! Do you realize what kind of risk I've taken to put you up here last night? Hoover himself will have me sent to the electric chair, like those bumbling German saboteurs who were dropped by U-boat off the Maine coast two years ago."

"He's referring to Operation Pastorius," Erik said to his brother by way of explanation. He had learned about Admiral Canaris's failed overseas *Abwehr* operation while being trained as a spy at the Agent School West in The Hague, but no doubt his brother had not been privy to such classified intelligence information. "It happened in '42. Seven of the nine captured Germans were sent to the electric chair, and the remaining two were locked away in prison, even though they had turned themselves in and foiled the sabotage operation."

"Exactly, it ended badly. Just like it's going to end badly for me if anyone sees you here! You must leave right now!"

"Calm down, Herr Krupp," bristled Wolfgang. "If anyone is drawing attention, it is you."

"But you can't be here! You must leave at once!"

"All right, we're leaving," said Erik. "But the Broadmoor is the perfect place for us to hide out. No one expects us here except—"

"Oh shit, there she is!" interrupted his brother. "Don't look! I don't think she's seen us!"

Despite the warning, Erik and Krupp both turned to look. Erik's mouth instantly opened wide with shock. Indeed, there on the sandstone patio outside the Lake Terrace Dining Room stood his mother, the Scottish interrogator who had grilled him along with Tin Eye in London, and Colonel Morrison.

And then, to his dismay, he realized that it was already too late: Morrison had spotted them. He pointed at them, barked out something to his two companions, and drew his sidearm.

"Oh my God, they've seen us!" cried Krupp in a panic.

The group on the patio started gesturing at them, alerting the fisherman along the banks and other people standing on the south end of the patio, who had stopped what they were doing to stare at them.

"Quick, we've got to get out of here, Brother!" said Erik, wanting to kick himself for his lapse of judgment and not following Krupp's advice.

Krupp threw up his hands in desperation. "I am ruined! I will see the electric chair for sure, now!"

"Don't worry, Herr Krupp, nothing's going to happen to you. We're leaving," Wolfgang tried to assuage him.

But Krupp wasn't listening. Instead, he was motioning vigorously. "Oh God, please don't shoot!" he blubbered to Morrison and the others. Suddenly, he started running towards the group, holding his hands up in surrender.

"Stop, Herr Krupp! Stop!" cried Erik but it was of no use.

The man kept running and screaming wildly: "Don't shoot! I captured them and am turning them in! Don't shoot!"

But Morrison and the others were too far away to hear what he was saying. Suddenly, all three of them came under heavy fire, not from the commandant and their mother's group as Erik had expected, but a new contingent of men in plainclothes that had emerged from a side door of the main hotel. He instantly recognized the man in charge of the new group: it was J. Edgar Hoover himself, the legendary chief of the crusading G-Men who saved the day in the American gangster movies. There were five men in his group, all in dark suits, three of them kneeling in a firing position clutching their U.S. government-issue pistols in a two-handed grip.

Erik yanked out his Colt 1911 .45 automatic he had pulled from one of the wounded American soldiers at his mother's house. He unleashed a blistering fire at Hoover and his G-Men, as his brother did the same with his own stolen U.S. Army service pistol. The tall man next to the FBI director was shielding him with his body, bravely protecting him from attack, while at the same time herding him back towards the door. The other three G-Men delivered covering fire at the same time, and then Morrison and the Scottish intelligence officer in the tartan trousers opened up with their sidearms.

Erik and his brother turned towards them, let rip, and were met with a furious counter barrage. Suddenly, Krupp's face opened up like a melon, brain and tissue exploding from the back of his cranium in a gusher, and he dropped to the ground like a hunk of meat.

"We need to take cover!" cried Wolfgang, and they quickly ducked into the nearby trees. Bullets licked after them from both of the enemy groups, sending strips of bark and splinters of wood in the air.

For a full minute, they didn't dare move or return fire as they were pinned down from several handguns and a noisy Thompson set in rapid-fire machine-gun mode. Then, after a momentary lapse in the firing to reload, Erik and Wolfgang both unleashed another volley at their attackers.

One of the G-Men went down clutching his leg.

Their shots were answered by a flurry of bullets that knocked down whole branches like a crosscut saw and whizzed past their ears like a flock of startled birds.

To Erik, it was like something out of an American Western.

The shooting echoed across Cheyenne Lake in a dull roar before slackening again. Both sides were forced to reload. He made eye contact with his brother hiding behind a thick-trunked cottonwood; the fierce U-boat commander, the scourge of the North Sea, calmly swept his pistol across the field of fire, searching for signs of the enemy. There was a hint of a smile on his face: Erik realized that he was actually relishing the combat, despite their desperate predicament.

It was then that he heard his mother's voice rise up above the momentary stillness of the lake.

CHAPTER 40

BROADMOOR HOTEL

"WOLFGANG, ERIK, CAN YOU HEAR ME?"

Erik looked at his brother, who shook his head, commanding him not to reply.

"Boys, you must listen to me! Can you hear me?"

"Yes, we hear you!" replied Erik. "What do you want?"

"For you to surrender!"

"No! Never!" shouted Wolfgang.

"Listen to me! You are completely surrounded. In the next five minutes, every policeman, FBI agent, and soldier in the area will be taking shots at you! You must surrender!"

"No, we will not surrender!" yelled Wolfgang defiantly.

"Listen to me! You have no chance of escape! You must give yourselves up!"

"No, goddamnit, we will never surrender!"

"Then you will die! And for what? A maniac dictator who would have his whole country destroyed, and all of his countrymen killed, before he gives up his power? Is that what you want to die for: your insane Führer and his twisted fantasy of a Thousand Year Reich?"

Erik felt a sting of anger, made all the worse because he agreed with her. But he could not give up on Germany, not now in his beloved country's time of greatest need!

All around, the Americans were moving into position. Stillness took hold of the air, like the great calm before the tempest. Morrison, another American officer, and one of the G-Men were making hand signals to one another and a third group of men. A moment later, the enemy had formed up into just two groups. One began a slow flanking maneuver around the south side of the lake; the other moved stealthily through the bushes and trees to the north. They were calmly moving in on them from two sides in a pincer movement, treading quickly but cautiously, pistols and machine guns at the ready. Morrison had obviously seen combat and knew what the hell he was doing.

Erik motioned to his brother to move back in a general retreat. As they did so, the world around them once again exploded with gunfire, coming this time from a new contingent of army officers across the lake. They were firing from the protective cover of the trees between the lake and the horseback riding and rodeo stadium. Residents of the hotel, they must have scrambled onto the scene to see what all the shooting was about. Erik and his brother both made themselves small behind a thick cottonwood. The bark splintered. Little puffs of smoke appeared all along the hotel across the lake and from the copse of trees nearest the golf course to the south.

Their position was untenable.

"Brother!" he called out over the heavy firing. "We have to get the hell out of here!"

"All right, on three we pull back towards the parking lot! We have to make it to the jeep—it's our only chance!"

On three, they dashed through the trees with bullets plucking at their feet and devouring foliage until they reached a sandstone wall.

They started to climb.

But as they poked their heads up over the top, they were peppered by a burst of gunfire from the other side of the wall and were forced to duck back down.

The situation was now desperate. With their backs against the wall, Erik scanned the area while his brother reloaded. He saw a flash of movement on the west side of the hotel, at the edge of the bushes. His brother saw it too, and they drew a bead and fired. The bullets rattled against the side of the hotel like a handful of gravel. A heavy grunt sounded, and Erik saw an FBI man fall into the bushes.

Again, they were blasted with gunfire, this time coming from across the lake and to the north. His head swiveled in the latter direction. He saw, to his dismay, that they were practically surrounded.

The damned Americans had outflanked them and were moving in for the kill!

The firing stopped momentarily as the Americans worked their way into better position in the encirclement. Erik felt around his body to see if he'd been hit. He couldn't feel any wetness, no sign of a tear in his U.S. captain's uniform, and he felt no pain anywhere. He must be all right.

Then he looked at Wolfgang: blood was seeping through his brother's jacket.

"Brother, you're hit. We've got to get the hell out of here and get you to a doctor."

"It's only a scratch. I'll be fine."

"All right, but we're going to have to make a run for it through those trees." He pointed to a little break in a stand of ponderosa pines to the south of the polo grounds. "Can you make it?"

"I'd better. Getting safely to those trees is our only chance."

He helped him to his feet and they were off, scrambling past the spa towards the pine trees, Erik covering the rear. From behind came the sound of guttural voices and shuffling feet. Suddenly, they were again under attack, bullets whistling through the air, peppering the perimeter wall that ran along the edge of the hotel, mowing down the flower gardens like a scythe. They delivered a rear guard answering blast and then Erik took his brother by the elbow and shoved him through the pines.

They nearly collided with a group of Sunday polo players rushing onto the scene.

"Out of our way!" yelled Wolfgang, and he fired a round over their heads with his service pistol to scatter them.

The woods turned to instant pandemonium as the polo players ran in every direction, pushing, shoving, trampling one another to get out of the way of the two Germans with the U.S. Army pistols and officer's uniforms.

"Which way?" yelled Wolfgang, suddenly disoriented.

"To the parking lot. It's our only chance!"

Pointing their weapons aggressively at the remaining polo players as a warning, they darted past them and dashed onto the street. When they were halfway across, Erik chanced a look over his shoulder and saw their pursuers flying out of the woods. Morrison was leading the pursuit with their mother Katherine, the Scotsman, and a motley group of uniformed military officers, G-Men, and non-uniformed men in civilian dress armed with pistols.

My God, it seemed like everybody in America had a gun! What was next? Schoolchildren with *Schmeissers*?

"They're coming after us!" he warned his brother.

There was a belch of smoke and a bullet whizzed past his ear, thunking into a car parked on the street.

"Keep moving!" he cried, and he wheeled around and returned fire with his .45.

Another group of five or six army officers came at them from the east. It was the group that had shot at them when they had tried to jump over the wall.

"My God, they're everywhere!" muttered Wolfgang.

"Quick, follow me!"

They made a mad dash for their jeep in the parking lot. But they hadn't taken five steps when Morrison's group charged into position to cut off their retreat. For the first time, Erik saw that his mother clutched a pistol in her hand. Would she really shoot her own son? he wondered as their eyes met. Once again, she called out to him and Wolfgang to give themselves up. But, to his relief, she didn't fire her weapon at him or his brother. He didn't want to have to shoot his own mother.

Instead, he raised his pistol to fire at Morrison.

But the split second before he squeezed the trigger, a crackling *rat-tat-tat* pierced the air and two of the men next to Morrison dropped to the ground. Erik heard the sound of screeching tires, and more machine gun fire rattling forth. One of the G-Men screamed out and clutched his stomach. With their charge abruptly blunted, Morrison and his contingent quickly snatched up their fallen comrades and ducked behind a pair of sparkling Rolls-Royces.

Erik turned to see who had fired the shots, wondering who had saved him and his brother.

No way—Kepler!

He was hanging out of the window of a cream-colored Chevrolet coupe, firing his machine gun while a man behind the wheel Erik didn't recognize frantically navigated the racing vehicle.

For an instant, he and his brother just stood there gawking in disbelief. Kepler's Thompson submachine gun smoked in his hands, and as their eyes met, Erik thought he saw a flicker of triumph beneath the man's stolen U.S. Army officer's cap. Kepler may have been wounded back at his mother's ranch house, but the man didn't look hurt now. He must have had his wound dressed by an actual doctor. They had deliberately left Kepler behind to be captured, not wanting to have to deal with the fanatical Nazi officer; but, by a remarkable twist of fate, he had escaped and was this very moment trying to rescue them. Joining up with him again seemed like a devil's bargain, but under the present circumstances they had little choice.

The coupe raced up next to them, Kepler ripping loose with another lethal spray from the Tommy gun, sending the enemy scattering for cover behind cars and trees.

"Quick, get in!"

Erik fired one last round of cover fire and jumped into the back seat of the open-topped vehicle along with his brother. The driver pressed his foot down hard on the gas pedal. They bolted up Lake Circle Drive, tires screeching and burning, bullets zipping all around them, one taking out the rear taillight.

The opposition had no cars in the immediate vicinity and was unable to follow in quick pursuit, allowing them to make the highway before hearing a single police siren. Erik saw squad cars and highway patrolman hurrying in from the east, but no one stopped them. Once it was clear that they had distanced themselves from their pursuers, Kepler peered back at them from his front seat, smiling triumphantly.

"No doubt you weren't expecting to see me again."

"No, but we're glad you came to our rescue," admitted Wolfgang. "I must say your timing was impeccable, Colonel."

"Be careful what you wish for, *Herr Kapitän zur See*. And that goes for your younger brother too."

"Too late for that," snorted Erik. "Who is your friend driving?"

"His name is Carl Weaver. He is a spy, like you."

"A spy?" said Wolfgang. "What are you doing way out here in the West?"

The man smiled and spoke with a flawless Hamburg accent. "Why saving the Fatherland, of course—just like you two!"

CHAPTER 41

BROADMOOR HOTEL

"YOU RUN A MIGHTY FINE HOTEL, COUNTESS," declared J. Edgar Hoover with an intimidating smile. "But I need those sons of yours delivered to me pronto. Now where do you think the devils have run off to?"

Katherine stared across the conference table at the little man—the FBI director was under 5'8" and deeply paranoid about it—and wanted to hit him over the head with a brick. It seemed unthinkable that he had *owned* her for the past three years, since the beginning of the war, but it was true. Technically, she may have worked for General William J. Donovan and the Office of Strategic Services, but it was Hoover who truly *controlled* her. After all, he was the one who took the most advantage of the classified information she gathered on Donovan's fledgling spy agency, and also the intelligence information she obtained from Otto Renault, her former lover and contact in the Resistance who fed her information on German military installations and Nazi collaborators inside Occupied France.

She looked into the eyes of the legendary man who had hunted down fugitives from Baby Face Nelson to Dillinger, Ma Barker to Bruno Hauptman. The FBI director's list of successfully captured most-wanted criminals also included eight bumbling German military saboteurs, six of whom were electrocuted until their blood boiled in their veins, as part of the roundup of the conspirators of Operation Pastorius, Hitler's failed plan to wreak mayhem and destruction against strategic American economic targets. He sat in his silk chair like an emperor beholden to no one. In the past two hours, Hoover had, by government fiat, set up his personal command-and-control center at her lavish five-star hotel to deal with the German escapees. His office was in the sumptuously appointed anteroom outside the Main Ballroom, which served as the primary work space for the fifty agents who were at this moment frantically following up leads.

"I don't know where my sons have gone," she replied honestly. "If I knew, I'd tell you, of course."

His beady eyes bored into her like a drill bit. "Just like you told me about your concierge Jurgen Krupp?"

"I never suspected that he would actually help them. Quite honestly, the Broadmoor Hotel is the last place I would have expected them."

"Even though they have stayed here many times before?"

"Yes."

"Pardon me for being skeptical, Countess, but that shoe just doesn't fit."

"And why is that?"

"This was the place they knew best. You family took summer vacations here for years."

"What are you saying?"

"I'm just wondering why you didn't tell Special Agent Tolliver any of this last night or this morning. Was it because you were trying to protect your boys?"

"I am not trying to protect anyone. I want them caught just as much as you."

"I'd like to believe you, honestly I would. But let's just say that at the moment, Countess, I'm a bit skeptical."

"I just don't want them shot down like dogs in the street. Any mother would feel the same way about her sons. And as for my employee Mr. Krupp, I believe he helped them out of a sense of loyalty to me."

"I seriously doubt that. All indications are that, prior to his death, Jurgen Krupp was a Nazi asset."

That was an outright lie, Katherine knew, but she held her tongue. Jurgen Krupp had lived in America for nearly twenty years and was an American citizen just like her. If he was guilty of anything, it was stupidity. He should never have helped Erik and Wolfgang. Clearly, his fondness for them as young boys, coupled with his sense of loyalty to her as his employer, had gotten him into trouble. In the end, it had cost him his life, and damn her sons for putting poor Jurgen in that position!

"Mr. Krupp was no Nazi. He was as much of an American as W.C. Fields. Like me, he came to this country because he hated war. And you know how we *Huns*, as you Americans so disparagingly call us, love our wars."

"Why you're almost making me teary-eyed, Countess. Almost. Now where do you think they went?"

"I already told you. I have no idea. But may I suggest Denver as a possibility? We used to visit there too during our summer vacations out West. We always stayed at the Brown Palace Hotel downtown."

"Is there anyone else they might know besides Krupp. What about the driver of the getaway car?"

"I didn't get a look at him. But it was my understanding that he was with Colonel Kepler."

"We can't rule out that your sons knew him too. The Nazi network in the United States may be small, but it is still a powerful entity."

"Don't you have a positive identification on the man yet?"

"No, but we will soon enough. Now what about the other three Germans you employ at your hotel?"

She took an invisible deep breath, forcing herself to remain calm and control her anger. "Otto Franks, Eva Niedecker, and Ellen Churchman are not Germans. They are American citizens just like me."

"Just like good old Jurgen Krupp. The man who hid your sons here at the hotel last night, gave them U.S. Army uniforms, and aided and abetted their escape."

"Why don't you question Otto and the others if you are so concerned about them?"

"Assistant Director Tolson is doing that right this very minute."

So that's where Mr. Tolson was. Since arriving at the Broadmoor, the two men had been inseparable until now, and they had booked adjoining rooms. But were they closet lovers? That's what her boss Donovan had intimated over the phone last night when she had called him to report the situation, informing him that she was cooperating with the FBI in tracking down the fugitive POWs. The OSS chief had warned her to be careful of Hoover. He said that he had a lot of dirt on the man, but he also readily admitted that the director probably had a significant amount of unseemly information on him as well. Donovan was a well-connected East Coast socialite, notorious gossiper, and womanizer—he had made flirtatious passes at Katherine on two prior occasions—and he had made as many enemies in Washington as his FBI nemesis. But she still found the Ivy Leaguer—her late husband John Templeton and Donovan had gone to Columbia together—a true creative genius. Unlike Hoover, "Wild Bill" was not mean-spirited, paranoid, or consumed with favorable publicity. He was a team player, more dedicated to the U.S. and its allies winning the war than the advancement of his own personal agenda. Consequently, he had a strong rapport with British Intelligence.

"I truly don't know where my sons have gone, Mr. Director. All I can say for sure is that they are desperate to get to a radio. They said they had information that could change the outcome of the war, and I believe them. That's why I want them stopped as much as you. They asked me to help them, but I refused. Instead, I shot the radio so they couldn't transmit their message."

"Am I supposed to applaud you for your patriotism when you're an OSS agent? By the way, does Bill Donovan know about our little arrangement?"

"No, of course not."

"But you did call him last night."

"What are you wiretapping my phones?"

"Just answer the question. Does Donovan know about our arrangement?"

"You mean does he know that every shred of intelligence I send him from France has been read a dozen times over by you and your G-Men before he gets to the first line? The answer is no."

"Don't get smart with me, and don't insult my intelligence by pretending that Donovan's an angel. Oh, the stories I could tell you about Wild Bill. It would make your head spin. Oh, that's right. You've been the source of a lot of those stories, so you already know what I'm talking about."

"I don't know what you've got against Bill Donovan. Is it because he once tried to have you fired as FBI director?"

"Tried and failed, Countess. Tried and failed. But that's not the problem I have with your Wild Bill. It's the fact that there can be one—and only one—intelligence czar in this fine country of ours. It's the only way that will work."

"And, of course, that someone is you."

"I didn't say that, Countess, you did. But I will say this. Your boss's idea to set up a super spy system with a bunch of communist-sympathizing Ivy Leaguers and European socialites like yourself, amateurs who don't know the first thing about intelligence gathering, is a terrible idea in the long, embarrassing history of terrible ideas. Not only that, but he has upset too many powerful constituencies, and left himself and his upstart agency vulnerable to attack. In the end, the army, president and congress will bring down Wild Bill Donovan, not J. Edgar Hoover."

"Somehow, I doubt that. And by the way, I don't much like being a pawn in your personal feud."

"As you can see, I'm almost getting teary-eyed, again. But enough of this chit-chat. Let's talk about what you're going to do for me."

"Are we in the territory of marching orders, or is this still the usual threats?"

"What's wrong with a little of both? So here's what you're going to do. You're going to keep an eye on the army, G-2, and that British intelligence officer MacGregor for me. You're going to be my eyes and ears as you help us—and ostensibly them—track down our three high-level escapees. At the moment, I don't give a damn about the other fifty-four POWs who escaped this morning during the general breakout. I just want those two dangerous boys of yours and Kepler. If you get a lead on their whereabouts—however small—you are to notify me right away. At the end of the day, this is going to be a Bureau collar. Is that understood?"

"So that's what this is about, you getting all the credit? Somehow that doesn't surprise me."

"Hunting down escaped Nazis is our job, not the army's or local police. We are the lead agency with the latest crime solving methodology. We do all the gritty legwork. We're the gristle, the guts, and the brains all wrapped up into one. Because of this fact and this fact alone, we *will* be the ones to receive the credit. It is only fair. And you, Countess, *are* going to make sure it happens."

"So I'm your insurance so you can beat General Shedd and G-2 to the punch, is that it?"

"I'm not going to dignify that with a response. But to show you that I am a reasonable man, I have a little present for you to help bring you up to speed on how we do things." He pushed a document across the table to her. "Here's a little article I published in *American Magazine* on how to hunt down escaped POWs."

She read the title aloud. "*'Enemies at Large: Here's How Uncle Sam Tracks Down These Dangerous and Desperate Foes When They Escape.'* By J. Edgar Hoover, Director of the Federal Bureau of Investigation." She looked up at him "Catchy title, but don't you think it's a little long?"

"Perhaps. But, believe it or not, that there is the most widely read article in America right now."

She read a few lines before glancing at the lengthy title again. "All right, I'll take a look at it. But it appears to me more like a blueprint to German captives on how best to escape rather than an FBI how-to-track-down-escaped-Germans pamphlet."

The pudgy, bulldog face compressed into an ugly scowl. "Don't be impertinent. You may find the article useful, not to mention enlightening, as you figure out how best to roundup those subversive Nazi boys of yours."

"My sons are not Nazis."

"They are part of the German war machine and a clear and present threat to our national security and way of life. How much more Nazi can you get than that?"

She quietly simmered, saying nothing in reply.

"There's something else. I understand that you have developed a romantic relationship with this Colonel Morrison."

She felt herself blush. "We don't have a romantic relationship. We are just friends."

"That's not what my sources and your face tell me."

She struggled to hold back her embarrassment and anger. "What's your point?"

"I'm instructing you not to let your feelings for the colonel interfere with our little arrangement."

"You really are a piece of work. Why did you blackmail me in the first place? I mean, there must have been others working for General Donovan better suited to give you top secret intelligence than me?"

"I wouldn't underestimate your usefulness, Countess. And blackmail is a strong word. Frankly, it is not a term I would use in connection with the United States government. I am not the criminal. It is your sons, pistons in the Nazi war machine, who are the criminals. I am just gathering critical intelligence and making sure the Bureau is on top of the situation, as is my duty. The dedicated men and women who serve under me deserve that much. Bill Donovan happens to be a reckless upstart in the intelligence game; he does far more harm than good. Mark my words, Wild Bill and his OSS will not survive the war. You giving me information from the French Resistance merely ensures that I keep an eye on the European situation first hand. Which is what the president and congress have authorized me to do."

"And what about the dirt you force me to give you on Donovan and the OSS? Is that not blackmail?"

Hoover smiled harshly. "As I said, blackmail is a word used for common criminals and I, Countess, am no criminal. But I do occasionally have to get my hands dirty. I suppose that's the price I have to pay to run the country—behind the scenes, of course."

"My God, will I ever be rid of you?"

"To do that, you need three things to happen, Countess. One, you deliver those sons of yours and Kepler to me. Two, America wins the war. And three, Bill Donovan and his OSS disappear for good. When those three things happen, you and I are done. I give you my word, or my name isn't J. Edgar Hoover."

CHAPTER 42

CAMP PERSHING

ONCE RECAPTURED GERMAN POW LIEUTENANT KRUEGER talked under duress, it took less than a half hour to locate the entrance to the escape tunnel in Officers' Compound 1A. According to Krueger, the Germans referred to it as the "revolving door." It was located at the end of the bathhouse next to the coal box. Morrison had his men carefully scrape away several inches of dirt, remove a heavy piece of plywood, and pull away four heavy potato sacks filled with sand—and suddenly there it was: a ladder leading down to the bottom of a carefully constructed shaft set eight feet below ground. The shaft was illuminated with electric lighting via thin extension cables, and its walls were shored up with solid wood planks. The tunnel branched off to the west from the main shaft, heading towards the mountains, and it too appeared to be well lit.

The tunnel was a remarkable feat of engineering, Morrison saw at once. He estimated that it must have taken at least six months to build such an intricate passageway. Which meant that the Germans had planned this escape for a long time, before he had even assumed command of Camp Pershing. He wasn't sure if all fifty-four of the prisoners who had escaped last night had gone through the tunnel, but Krueger had confessed that most had. Some of the men, the prisoner maintained, might have made it over the top or through gaps in the fence created by the tornado, but he wasn't sure how many. Although extra guards had been posted at all of the openings throughout the night, Morrison knew that a sleepy guard was no substitute for barbed wire.

"All right, I'm going in," he said to the officers and NCOs gazing down into the open conduit. "Captain Tanner, I want you to time Corporal McCall and me once we start through the tunnel, so we know how long it took the Germans to make their break. Now I need a flashlight. It looks like it's well lit down there, but a little more light wouldn't hurt."

"Colonel, you don't need to go down there," argued the captain. "I'll do it."

"No, I want to explore the tunnel for myself. Now where's my flashlight?"

Corporal McCall handed his own flashlight to him and was then given another to use for himself.

"Lieutenant Jorgenson, take two men and search this compound for digging tools. We need to know what the Germans had at their disposal to excavate this damned tunnel."

"Yes, Colonel."

"The rest of you meet us along the west fence line with the distance measurement wheel. How far away is it, Captain?"

"About a hundred fifty feet, sir."

"So our tunnel's probably a little longer than that, most likely within fifty feet of the fence. We'll meet you on the other side. Start your watch, Captain."

"Yes, sir."

Stuffing the flashlight into his pocket, he climbed down the ladder. A moment later, Corporal McCall followed after him and they started through the tunnel, crawling on their hands and knees. Moving in the lead, Morrison quickly realized that navigating through the narrow opening was a much more arduous task than he had expected. The space was narrow and confined, the air damp and stagnant as he struggled along on his elbows, belly, and knees, alternately crawling and pulling himself along. Every so often, he would halt to rest, shining the flashlight up onto the damp walls of silty loam. The sides and roof of the tunnel appeared to be covered with a damp crust of white caliche, which he realized must be why the walls were so hard and held so well, though planks of wood were also set at intervals of ten to fifteen feet to provide additional support.

As he penetrated further into the dimly lit tunnel, he came upon metal spikes driven into the walls at regular intervals as distance markers. There were also places where the walls had been cut out wider along the sides. These, Morrison surmised, must have served as rest areas, or places to turn around during the course of digging operations. After crawling along for several minutes, he came to an even bigger cul-de-sac where tunneling tools were stored: a pair of rock picks, three short-handled shovels, a rake, several spades, potato bags for hauling soil, and a cable of electric wire.

When he reached the end of the tunnel, he came upon a hinged piece of plywood that served as the door to the outside world. He pushed open the door and was greeted with fresh air. Unable to find the expertly concealed exit to the tunnel, Captain Tanner and his men were scanning the prairie thirty feet to the south. The hatch door was covered with buffalo grass and clumps of soil and was located less than twenty feet from the fence. The Germans had cut it close.

After helping McCall up out of the tunnel, he turned towards Tanner. "Captain, take an exact measurement of the tunnel's length and have two men crawl through it and make a detailed report of everything they see. How long did it take for us to get through?"

"Nine minutes, twenty-eight seconds, sir."

"It must have taken the Krauts at least a couple hours to get everyone through there. What time did Krueger say they escaped?"

"He didn't say exactly, sir. He just said it was some time after midnight."

"Well then, Captain, you need to talk to him again and get more out of him. I need to know when the tunnel was built, how they did it, and everything you can find out about the escape itself."

"Yes, sir. Am I to use physical force?"

"You are authorized to make Krueger and any others uncomfortable, put it that way. I leave that to your discretion, Captain. But I want that information and I want it within the hour."

"Yes, sir. But Colonel, do you…do you think we're in trouble?"

"Of course, we're in trouble. We just let fifty-four of Hitler's finest escape, on top of three of the most dangerous and wanted German officers in the *Wehrmacht*, one of whom happens to be a spy desperately sought by British and U.S. Intelligence. If we were in Hitler's or Stalin's army, we would have already been put before a firing squad."

The young lieutenant next to the captain turned visibly pale. "D-Do you think we're going to be court-marshaled?"

He looked at the expectant faces: these were his men, the soldiers under his command. He didn't want to alarm them unnecessarily, but he had to be honest with them. He also needed to pull them together and harden their resolve for the difficult days ahead. The second guessing had already begun by the army investigators, FBI, newspapermen, and general public, but it was going to get worse, a lot worse. The truth was that they were all in a whole heap of shit and heads were going to roll, starting with his. But he didn't want to scare the hell out of them.

"No, none of you are going to be court-martialed. So put that out of your minds right now. It is true that we all have been dealt a bad hand here, but we can't hang our heads. We have to make the best of an unfortunate situation and perform our duty to the utmost of our abilities. I will not tolerate anything but the best out of you all going forward. The past is behind us and I have taken full responsibility for that. No officer is to blame but me, and there will be no one court-martialed but me, I promise you. So my orders are this: do your job—do it well at all times and don't let any more goddamned Krauts escape—and you will get through this in one piece. That is all I have to say, gentlemen."

The words had scarcely left his mouth when a mud-splattered jeep came roaring up and screeched to a halt. It was Lieutenant Marks.

"Colonel, there's a call for you from General Bryan from Washington! He said for me to put him on hold and track you down, so I came to get you right away!"

"All right, let's go!"

He hopped in the jeep and they hurried to the small north administration building, which had been spared from the worst of the twisters, sustaining only minor damage to the windows, the west side of the roof, and the hand railings. He dashed into his new temporary office, closing the door behind him, and picked up the phone.

CHAPTER 43

CAMP PERSHING

"GENERAL BRYAN, THIS IS COLONEL MORRISON."

Without preamble, the assistant provost marshal on the other end said, "Is it true, Colonel, that it was a tunnel job?"

"Yes, General, I just took a close look at the tunnel myself. It's one hundred seventy feet long, and was dug at the end of the bathhouse. Right next to the coal box near the officers' barracks, Compound 1A. The tunnel is very sophisticated. I would estimate that it took the Germans at least six months, and probably damned near a year, to build."

"How many men escaped?"

"Fifty-four, but we've already recaptured seventeen and returned them to custody. We don't know if all of them went through the tunnel or not. Some may have gone through the fence. We're still repairing it from the tornado."

"Yes, I heard about the tornado. That may be the thing that saves your ass."

"Sir?"

"A terrible act of nature, cutting a swath of destruction and giving the enemy the perfect opportunity for mass escape."

"I hadn't thought of it that way, General. I'm just trying to recapture all the prisoners and get the camp up and running again."

"I still haven't received your report from the Seventh Service Command."

"I wanted to explore the tunnel first. I will send General Shedd a full report within the hour. I'm dealing with some logistics because of the tornado. We've brought in tents and extra MPs from Camp Carson to guard the prisoners and search for those still out, but we still have a shortage of food and hospital supplies."

"Were those two brothers or Kepler among the seventeen you've recaptured?"

"No, sir, they're still at large."

"So, you've still got those three Kraut bastards plus thirty-seven others out there missing. Do you have any leads on where they might have gone?"

"We've questioned several of those recaptured. We've applied a little pressure to one officer, Lieutenant Krueger, in particular. We managed to get some information. He said that most of the men headed south and west. I would say they're heading for Mexico or the mountains."

"Or Denver."

"Yes, sir, most likely Denver too. They can blend in there. The escape was a top-notch military operation with significant planning. Some of the men that were caught had compasses, maps, train schedules, food, cigarettes, and American-style clothing, correct to the last detail. We're scouring the farms and ranches looking for them, and FBI wanted posters have been printed up on the Walburg brothers and Kepler. We're getting the FBI the photographs and files on the others as we speak. Director Hoover's set up a headquarters at the Broadmoor. He was on vacation, but has now assumed command of the manhunt."

"Don't do anything to cross him, and that's an order. He's already making our lives miserable in Washington. He's been on the phone nonstop since your little meeting this morning. For God's sake, give him everything he needs and keep your damned mouth shut. With the tornado and everything, the provost marshal and the Seventh have got your back on this, but we won't hesitate to throw you under the bus if you mess with Hoover. No one wants to incur his wrath. I think you'll survive this, Colonel, but only if you steer clear of the director."

"I copy, sir."

"By the way, how many officers escaped?"

"Sixteen."

"Sixteen? I'm not going to lie to you, that's a lot, Colonel. Too many. How long after they escaped before you discovered they were missing?"

"We had a roll call on Sunday morning at 0900. That's when the shortage was first noted. My second-in-command, Captain Tanner, pulled me right away from the meeting with General Shedd and Director Hoover."

"That roll call just may save your ass too, Colonel. But by God, you do seem to be a cursed commander. First, there was that horrible business in Tunisia. Then Kepler and the work strike. And now, these damned Walburg brothers and the mass escape. The newspaper reporters are already breathing down our necks here in Washington, and now we have Hoover smothering us. Before this is through, he's going to make us look bad, I just know it. Bad luck has a way of latching onto certain people, Colonel, and you seem to be one of those damned people."

He felt a stab of anger, but held his tongue. Yet inside he couldn't help but wonder: *Am I really cursed?*

"I know that Kepler and the Walburg brothers are the top priority, but who in the hell do you think orchestrated this mass break?"

"It was Major Luger, I'm sure of it. He's Kepler's second-in-command. They're both hardened National Socialists and fought together in North Africa."

"All right, Colonel, I think I have a better picture of the situation and look forward to receiving your full report. But there is one more thing. What is the story with you and this woman Katherine Templeton? I understand she is the mother of these two Nazi spies."

"There's only one spy, General, and he is not a Nazi."

"Are you parsing words with me, Colonel? You should be more worried about being court-marshaled than whether some Kraut bastard is a National Socialist or not."

He said nothing, absorbed the body blow.

"So what's the story with this woman, Katherine Templeton? Is it true what my sources tell me, that you're having an affair ?"

"I am not having an affair with her. Who the hell told you that?"

"That's none of your damned business, Colonel. Regardless of the situation, I am ordering you to stand down. Now, is it true that this woman is their mother and that she employs your POWs at her ranch?"

"Yes, that is true."

"And you're having a relationship with her?"

"No, sir, I am not." *Or at least not yet anyway,* he thought. *Though I would like to.*

"You'd better not be lying to me, Colonel. I'll find out the truth, and so will the newspapers, and then no one can save your ass."

"This is Hoover's doing, isn't it?"

"You just stay away from that woman, and goddamn Director Hoover too. The last thing you need is more trouble right now."

"I promise you, we are not having a romantic relationship. She employs my prisoners and hosts parties at the Broadmoor for the Seventh, and that's it."

"Well, you'd better damned make sure to keep it that way, Colonel!" He hung up.

Jesus, what an asshole! Man, do I need a drink? He started digging through his drawer for his bottle, but his phone rang. He thought about not picking it up, but changed his mind.

"Colonel Morrison here," he said, expecting to be chewed out by another general or maybe J. Edgar Hoover prancing around in women's clothes.

"Jack, it's Katherine. How are you?"

Her voice was soothing and sexy, but General Bryan's warning still rang like a bleating klaxon in his head.

"Colonel, are you there?"

"Uh, yes, I'm sorry…I was…I was finishing something up."

"How are things going out there?"

"Uh, not too bad, all things considered. We've rounded up seventeen of the escaped POWs. You haven't spotted any hiding out around your ranch, have you?"

"As a matter of fact I have, and that's why I'm calling you. My foreman, Mr. Running Wolf, and two of my ranch hands just captured two of them. They were hiding out in a work shed in the east pasture. Mr. Running Wolf is returning the escaped POWs to you as we speak. He just drove off five minutes ago."

"I appreciate your calling to inform me. No sign of Erik or Wolfgang though, huh?"

"You would be the first person I would call, I assure you. Do you still question my loyalty, Jack?"

"They're your sons, Katherine. What do you expect me to do?"

"I understand that mothers and fathers everywhere in the world go to great lengths to protect their children. But I work for the United States government."

"Meaning?"

"Meaning it's my solemn duty to do everything in my power to ensure that enemy combatants are captured and brought to military justice."

"I believe you. But you should have told me about Jurgen Krupp."

"I didn't think—"

"You don't need to say anything more. But don't do that to me ever again. Otherwise, I *will* treat you like Bruno Hauptman."

"I'm sorry, Jack. I just wanted them to know what they are up against. I don't want my sons to be shot down like dogs, damnit. I told Jurgen that, if they came to him, to tell them to turn themselves in at Camp Carson. I also told him to tell them, in no uncertain terms, that I would be coming after them myself. You have no idea how hard it was for me to actually come out and say that."

"I told you this would happen."

"Jack, if I only—"

"I told you I don't want to hear any more about it. I'm in enough trouble as it is. The less I know the better."

"I just want you to know how terribly sorry I am. I should have told you."

"All right, I accept your apology."

"Enough to have dinner with me?"

Did she just say what I think she said? "Dinner?"

"I meant later tonight."

You know damn well you should say no! Oh shit, what do I do?

"I know you're busy with everything that's going on, but I want to see you. Please, at least give me the chance to apologize to you in person."

Again, an alarm went off in his brain, but this time instead of fighting it off, he was curious where this was all going to lead. "I can get away later…especially if you have information that would be useful to the case."

"Yes, I have information that would most definitely be useful. But the truth is that I don't want to be alone tonight."

Again, General Bryan's warning rang in his brain like an air raid alarm. He was torn: a part of him said, *Go, Go, Go!* like a quarterback about to run the perfect play, but the other, more cautious, military side of him said, *No, no, no! That way leads to trouble!*

Jesus, did he want a fucking drink?

But then he remembered that he hadn't had a drop since yesterday before the tornado, and he felt all the better for it. Just hearing her purring voice—a cross between Ingmar Bergman and Marlene Dietrich—made him go all fuzzy inside, and he realized that he didn't even need a dash of Jack Black or Old Forrester to feel the great lonesomeness inside him melt away. It was Katherine, he knew. Somehow, he could feel her changing him, making him feel younger. A part of him was powerfully, desperately in love with this remarkable, cultivated European woman.

"I want to see you too," he blurted, feeling like an awkward teenager.

"Will eight o'clock for dinner be acceptable?"

There was no turning back now as he felt a frisson of danger take hold of his body, like a fiery shot of whiskey. "Yes, ma'am, I'll be there."

"Good, I can't wait to make it all up to you."

He gulped. *Oh God, I'm really in for it now.*

And then he smiled.

CHAPTER 44

ARKANSAS RIVER WEST OF CAÑON CITY SOUTHERN COLORADO

"THE GERMAN-AMERICAN BUND IS NOT DEAD, GENTLEMEN," said Carl Weaver of the American organization established in the mid-1930s to promote a favorable view of Nazi Germany. "It has simply gone underground. There are many *Amerikadeutscher Volksbund* members all over the U.S. Each and every day, we loyal servants of the Führer do what we can for the Fatherland."

"I had no idea the network was so vast," said Erik, keeping a close eye on Kepler, who was applying a new dressing to his mangled shoulder.

"Me neither," echoed Wolfgang, also keeping a wary eye on the Nazi colonel in the corner of the log cabin.

"We are still powerful, which is why we have to be careful," said Weaver, who had been born Karl Ernst von Karman in Dusseldorf in 1913. "Bund members are closely watched by the American authorities, especially by that fat bastard Hoover and his G-Men."

Erik studied their host and rescuer, while still keeping a wary eye on Kepler. Weaver had piercing aquamarine eyes, a reddish-blond mop of tousled hair, and perfectly stacked teeth the color of ivory. They were in an isolated fishing cabin he co-owned along the Arkansas River, seventy miles southwest of Colorado Springs and a dozen miles west of Cañon City. Weaver had told them that he was a wealthy playboy, frustrated writer, and occasional fishing guide when he wasn't spying for his native Germany, but he had disclosed little else. Erik wanted to know more about the German-American as well as the extent of the *Abwehr* spy network in the United States.

"What do you do, Carl, when you are not writing, fishing, and rescuing German prisoners of war?" asked Erik affably.

"As I told you, I am in the intelligence business, just like you and Colonel Kepler."

"Is there much going on out here in the West?"

"More than you can imagine."

"Really?"

"There is the Rocky Mountain Arsenal, Fort Carson, and several other military installations and internment camps along the Front Range, as well as in the mountains. The Arsenal is northeast of Denver. The Americans work round the clock to produce deadly chemical warfare agents. Right next to it, they have the Rose Hill Internment Camp with three hundred German POWs. This nation of supposed 'softies' is manufacturing mustard gas, lewisite, and chlorine gas in huge quantities for its German final solution. They also make all kinds of munitions, including incendiary bombs. At this very moment, they are mass-producing a new, particularly lethal type of fire-bomb called a napalm bomb. It's an explosive mix of jellied gasoline that can destroy whole blocks of cities and forests in the blink of an eye. The Americans have limitless production capabilities."

"Then how can they possibly be stopped?" asked Wolfgang, who Erik could tell had been humbled by the United States' massive war production capability, infrastructure, and geographical enormity since his arrival in the New World.

"That task falls to you and your brother."

"No, it falls to me," said Kepler sternly, and he was up and on his feet, his fresh bandage fastened tightly about his shoulder. "We need to get to your radio transmitter this afternoon. Our time is running out."

"I'm afraid that is out of the question," protested Weaver. "By now, there are roadblocks at every road in and out of Colorado Springs, and guards posted at every radio station outpost. We might as well just surrender."

"We must report to the Führer as soon as possible. The fate of Germany hangs in the balance."

Weaver shook his head. America was his turf and he was the one in charge. "There has been no second-front attack in France, Norway, the Balkans, or anywhere else as of yet. There is still time to report to Berlin."

But Kepler was not one to be dissuaded. "This is not just about this so-called 'Operation Overlord' that Major von Walburg here has found out about. It is about something much bigger."

"And what is that?"

Kepler pulled out a gun and pointed it at Erik. "The time has come for you to tell us the full story, Major. Remember, I don't need you and your brother. I just need to know what's inside your fucking heads." He gritted his teeth. "Now you're going to tell me."

"Good Lord, put the gun away, Colonel," said Weaver. "We are all German soldiers here."

But Kepler ignored him and continued to point the Mauser Hahn Selbstspanner 7.65-mm pistol directly at Erik, who swallowed hard. "Tell me what I need to know so I can be rid of you, you insolent Prussian prick," he hissed.

"No, I will tell you nothing. My orders are to report directly to General Rommel and no one else."

"Damn your orders!"

"If you kill him, you can say goodbye to alerting the German High Command," Wolfgang reminded him. "Then where will you be? Without his special call sign, transmitting frequencies, and the information he has in his possession, you cannot succeed. They'll think it is all a fake. A message planted by the enemy. And then, they won't act on it. It will get buried in the hundreds upon hundreds of transmissions the *Abwehr* receives daily from all around the world."

"We'll see about that."

He cocked the Mauser.

Suddenly, a pair of shots rang out upstream of the fishing cabin, taking them by surprise.

All eyes turned to the windows. Now the faint sound of running footsteps and shouting voices could be heard.

"Shit," cried Weaver. "We're under attack!"

Erik listened. The noises sounded some distance off and appeared to be attenuated by the thick woods to the north. He wondered why, if people were shooting at them, the cabin hadn't even been hit. How could anyone be that bad of a marksman?

Another shot crackled through the valley. Now he could hear faint clomping sounds that sounded like animal hoofbeats.

Now that's strange.

He and the others quickly reloaded and checked their weapons, readying them for action, and went to the windows that faced uphill, away from the river.

Nothing.

And then suddenly, a deer appeared along the treeline across the clearing. The animal had been wounded from the shooting and was running towards the fishing cabin.

"Hunters," said Wolfgang laconically. "They're not after us. They're after the deer."

"Yes, but where are they?" wondered Weaver. "I don't see them."

Another gunshot echoed through the Arkansas River valley. But the shot missed the deer and the animal continued to run across the small clearing, hobbling but still moving quickly, angling for the south end of the cabin where the open terrain led to the river.

"God, they're lousy shots," said Kepler.

"That may be," said Erik. "But they're still armed and dangerous and headed this way. Look."

Three hunters emerged from the shadows of the woods into the bright sunlight. They were middle-aged men, beyond fighting age, and they wore jeans and cowboy hats and were thickly bearded like the colorful characters in Old Shatterhand's fictional Western world. Two of them aimed at the deer and opened fire. Struck by a pair of bullets, the antlered buck tumbled to the ground not fifty feet away from the cabin. Then it tried to rise to its feet.

The third hunter opened fire. This time the animal fell down and lay still.

It was then that the hunters spotted them staring at them from the open windows of the fishing cabin.

"Shit, they've seen us!" cried Wolfgang.

One of the men waved in a gesture of courtesy, letting them know they meant no harm and were simple hunters trying to scrounge up a wartime meal.

"Jesus Christ, this is the last thing we need," grumbled Kepler. "They're coming this way."

"We'll be fine," said Erik. "We just have to stay inside the cabin and not answer the door."

"If only it were that simple," said Weaver, who had turned away from the north-facing window and was now looking to the south, out the front window of the cabin and across the river. "Now we've got the police to contend with too.

With all that shooting, it's no wonder. Look, they've found our car."

"What, that can't be," gasped Kepler.

Erik turned with his brother and the colonel, stepped forward, and peered out the front window across the snowmelt-swollen Arkansas. On the road above the river, a black-and-white police car had indeed pulled up onto the turnout and a pair of uniformed officers with flat-brimmed hats were inspecting Weaver's 1942 Chevrolet "blackout special" coupe concealed in a stand of cottonwood trees. One of the officers was peering into the car while his partner was talking into his microphone, probably calling in the license plate numbers.

Erik couldn't believe his bad luck yet again. After everything he had endured since setting foot on U-521, was his true fate to die a violent death at the hands of the Americans and not be allowed to transmit his message to Germany?

"We've got to get the hell out of here," said Weaver. "In the next five minutes, the police are going to make us. Then they'll call in the cavalry, cross the river in force, and surround us. We need to go while we still have a chance."

"Go where?" asked Wolfgang. "We no longer have a car."

"We'll have to head downriver and steal one then," said Weaver. "It's our only chance."

"What about the hunters?" said Erik, pointing to the north across the small clearing. "They're still coming this way and will see us leaving."

"If they lift a finger to stop us, they will die. It is as simple as that," said Kepler, exchanging his Mauser for his Thompson. "We have three hundred rounds of ammo between us. We will not go down without a fight."

At that moment, another black-and-white pulled to a halt next to the other police car across the river. Erik felt his heart rate click up a notch. *Oh damn,* he thought, *here we go again.* He looked at his brother, who shook his head with consternation.

"This situation is getting worse by the minute," said Weaver. "Quickly now, everyone pack up your belongings and let's be on our way before more lawmen show up and we are *totally* surrounded."

CHAPTER 45

ARKANSAS RIVER

KEEPING TO A COPSE OF COTTONWOODS, they were able to slip past the police and the hunters and make their way downstream. Despite his wounds, Kepler was able to keep up with the others and move at a steady clip along the animal game trail through the trees. Erik couldn't believe how much stamina the bastard had or how tough he was. He was the very picture of the master Aryan race. With his butch haircut, sharp angled features, great physical strength and endurance, and heavy German accent, the Africa Corps commander was the exact image of the goose-stepping, Aryan super warrior so greatly feared by the American public and G.I. Here indeed was no ordinary man, the perfect instrument of warfare. All the same, Erik detested him and what he stood for.

For two miles, they clung to the southern edge of the foothills and line of bluffs that ran along the northern edge of the river, keeping to the narrow game trail that ran parallel to the Arkansas. Soon they came upon a prominent butte. It was notched into a series of caves that bored into a massive wall of lava rock. They threaded their way through tangles of pines and big blocks of the salt-coated basaltic andesite eroded from the cliffs. Several times flocks of birds scattered from the trees at their approach, darting and fluttering their wings, but they saw no other signs of life. After a while though, they heard the distant roar of rapids and what sounded like human voices.

They crept like coyotes down the hillslope for a closer look, carrying their bags filled with guns and food along with their canteens. With the late afternoon light filtering through an overhead canopy of pine trees, they peered down into the river valley. Nothing. They continued walking eastward until they could make out two distinct male voices. They seemed to be coming from behind the cliff, which jutted out prominently and obstructed the view of the river.

They continued downstream until they reached the cliff then crept on noiseless boots down the pine-needle carpet of the slope until the voices seemed to be directly below them. Here Weaver gestured for them to crawl through the grass to the cliff's edge to take a look. But Erik could feel that something wasn't right. The smart thing, he told himself, would be to turn around and leave, then strike north so as to be beyond the reach of the river and the car traffic on the road across the Arkansas.

Silently, they crawled towards the edge of the cliff, keeping hidden in the thick knee-high grass. Now they were a mere stone's throw away from the men and Erik felt his heart beating rapidly against his chest. Rising carefully to one knee, he peered over the edge.

A pair of elderly fishermen in heavy waders were putting their rods and tackle bags into their rubber raft along the water's edge. They appeared to be done fishing for the day and were preparing to paddle across the river to their car parked along the side of the road.

"Wait, we need that raft," said Kepler.

"He's right," said Weaver. "If we can float downstream, we can quickly put a dozen miles between us and our car. But I must warn you, the water down below in the canyon is quite rough."

"Well, if we have to take them, let's be quick about it," said Wolfgang. "They're starting to cross."

Erik saw that his brother was right. The anglers were pulling in the line and making ready to cast off from the bank.

Suddenly, Kepler jumped to his feet, taking them all by surprise. "Halt!" he commanded the two fishermen, covering them with his Tommy gun. "We need that boat!"

The two anglers looked up in startlement.

"Stay right where you are! We're coming to you!" commanded Weaver, pointing his Mauser pistol at them.

He dashed upstream to the right and slid down a grassy slope to the river bank. Erik and Wolfgang quickly followed while Kepler covered the two men with the Thompson. Once to the bank, they scrambled over a fallen tree and pile of sandstone boulders, charging downstream parallel to the river towards the two fishermen. As they approached, Erik saw that the two men had disregarded Kepler's and Weaver's orders to halt and had pulled the large rubber raft away from the bank. Now they were pushing it into the river.

Angered by their insolence, Kepler yelled, "Stop!" and opened fire with a quick warning burst from his Tommy over their heads from the bluff.

"Do what he says!" commanded Erik to the fishermen. "You will be shot if you don't hand over the boat to us right now!"

But instead of obeying, the two terrified old men snatched their paddles and began paddling hard for the far bank.

"Stop right now!" cried Wolfgang.

But it was too late as Kepler and Weaver both let loose with their weapons. The bullets ripped through the fishermen like a buzz saw, sending them both face down and spurting blood into the river.

It was then all hell broke loose.

On the road above the river, one of the black-and-white police cars they had seen upriver pulled up onto the turnout, and a pair of uniformed officers scrambled from the vehicle. Running along the bank for the raft, Erik felt his heart thunder in his chest as he saw the policemen draw pistols from their holsters.

"Quick, we have to catch up to the raft and climb in!" cried Weaver.

"Yes, it's our only chance!" agreed Erik.

Up on the bluff, Kepler opened up on the law officers with his Tommy, knocking down one and sending the other diving for cover behind the door of the vehicle. The two brothers and Weaver rumbled towards the raft in a direct beeline, splashing through the water. The cop had grabbed the microphone from his police car and was urgently talking into it, calling for reinforcements. Erik stumbled his way over the slippery, algae-covered river stones and grabbed the stern line of the rubber raft.

The officer chucked aside his mike and opened fire on the raft. Erik dove below the surface along with his brother as the bullets splashed along the gunwale, sending up a stream of water spouts. Sliding down the hillside on his back, Kepler blasted away at the officer again with his Tommy, spitting bullets all along the rocky ridge. Again, the lawman took cover, this time behind a huge granite boulder.

As Erik rose to the surface, he lost his footing on a slippery stone and staggered into his brother. The pair tumbled into the water in a tremendous splash, while the raft continued downstream.

But by then Weaver had waded into the stiff current and he now grabbed the stern line.

"Jump in!" he cried.

The policeman fired down upon them again.

But Kepler had popped in a fresh, 20-round box magazine into his Thompson and he now sprayed the hillside at the same time Erik and Wolfgang let loose with the Walther PPK 7.65-mm officer's pistols Weaver had given them. The cop was forced again to take cover and Kepler took the opportunity to quickly climb down to the riverbank to link up with them.

"Let's go, let's go!" he shouted as he splashed into the current.

Erik and Weaver fired a few more rounds to keep the policeman at bay.

Then they were off and heading for the Gorge.

CHAPTER 46

ROYAL GORGE, ARKANSAS RIVER

ONCE THEY WERE beyond the range of the lawman, they put away their guns. A minute later, they hit the whitewater and all four of them began working their paddles hard, putting their shoulders into it like oxen. Erik straddled the port gunwale with one leg in the river, his brother and Weaver occupied the same position to starboard, and Kepler took up the stern. Peering downstream at the narrowing canyon walls and ominous five-foot waves, Erik wondered how they were going to survive the next few minutes, let alone evade the authorities and track down a radio transmitter now that police knew their whereabouts.

Despite the sense of desperation, it was a surprisingly beautiful day on the river. The sky overhead was an untrammeled blue, the sun a sulfurous yellow. Soft willows and cottonwoods crowded the floodbanks, and hearty green pines were nestled along the rugged Precambrian bluffs flanking the valley. Though the serpentine Arkansas was running high, the water was clear since the vast majority of snowfall had yet to melt.

He looked over at his brother. Wolfgang was a stalwart presence, and Erik was glad that he was here. How wrong he had been to think his brother was still a stubborn fanatic no different from Kepler. Wolfgang was a different person from the rabid Hitler Youth that had tormented him when he was fifteen and sixteen years old in Berlin. Watching him paddling in the brisk current, Erik found himself once again proud of him, as he had been when they were school boys. The shirt sleeves of his U.S. Army captain's uniform were pulled up to expose powerful forearms, no doubt from swinging like a monkey through the narrow openings aboard U-521. As a longtime seaman, he looked natural and comfortable on the water, even if he wasn't behind the helm of a U-boat on the open ocean.

As they neared the mouth of the canyon, the roar echoing through the pegmatite granite walls was like the booming of 88s, and the waves swelled to the size of panzer tanks. The first big wave crashed into them head on, splashing water on their faces. The second slammed into the starboard gunwale, jolting them from their seats and spinning the raft off course. The third came in hard on the port gunwale, knocking the two brothers and Weaver into the middle of the flimsy rubber raft, which suddenly seemed like a child's toy boat amid the swollen, tempestuous Arkansas River.

"What are you doing, you idiots? Get up and paddle!" commanded Kepler over the roar of the rapids, his Thompson strapped over his freshly dressed shoulder as if his wounds meant nothing to him.

They struggled back to their positions and plunged their paddles into the water as another set of waves lashed furiously at the raft, pitching and rolling the vessel like an automobile swerving out of control on an icy road. But with their heads bobbing up and down in the swells and troughs, they were able to quickly develop a natural rhythm, synchronizing their strokes and shooting through the waves like a torpedo. Up ahead, two huge boulders forced the current into three separate flow channels, all of them frothing and dangerous looking.

"Which way, Brother?"

"Head right between them! That's where the current is swiftest!"

"Yes, that is the best way," agreed Weaver.

"Have you done this before?" Erik then asked the spy.

"Only once. And quite honestly, afterwards I felt lucky to be alive."

"And yet you urged us to do it?"

"Desperate situations call for desperate measures."

"Shut up and paddle!" commanded Kepler.

"All right! Hard paddle!" said Wolfgang.

Paddling furiously, they shot through the opening between the two boulders, and then onward down the river until they passed under the massive Royal Gorge Bridge, shimmering more than a thousand feet overhead. Before they could congratulate themselves on their achievement, however, they came upon another stretch of churning whitewater riddled with a terrifying maze of heavy boulders.

This time they chose right, but Erik saw instantly that it was a mistake.

In a stunning display of Mother Nature's sheer power, the raft was sucked into a giant trough, crumpled to three-quarters its size, and then shot up into the air as if from a cannon, knocking all four of them into the middle of the rubber raft. As they struggled to their feet, the vessel, suddenly unmanned, was thrown sideways in a great spasm, hoisted into the air, and then tossed into another trough, where it crumpled like a wilted plant and spun crazily around again before splashing down into another set of whitewater waves.

Then suddenly, they were out of the maelstrom and in slower water.

Erik pumped his fist in the air. "We fucking did it brother! We made it!"

"We haven't made it yet! Look at that!"

Wolfgang pointed to frothing stacks of five foot waves up ahead.

"No, look at that!" shouted Kepler, pointing to a new group of men with rifles. They were moving into firing position amid a cluster of boulders downstream, along the right bank.

Erik squinted. "Who the hell are they?"

"Whoever they are, they're not policemen or soldiers!" said Weaver. "They look like an armed mob of mountain men!"

"But who alerted them and how did they get here so quickly!" wondered Wolfgang aloud.

"They must have listened in on the police radio," said Erik, stunned at how quickly the tide had turned against them. "Half the state is out looking for us!"

"But where did they come from?" asked his brother. "These canyon walls are several hundred feet high!"

"I don't know, but we're goddamned fish in a barrel in this open raft!"

"These Americans have no honor!" snorted Kepler derisively in a violent staccato of *Berlinerisch*, throwing down his paddle into the water-filled raft in a fit of contempt for all things Yankee and jerking out his Tommy gun. "Carl and I will show this no-good rabble how we Germans put up a fight! You two keep paddling! This truly is a land of lawless gangsters!"

Along the bank, the armed civilian mountain men moved into position. Most of them were equipped with shotguns and rifles, but one man carried a pair of pistols in a hip holster like an old time Western gunfighter.

My God, thought Erik, *we truly have entered the world of Old Shatterhand!*

"Paddle hard to the left!" he called out to his brother. "We need to get to the far side of the river, away from those guns!"

"Damned gangsters!" bellowed Kepler, generous flecks of saliva spitting from his mouth. "Keep paddling!"

In that moment, to Erik, the Africa Corps colonel was truly the embodiment of the *Übermensch*—a Super Aryan steeped in a militant culture of authority and subordination, a member of the Nazi Master Race that laid claim to superior blood and breeding. Erik found himself hating the man a thousand fold more than the enemy they were about to engage. He seemed to represent all that was wrong with Germany.

"Quick, they're moving into position! Hard paddle!" cried Wolfgang.

They shot through a set of large rapids. Kepler and Weaver withheld from firing until they were three-quarters of the way through, and then they let loose with a furious burst, Kepler with his Tommy set in single-fire mode to conserve ammo, Weaver with his Mauser. Two of the enemy returned fire while the rest ducked behind the boulders, reassessing their courage and commitment now that the Germans were shooting back.

"Faster, Brother, faster!" cried Wolfgang. "We can slip past them!"

They paddled frantically, dipping and thrusting with all of their strength and agility, running the gauntlet as a salvo of gunfire exploded from the south bank.

Kepler and Weaver returned fire, but as they were hit by the next wave, they both lost their footing on the slippery rubber floor of the raft, and tumbled down into the water-filled interior. Emboldened now, the men along the bank let loose with their rifles, shotguns, and pistols as if it were the Gunfight at the OK Corral.

"Quick!" cried Erik. "Hard paddle!"

They stroked furiously. The raft smashed into a rock, pivoted, and realigned itself with the current as bullets buzzed like hornets all around them, ricocheting off the boulders and canyon walls. Somehow, Kepler and Weaver managed to scramble back into firing position and reload their weapons from Kepler's ammunition bag packed with spare magazines. They opened fire up ahead on the far bank, taking down one man, followed by another.

The enemy returned fire as they navigated through another set of rapids. The boat bobbed up and slapped down hard as they rode the crests and troughs of the fat waves. There was an abrupt whooshing sound as a bullet slammed into the starboard gunwale, but to Erik's amazement, the whoosh turned to only a light hissing sound and the raft seemed to be deflating slowly enough that they should be able to make it through the rapids.

And then, Lady Luck changed hands again.

CHAPTER 47

ROYAL GORGE

SUDDENLY A PAIR OF POLICEMEN armed with pistols crashed through the foliage downstream of the civilians and dashed towards the river bank. At the sight of the new interlopers, the two brothers again picked up their pace, paddling frantically. The policemen slid down the bank and crouched behind a pair of boulders as Kepler and Weaver unloaded on them and the civilians just upstream from the men in blue. As the Nazi colonel again changed out his spent magazine for a fresh one while Weaver kept up a suppressing fire, Erik could hear the cops shouting out to the civilians to give cover fire so they could maneuver into position for a better shot.

"Where do these people keep coming from?" cried Wolfgang over the sound of the gurgling whitewater.

"I don't know," confessed Erik, "but they are beginning to irk me! They are relentless!"

Glancing downstream and to his right along the narrow-gauge railroad tracks, he watched with dread as both the civilians and the policemen another hundred feet downstream opened fire. He continued paddling hard, scanning downstream along the left bank for a route that would put some distance between themselves and the enemy as they continued to run the gauntlet. Unfortunately, they were coming to the most turbulent run of whitewater they had seen yet—with walls of water the size of Tiger tanks. But then he noticed that several hundred feet further downstream, the whitewater dumped into a little basin and the current slowed before making the final stretch down into Cañon City.

A plan quickly formed in his mind.

"We've got to run those rapids and then pull over to the left bank after we get through them. There will be more of the enemy waiting for us downstream. We need to get off this river, or we will die!"

"Yes, that is a good plan," agreed Kepler. "But you two had better paddle like crazy, or we won't make it through the first set of rapids!"

"All right, Brother—hard paddle!" cried Erik, and they plunged ahead, blasting through the frothing whitewater while Kepler unleashed his Thompson submachine gun at the enemy, this time in automatic rapid-fire mode, yelling like a fanatic as he sprayed the south side of the canyon. The civilians they passed on their right and the two policemen further downstream returned fire, the rounds zipping through the river, leaving traceries at the edges of the backeddies.

"Uh-oh, I'm afraid we've got more company," declared Wolfgang, as a pair of men in dark suits—men that looked so completely out of place that Erik knew at once they had to be FBI agents—scrambled down a gently sloping wall of quartz-rich graphic granite and banded injection gneiss on their left.

"*Mein Gott*, now we've got G-Men!" cried Weaver.

Like actors making a grand stage entrance, the two FBI men slid down the bank, parted through a pair of boulders, and opened fire just upstream of the point where the rapids dumped into the deeper pool of quieter water. Now a murderous enfilade of bullets tore away at the Germans from both sides of the river, rattling and splashing all around them in plumes of spray, drilling into the raft, and—

Weaver took a bullet in the chest then another in the face. The spy buckled and spasmed as the bullets drove into him, his face dissolved in a misty spray of blood and bone, and he tumbled over the side.

And then Erik felt a sensation in his left arm like a sharp, hot knife.

Dropping his paddle, he saw a tear in his uniform and a grazing wound just below the elbow, dribbling blood. He quickly retrieved the paddle and resumed paddling, but he felt a dreadful pain. Luckily, the ice cold river water splashing up onto his wounded arm dampened his agony.

Another bullet, this time delivered from one of the G-Men, pierced the raft. Kepler—and now his brother Wolfgang who had pulled out his Walther PPK—let loose with bursts of gunfire. Another of the civilians, who were upstream now, went down, followed by another. Then one of the policemen was knocked backwards and, as he fell against a rock, his finger accidentally pulled the trigger and he shot his nearby partner in the head, killing him instantly.

"Here comes the quiet water!" shouted Erik. "Pour into them so we can get off this damned river!"

While Wolfgang kept up a hot fire, Kepler reloaded his Tommy again, and together they let loose with a withering fire at the enemy. One of the FBI agents grunted heavily as a spray of blood erupted from his chest, courtesy of Kepler. But the two remaining civilians and the lone G-Man still standing returned a blistering fire that riddled the already floundering raft with bullet holes. The port and starboard gunwales began to collapse like a wilted flower.

With water gushing in from all sides, the boat slowed and they truly were fish in a barrel. The FBI man with his pistol and the civilians armed with rifles took advantage of their opportunity and poured in more devastating rounds.

"We've got to bail out!" cried Wolfgang.

And then Erik saw his brother flinch at the sight of something along the north bank. A rifle crackled and he clutched his chest, staggered, and toppled over the gunwale into the river.

"No, Brother, no!"

Another fusillade ripped into them from both banks. Feeling a surge of anger, Erik looked left and saw that the shooter was the remaining G-Man. Dropping his paddle, he pulled out his own pistol and immediately put two bullets into the man, who had not crept far enough around the boulder he was hiding behind to reload his weapon and had become exposed from the river. At the same time, Kepler managed to take down one of the civilians, leaving only two remaining enemy combatants. But the last two men standing had had their fill and quickly took refuge behind a large boulder fifty yards upstream.

With the enemy vanquished, at least for the moment, Erik returned his attention to his brother while Kepler again reloaded and switched his Thompson back into single-shot mode to conserve ammunition. He spotted Wolfgang splashing through the whitewater, paddling and kicking furiously with his arms and legs to stay afloat while at the same time working his way towards the bank. Thankfully, he was close to reaching the little oval basin of calm water, and he didn't appear to be so badly wounded that he could not swim under his own power.

"I'm going in after him. I need to make sure he's all right!"

"Get him to the bank, damnit!" commanded Kepler. "I'll meet you there, just below that big rock!"

Scanning the river and bank where the colonel was pointing, Erik nodded in affirmation. Then he jumped overboard and floated downstream with his head up and feet facing downstream, stroking with his arms until he managed to reach his brother. Together, they worked their way through the bubbly vortex towards the bank as the crumpled, bullet-riddled raft drifted past along with the paddles and floating fishing equipment. Eventually, the current had slackened enough that they could stand up. Clutching their wounds, they managed to scramble over the slippery boulders to the north bank, where they collapsed and struggled to catch their breath.

"Well, Brother, what did you think of our American reception committee?"

"I think we are lucky as hell to be alive."

"I don't think these Yankees like us very much."

"They just don't know us yet. If we settle down here after the war, they will get to know us better and then they will grow to like us. After all, they positively love General Eisenhower and Babe Ruth, and they are as German as Frederick the Great."

"Shut up, you two! Why would you want to live in this land of decadent gangsters and nigger-Jews?" snarled Kepler, his wet boots squeaking on the rocks. "Come on, let's go!"

"No, we need a moment to rest," protested Erik. "In case you hadn't noticed, Weaver is gone and we have just been shot."

The Africa Corps colonel crowded in close to them, quickly inspecting their wounds. "Those are nothing—mere flesh wounds! Now let's get moving!"

"Fuck you! You don't give the orders around here!" growled Wolfgang. "I told you we need to rest a minute and dress our wounds!"

"And to that I say, 'No, you lazy Prussian bastards!'" He jabbed them both with his Tommy gun. "Get up! The fate of our country hangs in the balance and there is not a minute to spare!"

CHAPTER 48

BROADMOOR HOTEL

THOUGH IT WAS THE SABBATH, the director wore a blue-pinstripe, three-piece suit and dandy black-and-white leather shoes that would not have looked out of place shuffling the jitterbug on the Jungle Room dance floor. Hoover and his heralded G-Men had by now completely taken over three-quarters of the Broadmoor Hotel, and he and Katherine were sitting in his newly created FBI command-and-control center. The director had been talking for five minutes straight. When his mouth finally stopped flapping, Katherine didn't dare say a word. Instead, she just stared at him, suppressing the temptation to swat him with the stag-gripped .45-caliber pistol she had concealed beneath her dress, preferring to let her eyes do the talking in response to his latest verbal assault on her dignity and patriotism.

"Now, I'm only going to say this one last time," Hoover said in his affected yet threatening mid-Atlantic voice that came out at such a rapid clip that his stenographers seldom could keep up. The FBI director had been a stutterer as a boy, which he had overcome in adulthood by teaching himself to talk in the fast-talking style of a legal prosecutor. "You will stand trial for treason, or be deported as a foreign undesirable, if you do not cooperate with our investigation to the fullest extent of the law."

"But I am cooperating to the fullest extent of the law."

He gave a skeptical smirk. "Are you now?"

"How am I supposed to know where they went after the river? I don't know every nook and cranny in the mountains north of Cañon City."

"I told you not to lie to me. Why didn't you tell me about the Bund meeting you attended with your concierge Jurgen Krupp and that Nazi spy Weaver?"

"It was 1935. I had no idea then that we would one day be at war with Germany. I only went to the meeting to be introduced to fellow Germans living here in America."

"You withheld information from me deliberately. You wouldn't call that being deceptive?"

"I didn't even know who Weaver was at the time. There were twenty other people at the meeting."

"You say that, Countess, and yet your story just doesn't ring true. You think I'm a cruel-hearted son of a bitch, but tell me you wouldn't have the same suspicions if you were in my shoes?"

"I don't care how it sounds. What I'm telling you is the truth."

"But how do I know that you're not a double agent? Just because you work for the OSS doesn't mean that you aren't also working for the Germans."

"That's ludicrous and you know it. You know perfectly well that I am no Nazi. I left Germany to escape Hitler, and I am now an American citizen."

"You're an American citizen for as long as I say you're an American citizen."

"Is that a threat?"

"No, it's a promise. You're a U.S. citizen as long as you tell the truth and provide useful intelligence. That's the agreement, remember?"

He fixed her with an intimidating glare. She said nothing and they fell into a simmering silence. What could she say to a man who was so powerful that he controlled not only her, but Commander-in-Chief Franklin Delano Roosevelt himself?

For a brief moment, she tried to imagine herself somewhere else. To her surprise, the picture that came to her was of her and Jack Morrison sipping gin fizzes together on her front porch later tonight. She wondered if he really would be there at eight o'clock as they had planned. On the one hand, she hoped to see him, but on the other, she was scared. With everything that was happening, it was definitely a bad time for her to be involved with an American military officer. But he seemed so genuinely caring and decent; she couldn't help but wonder if it were not worth the risk.

He didn't seem like most men. He was strong yet gentle. He treated her as an intellectual equal, something completely foreign to the vast majority of men she worked alongside at the OSS and army. And he had a certain humble charm and vulnerability about him.

"I'm running out of patience," bristled Hoover, snapping her from her momentary escape. "I want to know where those damned sons of yours have gone and who else might be sheltering them?"

"I've already told you, I don't know."

"That's not good enough."

"You have the list of people that were at the Bund meeting. And you've already interrogated my three employees: Otto Franks, Eva Niedecker, and Ellen Churchman. As I've told you before, all three of them are American citizens."

"That doesn't mean they're not also Nazi subversives."

"That's unlikely and you know it."

"Unlikely or not, you're going to have to give me more. Those murdering sons of yours have killed more than ten men. They've gone on a bloody rampage."

"They are soldiers. It is their job to fight the enemy. But even then, I can guarantee that Colonel Kepler is the one who has done most of the killing. That man is ruthless."

"Is that the information you got from General Shedd and your British friend MacGregor?"

"You're the one who wanted me to spy on them."

"And what have you found out?"

"Nothing so far. I've been working primarily with your agents. Special Agent Tolliver wants me to go with his team into the mountains and broadcast over a loudspeaker to try to get my sons to surrender. Personally, I think it's a ridiculous idea, but as I told you, I am cooperating fully. We're leaving in half an hour."

"So what you're telling me is that there was no special place your family used to go to in the mountains? Somewhere these fugitives could be hiding out?"

"I can't think of anywhere. During our family summers out West, we went on motor car drives to Florissant to see the fossils, Royal Gorge to see the bridge, and to Manitou Springs, Pikes Peak, Cripple Creek, and Leadville. But we didn't know anyone in those places. We also used to stay at the Brown Palace in Denver and the Stanley Hotel in Estes Park, but as I told you, we didn't have any friends there."

"You'd better not be holding back on me. I'm warning you."

"You seriously can't expect me to track them down when I haven't seen either of them in years. I have no idea where they could be."

"Then you'd better try harder. Remember our deal: if you get a lead on their whereabouts—however small—you are to notify me right away."

"I am quite aware of our blackmail arrangement, Mr. Director. You don't need to lecture me again by telling me that the escaped prisoners are the responsibility of the Bureau, not the army, G-2, OSS, or British Intelligence. I understand your goal: you want to make sure that the FBI is the lead in making the arrest, and you're using me as your personal pawn to achieve that goal."

"You're mistaken, Countess, if you think this is some power grab on my part. This isn't about me. It's about which governmental agency is in the best position to hunt down and capture these at-large POWs. It's about which one has America's best interests and its ultimate protection at heart. America believes in me and my G-Men, Countess. They know that we are there for them in dangerous and troubled times like these. That's why I am the son of a bitch I am, and for no other reason. It's the same reason our General Patton is the way he is. And you can quote me on that."

"And if I do what you ask, will you finally leave me alone?"

"I already told you the answer to that question, Countess. If you want your freedom, you'd better deliver those sons of yours and Kepler to me pronto."

"And that's all?"

"No, like I told you before, America also has to win the war and you have to deliver Bill Donovan's head to me on a silver platter. Once all three of those things are accomplished, I promise you, *fräulein*, you're free as a bird."

She shook her head in disgust. "It is rude to call me *fräulein* when you know perfectly well I am a widow. You're a cold hearted bastard, J. Edgar Hoover."

"No, I represent law and order, and my dear departed mother thought the world of me."

"So I've heard. I've also heard that both your mother and father were of German ancestry. Don't you find that a tad ironic?"

Hoover gave a puzzled expression, as if the very concept of irony was completely alien to him. "Ironic? Ironic how?"

"Oh, one day you'll figure it out. After all, you appear to be a rather sharp fellow—for a lowly Hun."

CHAPTER 49

BROADMOOR HOTEL

WHEN COLONEL TAM MACGREGOR saw Katherine Templeton pacing alongside Cheyenne Lake, he imagined himself as an Old Master painter rendering the scene. She was a remarkably beautiful, captivating woman whom he could swear had to be at least a decade younger than her actual age of forty-eight. Her long blond hair was swept back by the wind, her cheeks flush like a rose-colored sunset. At her feet, the sunlight sparkled off the cobalt-blue surface of the lake and white-headed geese bobbed and honked contentedly at one another. Beyond the lake, the backdrop of Cheyenne Mountain rose up like a precious jewel against the pastel skyline. For a moment, he forgot about the war and the bloody Nazis, the meddling, churlish Churchill and fanatical Hitler, the madness and secrecy and killing on a massive scale never seen before in the annals of civilization.

There was only a beautiful woman, a lake, and a mountain rising up against a sparkling Western sky. It was a vast and wondrous country out here. It made his head spin in a pleasant way, and he knew that's why the Countess von Walburg had escaped Nazi Germany and come to this uniquely special montane region that was so utterly majestic.

He watched her surreptitiously from the Lake Terrace Dining Room. He and General Shedd had just finished a meal of pan-seared Colorado mountain trout, served with two poached eggs, parsley potatoes, and Meunière butter that had been the best meal he had had in five long years. Since the Blitz, London had survived on heavily-rationed Dickensian gruel and he had lost twenty pounds.

"General Shedd, would you mind terribly if I had a quick word with Mrs. Templeton?"

The general looked at his watch. "That's fine. We have fifteen minutes until our briefing with Director Hoover. I'll go with you."

"Ah, I'd prefer to speak to her in private if you don't mind."

The general hesitated. "All right, but for God sakes don't say or do anything that is going to get either of us into any trouble. I'll grab a smoke."

"Thank you, General. I won't be but five minutes."

He walked outside onto the patio and headed towards the lake. Katherine Templeton looked up when he reached the grassy bank a few feet away.

"Lieutenant Colonel MacGregor, are you spying on me?"

"No, I just came by to chat for a moment. General Shedd and I are about to meet with Director Hoover."

A look came over her face, and he knew he had struck a nerve. "I take it you are not too fond of the director. Well then, it appears that you and I have something in common."

"Oh we do, do we?"

"The man harangued me yesterday, and I quote: 'Even one escaped prisoner at large, trained as he is in the techniques of destruction, is a danger to our internal security, our war production, and the lives and safety of our citizens.'"

She smiled. "That was a very good impression."

"Thank you. But there's just one problem with it. General Shedd showed me statistics from the provost marshal demonstrating that, since the war began, there has not been a single case of military sabotage or assault on an American citizen by a fugitive German, Italian, or Japanese prisoner of war. POWs don't escape to blow things up—they escape to return to their homeland, or to sip a pint for a day or two as a free man, or to cause chaos and confusion for a short time period."

"They also escape to alert the German High Command."

He smiled. "Yes, there is that too."

She crossed her arms. "Is there something you're trying to tell me, Colonel? I know you're British, but you don't have to be quite so oblique."

"We know about your relationship with Director Hoover. We *know*—and we want to help."

"Who is *we*?"

"British Intelligence and, believe me, we know everything. Funny, but we don't take too kindly to blackmail across the Atlantic either."

"May I ask how you came by this information?"

"Let's just say that Sir William Stephenson, head of British Security Coordination in New York City, is a very good friend of your boss General Donovan. They're both worried about you."

She raised an eyebrow. "Worried about me?"

"General Donovan thinks that, when the proper time comes, you could be an asset on the ground in France and Germany in identifying Nazi collaborators. You're fluent in German, French, and English and are of a certain age that tends to command respect and not draw attention."

"I suppose I should take that as a compliment."

"You should. Let's just say we have our people in the Maquis too, but your contact in France is a gem."

"So your people have known about me for some time?"

"Not my people, MI6. Our sister service that's supposed to only handle foreign intelligence, but in fact makes our lives miserable just as your Director Hoover makes things miserable for your beloved Wild Bill. But they only told me late last night. That's when I found out that you are not only OSS, but in effect a domestic double agent because you are also being controlled by the director of the FBI. Rather strange world we live in, isn't it?"

"I'll say. So were you under orders to reach out to me on your important visit to the states?"

"Not when I first came here. I received orders only this morning."

"So you're killing two birds with one stone. I suppose that's the British way?"

"Seems to be the order of the day in the intelligence game. It's rather like cricket. But there's also another reason I wanted to talk to you."

"Another reason? My, you British *are* full of surprises."

"I'm opening up a back channel."

"A back channel?"

"From your boss Donovan. The FBI has bugged your phones."

"I already knew that and I don't give a damn."

"Hoover has cut the army and myself out of the loop and is pursuing the case as he sees fit. Oh, he's keeping us briefed on developments, but you can rest assured that if the FBI finds your sons or Colonel Kepler, they will take their time about handing them over to us. And time is the one critical thing we do not have on our side."

"I understand your situation. Whatever secret Erik has could cost us the war. I know my son—and that's how I know he isn't exaggerating."

"It's a rather dicey situation, as you Yanks like to say. The truth is we need to track down the three escaped Germans before Hoover, or we may never get the chance to interrogate the prisoners. The man is a wild card and his vanity knows no bounds. He could hold onto them for a day to give press conferences promoting himself and putting his beloved Bureau in the limelight. We can't let that happen. That's why I've been authorized from both Sir William and General Donovan to open a backchannel with you. We need to know the instant Erik and Wolfgang are taken into custody, or their location becomes known."

"Known to whom?"

"Well, to be quite honest, known to you."

"Are you suggesting that I would aid and abet the enemy?"

"No, I am not suggesting that. But my gut feeling is that they may try to reach out to you. After all, you are their mother."

"Not quite the mother-child reunion I envisioned when I was a young woman."

He stared out at the honking geese, watched as they flapped their wings, sending symmetrical ripples through the water. "This war makes things rather complicated, doesn't it?"

"Yes, it most certainly does."

"But can I count on you?"

"Yes, you can count on me. But I have just one question."

"Of course?"

"What is going to happen to my sons when they are found?"

"I don't know for certain, but I suspect it could get rather unseemly."

"That's what I was afraid of. In that case, consider the backchannel open." And with that, she drew her linen jacket around herself and moved off towards the flock of geese on Cheyenne Lake.

CHAPTER 50

GRAZING BIT, COLORADO

THEY STOOD IN THE DUSKY SHADOWS like stalking hyenas, peering into the windows of the small ranch house, taking measure of the occupants. There was only a middle-aged man and woman quietly eating in the kitchen, simple country folk by the looks of them, with no children, or at least none that Erik could see. There were no guns or other weapons visible, though the rancher and his wife no doubt had sharp cutting knives in their kitchen drawers. But knives were no match for loaded guns. A fresh oven-baked apple pie—how exquisitely American, he thought cooled tantalizingly at the open kitchen window, causing him and his two companions to salivate. After their misadventure on the river and subsequent harrowing trek over rough and uneven mountains trails, under the constant threat of capture, all three of them were famished and dying of thirst. His gaze shifted to the rusted Ford truck parked next to the barn. *That will come in handy too—after we eat.*

"I will take them from the front and you two will cut off their escape from the back," commanded Kepler, who had, in less than five minutes, apparently worked everything out.

"No," said Wolfgang. "We will all go in through the front door and take them by surprise. There is no reason to fire a single shot. We will get food and water, take their truck, and be on our way with no one hurt."

"Are you disobeying a direct order?"

"Fuck you. You are not my superior officer. We are of equal rank."

"He's right, Colonel," said Erik. "But I'm afraid you're both wrong about who's in charge." He looked at Kepler. "Your English stinks and sorry, Brother, but you are not a spy, so I will be doing the talking. Follow me. I am in charge and I say no one gets hurt."

Before they could countermand him, he stepped from beneath the tree and started for the front door, keeping his eye on the rancher and his wife eating their dinner at the table.

Behind him, he heard his brother cry out in an exasperated whisper, "Wait, Brother, wait!" and Kepler curse "Damn your impudence!" but, despite their protests, they tiptoed quickly after him.

When he reached the front porch, his boots creaked on the wooden floorboards. He instantly froze. The sound, though miniscule, seemed as loud as a crash of thunder and he waved the others to halt in their tracks.

They stopped.

Erik listened closely, barely taking a breath.

But no unusual reaction came from the ranch house: the rancher and his wife continued to talk in low voices over their dinner. Slowly, Erik felt his muscles relax and his heart beat returned to normal.

He waved them forward.

They assembled at the front door. Here they paused to listen and quietly check their weapons one last time: snicking off safeties, inspecting chambers, counting magazines as quietly as mice. On the front door was a white service flag with two blue stars and one gold star with a blue rim, signifying three family members serving overseas in the U.S. Armed Forces, one of whom had died during service, most likely killed in action. It struck Erik as strangely surreal that the war had impacted people so far removed from European or Pacific battlefields.

The sight of the simple little flag made him feel sad and lonely inside, and he wondered if he would ever make it home. Did he even want to return home? With all the Allied bombing, millions of dead amid the rubble, and Hitler and his Nazis still in power, what was there to return to?

When they were finished with their weapons check, Kepler gave a hand signal, still convinced that he was in charge, and then it was *"Los! Los! Los!"* without actually uttering a single syllable. Erik felt a surge of dread, fear, and excitement shoot through his veins as they stormed inside the ranch house and charged for the kitchen like a wolf pack.

They caught the husband and wife completely by surprise.

A look of mortal fear blossomed on the woman's face and she screamed. The man reached quickly for a shotgun leaning against the wall that had been hidden from the Germans' view. The news of their escape must have been all over the radio, and the man had kept his gun close by to defend himself and his wife.

"Stop, we mean you no harm!" Erik warned them.

But he was too late.

The rancher, more spry on his feet than Erik would have thought possible, had already grabbed the shotgun and, as he turned to fire, Kepler unloaded on him in single-shot mode with the Tommy.

The man was driven back by the impact and fumbled the shotgun in his hands. It clattered harmlessly to the floor with a loud thud.

"Stay down! It's over!" cried Erik, quickly stepping between the man and Kepler and kicking the shotgun to the side.

His brother picked it up with one hand, while covering the man and his wife with his pistol in the other.

"Quickly, get something to stop the bleeding!" Erik snapped at the terrified wife.

She hesitated, frozen with fear.

"Do you want your husband to live or not! Now get a rag or towel! We've got to stop this bleeding!"

Quickly collecting herself, she tore off her apron, handed it to him, and began rummaging through the kitchen drawers for something more substantial. Meanwhile, Erik and Wolfgang helped her husband to a chair as Kepler grumbled under his breath and began greedily devouring the chicken and roasted potato dinners the man and woman had been eating before the attack. Blood poured from the rancher's shoulder wound in a crimson torrent, but they were quickly able to get the bleeding under control with the apron and a pair of dishtowels the woman retrieved from the kitchen drawer. The rancher groaned and cursed in a suppressed murmur every so often as he was being bandaged up and his wife applied pressure to the wound, but other than that no words were uttered. These Colorado mountain folk were certainly tough, hardy Americans, thought Erik, amazed at the husband's and wife's composure under such terrifying circumstances.

With the rancher and his wife under control and posing no threat, they rummaged through the refrigerator and cabinets for food and drink, placed it onto the table, and pitched in. By then, Kepler had inhaled all of the chicken and potatoes and wanted more. For several minutes, no one spoke as all three famished POWs replenished themselves with cheese, raw eggs, bread smeared with butter, milk, cold hominy grits, and slices of meat. The rancher and his wife looked on stoically, but inside Erik knew they must have been terrified out of their wits.

"Everything is going to be fine," he reassured them. "We just need some food and clothes and to borrow your truck. Then we will be on our way and you can return to your lives. We are sorry for the intrusion."

"Speak for yourself," snarled Kepler through a mouthful of smoked ham and cheddar cheese. "You shouldn't have pulled that shotgun on me, old man. You are going to pay for that."

"He's already paid for that," snapped Wolfgang. "There is to be no more shooting."

"That depends on if he and his wife tell us what we need to know."

Despite his wound, the rancher squinted at Kepler with unconcealed disdain. "You're the escaped Krauts. The first three the ones they want bad." His face had already turned a shade paler from blood loss, but his chin projected with proud defiance. Erik could tell he was a tough, stubborn old coot.

"You don't ask the questions, old man. I ask the damned questions."

"You're the one called Kepler, the Africa Corps colonel. They said you were the worst of the lot, the most dangerous and deadly."

"I told you, I ask the goddamned questions. But whoever said that is right: I am a dangerous and deadly *Kraut* so you had better watch your fucking tongue!"

The old man was unfazed by the threat; Erik figured he had probably fought in the Great War and had seen a German soldier or two in his time, even if it was only through the sight of a rifle.

"It was the FBI that said it. There was a G-Man here not but an hour ago. He gave us wanted posters."

"They're right over there," said the woman, pointing to several sheets of paper on the counter. "The FBI man said you might be coming this way."

Kepler eyed them both sharply, still covering the man with his Thompson. "Get the posters," he snapped to Erik, but Wolfgang was already up from his chair and heading for the small pile of papers.

He quickly thumbed through them. "They have posters for all of us. Just like Billy the Kid and Jesse James."

"What about the others that escaped? Are there posters for them too?"

"There are pictures of the other escapees. I don't know if it's all of them or not."

Kepler turned back towards the rancher and his wife. "How many POWs have been caught?"

"The radio and the FBI man said it was thirty-six so far. Thirty-six of fifty-seven total."

"So there are still twenty-one of us at large," said Wolfgang.

"Yes, but they want you three the most." He tipped his head towards Wolfgang. "You're the U-boat captain, von Walburg." He turned to Erik. "And you're his younger brother, the spy. Funny, you two don't look so bad to me."

"We'll take that as a compliment," said Erik with an ingratiating smile. "But remember, looks can be deceiving."

Kepler frowned. "Shut up you two. We're not here to fraternize with the enemy." He pointed the Tommy at the rancher, drawing an ever so subtle twitch. "I'm sure the police have set up automobile checkpoints. What is the best way out of here to avoid them?"

"I don't rightly know. I don't know where the checkpoints are."

"You are lying. Where will the police be?"

The man said nothing.

"I said where will the goddamn police be posted?"

"Now, listen here fella, I don't much like being talked to that way. It's bad enough that you goddamn Krauts bust into my home and threaten me and the missus."

His wife, whose eyes had been pleading with him to cooperate, now shot him a scolding glance. "Now Arvid, we need to tell the man what he needs to know." She smiled gingerly at Kepler. "The police will be guarding every main road in and out of Cañon City. So if you're going to steal our truck, which you are no doubt going to do, you will need to use County Road Number—"

"They're not taking my damned truck!"

Kepler gave a malicious smile. "Is that so, old man? Now hand over the keys!"

"Nope, I won't do it."

"And why the hell not?"

"I just put a new engine in it and it cost me four hundred dollars. And my wife and I don't know where the roadblocks are because we haven't seen them."

"Your stubbornness is going to get you killed, old man. Now hand over the fucking keys, or die!"

"No, sir, I don't believe I will."

"Shame on you, Arvid, I'm giving them the damned keys!" Before her husband could stop her, she rose from her chair, went to the kitchen drawer, fished out a set of keys, and handed them to Kepler, who quickly pocketed them without taking the machine gun off her husband.

"There, that's better," he said, smiling mirthlessly. "You should listen to your wife, Herr Cattleman. What is your deal? You want to be a tough guy like James Cagney?"

"I never said I was tough."

"Oh, but you gangster Americans always root for either the tough-guy criminal or the underdog, don't you?"

"I said I don't know where the roadblocks are and that's the God honest truth. We ain't seen 'em." His mouth formed a stubborn line. "But in the end, it won't matter."

Kepler frowned. "What's that you say?"

The woman gripped her husband's unwounded arm to stop him from saying what she was afraid he would say next, but Erik saw that he was a stubborn man, unafraid of these escaped enemy combatants that had invaded his home. To his own detriment, he would speak his mind and no one, not even his wife, was going to stop him.

"They're going to catch you Nazi bastards, mark my words. And when they do, they're going to send you to the electric chair." Now he waggled an admonishing finger. "Or maybe they'll hang you, or put you in front of a firing squad. Either way, I'm looking at three dead Nazis. And that's three less of Hitler's finest our two boys will have to fight when they cross over into France, Belgium, and Germany, by thunder!"

His lips were set in a stubborn line and they quivered with this last remark, his emotion and hatred worn raw and open like his fresh wound.

His wife was quick to protect him. "My Arvid didn't mean that, honest he didn't. He's just been shot up is all, and we lost our oldest, Arvid Junior, in Sicily. He's just upset and didn't mean anything by it."

Thinking of the service flag in the window, Erik looked into their pained eyes. She and her husband had obviously been ravaged by the loss of their soldier son, and they continued to be haunted by the possibility of losing their two remaining boys fighting overseas. He felt badly for them.

"I am not a Nazi," he said quietly to the woman and her husband. "And neither is my brother. We are just loyal to our country. The same as you and your sons."

"You boys are nothing like us, you jack-booted, goose-stepping thugs!" roared the rancher, suddenly aroused with fury. "You're all Nazis—every last damned one of ye!"

"We are not either. I agree with you that Hitler is a mad man and must be stopped. We all know that he—"

"Shut up, the both of you!" Kepler was up and on his feet now, his customarily glacial-blue eyes blazing, the Tommy locked in snugly to his side, pinned by his muscular forearm covered with bristly hair.

Erik looked straight up the gun barrel and thought: *Is this really the way I am going to go, killed at the hands of a fellow German officer?*

CHAPTER 51

GRAZING BIT

THE KITCHEN WAS GRIPPED with a tense silence. With Kepler looking ready to explode with violence, Erik knew that his only chance was to calmly diffuse the situation.

"It's all right, everyone just stay calm," he said in a soothing voice, holding his hands up, and he instantly regretted how feeble and impotent he must look and sound to the others. "Let's finish our food and be on our way. There's no reason for anyone—on either side—to lose his head."

"Shut up!" snarled Kepler. "That means everyone!"

Erik watched in horror as the Africa Corps commander snicked the Thompson from single-shot to automatic fire, ready to open up with a lethal spray of bullets.

"Now you, Major, are going to tell me everything I need to know so I can be rid of you and your nigger-Jew, jazz-loving brother once and for all. What a fool I was to think that you spoiled Prussian bastards were actually patriots of the Fatherland despite your many failings. Now you will tell me everything you know, or I will shoot down these American swine you seem to want to protect even though they spit on your honor. Tell me now—or I will kill them both. Start with Double Cross. What is it and why is it important?"

Erik said nothing.

"Don't play dumb with me. I heard you and your brother whispering. Tell me now, or Rhett and Scarlett die. What is Double Cross?"

He glanced at the rancher and his wife, saw the pleading mingled with the hate in their eyes, and he felt miserable inside. "If I tell you, you will just kill me."

"If you tell me, I will have no reason to kill you. With all three of us in play, we will have three times the chance of successfully alerting the High Command. But if you don't tell me, I can guarantee these Americans whom you envy so much, who have already lost a son in Sicily and are about to lose their other two in the hard-fought battles yet to come, will most certainly die. And for what? Because you stubbornly refused to tell me what I needed to know?"

Still, he hesitated. But after looking one more time into the woman's haunted, withered face, he relented.

"Very well, Double Cross is the name British Intelligence has given to its program of turned German agents living in England. I believe they have rounded up every agent sent by the *Abwehr* to spy for Germany and turned them into double agents that they control from London."

Kepler gave a skeptical snort. "That's preposterous. How could they have captured every agent?"

"Because most of the men and women Admiral Canaris has sent over have been poorly trained, bumbling fools. The rest immediately surrendered themselves upon being airdropped or delivered by submarine to the British Isles."

Kepler still looked skeptical. "Everyone except you, of course."

"I wasn't sent by Canaris—I was sent by my father and General Rommel. And I had two other things going for me that the other operatives did not: I observed strict radio silence, up until two weeks ago anyway, and I had a perfect cover."

"And what was that?"

"I posed as a Swedish industrialist named Henrik Carlsson. By a stroke of luck, he happened to be working for British intelligence. Carlsson had top-level security clearance and I had perfect forgeries of his papers and was fortunate enough to look very much like the man. I have been posing as Carlsson for the past four months. Thankfully, we never bumped into each other until three weeks ago."

"So what do these Double Cross agents do?"

"They deceive the German High Command about the locations of amphibious landings, air attacks, and the like by sending out mostly false intelligence with the occasional nugget of real and seemingly important information that is, in fact, totally harmless. They do this to keep the charade going, to keep the Germans hooked. Double Cross brings spectacular military advantages for the Allies. By sending out false reports that our German intelligence latches onto, the Allies are able to force us to move large numbers of troops to locations where no invasion will ever take place. They are able to completely nullify any intelligence we gain. They know our every move beforehand and then they feed us false intelligence to make us do what they want us to do. In short, they control us. That is what I have discovered, and that is why I was sent to England in the first place. My father and General Rommel both had suspected as much, but they wanted confirmation before taking it to the OKW."

"But if what you say is true then that means the Allies have cracked our radio codes. That cannot be."

"Don't ask me how they did it, but that is precisely what has happened. The Allies have cracked our codes and they are using that to undermine and deceive us every hour of every day. And now the British and Americans are about to pull off the biggest deception of the entire war."

Kepler's eyes took on a knowing gleam. "Overlord."

"Yes."

"So you discovered not only where the primary cross-channel invasion is going to take place, but where the secondary, follow-up assaults will occur. That is why that British officer has come all the way across the Atlantic to Colorado, U.S.A. He is here to track you down and make sure you haven't let the cat out of the bag. So where will the main attack take place?"

"Normandy."

"Normandy? And what about the subsequent landings?"

"I believe it will be southern, Vichy-controlled France, but I am not one hundred percent sure."

"How do you know it will be Normandy?"

He told him about the partial copy of the Supreme Headquarters Allied Expeditionary Force official, stamped invasion plan packet he had stolen. And the amphibious training exercises he had observed with his own eyes at Slapton Sands. And the dummy tank he had seen deflated by an ornery bull's horns southwest of Dover. And the British agent he had killed in Hyde Park. And the seemingly random, but actually interconnected, nuggets of intelligence he had picked up from various sources in London. When he was finished, everyone looked at him in a new light, as if somehow in the passage of the last five minutes he had transformed from a simple soldier on the run to a larger-than-life Harry Houdini, Sir Edmund Hillary, or Albert Einstein. He was no longer just an ordinary man, but someone who had achieved the impossible and now stood poised to change history.

"Oh my God," gasped the rancher's wife, her whispering voice as much a plea for divine intervention against the Axis cause as an exclamation of surprise.

Kepler's wintry-blue eyes took on a fanatic's gleam and Erik was reminded of the *Parteiadler* of the Third Reich—an eagle violently clutching a swastika in its claws. "The Führer is going to be very pleased with this information. I will tell him first thing tomorrow morning."

"You?" said Erik. "What about us?"

"I'm afraid, *der Schwächling*, that you were right: I don't need you or your brother any longer. I can transmit from the Cheyenne Mountain radio tower on my own and make the announcement to the High Command directly."

"You Nazi bastard," seethed the rancher. "You'd not only betray your own troopers, you'd gun down your own mom and pop, wouldn't you?"

"For the Fatherland, I will do *whatever it takes*, as you gangster Americans like to say."

Erik watched with resignation as Kepler turned the Tommy on him and his brother.

"You still need the call sign and transmission frequencies," Wolfgang reminded him, making a last ditch effort to buy them time. "Without those, neither the SS nor the *Abwehr* will believe you."

"Oh, I think they'll believe the commander of the 21st Panzer Division, *Herr Kapitän zur See.* Don't you?"

No one said a word or made a move. Glimpsing into the future, Erik saw the last bloody moments of his life unfold in black-and-white slow motion, like a war newsreel.

And then, the fuzzily glimpsed future turned into a damnable reality.

CHAPTER 52

GRAZING BIT

COVERING THE THREE MEN with his Tommy with his right hand, Kepler then took everyone by surprise by reaching out and grabbing the woman with his left, taking her in a taut hold. Erik was stunned by the alarming quickness of the Nazi colonel.

"Put down your weapons, or I kill her!" he warned them. "Do it now!"

Wolfgang raised his pistol in defense, but Erik waved him off. "Do as he says, Brother. He isn't bluffing."

"No, I'm not giving up my weapon. He'll just kill us all anyway."

"You let her go, damn you!" roared the old rancher.

Kepler glared flints. "Shut up, all of you! She is my captive and I am leaving with her. If you do exactly as I say and drop your weapons, then you will live. Otherwise, I will kill you all where you sit. Which is it to be?"

Erik looked at his brother.

"I'm not giving up my gun, damnit."

Kepler tightened his grip around the woman's throat. "I'm not going to warn you again. Put down your weapons, or I'll kill her and all of you, too, right here and now!"

Slowly, Erik set down his pistol on the kitchen table. Kepler looked hard at his brother, waiting for him to do the same.

But he wouldn't give up the weapon.

Kepler let loose with a warning shot over their heads then calmly flicked the Thompson to automatic fire. "If I have to tell you again, I'll spray you all with bullets! Put your guns down or you all die!"

"No, I will not," countered Wolfgang, and he pointed his Walther defiantly at Kepler. "I have had enough of taking orders from you, you bastard."

Keeping the Tommy pointed at them, Kepler gripped the rancher's wife in a vise-like head clamp and started backing up in the direction of the hallway that led to the front door.

"Please don't take my wife," pleaded the rancher. "Take me instead."

"You are of no use to me, old man. But your wife can get me through the police checkpoints in that fine truck of yours."

"Without my designated call sign and transmission frequencies, the High Command will never believe you," said Erik. "You need me. In fact, you need me and my brother both. Just give up the woman and we'll go with you. Together, we'll deliver the message to Germany."

"Sorry, but now that I know about Double Cross I don't need anyone but the woman. Now we're going down that hallway. Stay where you are or I'll open up on all of you. Your pistols are no match for my machine gun. I'll split all three of you wide open before a single one of you can get off a shot."

At that, Wolfgang rose defiantly from his chair, keeping his pistol locked onto Kepler in a two-handed hold.

Kepler appeared surprised by the maneuver. "Stay where you are, I'm warning you," he said. "If you come closer, I will shoot."

"No, it is you who should put down your weapon and surrender at once or I'll shoot you."

"Don't fuck with him, Brother. He is the one with the Tommy."

"I don't give a damn. He's not leaving this ranch alive."

His brother's voice was unnaturally calm and quietly commanding, and Erik couldn't help but think, *You don't know who we're dealing with. Kepler is a fanatic and does not care about human life.* And then he was struck with another thought. *I shouldn't have given up my gun. Wolfgang is right; the Nazi bastard will probably just kill us anyway, so I should have held onto it.*

He glanced at his Walther on the table and decided to call Kepler's bluff. In a quick motion, he picked it up, stood up from his chair, and pointed it at Kepler. The Nazi colonel flashed a combination of surprise and anger, but as before with Wolfgang he didn't shoot. Erik had been right: Kepler was bluffing and didn't want to risk getting shot or them accidentally killing the woman and thereby ruining his chances of escape. He knew that having the rancher's wife in the truck with him offered him the best chance at clearing the police checkpoints.

"Put the Tommy down, Colonel, or we will shoot you down like a dog," Erik then said, feeling the adrenaline rush of the moment swirl through his body like a shot of fine Irish whiskey.

"You are brave, but stupid," said Kepler, grinning harshly.

He quickened his backwards pace towards the hallway entrance, and Erik thought to himself, *Damn—only five more feet!*

"Put the gun down, Colonel," said his brother. "You are not going to get out of here. As soon as you turn and make a run for that truck, we're going to open fire on you. You can't drive and shoot at the same time."

Erik moved to his right and took a step closer to Kepler as Wolfgang methodically mirrored his movements on his left, tightening the noose. The room came to a tense standstill as they all stared at one another. The Africa Corps commander looked on with anticipation like everyone else in the room and then took another careful step backwards, gripping the woman tightly.

"Stop right there," ordered Erik. "You're not going to get off this ranch alive so you might as well stand down and drop your weapon."

"No, if he agrees to release my wife, we need to let him go," said the old rancher, who had softened considerably now that Kepler had taken his wife hostage. "Please, Colonel. She has nothing to do with this. Go on and take my truck, but please leave her. I'm begging you—don't take my Margaret."

Kepler shook his head defiantly. "Can't do it, old man. She's coming with me." Keeping his Tommy pointed at his captive's neck, he continued to back towards the hallway entrance.

It was then it happened.

In a sudden pre-meditated movement, the surprisingly agile woman twisted her body, jerked away from Kepler's grip, and darted towards the kitchen stove. Kepler depressed the trigger of the Tommy, letting loose with a spray. A deafening *rat-tat-tat* blast shook the room and was answered by a crackling belch of return fire. The rancher's wife screamed as she saw the bullets tear across her husband's chest, opening him up like a tin of sardines. He fell back is his chair to the floor as bullets nicked and whined all around the kitchen in an ear-splitting roar, showering the combatants with sundry chunks of wood, lathe, and plaster from the walls and ceiling.

Using the kitchen table for protection, Erik ducked down and fired his own weapon. But Kepler had already wheeled to draw a bead on him and his brother. With a maniacal glint in his eyes, the Africa Corps commander swung the Thompson back and forth like a flamethrower, his knuckles white from squeezing the trigger so hard.

The machine gun bucked like a runaway half-track. The simple western landscape painting of a lonesome cowboy on a horse behind them clattered to the floor riddled with bullets.

Erik dove to the floor as a pair of answering shots came from his brother's deep-throated Walther. Kepler fired again, reached out, grabbed the woman, and dashed down the hallway, shooting over his shoulder as he ran.

Erik and Wolfgang didn't dare return fire for fear of hitting the woman. They looked at one another.

"Are you okay, Brother? Were you hit?" asked Erik.

"No, I'm fine. Let's go get him."

"Give me one second. I have to change out my magazine."

"All right, but hurry. We *have* to stop that bastard!"

He bolted from the room, his powerful legs churning like a racehorse. As Erik reloaded, the sound of his brother's choppy footsteps receded down the hallway and faded out for a moment before becoming audible again through the open kitchen window. He quickly surveyed the room. The little country kitchen had turned into a combat zone. The rancher lay in a pool of blood, glossy and deep vermillion against the pine wood floor. Erik felt nauseated. It was unthinkable that such carnage towards an innocent non-combatant could have taken place in the blink of an eye.

With his Walther now reloaded, he started for the hallway. Outside, he now heard an exchange of heavy gunfire followed by the slamming of a car door.

Damn, don't tell me Kepler's going to get away?

He dashed down the hallway, gripping his pistol in his hand. Another thunderous exchange of gunfire rocked his ears followed a moment later by the sound of a firing engine. As he made it to the front door, he heard a great commotion in the direction of the barn: running boots, squealing tires, hot gunfire. He pushed open the door and stepped into the night.

He saw his brother shooting at the tires of the old Ford pickup truck as Kepler struggled to steer the contraption towards the main road with the rancher's wife held captive in the passenger seat next to him. Erik opened fire, too, but the

Ford raced down the dirt road, broke hard to the right, and disappeared into a thick grove of pine trees.

"Damnit, we should have killed that bastard on the river when we had a chance," cursed Wolfgang.

"What's done is done. Somehow we have to find a way to get to the Cheyenne Mountain radio tower before him."

"That's going to take a miracle. We have no transportation."

"We still have to try. There's no guarantee Kepler's going to get through. Unlike us, he has a strong German accent. If questioned at a roadblock, he'll probably be caught even with the rancher's wife helping him. We might have a better chance on foot. One way or another, we have to finish what we started."

"The Cheyenne Mountain radio tower? You really think we can make it?"

"We have no choice. We have to at least try. Besides, even if Kepler does manage to get their first, I don't see how German intelligence would actually believe him without the call sign."

"Unfortunately, traveling might be more difficult than you think, for me at least."

"What are you talking about?" And then he saw.

His brother had turned his body towards the porch light and pulled aside his torn shirt to expose a bullet entry and exit wound through the edge of his ribcage.

"That Nazi son of a bitch got me in the ribs," said Wolfgang with a heavy groan. "I'm not sure I can make it."

"Good lord, and here I thought I was the wounded one. But mine is just a scratch compared to yours. I guess I have no excuse not to try to be the hero now."

"You're right, you don't."

"Here, let's get you inside and bandage you up. Then we'll head out together. If I'm going to die with anyone in a foreign land, I want it to be you. We've got to be able to find an automobile somewhere."

"I am badly hit, *Brüderlein*. I will only slow you down whether we find a car or not."

"I don't care. We need to do this together, and if we are to die, I want to be there with you at the end. You're my brother."

"All right. But I think we have to ask ourselves one thing. Is there any hope left for our Fatherland at all?"

Erik felt his heart sink. Never in his life had he heard his older brother utter such words of defeat. Was this really the Hitler Youth, Democratic Socialist Party member, illustrious U-boat commander—the infamous 'scourge of the North Sea' himself—talking! It made him fear for the long-term survival of his beloved country to hear such resigned, defeated talk coming from his tough-as-nails brother.

It sounded totally alien.

"The war is lost, brother," continued Wolfgang despondently. "I have known this in my heart since we boarded the train in New York for Camp Pershing. We have no chance against these powerful Americans and their even more powerful democracy."

Erik looked at him, still unable to believe that this was his brother talking.

"Damn you, Wolfgang, we can't give up. We are Germany's last hope. We must turn the enemy back into the sea and negotiate for peace from a position of strength. General Rommel and Father believe this is the only way. Regardless of what happens to Kepler, we must broadcast our message to Rommel and the High Command and then all of this madness will have been worth something."

His brother looked at him, lower lip trembling with emotion. For the first time Erik could remember, there were tears in his eyes.

"You are right, *Brüderlein.* We have to finish this."

"Good. Now do you think you can walk, at least until we find a car?"

"Yes, I will find a way. But first let's get some food and medicine from inside. Then we will hit the trail."

Erik smiled. "That's the spirit. Now that's the big brother I remember."

And with that, he helped him hobble back inside the house.

CHAPTER 53

LEFT HAND RANCH

AFTER THEIR LATE DINNER, as they stepped onto the front porch, Katherine heard the voice of Jack Running Wolf rising up into the night along with the gentle beat of a parfleche hand drum. The nasally song drifted up into the sage-scented air and made her feel safe and secure, as if guarded by powerful ancient spirits. She had heard the song many times before—it was the Comanche's favorite—and it always managed to tug at her soul and make her feel a kinship with the past and everything around her in the present. She could see him standing on the hill to the north, a dark silhouette tapping at a hand drum, his trusty rifle slung over his shoulder and just visible against the moonlit backdrop of night sky.

"What is he singing?" asked Colonel Morrison softly, his head cocked in the direction of the hill with the lone Indian.

"It's an old Comanche war song. He's calling out to his animal spirit—the wolf—to give him a brave heart and a steady bow and lance before the enemy."

"It's beautiful."

"Jack told me it was first sung by his people the night before they battled the Cheyenne over a hundred years ago along the Red River. Now he's singing the song for the new enemy."

"The new enemy?"

"Your escaped Germans."

"*My* escaped Germans? Well then, if you're going to put it like that, I'm going to hum along with him, because nobody wants those sons of bitches more than I do. Don't forget, I still have twelve of the bastards out there—and two of them happen to be your sons."

"You still don't trust me, do you? You and J. Edgar Hoover."

"Of course I trust you, or else I wouldn't be here."

"That makes me feel better. Would you like to go for a walk?"

"That's a swell idea. We have to do something to work off that incredible meal Kate cooked for us and all that fine wine we drank."

"Yes, I'm still feeling a little tipsy."

"Good, I might be able to steal a kiss from you."

"Oh, I don't think you'll have to steal it."

She winked at him and they laughed. Then they stepped down from the porch and headed off to the south in the opposite direction from Jack Running Wolf and his lonesome Comanche song.

After a short distance, she felt his hand take hers. The warmth spread over her like a winter hearth.

She found herself wanting to feel it all again, the closeness of a man, the burst of passion, the idle playfulness afterwards. She thought of her late husband John Templeton. Was one year of mourning long enough? How long did she have to wait before she was allowed to spread her wings for another man? When the time came, would she even be able to remember what to do? Ruefully, she thought: best to just let it happen naturally.

They walked on with their arms linked together, the warm fuzzy feeling coming all over her, clouding her brain. But it felt good, just walking like this, arm in arm, content. Up ahead in the cottonwoods, she heard the hoot of a night owl. They stopped for a moment to look up at the North Star, a white, twinkly pinprick against the black, velvety curtain of night sky.

His voice broke through her thoughts. "I probably shouldn't be telling you this, but I may not be around much longer."

"What? You're leaving?"

"Not by choice. Your illustrious hotel guest fired off an angry telegram to Secretary of War Stimson stating that I am an incompetent numbskull. There's talk that I am to be court-marshaled."

She squeezed his hand. "Hoover? Hoover did this to you?"

"The man is a piece of work. You had better watch your back. With one phone call, he could have you on the next ship back to Hamburg—or the main villain in the next military tribunal. Even the president's afraid of him."

"I don't know what to say, Jack, except this is terrible and undeserved. I mean, you and your men have already recaptured all but twelve of the nearly sixty escapees."

"Actually, we've only brought in twenty-five. The rest of the prisoners turned themselves in or were recaptured by the police and FBI. And of the ones recaptured, we still haven't caught the most important ones. There's a lot of pressure coming out of Washington and heads are going to roll on this one. Starting with mine, apparently."

"I'm sorry, Jack, truly I am." She sighed. "I spent all afternoon driving up and down between Cañon City and the Springs, calling out from a megaphone for my sons to surrender themselves. My voice is still hoarse, and Agent Tolliver wants me back at it tomorrow at 6 o'clock sharp. But why the FBI and army think they would be willing to surrender to me when I haven't seen Wolfgang in more than a decade and Erik in more than four years is beyond me."

"You're their mother. The powers that be consider you a magnet."

"I abandoned Wolfgang, and Erik abandoned me. That doesn't make me much of a mother, or the three of us much of a family."

"Maybe one day that will change. We live in tough times, Katherine. We've all been torn inside out by this damned war."

"You can say that again, Jack Morrison," she said, looking into his moonlit eyes. "You can say that again."

CHAPTER 54

LEFT HAND RANCH

HER VOICE was filled with compassion, the gibbous moon lent her face a gentle glow, and suddenly he wanted more than anything else to take her into his arms. But instead, he suppressed his desire, gave her hand a little squeeze, and they continued walking through the tall prairie grass.

When the moment was gone, he wanted to kick himself.

She wanted you to kiss her, goddamnit! She was expecting it, you dumb lug!

They walked up a small hill. When they reached the top, they stared up again at the stars. In the distance, Morrison could still hear the faint singing and drumbeat of Jack Running Wolf. It harkened him back to the days of mounted warriors in bright feathered headdresses and bone breastplates, and vividly painted horses preparing to do battle on the high plains. More importantly, it reminded him of his young glory days fighting as a cavalryman under Black Jack Pershing and chasing Pancho Villa all over Northern Mexico.

"I want to thank you for inviting me here tonight," he said in a whispering voice, still feeling like an idiot for not acting on his opportunity.

"No, I would like to thank you."

Suddenly, she took him off guard by leaning forward and giving him a soft, moist kiss on the cheek.

He smiled like a kid at a ballgame. "Am I dreaming, or did you just kiss me?"

"It was only on the cheek. Here try this."

She kissed him again, this time on the lips. They tasted fresh, like wild cherries. They leaned into one another and kissed again. He felt his head spin in a pleasant way as her bosom pressed against his chest. When they gently pulled away, his body tingled all over.

She smiled up at him mischievously. "You are an intriguing man, Jack Morrison. I wanted to do that the first time I laid eyes on you."

He was at a sudden loss for words. She actually found him attractive? Well, not really…she had said *intriguing*, but that was still good, right?

He let out a little sigh of satisfaction. He couldn't remember any woman ever kissing him like that before, not even his beloved Elizabeth. He felt uncomfortable, yet inside he was soaring with delight. He thought: what a wonderfully brazen woman.

And then he thought of his late wife.

Oh, dear Elizabeth, I am so sorry. I don't know what's come over me.

"What's the matter, General? Cat got your tongue?"

"Why do you sound more and more like Marlene Dietrich now that we've kissed."

"Because when romance hits me, my German accent returns in full force."

"It's like the purr of a cat."

"Should I take that as a compliment?"

"Most definitely, ma'am."

"Remember, its Katherine, not ma'am. I'm not in an old folks' home, not yet anyway."

"You caught me off guard. That first kiss…I didn't expect it."

"I don't see how. That whole time we were walking up the hill, all you were thinking about was how badly you wanted to kiss me. And then, when you didn't, you became angry with yourself."

"Wait a second. How could you have possibly known that?"

"Remember, I'm a spy. It's my job to read people. But I must confess it shouldn't be so easy to take a U.S. colonel off guard."

"Never before have I faced such a daunting adversary. *Wehrmacht* panzer divisions I can handle, but a gorgeous woman with a voice and a figure like Marlene Dietrich…now that's something all my years of combat training never prepared me for."

His remark brought a sardonic parting of her lips. "They say it is a man's world. If that's true, why do men always become weak-kneed and soft-voiced in the presence of a woman?"

"Only some women elicit that response. And you happen to be one of them."

"I will take that with me to my pillow tonight."

She drew close again and kissed him on the lips. He felt his head spinning and himself growing hard and he could have sworn he was ten years younger. He knew in that instant that he had fallen completely head over heels for her.

After a moment, she pulled away and looked him in the eye. "Tomorrow, we are going to catch those sons of mine before Hoover, General Shedd, or the police shoot them down like dogs. I don't know how we're going to do it, but we have to find a way. The longer this thing draws out, the more trigger-happy the authorities are going to get and the more killing there will be. We have to find them first."

"I want them as badly as you do."

"I know you do. I also realize that you were right: I don't want to lose those boys."

"They're not boys anymore."

"They'll always be my boys in my heart. Always."

He said nothing, knew she was telling it straight up. *God what a woman!*

"In just this past year, I've lost a husband and a son. I don't want to lose Erik and Wolfgang again now that they have come back into my life. I didn't realize how much I missed them until I saw them again."

"I told you those maternal instincts would kick in."

"Look, I want them behind barbed wire. I just don't want them to die."

"I know how you feel, and I can't say I blame you. But you're walking a dangerous line here, and you and I both know it."

"That may be, but you have to admit that catching them alive would help you redeem yourself with the provost marshal and allow me to get at least a partially clean slate with Hoover. You do want to save your job, don't you?"

"I don't know. To be honest, I'm not sure I give a damn anymore. But I do know two things for certain."

"And what would those be?"

"I definitely want to catch that bastard Kepler and those two wily sons of yours."

"And the second?"

"I want to be with you."

"Oh Jack, I want to be with you too. Now why don't you just get it over with and kiss me again? I know you're thinking about it."

"You're right, I am," he said, pulling her into his arms. "In fact, I can't get you out of my mind."

DAY 7

MONDAY

JUNE 5, 1944

CHAPTER 55

TWO FEATHERS CREEK, COLORADO

WOLFGANG VON WALBURG cupped his hands into the mountain creek and splashed some water onto his face. He was numb from exhaustion, having struggled to keep up with his brother's furious pace all night long and throughout most of the morning. The icy cold water revived him instantly. For a blissful moment, he forgot about his bullet wounds and blistered feet and instead imagined himself back at the Tiergarten with Erik in the summer of '31. It was three years before Erik and Max would leave for America with their mother, and he and Erik were having fun running through the trees, pretending to be knights in shining armor as they battled with wooden swords and shields painted with the ancient family crest. That was the closest they had ever been, he realized—until now. Somehow, their common goal of saving the Fatherland, being on the run against a common enemy, and their mutual hatred of Kepler had brought them closer together, putting their bitter past behind them.

They were friends and true brothers once again.

Despite their newfound respect and common cause, they had been forced to separate an hour ago. Knowing he was slowing his brother down, he had told Erik to press onward to the Cheyenne Mountain radio tower without him. He would only continue to hold him back. His brother had agreed, so they split up and Erik had quickly pushed ahead without him. Wolfgang was proud of his younger brother for his tenacity, but also his humanity. He knew now why his mother, though she never would have admitted it to him, had always loved Erik the most. Not only was he the most like her, he was a remarkable young man and a true hero of Germany.

He was pulled from his reverie by the sound of voices coming from upstream and across the mountain creek. He looked up to see a pair of boys mounted on horseback. They were perhaps thirteen or fourteen years of age and starting to ford the body of water, which, though only thirty feet across, still roared like a freight train. Compared to the swollen, deadly Arkansas River that he had barely survived yesterday, the creek before him was a mere rivulet. But the water was still running high and fast in early June.

When he spied the two boys, he pulled back into the copse of pine trees so they wouldn't spot him. To his surprise, they cradled rifles in their arms. Maybe they were out hunting rabbits or deer.

As they began traversing the creek, the water rose quickly around their horses' legs, then up to their bellies, and finally up to the stirrups as the water streamed around the little dams formed by the animals' muscular frames. The boys tried to angle their horses slightly upstream to keep in a straight line, but the current was too strong and the horses zigzagged. Every so often, the animals paused to brace their hooves against the sweep of water and pawed ahead to find purchase on the rocky bottom. They stumbled several times, but each time they were able to regain their balance and hold steady in the current.

And then, the roan horse out front froze.

The boy gave the horse a swift kick and worked the reins, but it wouldn't budge. He kicked it again, but to no avail, as the other boy bunched up close behind him.

Wolfgang had a horrible feeling something bad was about to happen.

With eyes wide with terror and nostrils flaring, the lead roan horse reared up out of the water and backed into the other horse, a speckled gray.

"Steady, boy, steady," muttered the boy in the rear to calm the animal down.

But it was too late.

The roan rammed hard into the speckled gray, knocking it backwards, and in the next instant, both terrified animals reared wildly.

Both boys were tossed into the river, their rifles flying into the air like batons and sinking beneath the whitewater surface. The horses splashed towards the bank as the two boys plunged downstream into a swirling vortex of white bubbly foam. They were quickly pulled under in a suck hole before breaking the surface for a moment, only to be dragged under again.

At that moment, a police car and a truck with a horse trailer pulled up along the side of the road. A policeman in a blue uniform and another man emerged from the vehicles. They were a hundred yards upstream and even with the two boys, who had managed to swim out of the suck hole and were now drifting downriver towards Wolfgang.

The policeman and the other man yelled down to the two boys. But the current was swift and the boys couldn't hear them and were already in trouble. Their heads popped up for a second and then went under again, their arms flailing for the surface.

Damnit! What should I do? Should I save them?

He looked upstream at the cop and the other man. They had spotted him and were now scrambling down the talus slope and waving their arms at him to help. If he rescued the boys, he was as good as captured. But if he backtracked upslope, while the policeman and the other man tried to rescue the boys, he could steal the police car, drive to the Cheyenne Mountain radio station, and perhaps save Germany.

He looked back at the boys.

They had managed to push away from a pair of boulders with their feet and were floating downstream again.

The cop and the other man cried at him to help them.

Shit, what should I do? You know the answer, you fool. There is only one choice: to save Ger—

Hell no, I can't do it!

He scrambled down the bank and splashed into the frigid water.

He saw the two boys duck under the surface to avoid a fallen tree limb. But then they were thrown into a clump of boulders. The head of the one out front struck a big block of sandstone and he was sucked beneath the surface. When he resurfaced a moment later, his body had gone slack in the water and the other boy was struggling to catch up to him.

Behind him, Wolfgang heard the shouting of the two men and crash of underbrush. Turning, he saw them charging towards him through the trees. He turned back again and saw the boy's limp body floating face down in the water, the waves tumbling over him as his friend paddled in vain behind him. If he could get out far enough without being bowled over by the current, perhaps he could reach out and grab the two boys and haul them to shore.

He splashed out into the deeper water, holding on to the spindly branch of a fallen cottonwood.

This was it: he had only one chance.

Clutching the branch, he reached out to grab the unconscious boy first. But just as his hand clamped around the boys wrist, he lost his footing and was swept up in the current.

He went under and spun crazily, losing control of the boy. For an instant, he was completely disoriented, unable to tell up from down. He saw gravel bouncing along the bottom and fragments of wood and plants dancing hysterically all around him.

He kicked upward and broke the surface, gasping for air. The boy was just ahead of him. With three powerful strokes, he closed the gap between them and once again took hold of the boy with one hand, while slowing up and reaching out to grab the other boy with his other. With a series of desperate kicks, he was able to make it to less turbulent water. He dragged them both along until finally the current had slackened enough that he could stand up. Touching down on the pebbly bottom, he gave a sigh of relief: the feel of solid ground beneath his feet was reassuring.

He heard a cheer rise up from the bank from the two men.

But as he looked down at the unconscious boy his heart sank. He wasn't breathing!

He hauled him up onto the pebbly bank and, with the help of the other boy, dragged him onto the grass. Rolling him onto his back, he began pushing down on his stomach. No response. He pushed harder. Still nothing. He tried again, and this time the boy shuddered and began coughing up water. A moment later, the boy looked up at him with a mixture of fear and surprise, his eyes big as plums.

Behind him, Wolfgang heard a crashing sound in the brush. He spun around to see the policeman and the other man dashing up. The cop had his gun drawn.

He saw his life flash before his eyes. God Almighty had rewarded him with a rich, full life, albeit a short one, but it was time to surrender before the enemy and face the hangman's noose. After all the killing of the past two days—not only of soldiers, but innocent civilians—surely the Americans would put him to death for his crimes, even if they had been committed while trying to escape.

"Thank you, kind sir. Thank you for saving my boys!" the man in civilian clothes blubbered, taking Wolfgang in a ferocious bear hug, tears of relief pouring from his eyes.

The cop holstered his pistol, smiled like John Wayne himself, and slapped him on the back. “You done good! What’d you say your name was?”

Thinking quickly on his feet, Wolfgang adopted a Texas accent—an exaggerated southern accent being the easiest to master and most convincing as long as you weren’t around a born and bred southerner. “Jasper Rogers is the name. I hail from the Lone Star state.”

“Texas?” said the father of the boys, who, Wolfgang saw now, were twins. “Well, to be honest, we Coloradans ain’t too partial to Texans. But I expect we can make an exception for a genuine hero.”

“I reckon that’ll do just fine,” said Wolfgang, smiling dutifully.

“Boys, what do you say to this here gentleman who saved your bacon?”

“Thank you, sir.”

“Yeah, thanks, mister.”

“I warned them not to go out on their own hunting Krauts—and what the hell do they do? They take my Remington bolt action and my Winchester ’67, saddle the horses, and head on out to kill goddamned Heinies!”

Wolfgang rewarded the boys with a look of approval. “These two young whippersnappers did that? Well, I’ll be damned.”

The man nodded vigorously. “Boys, I’ve got to say I love the enthusiasm, but Kraut-killing is man’s work. You two boys are in a heap of trouble, I’m telling you.”

“I’ll say,” said the policeman. “Where are your weapons, boys?”

They cast a guilty glance at one another. “We lost them in the river.”

“Well, I’m going to have to tan both your hides when we get home,” said their father. “But I am glad to have you both alive.” He pulled them in and gave them a crushing hug. “We best get home to your ma now. She’s been worried sick about you. With these murdering Krauts on the loose, the whole state’s up in arms. You haven’t seen any of them, have you, mister?”

He felt like he was about to faint, but forced himself to remain steady. “As a matter of fact, I have. I came out here on my day off to go fishing, but unfortunately I ran into a pair of those escaped Germans you’re talking about. They beat me up and took my fishing rod, sleeping bag, wallet, everything I own.”

Slowly, the policeman took a step back and drew his pistol. “How do we know you’re not one of those escaped Nazis?”

He did his best to look stunned. “Because you will find that I am employed as a ranch hand at Left Hand Ranch. If you’d be kind enough to take me there, you will receive a handsome reward from the owner. Also, if I was a bloodthirsty Nazi, would I rescue these two fine boys here?”

The cop just looked at him. “Left Hand Ranch, you say?”

“Just a few miles east of Colorado Springs. I promise it will be worth your while.”

The cop hesitated, looked him over, the .45 gripped tightly in his hand.

“He saved my boys, Jackson. No Nazi would do a thing like that. I think he’s telling the truth.”

The cop continued to look him over. “You telling the truth, son?”

“Yes, sir, as the Lord is my witness. Please take me to the ranch. And as I said, you will receive a handsome reward."

Several seconds passed before the policeman gave a little nod and holstered his weapon. "All right, I'll take you there. I don't want any reward money because I'm not allowed to take it. But you damn well better be telling the truth, or I'll shoot you myself. Oh, and also, I'm going to have to handcuff you to the door."

"If it makes you feel safer," said Wolfgang through a neighborly American smile, though he felt like he was about to pass out. "All I want is to go home."

CHAPTER 56

HORSESHOE BUTTE, COLORADO

ERIK stared down at the main dirt road and side road teeing into it from the western flank of a rugged butte whose name he did not know. To his surprise and relief, there were no posted guards or roadblocks of any kind. The trail he had been following northeast for the last two hours, since he had left his brother, was the width of a skinny horse. It zigzagged in a series of switchbacks, cutting through clusters of piñon pine and outcrops of ripple-marked sandstone and porphyritic granite.

He stopped a moment to rest beneath a shady pine tree. A part of him felt as though he had abandoned his brother, but he knew that going their separate ways was the right thing to do. Wolfgang had been struggling to keep up for hours, and Erik had been relieved when his older brother had insisted that he continue on to Cheyenne Mountain without him.

He took a pull from his canteen and rummaged through his shoulder sack for some food. He pulled out a small loaf of bread—the one thing he did not like about America was its thinly sliced, insipid white bread—and a hunk of cheddar cheese and wolfed it down. He finished off the hasty meal with a green apple and another swig from his canteen.

That was when he heard the sound of an automobile engine.

The noise reached up to his ears before he saw any sign of the vehicle. He started down the footpath to listen, keeping his eyes peeled in the direction of the sound, which was growing louder.

Suddenly, it appeared: a tan sheriff's car, rising up over the adjacent hilltop before slinking down into the dusty brown valley like a stalking predator. Then he thought he heard the faint sound of a second vehicle. He fixed his eyes on the road, waiting. Seconds later a hunter-green Plymouth materialized in the distance, coming from the other direction. The sheriff's car drove up and parked in the middle of the main road, leaving only a small lane to pass on the right. A county sheriff in a tan cowboy hat stepped out of the car, grabbed a pair of barricades from the trunk, and set them up along the open lane to form a blockade.

A minute later, the Plymouth pulled up and parked on the side of the road. Two men in dark suits and sunglasses stepped from the vehicle. The sheriff in the cowboy hat stepped over to talk to them. By the way they were dressed Erik knew they had to be FBI agents. They walked with the sheriff to a shady area next to the road, where they all pulled out cigarettes and began smoking and talking.

If I can get the FBI car, I can get to the radio tower in less than an hour. But how can I steal it without getting shot?

While his mind worked through the options, he started down the mountain, hugging closely to the gnarly juniper and piñon along the zigzag trail. When he reached the next switchback, he again came to a halt and peered down at the sheriff and G-Men, still smoking and talking.

To his surprise, he saw a stirring in the trees to the right of the men. A head and upper torso poked through the leaves like a Roman bust. There was someone else watching them, a man by the looks of it, though given the distance and sun in his eyes, Erik couldn't be certain. But who was this individual and why did he appear to be sneaking up on the sheriff and FBI agents?

The foliage shook again and the head disappeared. He felt a sudden frisson of danger, a little warning bell, as he continued down the zigzag trail, trying to steal a closer look. His sixth sense told him something wasn't right.

Why was this man acting so surreptitiously?

He popped the magazine on the Walther PPK his brother had given him and checked it. He only had six rounds left and one spare magazine remaining for a total of thirteen shots. Hardly enough if he got into a heavy gun battle like at the river, but it would have to do.

He hurried down the trail, keeping his eyes on the sheriff and FBI men talking and smoking, as well as the trees beyond where the new interloper had been watching them. He didn't see any movement. He kept walking, keeping himself carefully concealed by the mountain foliage as he strode down the trail.

A pickup truck loaded with hay bales drove in from the west. The sheriff stepped out, halted the truck, and spoke to the driver a moment before checking in the back and then waving the truck on. He then returned to the FBI agents smoking on the side of the road.

Erik headed down the mountain until he came to a fork in the trail. He turned left, following the path that ran along the slope towards the men. The trail was surrounded by drab gray rocks and scrubby brush that allowed him to blend in. He kept a vigilant eye out as he walked, still trying to spy the mysterious man sneaking up on the sheriff and G-Men.

It was then he saw him again, creeping out of the trees.

His eyes bulged with shock: *Kepler!*

He saw at once that he had been hurt yet again for he limped when he walked. But despite his gunshot wounds and limp, he still looked formidable, like some sort of Phoenix arisen from the ashes or Rasputin willing himself to live on and fight another day. But what had happened to the rancher's wife? Even with her providing female cover, Kepler must not have been able to make it through the checkpoints, or for some other reason had been forced to abandon the Ford truck. Had he killed the woman or simply let her go because he no longer needed her? In any event, it no longer mattered: the son of a bitch was right here before his eyes and obviously had not made it to Cheyenne Mountain, which in itself was a miracle. Maybe there was a God after all and he was giving Erik a legitimate chance to save his beloved Germany?

He continued to study Kepler closely. The Africa Corps commander's expression was one of fierce determination as he emerged from the trees and darted behind the Plymouth, his lethal Thompson tight against his hip and ammo-filled pack strapped to his back. *My God, he's still got the Tommy?* The sheriff and two FBI men still hadn't spotted him as one of the G-Men tossed his cigarette butt onto the gravel road and stamped it out with his foot.

At that moment, it dawned on Erik that the elusive Nazi bastard was about to beat him to the punch and steal the car meant for him!

Except Kepler wasn't just going for the car, he realized—the colonel was going to take these men down right now, making sure to leave no witnesses or authorities behind to come after him!

Despite his hurt leg, Kepler crept along the driver's side of the Plymouth at a quick clip, keeping his head below the roof. Then, like a lion, he suddenly leapt out, firing from his hip with the Thompson. Taken completely by surprise, the sheriff and two FBI men convulsed like gangsters in a Hollywood movie as a half-magazine of bullets sprayed into them. Only the sheriff managed to clear his holster, but even he was riddled with three or four rounds before his finger touched the trigger, the shot driving harmlessly into the ground.

The victims fell one, two, three to the dirt road with a heavy, meaty thud.

My God, he's killed them all, Erik thought grimly. Kepler quickly rummaged through the pockets of the G-Men until he found a car key.

It was at that moment he spotted Erik.

The Nazi scowled at him, stood up, and opened fire with his Tommy. Erik ducked behind a large boulder of sandstone and drew his German-made Walther.

"You Prussian bastard!" hissed Kepler from across the dirt road. "I don't know what kind of special luck you have, but I am telling you that it ends right here and now. I am going to finish you off once and for all."

"You can certainly try."

"Where is your brother? Or did he not make it after I shot him?"

"You barely nicked him. In fact, he's sneaking up behind you right now."

"You're a liar."

"How can you be sure? By the way, what happened to the truck and the rancher's wife?"

"That brother of yours got lucky. The gas tank was barely filled to begin with, and he must have punctured the bottom of it when he shot at us. We ran out of gas after only a few miles."

"What about the woman? Did you let her go?"

"What do you think?"

"You bastard."

"Look at the bright side. At least she is reunited with her husband and her sons."

"You're going to burn in hell for your sins, you know."

"No, I shall be talked about for a thousand years for my heroism. That is the definition of a true *Übermensch,* is it not?"

"You think you are a Superman! But you're nothing but a monster—just like Hitler, Göring, and Goebbels!"

"You are a defeatist and an embarrassment to the Reich, and so is your brother!"

"He is twice the man you'll ever be! Goethe would be proud of him, but not a sick fuck like you!"

"You and your brother are disloyal cowards, abominations to the flag you serve under! You swore an oath to our Führer!"

"No, I swore an oath to Germany! Hitler is not my leader! He belongs to fanatics like you!"

"You *schwein*, I have heard enough of your treasonous talk! It is time for you to die!"

In a lightning quick movement, he leapt up from his crouching position and let loose with the Tommy. Erik ducked behind the massive boulder, crab-walked to his right, raised the Walther, and returned fire with a blast of his own that punctured the side of the Plymouth. Kepler moved towards the rear of the car, switched from automatic to single-shot fire, and hurled another round at him, forcing him to again take cover.

Wanting to conserve his ammo, Erik didn't fire back right away. Instead, he waited.

But there was nothing, not even the click of the Tommy or sound of a light footfall on the dirt road.

He quickly surveyed his surroundings, his muscles tense as brick. He couldn't stay here pinned down behind this rock. Though providing protection, it severely limited his mobility. He needed to be able to maneuver into position for a better shot and stay on the offensive. But he also had to be somewhat cautious; after all, Kepler had a machine gun and all Erik had was a pistol with eleven more rounds. He would have to make every bullet count.

Now, finally, he heard noises from his enemy: the click of a fresh box magazine being popped into place followed a few seconds later by the squeak of a car door.

He moved to his left. From his combat training, he knew you were never supposed to look over an obstacle when under attack. You were supposed to remain in a crouched position and look around it, so as to avoid counterfire. Using the rounded edge of the boulder for cover, he popped up like a jack-in-the-box and let loose with a quick shot at his adversary, who had slithered into the driver's seat of the Plymouth. His single shot was met with an automatic blast from the Thompson as Kepler leaned out the open window and let rip, his expression one of fanatical resolve.

Again, Erik ducked down.

Rat-tat-tat. The bullets whizzed past—slamming harmlessly into the cottonwoods, slicing off leaves and limbs—and then a burst ricocheted off the boulder behind him in a high-pitched pinging sound, tearing at him like a swarm of angry Spitfires and echoing off the walls at an earsplitting decibel. He scrambled closer to his right for more protection, but the bullets moved from left to right like a buzz saw and he felt a stinging sensation in his arm.

Verdammt, the bastard's gotten me again!

He fell back heavily and slumped against the sandstone boulder, feeling a rush of warm blood just above the elbow. But he quickly realized that the wound wasn't from a bullet; the ricochet had dislodged a sliver of rock that drove into his arm. He pulled out the angular-shaped slice of feldspar, grimacing in pain as he did so. Luckily, the rock sliver hadn't hit bone, but he was going to bleed, and bleed badly.

Wincing in pain again, he heard the Plymouth fire up.

Shit, he's getting away!

Crawling to his right, he jumped out from behind the boulder and took aim. But his adversary was already gunning the engine and pulling out onto the dirt road. For an instant, their eyes met. Kepler had his left hand on the wheel and his right on the Tommy, the nose of which extended out the window, pointing straight at him. There was a crazy glaze in his eyes like a rabid dog as the submachine gun exploded, spitting bullets like a crackling thunderstorm, blasting Erik's ears with a deafening roar.

Again, he ducked down and returned fire, but both shots missed as Kepler raced down the road. In his last act of defiance, he shot out the right front tire of the sheriff's car, deflating it instantly. Erik watched dejectedly as the Plymouth roared down the main road and disappeared around the bend.

How could I have let him get away?

But then he looked at the sheriff's car. Maybe he could still use it. He ran to the dead lawman. Quickly rummaging through his pockets, he found his set of keys, grabbed the fallen man's hat, sunglasses, Colt pistol, and ammo belt, ran back to the car, and fired the engine.

There was no time to change the tire. He would just have to drive on a mangled rim and hope he could catch Kepler before it was too late.

CHAPTER 57

LEFT HAND RANCH

KATHERINE trudged up the front porch steps, feeling the exhaustion all the way to her bones. Driving around all day with Agent Tolliver to track down her escaped sons, she was sunburnt and covered in dust, grime, and sweat. As she made it to the top stair, Jack and Kate Running Wolf appeared at the doorway.

"Whoa, ma'am, you look like you've been to hell and back," observed Jack, looking her up and down.

"You can say that again," gasped Kate. "What did the FBI do to you, drag you behind a car?" She rushed forward to help her.

Katherine wiped the sweaty dust from her face and took Kate's hand. "I just feel a little faint is all. It was so hot and dusty on those back roads."

Kate helped her into one of the porch rocking chairs. "Where did they take you?"

"All over." She let out a weary sigh as she leaned back in the chair. "We must have covered every back road between Colorado Springs and Royal Gorge. They gave me a megaphone and had me call out in English and German for them to give themselves up."

"You never saw them boys?" queried Jack.

"No. They're probably deep in the mountains by now. What time is it?"

Jack looked at his watch. "A little after four. You've been at it since sunup—no wonder you're exhausted."

"I'll fetch you a lemonade," said Kate, and she went inside.

Jack pulled back one of his deerskin-wrapped plaits and sat down in the rocking chair next to her. "You truly do look like those G-Men dragged you behind a car. Why did they treat you so bad?"

"I think they're mad at me."

"Why should they be mad at you? You didn't do nothing wrong. You're helping them. Hell, you're not just helping them. You're a government agent just like them."

"Yes, but I'm afraid the FBI and army don't consider the OSS a legitimate wartime entity. But more importantly, they're angry about all the killing. They consider my sons not so much wanted prisoners of war but common criminals on the run."

"Yes, ma'am, I see your point. As long as them boys are still out there, they pose a danger."

"It's even worse than that, Jack. What they know could be devastating to our country. That's why a British colonel flew all the way out here to the Rocky

Mountains to find out what Erik and Wolfgang know and to make sure they haven't reported it to the German High Command."

"But it's still not your fault. Them boys haven't been yours for quite some time now. They're Krauts and you're a true red, white, and blue American. You're not as American as me, of course, 'cause I'm Comanche, but you are still Grade A Yankee."

He gave a toothy grin and Katherine chuckled. Two minutes later, she was sipping the lemonade Kate had brought her and watching a black-and-white police car churning up a dust cloud as it swung off the main county road and onto her winding driveway. The vehicle clattered its way up the road, passing a series of adobe outbuildings, granaries, and horse and cattle corrals before coming to a halt out front. A uniformed policeman stepped out and helped a handcuffed man out of the car.

Wolfgang!

She jumped up out of her chair, feeling a powerful wave of motherly relief. But what had happened to her other son?

She moved quickly to the top of the porch steps.

"You Katherine Templeton, the owner of this here ranch?" the policeman called up to her.

"Why, yes I am."

Wolfgang abruptly stepped in front of the policeman. "Hi, ma'am, it's me—Jasper Rogers, your third favorite ranch hand," he said in a Texas twang that was surprisingly authentic sounding. But then she remembered that he and Erik both had been quite accomplished little actors growing up in Berlin, and it didn't seem so remarkable. "It seems I got into a little scrape with those escaped German fellows and the sheriff here was kind enough to drive me home. They took everything: my wallet, fishing rod, sleeping bag, and tent. They held me up at gunpoint."

"Ma'am," interrupted the policeman, taking Wolfgang by the arm. "Is this man telling the truth? Does he work for you?"

She hesitated, looking quickly at Jack and then back at the policeman. "Why he most certainly does, officer. But he is fibbing about one thing."

"And what would that be, ma'am?"

"Jasper Rogers here is actually my *favorite* ranch hand."

"Thank you kindly, ma'am," said Wolfgang, beaming. "I'm right happy to be number one."

The policeman allowed himself a little laugh. "All right, ma'am, with all of these escaped Krauts on the loose, I had to be sure."

"Thank you for bringing him back, officer."

"My pleasure, ma'am."

They exchanged a few more words. Then he withdrew a key, unlocked the handcuffs, set the prisoner loose, and was on his way. When the police car was a third of the way to the main road, she summoned Wolfgang to sit down in the rocking chair next to hers. Jack and Kate Running Wolf stood nearby, eyeing them closely, anxious to hear every word.

CHAPTER 58

LEFT HAND RANCH

SHE LOOKED AT WOLFGANG SHARPLY. His clothes were practically tatters, and he was covered in blood and grime.

"There is only one reason for you to be here," she said tartly, not wanting to show him any sympathy despite his obvious wounds. "And that is to surrender to me."

He nodded solemnly. "Why else do you think I'm here?"

"Where is your brother?"

"I don't know. I was wounded and he went ahead of me."

"Where?"

"I wish I knew."

"I don't believe you. What about Colonel Kepler?"

"He drove off in a truck and left Erik and I behind. We considered it good riddance."

"Damn you and that brother of yours for getting caught up in this murderous rampage. I should have shot you both myself yesterday at the Broadmoor when I had the chance. I had you both in my sights, believe me. It would have been a lot quicker and less painful than what you're going to go through now."

He appeared taken aback by her savage honesty. "You would shoot *your own* sons?"

"You two are no longer my sons. You're brutal, ruthless Nazis." She turned to Jack. "Please fetch some rope so we can tie up the prisoner. And while you're at it, grab my shotgun and get a weapon for yourself. I may just want to get it all over with and shoot him myself. Hoover is going to put him to death anyway. That's what he does with German spies and soldiers that he doesn't much care for."

The Comanche smiled. "Yes, ma'am—with pleasure." And he was off.

She looked back at her son, who had paled slightly. But he was still a portrait of strength and grace: over six feet tall with exquisitely chiseled features, a regal Prussian brow, and blue eyes that glittered like precious gemstones. Even wounded, soaked in blood, and covered in dirty filth he was a supremely handsome devil, the very picture of her first husband in his late twenties.

Damn him!

He smiled thinly. "Seriously mother, I don't think you would kill your own son."

"I wouldn't bet on that if I were you. Not after the death and mayhem you, your brother, and that maniac Kepler have wreaked on innocent people."

"It is war, Mother. Wasn't it your General Sherman who said war is hell?"

"That's not funny. You have killed innocent people."

"I have killed only one man—on the river—and wounded three others and that is because they were shooting at me. I don't want to kill anyone else, and that is precisely why I have turned myself in. I also wanted to see you, as a free man and as your son. You see, I love you mother. I have loved you all these years even as I have hated you. You abandoned me, but I want you to know that I forgive you."

For a moment, she saw him not as a twenty-eight year old prisoner of war, Nazi Party member, and enemy combatant, but her ruddy-cheeked twelve year old son that she had adored. She was gripped with a sudden urge to hug him, realizing how much she had loved him all these years too. A part of her had never given up hope for her oldest son, she realized, despite all her tough talk. But then Jack Running Wolf reappeared with rope, a twelve-gauge shotgun, and a pistol and the reality of their current relationship returned.

"Tie him up, Jack," she commanded as she took a pistol from him. "He may have surrendered, but he is still dangerous."

"My pleasure, ma'am. Do you want me to hog-tie the rascal?"

"No, Jack, just tie his hands in front. With his wounds, that will be enough."

"All right, if you say so, but I still think we should just shoot him. It would save everyone a whole lot of trouble."

As the Comanche stepped towards Wolfgang, her son held out his hands compliantly so they could be bound. Then he turned towards her, his eyes pleading. "What I have done I have done for Germany. I never wanted to kill anyone—and neither did Erik. We only shot men that were trying to kill us. And just so you know, it was Kepler who did most of the shooting *and* killing, and he's the only one who killed civilians."

Katherine could tell his words were genuine, but it was doubtful whether they would ultimately matter given the death toll. "What happens to you will be for a military court to decide. But you should know they'll probably send you to the electric chair. Will you still think all this was worth it then?"

"It was always worth it to try to save Germany from self-destruction. Erik's task was always a noble one. I just didn't see it at first."

She continued to study his face as Jack Running Wolf began tying his hands together. "What is it that you two know? What is so important that you would be willing to die for it?"

"We know the Allies' deepest, most classified military secret. That is why they have sent a British intelligence officer halfway around the world after us. But if I tell you this secret, you will be as much of a threat as us."

"You let me worry about that."

He nodded towards Jack and Kate Running Wolf. "What about them?"

"That's their decision."

"We want to hear," said Jack Running Wolf, after looking at his wife and receiving a little nod.

"Very well," said Wolfgang, and he proceeded to tell them about Henrik Carlsson, Double Cross, and Overlord—the planned attack at the beaches of Normandy and the deception at Pas de Calais, where the German High Command was being misled to believe the principal thrust would take place. At first, it seemed too extraordinary to believe—how could her own son possibly sneak into Britain and learn such critical and carefully guarded secrets?—but the more she listened, the more she realized how much it all made sense. After all, once you had top-level security clearance and virtually unlimited access to both military and non-military installations, you could gather, synthesize, and analyze all kinds of important data into a meaningful picture. She saw at once how all that was needed to expose the Allies' plans and bring the whole house of cards down was one resourceful, motivated, and plucky spy with access to a handful of classified secrets.

That someone was her son Erik von Walburg.

Damnit, she thought, *I have to find him.*

"Where is your brother?" she demanded.

"I told you I don't know."

She slapped him across the face. "Don't lie to me. Where the hell is your brother?"

He looked at her with a mixture of stubborn pride, hatred, and hurt in his eyes. But still, he said nothing.

She slapped him again, harder this time. "I said where is your damned brother?"

"I don't know, but I do know where he is heading. The only problem is he has very little chance at success. Kepler has most likely beaten him to the punch."

"Are they headed for Cheyenne Mountain? Is that where they're going to try and make their radio transmission?"

He said nothing. She slapped him again, this time so hard that it jerked his head to the left.

"You start talking or I'm going to have Jack here shoot off your goddamned foot!"

She motioned to the Comanche, who looked more than willing to perform the feat. He cocked his twelve-gauge and pointed it at Wolfgang, who stared warily down the steel barrel. Katherine saw a bead of sweat bead his brow.

"Just his left foot, Jack. That way we still have his right foot as a bargaining chip if he doesn't talk."

The Comanche grinned obligingly and pointed the shotgun at her son's left foot.

"You wouldn't really have him do such a thing? I am your own son."

"No, you are the enemy. Let him have it, Jack."

"Wait, wait!" cried Wolfgang, seeing that she wasn't bluffing. "I'll tell you what you want to know, but I must warn you that you're probably already too late."

"Start talking then. Make it quick."

"All right, all right, just don't shoot. When last I saw Erik and Kepler, each was headed separately for the Cheyenne Mountain radio tower. Kepler in a truck he stole from a rancher and Erik on foot. From Cheyenne Mountain, they can broadcast all the way to Berlin the intelligence which Erik has in his possession and which, unfortunately, Kepler now knows. Since Kepler got hold of a truck, he is the favorite to get there first. But perhaps he has been caught by the police and Erik will be the one to get there and make the broadcast. I don't know. All I know is that is where they were both headed last time I saw them."

"My God, we've got to stop them." She looked at Jack Running Wolf. "Keep covering him with that shotgun. I've got to make a call."

She ran into the house, went to the phone, and dialed a number. Moments later, she was connected with Colonel Morrison.

"Jack, it's me. I need your help."

"Katherine? What is it? What's going on?"

She quickly explained the situation. "We need to get to that radio tower and stop them," she said once she had told him everything.

"Listen to me, Katherine. I want to help, honestly I do. But I've been relieved of my command. I just found a few minutes ago. I have been taken off active duty, perhaps permanently, pending the results of a court-martial investigation."

"But, Jack, I've got to have your help! The only way my sons don't see the electric chair is if we can stop Erik and Kepler!"

"Those boys of yours are probably going to see the chair no matter what we do. Do you know how many people have been killed?"

"Damnit, Jack, they're my sons! If I don't protect them, who will? Just come with me please. You already have Wolfgang because I'm handing him over to you, but now you have a chance to capture Erik and Kepler. They certainly can't relieve you of command if you capture all three of them. They'll have to give you a medal, and you can make sure Erik and Wolfgang don't see the chair. Please you have to do this for me! They're all I've got left!"

She tried to hold back the tears, but there was no way to stop them and she began to sob. Suddenly, she wanted more than anything else to have her sons back in her life, if not now then at least when this terrible, terrible war was over. The phone went silent on the other end. All she could hear was the light sound of his breathing as she struggled in vain to choke back the tears. Nothing in life to this point had prepared her to deal with the powerful, conflicted emotions she felt inside. And then, the words she wanted desperately to hear came through over the telephone line, as if by magic.

"All right, I'll be there in twenty minutes."

"Thank you, Jack. You won't regret this!"

She quickly hung up and dialed another number. After being routed from a secretary and receptionist, she heard the voice she wanted to hear.

"Frederick, it's Katherine!"

"Katherine, what on earth is going on?"

"I need you to meet us at the Broadmoor in one hour. And bring our mutual friends Mr. Gardner and Mr. Jamison!"

"What's going on? What are you up to?"

"Frederick, as my lawyer, you're just going to have to trust me. Right now, I need you to not ask questions and get in touch with Mr. Gardner and Mr. Jamison. Then pick them up, drive them to the Broadmoor, and wait for me in the lobby!"

"Gardner and Jamison? What is going on, Katherine?

"You've got to trust me, Frederick! Meet me at the Broadmoor in one hour!"

"But Katherine—"
"Just be there!" she cried, and she slammed down the phone.
There was only one thing left to do: she had to call Wild Bill Donovan.

CHAPTER 59

CHEYENNE MOUNTAIN

FEELING A THROBBING ANTICIPATION, Erik studied the lines of fire and points of ingress and egress at the radio tower building on top of Cheyenne Mountain. There was no sign yet of Kepler; the only personnel were a pair of second-rate U.S. Army sentries. Gangly and pimple-faced, they couldn't have been a day over twenty, and they moved about the adobe structure in bored, mechanical motions. If they had been front-line caliber troops, they would have been sent to Italy to take Rome or to England for the planned invasion of Western Europe, instead of being posted on guard duty at this western backwater.

There were two cars in the parking lot along with the guards' lone military jeep, suggesting that at least two radio broadcasters were inside performing their routine job, in addition to the two posted sentries. He would have no trouble with the broadcasters; they would surrender instantly. It was the two sentries that he had to worry about, though they seemed about as threatening as a pair of St. Bernard's.

But could he get past them without being seen? Even as ill-trained and unsuspecting as they were, that prospect seemed unlikely. Somehow, he would have to subdue them.

Since his arrival, they had mostly been smoking cigarettes, jabbering, and horsing around, but for the past five minutes, they had stopped fooling around and were pacing back and forth in front of the radio control building, automatic rifles slung languidly over their shoulders. One of them was whistling some ditty to himself that he had probably picked up from the radio, while the other hobbled along with a gimpy club foot and every so often picked his nose. Erik knew they would pay dearly for their inexperience and carelessness; however, he had not anticipated that it would come about so quickly as the bushes quietly parted and a face appeared like some sort of ghostly apparition.

It was the elusive Colonel Kepler, once again like a Phoenix arisen from the ashes, and his sudden, terrifying appearance took Erik's breath away. Somehow the Africa Corps commander must have taken a detour or been detained en route to the radio tower, and Erik realized that he was lucky to have preceded him here. But it was more than that: it was his destiny to stop this madman and make the broadcast himself. Erik could feel it deep down to his marrow: this was *his* moment, *his* destiny, and nothing was going to stop him. Though wounded, Kepler still moved with his usual cat-like quickness and sense of military precision. And he still had the Tommy strapped across his shoulder and his ammo-filled pack. But right now he didn't need the submachine gun as he closed in on the unsuspecting sentry to the left with a large, serrated knife.

It was over before Erik could count to three. The left hand moved from left to right across the throat, severing the carotid artery and sending up a feathery spume of blood that sprayed a nearby pine tree. The young man made a revolting gurgling sound and clutched helplessly at his throat as Kepler pitched him into the bushes like a discarded animal carcass.

Erik was stunned.

Kepler was a true killing machine, the perfect Aryan warrior: no doubt, no guilt, no emotion. With trepidation, he suddenly realized that he was no match for the Nazi if it came to a hand-to-hand fight.

The man truly was an *Übermensch.*

Feeling a mixture of fear and dread, Erik moved forward quickly around a thick-trunked ponderosa pine and tucked himself behind a boulder. He was now only fifty feet from the other guard, who was pacing on the west side of the building near the parking lot.

Like a predatory cat, Kepler navigated around the north side of the building and slinked in silently for his second kill.

But the second guard had sensed that something wasn't right. He stopped pacing, took his rifle in both hands, and assumed a defensive crouching position.

Kepler came in from the American's left, this time with a small arm's pistol instead of his knife or Tommy. The first gunshot struck the victim in the neck. The guard staggered back and instantly dropped his weapon. Without breaking stride, Kepler fired again and then a third time. The back of the guard's head separated from his body as the pair of shots bored through his brain and blew out the rear of his cranium in a misty spray of brain matter, bone, and crimson blood. He collapsed on the pavement in front of the radio tower with a dull thud—dead before he hit the ground.

Again, Erik was stunned at the swiftness of the violence.

He felt a mixture of shock, awe, and animal fear: the lightning quickness and sheer savagery of Colonel Franz Kepler was truly astounding.

And then, the killer turned the corner and disappeared, ghostlike, into the radio building.

Erik knew then what he had to do: somehow he had to find a way to kill the *Übermensch.*

But it was not going to be easy.

CHAPTER 60

COLORADO SPRINGS

"I HAVE JUST HANDED YOU the biggest scoop since Pearl Harbor, and all I want in return is your word that you will honor the truth and not be bullied by the powers-that-be into creating a false history. The question is, Jason, are you up to it?"

Katherine Templeton's fierce gaze was directed at the man sitting in the middle of the backseat of her spacious Duesenberg SJ—Jason Gardner, chairman, publisher, and chief editor of the *Colorado Springs Gazette*. To his left sat her attorney, Frederick Barstow III, and to his right was Gazette photographer Henry Jamison, who had done several impressive promotional shoots at the Broadmoor for the newspaper. Jack Running Wolf was driving the sleek, luxurious, 320-horsepower vehicle, his face a study in focused intensity as he negotiated a tight turn, leaving behind the picturesque Broadmoor Zoo in their wake. They were following behind Colonel Morrison in his U.S. Army jeep, which also bore her son Wolfgang, manacled and already interrogated, and two of Morrison's officers. Massive Cheyenne Mountain loomed above to the west, its piney forest casting late afternoon shadows all across its crystalline-granite face.

"Well, Jason?" She raised a stern eyebrow as she saw that the *Gazette* publisher was wavering. "Do you think you can do it? I need you to promise me."

"I already said I would."

"No, you are going to officially promise me and then I am going to hold you to it. My lawyer, Mr. Barstow here, is my witness. There is too much at stake and threats to national security tend to be grossly exaggerated during times like these. I need to know that I can count on your discretion in this sensitive matter and that you will uphold the truth even when your back is against the wall. And your back will be against the wall, Jason, I can assure you."

"Katherine, you know damn well you can count on me. You've only told me what General Donovan has authorized you to tell me, so I don't understand the big deal. You let me and my in-house counsel worry about the *powers-that-be*."

"I am not talking about that, Jason. I am talking about the fact that my two sons are not ruthless murderers—they are German soldiers and escaped POWs protected under the Geneva Convention."

"But they've killed people, Katherine. The death toll is over twelve now, I'm told."

"I know it's a bad situation. But according to my son Wolfgang, it was Kepler who did most of the killing. And let's not lose sight of the fact that Erik and Wolfgang are soldiers fighting against other soldiers and police that have been shooting at them and trying to capture them. They are not outlaws. In fact, what makes them the most dangerous is the fact that they know the Allied plans for the invasion of Europe and have severely compromised the British security network."

"I understand the situation, Katherine. Wolfgang has surrendered himself voluntarily and told Colonel Morrison everything he knows, and Erik is still at large and believed to be trying to get to the Cheyenne Mountain radio tower along with this Colonel Kepler to broadcast to the OKW. I know you can't tell me any more than that except that it is *absolutely vital* to the war effort that Erik and Kepler be stopped. And I also know that you can count on me to uphold the truth in this matter and not go off on some sensationalist Hun-bashing rant like every other newspaper in the country."

"That's right, Jason. That's not the story here. The story is about catching three German officers before they can alert the Reich and drive the Allies back into the sea, thereby forcing a settlement or dragging the war out for another five years. It is also about making sure they are treated like prisoners of war in accordance with the Geneva Convention. German soldiers are under orders from Hitler to try and escape and cause havoc—and our troops held captive in POW camps overseas are under the same orders from their commander-in-chief."

"This is a once in a lifetime opportunity for you Jason," said her lawyer Barstow, "and you can't blow it. This is not going to turn into another Operation Pastorius, where the rights of the accused are cast aside by that pompous, headline-seeking ass J. Edgar Hoover. In this case, the rule of law will be obeyed. Even prisoners of war have rights. All Mrs. Templeton wants is fair play for her sons and for you not to disclose that she is an OSS officer, unless of course, we ask you to disclose it."

"I understand your position and intend to uphold my end of the bargain." He turned back to Katherine, seated in the front passenger seat. "For the last time, I give you my word as a publisher, close friend, and gentleman that I will report the facts of the case fairly and honestly. Now please tell me that satisfies you."

They held each other's gaze for a long, tense moment.

"Very well, Jason, I am satisfied." She felt a sense of relief as the Duesenberg took a tight turn and started up the Russell Tutt Scenic Highway, a zigzagging road carved into the mountain. The highway had originally been named the "Wonder Road" because of its breathtaking views of the Rockies and the glorious vistas of the Broadmoor Hotel and city of Colorado Springs below.

"So is the plan to capture your son Erik and Kepler at the radio tower?"

"We don't know if either Erik or Kepler will be there. But if they are, Colonel Morrison intends to take them into custody. If neither of them is there, you and Mr. Jamison will take my son Wolfgang's testimonial, while Mr. Jamison captures it all on film in the presence of my lawyer. We need to properly document the truth before General Shedd and the cavalry arrive."

"So you're sure the General's going to be there?"

"He's not the only one. Colonel MacGregor of British Intelligence has been contacted as well."

"What about the FBI? Have they been notified?"

"No, I am happy to say they haven't been invited to our little shindig. You see, General Donovan and Director Hoover don't like each other very much. In fact, if you gave them half a chance, they would probably rip each other's throats out."

CHAPTER 61

CHEYENNE MOUNTAIN

AT THE SOUND OF THE FIRST GUNSHOT, Erik dashed for the front door of the radio transmitter building, Walther PPK in hand. He almost didn't care about making his own broadcast; his primary goal, the thing that he most desperately wanted, was to kill Kepler. He would love to strangle him with his bare hands and watch the panic fill his eyes, up close, as the murderous Nazi knew he was about to die.

He reached for the door handle and tried to turn it, but it was locked.

Damnit!

He shot off the lock with his pistol, jerked open the door, charged into the control room, and nearly tripped over a dead radio operator with a pool of blood seeping from the exit wound in his head. Kepler abruptly turned away from a second operator wearing a radio headset that he had been giving instructions to and pointed his Thompson at Erik.

But the Tommy didn't fire.

Erik looked at Kepler, wondering why, improbably, he had been spared from a barrage of lethal bullets. Then he realized that the machine gun had jammed.

He raised his pistol to fire.

But Kepler was quick.

He lunged forward and swung the Tommy at him like an American baseball bat. Erik tried to crack off a shot, but as he squeezed the trigger, Kepler managed to knock his arm to the side and the shot drove into the radio operator, who toppled from his seat at the control panel to the floor like a slab of beef.

Kepler swung at him again with the machine gun. This time, Erik took a fierce blow to his ribs and grimaced in agony. Fearing for his life, he again tried to raise his pistol to fire, but Kepler swung the Tommy in a tight arc, knocking the Walther from his hand to the floor.

Now, he was alone against the *Übermensch* as well as weaponless.

He lowered his shoulder and charged into him, letting loose with a battle cry as he exploded into his midsection like a rugby player. He knocked him to the floor and, as Kepler fell back, he somehow managed to jerk the Thompson from his grip.

Kepler pulled his pistol from his waistband, but Erik knocked it from his grasp with the Tommy. But again the colonel recovered quickly. He withdrew the serrated knife that Erik had seen him use outside to dispatch the guard. Erik swung the Tommy at him, but Kepler parried the blow with the giant knife. He then followed up with a deadly thrust of his own, the razor-sharp knife glinting in the overhead artificial light like a hideously crafted jewel, his face twisted into a terrifying grimace.

Erik knocked aside the knife thrust and swung at his adversary's face with the Tommy, missed, and drove aside another thrust before taking a short, quick slash to his upper arm and another across his chest.

He grimaced in agony, felt his arm go numb.

Sensing victory, Kepler began slashing the knife with renewed vigor. On the defensive, Erik dodged and leapt back with each swing of the glittering blade, struggling to deflect the blows using the steel alloy barrel of the submachine gun. The Nazi came at him like an enraged bear. Erik knew he wouldn't be able to match his hulking adversary for long at this furious pace, not when he had sustained multiple wounds over the past two days as well as two new fresh ones. His only chance was to find a quick opening and deliver a crippling blow.

Somehow, he had to turn Kepler's primary strength, his aggressiveness, against him and thereby make it a weakness.

He raised the Tommy high, deliberately leaving himself open to a stab, and, when Kepler predictably stepped forward to run him through, Erik stepped to the side and brought the machine gun crashing down on Kepler's left hand. The colonel gave a primal scream. For an instant, Erik thought he had crippled him. But all he appeared to have done was drive Kepler's hand inward so that the blade penetrated his other hand, cutting away a slice of his right thumb.

The colonel was maimed but not neutralized.

Erik lunged at him and drove him into the wall, jamming the stock of the Tommy gun into his throat, bringing the weight of his whole body down on top of him while holding his head up and away, as he had been taught during his spy training at Agent School West at *Park Zorgvliet*. He didn't want to shoot Kepler or cut him with a knife: he wanted to choke the life out of him, slowly, deliberately, so his last moment on earth would be not so much painful as filled with pure terror. He wanted Kepler to die knowing that he had not accomplished his goal of changing the course of Germany history, that murderous Nazi thugs did not deserve to be the ones to rise up to help the Fatherland. The future of Germany had to be about something more than the Franz Keplers of the world. The trail of bloodshed and mayhem that he had wreaked across Colorado had come back full circle to snuff out his meaningless Nazi life.

He pressed the stock down hard on Kepler's Adam's Apple, saw his eyes bulging with panic.

All he wanted was to kill!

He could feel Kepler flailing beneath him in a final death struggle, hands clawing like the eagle's talons of the *Parteiadler* of the Third Reich, legs kicking frantically. He embraced the hate raging inside him; he would have his vengeance right here and now. It made him feel good inside, deliciously good, to see the life slowly draining from the Nazi maniac who had taken the lives of so many innocent people, this Hitler in miniature.

And then, from out of nowhere, he felt a sharp blow to the back of his head.

He felt suddenly light-headed and disoriented. The Tommy gun slipped from his hands and clattered to the floor. He looked groggily at Kepler and saw that he had managed to grab some blunt object, a paperweight, he realized. He tried to move, but his body didn't seem to work, and the world turned fuzzy.

Damn, I have failed. Now he is going to kill me.

Kepler pushed him away, kicked aside the Tommy gun, climbed to his feet, and greedily sucked in air. His face had a purplish hue from being nearly choked to death, and blood gushed from his smashed nose, but he was very much alive and clearly poised to seek vengeance.

Still only half-conscious, Erik cursed his misfortune.

The tide had turned and now it was his turn to die.

Kepler picked up his Walther PPK and calmly pointed the pistol at him, poised to deliver the *coup de grâce*.

CHAPTER 62

CHEYENNE MOUNTAIN

ERIK LOOKED UP at him through a hazy world of pain. Slowly, the feeling returned to his arms and legs and his brain seemed to be working properly. All the same, he was powerless to stop Kepler from killing him and wasn't sure if he even wanted to resist. What was the point when his beloved Germany would be bombed, plundered, carved up, and sent back to the Stone Age once the Allies secured a beachhead at Normandy?

"You are no German soldier, *der Schwächling*," snarled his hated adversary in his native tongue—*auf Deutsch*. He cocked the pistol, his eyes aflame with the craze of a true zealot. "It is traitorous cowards like you who will cost us this war. And for that unpardonable sin, you must die a violent death."

Erik glanced around the radio room. What a tragic place to take one's final breath. The two dead bodies lying in awkward, bloody repose on the floor, when taken in along with the monster standing above him with the pistol, served to reinforce the idea that this was his Waterloo—his final tragic battlefield.

The war—and his own death—had come all the way to America.

And then, Kepler did a shocking, unexpected thing. While keeping the pistol trained on Erik, he sat down in the radio operator's chair, donned a pair of headphones, and began casually fiddling with the radio control frequency knobs.

Wait, he wasn't actually going to—

"I know what you're thinking, *der Schwächling,*" pronounced Kepler in a cool, ascetic voice. "I should attack while he is distracted with his broadcast. Won't that give me a chance to live? The answer is a resounding no. I will shoot you down like a dog before you close within five feet of me because I am a crack shot and can easily juggle several tasks at one time. You know why that is, *der Schwächling*? It is because I am a true *Übermensch*. The world will always belong to me and men like me. We are the Aryan ideal—the true embodiment of *Superman*—not this foolish American creation in tights who leaps from tall buildings and flies faster than a locomotive."

"You've gone stark raving mad. With men like you in charge, the war truly is lost."

"No, we are preparing for the final victory," he said, adjusting a control knob and pulling the microphone towards him. "What I am about to do will ensure immortality for me and the triumph of the Thousand Year Reich."

"With men like you, there is no hope for Germany. Everything is lost—even an honorable peace."

"Shut up, *der Schwächling*. Shut up and listen to the sound of history being made. Then afterwards I will gladly kill you."

"You are a curse and abomination to the Fatherland."

"No, I am the future of Germany."

He made one final adjustment to the frequency setting. Then he cleared his throat and launched into his speech.

"Greetings, *mein Führer*. Greetings to you and all of our brave German comrades fighting on behalf of the Fatherland. This is Colonel Franz Kepler, commander of the 21st Panzer Division, Africa Corps. I am calling out to you, my beloved Führer, to the German High Command, and, indeed, to all the world to tell you about the American and British plans for the Allied invasion of France at Normandy and the top-secret inner workings of the British Double Cross spy system…."

As Kepler launched into his speech, Erik remembered back to their first confrontation back in Tunis, to all the unnecessary killing the man had done here in America, and knew he could not let it end like this.

He would rather die than let it end like this.

Though still groggy, he slowly forced himself to his feet. Kepler smiled wolfishly, daring him to make a move, and continued speaking into the microphone with the pistol pointed at his chest as if nothing unusual was happening, his stentorian voice carrying over an entire ocean all the way to the Reich Chancellery at 77 Wilhelmstrasse in Berlin. The broadcast no longer meant anything to Erik; all he wanted was to kill Kepler, to kill the monster that his beloved Germany had become, in effect to kill the Führer who had led his country to total destruction. He realized that alerting the High Command would amount to nothing: the war was lost and Germany would be annihilated—and deservedly so. He had deluded himself into thinking that he could make a difference by securing an honorable peace and sparing his beloved Germany from total destruction.

Now what was there to live for?

Nothing, he decided. All he cared about was destroying Kepler.

He looked at the object of his fury. He had no weapon except his bare hands, and once again, he envisioned himself choking the life out of the Nazi. Kepler's smile widened and his eyes lit up with challenge as he spoke dramatically into the microphone, triumphantly reciting the planned order of battle for the main invasion at Normandy, which was not to be followed by secondary attacks at the Pas de Calais or Norway but rather in Vichy-held Southern France later in the summer. The moment seemed to last forever, like a breath taken and held. Erik quickly scanned the room for a weapon—something, anything to kill Kepler with—but the only thing nearby was the bloody paperweight on the floor. And it was more than five feet away.

He looked back at his adversary, his mind racing.

"You are finished and so is Germany! You both deserve to die!"

Kepler's finger clasped around the trigger and a crazy gleam filled his eyes. "No, it is you who are finished, *der Schwächling*! You are nothing but an American weakling!"

Then he pulled the trigger.

CHAPTER 63

CHEYENNE MOUNTAIN

"MY GOD, HE JUST SHOT HIM!" exclaimed Lieutenant Colonel Tam MacGregor as his body slammed against the rear side door of the army jeep. Once again, the driver jerked the hand-throttle and the vehicle lurched forward like a racehorse, slipping on the gravel with a perilous hundred-foot drop-off below on their right. They were blasting up "Wonder Road" that led to the top of Cheyenne Mountain, and Kepler's half-crazed voice came over the car radio like Adolf Hitler at Nuremberg. Tam could already picture the mass slaughter as the Allied troops disembarked from their Higgins boats at Normandy, where disastrously, the Germans now knew the primary attack would take place.

They had to get to the top of the mountain and stop him!

"Goddamnit, Sergeant, can't you get this contraption to go any faster!" snapped General Shedd, a soggy cigar protruding from his mouth.

"I can sure as hell try, sir!" The driver downshifted again, slapped his boot down on the accelerator. The engine screamed as they stormed up the zigzagging mountainside highway.

"I'm going to try and get Colonel Morrison on the radio again!" cried Tam over the roaring engine. "He may not be picking up the broadcast and could be walking into an ambush!"

"Yes, you do that, Colonel! You tell him that I want that Kraut bastard in our custody in the next five minutes, goddamnit! But he is not to be shot, is that understood? Your bosses at MI5 and my intelligence cohorts at G-2 both want him alive! They need him to make a follow-up broadcast to take back everything he's saying right now!"

"Yes, General, I am well aware of our orders!" said Tam, holding on for dear life. He found the man a blood-and-guts prima donna, as so many of the American generals seemed to be. But then again so was Monty, and the war-hardened British people worshiped him more than even Churchill himself.

He quickly radioed Morrison. "Colonel, it's MacGregor here again. Are you hearing this?"

A hiss and crackle followed by Morrison's voice. "Hearing what?"

"On the radio, man—tune to 850! Kepler's taken over the control room and is broadcasting all the way to Berlin! The bloody bastard is this very moment deciding the outcome of the war and must be stopped! Where are you?"

"We're almost to the top!"

The jeep teetered on the next turn and Tam was nearly thrown from the vehicle. He fumbled the radio phone onto the floor of the jeep as he was forced to grip the handgrip with both hands.

"Colonel MacGregor, are you there?"

He picked up the radio phone. "We had a bit of excitement back there, but it's under control now! Now about Kepler, he's armed and dangerous! He just shot Erik von Walburg!"

"What?"

"Shockingly, he stopped broadcasting just long enough to shoot the man. No doubt Walburg's dead. Colonel, you must stop Kepler, but he needs to be taken alive!"

"Alive? Why?"

"We are going to need him to make a follow-up broadcast refuting his claims of Normandy as the primary attack site and saying it is Pas de Calais!"

"Here, give me that goddamned thing!" blustered Shedd, and he snatched the handheld radio from Tam and hollered into the mouthpiece while chomping his soggy cigar.

"Colonel, I am giving you a direct order! You are to take that radio control room by force, terminate the broadcast, and take Kepler and Walburg, if he is still alive, prisoner. Do you understand me, Colonel!"

"It's going to be hard to take Kepler alive."

"I am giving you a direct fucking order, Jack! I want Kepler alive! G-2 and British Intelligence need him alive, I repeat alive! Do you copy?"

"Yes, sir, I copy loud and clear! I'm just telling you it won't be easy!"

"Nothing in war is, Colonel. Now if you do this right, I may just get you your goddamned job back! What do you say?"

"With all due respect, General, you can take my crappy job baby-sitting Nazis and shove it up your ass! All I care about is getting my hands on that son of a bitch Kepler!"

"Well then, get after it, Colonel! That's the goddamned spirit! And remember, I want that Nazi son of a bitch alive!"

As the general signed off and handed the radio back to him, Tam peered down the mountain and saw a car three switchbacks below, following them up the zigzag road. He pointed down at the vehicle, which, as it came into better view, he realized was a German-manufactured Mercedes-Benz 770 W150. The massive, eight-cylinder, 7,655-cc-engine luxury car was favored by upper echelon members of the *Oberkommando der Wehrmacht* as well as high-ranking Nazi Party officials, including Hitler himself.

Who in the hell could that be?

Shedd quickly echoed his thoughts. "Goddamnit, who the fuck is that coming up behind us?" he thundered over the roar of the jeep's engine.

"I'm not sure, General," said Tam. "But it looks like we may have more bloody Nazis on our hands."

CHAPTER 64

CHEYENNE MOUNTAIN

AS THE DUESENBERG SJ squealed out of the final turn, Katherine gazed up at the massive radio transmitter cresting the North Peak of Cheyenne Mountain. Though she had observed the radio tower countless times before—in fact, she saw it whenever she was in town at the Broadmoor—somehow it looked more dangerous and menacing today, especially viewed up close. After all, it was no longer just a radio tower, but rather, if Erik succeeded in his mission, the means by which the Thousand Year Reich might become a horrifying reality.

She wondered if her son or Kepler were here. There were two civilian cars and a jeep parked out front, and another car with a flat tire and badly damaged rim that had been abandoned on the steep incline two-thirds of the way up the mountain. But there was no sign of either Erik or Kepler.

Jumping out of his jeep just ahead of her, Morrison stepped quickly to her car window, an urgent expression on his sun-burnished face.

"Kepler's in there," he declared. "He's in there broadcasting right now and we're going in after him."

"There's no sign of Erik?"

"He's in there too, Katherine, but he's been shot. We're going to go in and help him."

Looking towards the bushes, she saw a pair of army boots sticking out. She started to push open the passenger door, but he shoved it closed.

"No way, Katherine—you're not going in there. You let me and my men handle this! You have done enough."

"Done enough?"

"The record clearly shows that you've done all you could to stop all this. And that goes for your sons Wolfgang and Erik too. Kepler wouldn't have shot Erik if he hadn't been trying to stop him."

"I don't care about me! My son is wounded and I must—"

"No, that's out of the question! Now, stay in the car and wait for General Shedd and Colonel MacGregor. They're right behind us!"

"Shit, there he is!" cried Jack Running Wolf from the driver's seat.

Morrison spun around. "General Shedd? He's here already?"

Katherine pointed towards the radio building. "No, he's talking about Kepler!"

Morrison spun around again. Seeing the Africa Corps commander in the flesh, he instantly tugged at the Colt .45 semiautomatic service pistol in his holster. Now that he was distracted, Katherine shoved open the door and scrambled out of the Duesenberg.

Clutching a pistol in his left hand and wearing a heavy U.S. military overcoat, Kepler stepped calmly down the walkway towards the parking lot, a triumphant expression on his classically Aryan face. Slowly, the others stepped from the car, keeping their eyes fixed on the terrifying Africa Corps colonel, who held a pistol to his temple as if about to take his own life. Meanwhile, *Colorado Springs Gazette* photographer Henry Jamison began surreptitiously filming with his 8-mm camera.

At the end of the walkway, Kepler stopped and stood next to a ponderosa pine tree. "You are too late for the show, ladies and gentlemen," he said as if he was P.T. Barnum and they had just missed the circus. "I have made my broadcast to the German High Command—indeed to all the world—and my Führer, the world's only true supreme commander, knows that your great attack on Fortress Europe will be at Normandy and not the Pas de Calais. With that knowledge, we shall drive your invasion force back into the sea and never allow the Allies to establish a beachhead."

"Put down the gun, Colonel!" snapped Morrison, who Katherine saw had moved to the right and trained his pistol on Kepler's chest. "Do it now!"

The German gave a knowing, self-congratulatory smile, keeping the pistol pointed at his temple. "Stand back, or I will shoot myself."

"I said put the gun down or I will fire!"

"No, you won't. You are under strict orders to take me alive."

Katherine looked at Morrison, who was doing his best to remain poker-faced, but his expression still betrayed him.

"I knew it. How else would you be able to undo the damage if you don't have me broadcast a new message denying the validity of the original? But you will never take me alive. When your invasion force is repulsed at the beaches of Normandy, Allied morale will slump and it will be at least a year, and probably longer, before another attempt can be made on the continent. During that time, we will be able to focus our efforts on driving Stalin's Red Army back to Moscow."

"Put the damned gun down now!" commanded Morrison as Katherine withdrew her own pistol and started off to the left with Jamison's camera rolling.

At that moment, an army jeep screeched into the parking lot. Katherine saw General Shedd and Colonel MacGregor jump from the vehicle carrying military sidearms.

"For you and your countrymen, the war is lost," continued Kepler in his half-crazed monotone, addressing both her group and the new arrivals in the jeep. "We will drag it out for another decade if we have to. You soft Americans don't have the stomach for a grueling, protracted bloodbath and will opt for peace. Your supposedly great democracy is your Achilles Heel. When we drive you back into the sea, there will be great misery and bloodshed and, with all hope lost, your civilian population will want to pack it in. That is because German determination and discipline are superior to American liberalism and decadence. You people are too soft and weak to rule the world."

Katherine felt her anger rising. "That is where you are wrong," she said defiantly as she moved into position, her gun trained on Kepler. "America will never give up until Hitler has taken his final breath and Germany has been de-Nazified. The days of men like you are numbered and you will never be welcome in the post-war Germany. Your time is finished."

Morrison looked at her sharply. "Katherine, I told you to stand back."

"I'm not going anywhere. Not until I know what has happened to my son."

Suddenly another car—to Katherine's surprise it was a Mercedes-Benz 770, the type favored by Hitler and other high-ranking Nazi party officials—came screeching into the parking lot. Racing up behind the lead car was a fleet of official-looking vehicles with U.S. government plates. Everyone stood there gaping mouthed as none other than J. Edgar Hoover stepped from the lead Mercedes, which, unlike the other vehicles was obviously not government-issue. Katherine suspected it must have been confiscated from some big-wig criminal. The FBI director strode forward with an air of authority as a dozen field agents tumbled out of the follow-up vehicles and quickly surrounded him like a Secret Service personal protection detail.

"Well, well, if it isn't the big G-Man himself—Mr. J. Edgar Hoover," snorted Kepler derisively as he recognized the legendary law enforcement and intelligence czar of German ancestry. He flipped back his overcoat like a gunfighter. "This is getting better by the minute. Now we truly do have a Mexican standoff, as you racist Americans are so fond of saying in your gangster movies."

Hoover squinted like an old time gunfighter as he stepped cautiously forward, but he said nothing. Katherine felt a portent of violence in the air. Kepler's intense gaze darted between Hoover, Morrison, and herself like a ticking time bomb. She took two steps forward, keeping her pistol trained on Kepler's heart.

With gun in hand, Hoover came to a halt next to Morrison, General Shedd, Colonel MacGregor, her handcuffed son Wolfgang, and the army sergeant guarding him. "We'll take it from here, General," the FBI director said to Shedd in a tone that left no doubt as to who he believed was in charge.

"We have it under control, Mr. Director," replied Shedd coolly.

"If you have it under control, why is Mrs. Templeton armed? We need Kepler alive."

"Put down the gun, Katherine!" said Morrison. "Stand down! We've got this!"

"You heard him—put it down!" echoed General Shedd, and next to him Jack Running Wolf, Tam MacGregor, and her lawyer Frederick Barstow urged her to do the same but with their eyes.

Ignoring them all, she took another step closer to Kepler, keeping her pistol trained on his heart. His heavy U.S. military overcoat seemed out of place in summertime, even here in the cool mountains, and she wondered if he had other weapons concealed beneath the coat.

Meanwhile, the crowd had grown to more than twenty armed men. They had all drawn their firearms and now began to fan out around Hoover and Shedd and towards Kepler in an umbrella pattern. But the German quickly waved them off and demanded that they stop moving.

Katherine froze.

So did Morrison and the others. As the tense seconds ticked off, they stood still with their guns aimed at Kepler, each and every face as rigid as stone, as Jason Gardner and Henry Jamison of the *Gazette* continued to capture the historic scene on a notepad and movie camera, respectively.

She squinted at Kepler. "What have you done with my son?"

"He is dead. I killed him."

She felt a crushing wave of sadness, but she forced herself to remain stoic. "Why?"

"Because he was a coward and traitor to the Fatherland. He swore an oath to our Führer, yet he violated that oath. And you should know *der Schwächling* died begging for his life."

She felt a surge of hate. "You liar!"

"Stop it, Katherine!" said Morrison. "He's just goading you! Now put the gun down, Colonel, or I'll shoot you myself!"

"If you were going to shoot me, you would have done so already. But I will make it easy for you weak-kneed Americans."

Slowly, he set his gun down on the pavement. Then he kicked it towards the group.

It came to a stop right in front of Hoover.

"Go ahead and pick it up, Mr. G-Man," he dared him. "I surrender."

No one moved a muscle.

For a tense moment, the FBI director and everybody else in the parking lot stared back and forth between Kepler and the gun, not trusting him. Like the others, Katherine had a terrible feeling that he had some clever trick up his sleeve and was faking his surrender.

She raised her .45 a half-inch, locking onto his determined face.

That was when she saw her son Erik shambling down the walkway behind him, carrying a gun in his hand.

CHAPTER 65

CHEYENNE MOUNTAIN

SHE SUPPRESSED a gasp of joyful relief as she didn't want to alert Kepler. Then she saw that her son's face was pale as a vampire from blood loss and his shirt was covered in blood. She felt a sense of motherly panic. My God, how many times had Kepler shot him? He looked as though he was clinging to life by a slender thread. And yet, he also had a look of fierce determination, as if no one was going to stop him from doing what he was about to do.

"Kepler!" he called out. "Turn around, you bastard!"

The Nazi colonel didn't budge. Instead, he gave a knowing smile, as if he had expected something like this all along or didn't care, and she knew in that instant that he did indeed have some sort of weapon concealed beneath that damned heavy jacket of his.

With lightning quickness, he ducked behind the pine tree, yanked the pins out of a pair of hand grenades, and tossed one grenade towards Hoover and his FBI men and the other towards Morrison and the military personnel.

"Grenade!" someone shouted, and everyone dove for cover.

Now protected by the tree, Kepler yanked out a Tommy gun from beneath his heavy jacket and opened fire at the scrambling and diving bodies.

Katherine couldn't believe her eyes as she saw a dozen men instantly torn to shreds from the two incendiary devices and the rattling Tommy gun. A disemboweled General Shedd staggered towards her carrying his guts in his hands like a coiled rope. A moment later she saw her lawyer, Frederick Barstow, and the publisher of the *Gazette*, Jason Gardner, cut down by a burst of gunfire. Then, to her dismay, Jack Running Wolf took a bullet in his arm and his Colt revolver flew from his hand. Shocked by the sudden violent change in circumstances, she took cover from the fusillade by ducking behind the Duesenberg.

Off to her right, she saw Morrison and her son Wolfgang returning fire, their jaws clenched tight as puffs of smoke blossomed in front of their faces. Her son must have grabbed a gun from one of the dead FBI agents and was firing the weapon in a two-handed grip wearing his handcuffs. Her other son Erik, though severely wounded, was shooting at Kepler from the trees next to the radio building. But Kepler had the Tommy and still plenty of ammo.

She heard a footfall to her left accompanied by a light clicking sound. Peering in the direction of the sound, she saw Henry Jamison of the *Gazette* still faithfully filming the scene with his 8-mm camera. He was crouching down behind the rear fender of a jeep, oblivious to his personal safety, his camera sweeping across the battlefield as if he was Ernie Pyle reporting from the front lines of

Europe.

Scrambling to her knees, she peered over the hood of the Duesenberg so she could have a better view of Kepler. He had moved to a new position behind a thicker-trunked tree, and he now unleashed another burst into Hoover and the remaining cluster of army officers and FBI agents that had taken refuge behind the Mercedes, a contingent now reduced to six men total. They returned fire and both sides began blasting away at one another in a close quarters' gunfight.

With Kepler distracted by Hoover and all the other guns, Katherine realized she had a chance to bring him down herself. She took careful aim with her pistol. A part of her wanted to kill him badly, but another part, her gentle womanly side, was reluctant to shoot another human being. Even though she worked for the OSS and knew how to handle a gun, killing another person went against everything she stood for.

But she had to do something.

Taking a deep breath, she opened fire from behind the Duesenberg. But Kepler, now alerted to her threat by some sort of sixth sense, turned away from Morrison, pointed his Tommy straight at her, and let loose with a clattering burst.

A pair of shots whizzed past her ear, and she returned fire, missing.

In response, Kepler fired another burst. This time, she felt a deep burning along the left side of her stomach. Emitting a shriek, she fell next to the front fender of the Duesenberg. Slumping against the automobile, she felt a rush of warm blood inside her blouse. A dizzy sensation took hold of her brain as the crimson fluid seeped through and dripped onto her skirt. Morrison and Wolfgang both rushed over to help her.

Now Kepler popped out from behind the tree and made a suicidal charge, yelling "*Ich grüße dich, mein ewiges Deutschland!*" *I greet you, my eternal Germany!*

Wounded but enraged, Katherine started to squeeze—

But there was no need for her to fire as Kepler's face registered sudden astonishment and a half-dozen red blots appeared on his jacket from Erik, Wolfgang, Morrison, and J. Edgar Hoover himself, who all closed in on him and let loose simultaneously from four different directions. There were six more concussive impacts and then the Nazi was standing there, teetering like a puppet, the gun in his hand pointing towards the heavens, his eyes taking in the world with an expression of glazed disbelief mingled with militant triumph. He stood there for what seemed like a lifetime before staggering and falling to the pavement.

For several seconds, everyone in the parking lot froze and no one said a word. Even Hoover was momentarily paralyzed and speechless. It was as if a terrible storm had passed and everyone was surprised to be alive.

Then slowly and cautiously, by ones and twos, they began to make their way over to the body. Clutching at her wounded stomach, Katherine stepped forward to have a closer look. Kepler laid face-down curled up in a half-fetal position, his legs tucked into his body and his long jacket crinkled up around him. Morrison and her two sons reached him first, followed by Hoover and his two remaining G-Men, Colonel MacGregor, and Jamison, with his rolling camera, as the cries of the dying and wounded rose mournfully in the crisp mountain air.

"Turn him over," commanded the FBI director. "I want to see his face."

Morrison kicked at the body, saw no movement, and started to turn him over.

Kepler's left arm came free. It was then Katherine saw the extracted firing pin clasped between his fingers and the hand grenade in the palm of his hand.

He gave one last triumphant smile.

"One final present for you, Mr. G-Man," he croaked, and his palm opened up and the grenade dribbled onto the pavement and rolled towards the FBI director.

"Grenade!" shouted Morrison.

"Get down!" screamed Erik, and he jumped onto the pavement, snatched the grenade, and tossed it towards the bushes as Wolfgang tackled Hoover and pushed him to safety and Morrison dove in front of Katherine to shield her from the explosion.

But the blast still ripped through the panicked crowd.

Katherine felt herself driven hard to the ground as slivers of metal flak tore into her flesh. There was a momentary burst of pain like shooting darts and the next thing she knew the world moved in slow motion. She lay immobilized on the pavement, unable to hear because her ears rang so badly.

Then the moment passed.

Suddenly, the world moved at normal speed and she could hear again. A tumult of sound hit her from all directions: voices screaming and shouting, feet running towards her, wounded men groaning. On the pavement next to her, she saw that Jack Morrison was not moving at all.

My God, poor Jack—you shouldn't have tried to save me, she thought.

She tried to get to her feet, but could not, feeling weak as a baby.

She touched her fingers to her stomach and felt the warm blood. She felt a dull, numbing pain instead of an agonized throbbing, which she knew was bad because it meant that her wound was quite grave. She squeezed her left hand against her stomach to clamp shut the flow of blood, feeling overcome by a great weariness.

"Hold on, Mother!" she heard a pair of voices say, voices that sounded like angels, and she saw her handsome young boys kneeling over her. "You're going to make it! Just hold on!"

Then the world slowed down again.

She looked up at the faces, but her two boys were no longer there and everything was blurry. She felt lightheaded, ethereal, and the sensation reminded her of the time she was thrown from her horse as a little girl in Prussia. She felt arms reaching out and touching her. She desperately wanted to say something, but she could not find the energy for words.

Her mind went back to her early motherhood. She longed for those simple, pastoral days of her late twenties and early thirties when there was no war and life had seemed so simple and beautiful. She pictured her three wonderful sons as adorable, cherubic, pink-bottomed babies. The mental image of the three of them, so young and innocent, and her chivalrous husband hung there in her mind for a long moment and she felt a profound yearning to travel through time and visit the past and for the world to be...simple again.

For there to be a world without war, again.

As she closed her eyes and traveled back to those halcyon days, she heard the voice of Henry Jamison of the *Gazette* trickle through the fog of her consciousness.

"Well, if that doesn't beat all. Those two Kraut brothers just saved J. Edgar Fucking Hoover himself!"

Now there's irony for you, she thought dreamily, and then she saw white pinpoints of light, stretching to infinity, and she knew that she and her new love Jack Morrison had both, together, met their end.

DAY 8

TUESDAY

D-DAY: JUNE 6, 1944

CHAPTER 66

EAGLE'S NEST, BERCHTESGADEN
GERMAN-AUSTRIAN BORDER

UNABLE TO SLEEP YET AGAIN, Adolf Hitler—"the Bohemian corporal" as Field Marshal Gerd von Rundstedt, commander of the Atlantic Wall forces that were to repel the Allied invaders back into the sea, disparagingly referred to him—stood before his bathroom mirror, splashing some warm water on his face. The sorry state of the war, his digestive problems that gave him unbearably bad flatulence, and the painful tremor in his left arm—tonight all of the usual suspects were acting in concert to make his insomnia particularly troublesome. My God, how could he be expected to run a war when he couldn't even sleep! The very thought of getting *absolutely no* rest before tomorrow's scheduled meeting outside Salzburg—where he was to meet with the new Hungarian prime minister and diplomats from Bulgaria, Romania, and Hungary to demand more money for the German war effort—made him angry.

So very, very angry.

His private physician, Dr. Morell, had administered an injection and a sedative just before bed to help him sleep, but it had not worked at all. He might as well pace the hallways all night pondering his troubled thoughts as rely on the glandular concoctions of his official Reich Injection Master. Why only four hours earlier he had been discussing films with Eva and Goebbels, and they had been laughing and joking and having such a wonderful time talking about his all-time favorite film, *King Kong,* that he was sure he would sleep well tonight.

But it was not to be. It made him so mad.

Through the open bathroom door, he looked at his beautiful mistress, who lay in his monstrously huge and well-appointed bed, her ample breasts rising and falling in a gentle rhythm. He looked back at his face in the mirror. He hated to admit that he no longer looked anything like the powerful leader who had inspired millions at the Nuremburg *Reichsparteitag des Sieges*—Rally of Victory—over a decade earlier. He looked tired and depressed, like a man who was losing a world war.

His skin was sallow and chalky as if he had jaundice. The eyes beneath his spectacles were puffy and bloodshot from lack of sleep. And he had become pulpy and bloated from lack of exercise and massive doses of medication he took intravenously and orally to make it through the toll of daily life. Of course, he had never been the tall, blond, blue-eyed model of Aryan perfection, but even so he had slipped dramatically these past few months as the Red Army pushed westward and American and British tanks rolled towards Rome. Why his hair was even streaked with gray not only at the temples, but all over his head, and it wasn't a handsome, dignified, silvery gray but the drab color of a wharf rat. And lately he had taken to shunning bright lights and wearing a cap with a huge visor to shield his eyes, as if he were a hermit. Was he truly falling apart or was this simply the unpleasant reality of middle-age?

Letting out a weary sigh of resignation, he studied Eva's reflection in the mirror lying peacefully in their bed. *How does she sleep like a baby when the whole world is at war?* he wondered, and then he heard a light rap and familiar voice at the door.

It was his personal valet, *SS Obersturmbannführer* Heinz Linge.

He went to the door and opened it. He was surprised to see standing next to his valet General Jodl. Both the general and Linge looked terrified to be waking him up in the middle of the night.

"You can relax, gentlemen." He spoke in the gentle voice he used only in the presence of attractive female company and his staff when he didn't want to frighten them with his erratic mood swings, which, with the recent setbacks along the Eastern Front and in the Italian theatre, he was having increasing difficulty in controlling. "I was already up. But I must say that I hope your presence here at this time of night is a harbinger of good news for the Reich, perhaps a small success in the field to offset yesterday's capture of Rome by the Allies?"

Linge clicked his boots together and gave the official Hitler salute. "*Jawohl, mein Führer*. I apologize for the interruption, but *Generaloberst* Jodl has important news as you have intimated. I know you gave strict instructions not to be disturbed, but I think you will be pleased to hear what he has to report."

The general stepped forward, greeted him with the Hitler salute, and handed him a sheath of paper. As the Chief of Operation Staff of the German High Command, Alfred Jodl was the senior officer responsible for briefing Hitler on important military matters on a daily basis. The Nazi leader brought the message to his baggy, bespectacled eyes and began to read. Like his American counterpart FDR, whom most Americans didn't even know required a wheelchair, Hitler kept the German people from knowing he wore glasses and was rarely, if ever, photographed wearing them.

He read the message twice. It was from Friedrich-Adolf Krummacher, the head of the OKW Intelligence Branch, and it gave a complete summary of the forthcoming Allied order of battle in Occupied France and the intelligence upon which it was based. When he was finished, he handed the message back to Jodl.

He would remember all of the facts in the message; his physical health may have been deteriorating, but his command of military details was still first-rate. Following briefings, he often received accolades from his generals, who were unanimously impressed with his attention to detail and remarkable memory.

"Interesting. So we are to believe that the main invasion will come at Normandy and not the Pas de Calais? Come, General, we shall go outside. I don't want to wake Eva."

"If that will be all then, my Führer, I shall bid you goodnight," said Linge, and he again clicked his boots and gave the Hitler salute before turning precisely on a heel and starting down the plushly furnished corridor.

Careful not to wake his mistress, Hitler led Jodl quietly to a sweeping balcony that, if it had been daytime, would have looked out onto thick alpine forests and lush meadows straddling the German-Austrian border. The "Eagle's Nest" included not just a resplendent mountaintop chalet, but a vast, labyrinthine military command-and-control center that served as the Führer*'s* second seat of government, as well as his planned refuge of last resort. Despite his insomnia, Hitler felt at peace here. After all, this salubrious mountain region was where he had put the finishing touches on *Mein Kampf*, and, accordingly, many of his countrymen referred to it as the "cradle of the Third Reich."

"What do we know of this man Kepler who made this report on the radio?"

"According to the Swiss legation, he has been at Camp Pershing since a month after the surrender of Tunis in May of '43. He was commander of the 21st Panzer Division, the last to surrender."

"A true patriot to the Fatherland. And what of these von Walburg brothers who escaped with him and that he has reported were killed in action? What is their story?"

"You awarded *Kapitän zur See* Wolfgang von Walburg the Knight's Cross of the Iron Cross with Oak Leaves and Swords just this past fall. He is a hero, the top U-boat commander in the North Sea."

"Oh, yes, 'the scourge of the North Sea', as Mr. Churchill calls him. And it was his brother Erik who reportedly obtained all of this critical intelligence in England. So they are both heroes of the Fatherland."

"Yes, my Führer."

"And this younger Walburg was sent by General Rommel and his father, General von Walburg, as an independent spy and was not sent by Canaris?"

"That is correct."

"Are we sure we can trust this young man's word?"

"I believe so. He comes from a very fine military family and long line of German patriots. His great-great grandfather fought with Frederick the Great."

Leaning against the balustrade, he took his palsied and useless left arm by the elbow with his right hand to keep it from shaking uncontrollably. "But Normandy, Herr Jodl—Normandy!" he snapped in a sudden burst of pain. "All of our intelligence up to this unusual broadcast has indicated the Pas de Calais as the main thrust of the Allied invasion. Normandy is merely a feint. How can we be sure of this man?"

"General Rommel has vouched for him. Vouched most vociferously and insolently, I might add. In fact, he requests that you release Panzer Group West from Paris immediately to him and Field Marshal von Rundstedt."

He released a little sigh as the shaking began to subside. "The Desert Fox can be presumptuous at times. Is this Erik von Walburg a Party member?"

"Well, no, but his father and brother are."

"Hmm…not a Party member. But that is not what concerns me most. It is this Double Cross. Am I really to believe that our codes have been compromised and that every one of our agents in Britain is, in fact, a double agent? Somehow, I cannot bring myself to believe that. It was my understanding that our codes were impenetrable."

"It is rather…hard to believe, my Führer. But the radio broadcast appears genuine. And we have more supporting information. In addition to the broadcast, our intelligence picked up fourteen cryptic messages today by the French Resistance that an attack is imminent. The Seventh Army at Calais has raised its state of alert, but we have done nothing yet at Normandy. If that is where the main thrust will be, shouldn't we mobilize the panzers as soon as possible?"

Hitler didn't reply at first. He felt like he was tipping to the right, an unpleasant sensation that he regrettably had to endure these days, and he quickly felt his pulse. *Why do I always feel slightly off-balance?*

"I don't know, Jodl," he said when he realized that his pulse was normal, "I think it could all be a trick."

"A trick? But *mein Führer,* the radio broadcast. We recorded it, or most of it. I've heard it myself and it appears completely genuine. General Rommel is most insistent as well."

"But it contradicts everything we have learned from our best agent in England."

"You're referring to Juan Pujol Garcia, code named Arabel?"

"Yes, Arabel. That man deserves the Iron Cross."

"I know how much you value the Spaniard. But if Arabel has been compromised, then none of what he has said up until now is true and we have been deceived. That would make him not our best agent, but our worst enemy."

"Come now, Jodl. Arabel has never been wrong before."

"But if it's all fake then—"

"Don't interrupt me! I tell you that this Kepler broadcast based on von Walburg's intelligence is just not credible. All of our intelligence to date has pinpointed the Pas de Calais as the main thrust of the attack. Agent Arabel has been a godsend to us. All of the reports received in the last month from him have confirmed, without exception, that Calais is where the primary wave will be. His reports have always been exceptionally accurate—indeed, I might even say flawless."

"Yes, but what if Walburg is right and Double Cross is real? Then we have a most powerful weapon at our disposal. We can simply do the opposite of what Arabel tells us and win the war. We can drive the Allies back into the sea, never to return!"

Hitler didn't like the pleading desperation in his subordinate's voice. It sounded unbecoming of a *Wehrmacht* officer. "No, no, no, Jodl, I tell you this whole Double Cross thing is a farce! The British are clever, but they are not that clever. And the Americans. Ha! They don't even know what intelligence is. Their Office of Strategic Services headed by that crazy 'Wild Bill' Donovan…why they're nothing but a bunch of amateurs and cowboys. And that bloated carcass J. Edgar Hoover…don't even get me started about him and his overrated G-Men!"

"I understand your position, my Führer, truly I do. But I don't think we can dismiss the broadcast entirely. Even General von Rundstedt—"

"Don't talk to me of *der alte Herr!* At sixty-eight, that old goat Rundstedt couldn't spot an amphibious attack if the enemy had secured the beachhead!"

"But both he and Rommel are in agreement, a true rarity. They call upon you to release the two reserve panzer divisions—the 12th SS Panzer and Panzer Lehr—in order to make them available for counterattack in Normandy. They also request that 1st Panzer Division begin moving immediately from Pas de Calais towards Caen."

"That is out of the question. Normandy is nothing but a diversion."

"But my Führer—"

"Rommel and Rundstedt cannot have their panzers. That is all I have to say on the matter." He grabbed his left arm again to keep it from trembling. "Oh, Jodl, how my field marshals have let me down? Sometimes, I wish I could simply retire up here in these beautiful mountains and live out my final years devoted to reading, meditation, or running a museum. Think of it, a Reich Museum—wouldn't that be wonderful?"

"Yes, my Führer, it would. But suppose Double Cross is a reality and all the intelligence we have been receiving is false? Don't you think we should take precautions?"

"Double Cross simply cannot be, Jodl. It cannot be for the simple reason that the greatest nation on earth—our beloved Fatherland—could not possibly have been duped in such a manner. It is not possible. We—and we alone—are the true Master Race, the very pinnacle of perfection. We do not make such mistakes."

"But suppose it is true? Will not history judge us poorly if we do nothing? As General Rommel said, 'If we can't throw the enemy into the sea within twenty-four hours, then it will be the beginning of the end.'"

He felt a wave of bile in his stomach and his anger resurfacing. He waved his hand dismissively. "Ah, the Marshal Laddie says many things."

"The Marshal Laddie? Don't you mean the Desert Fox?"

"Don't mince words with me, Jodl. You know that I am very fond of Rommel, but he suffers from what I like to call African sickness."

"African sickness?"

"Pessimism is a most destructive force. Only optimists can pull anything off these days. That is why I need my field marshals to be eternally optimistic."

"I am optimistic, *mein Führer,* it's just that I think Herr Rommel—"

"That's enough, Jodl. I have made my decision. The enemy's attack will come at the Pas de Calais. And when he attacks, he will achieve no success. That is a given. And once defeated, the enemy will not attempt another amphibious invasion in the West. Mark my words, Calais will be the Allies' Waterloo. Even my astrologer thinks so."

"Your astrologer? And if the attack comes at Normandy?"

Hitler laughed easily, finally feeling himself ready for sleep. "It will be nothing more than a diversion. A very small—and insignificant—diversion!"

Jodl bore a mixed look of exasperation and resignation, as so many of Hitler's generals did after another pointless debate. "Very well, my Führer. I will leave you to your rest."

"Come now, Jodl, there is nothing to worry about. When the main attack comes, it will be repelled with ease. And when it comes, it will be at the Pas de Calais *not* Normandy. That I promise you!"

CHAPTER 67

POINTE DU HOC FORWARD OBSERVATION POST NORMANDY COAST, OCCUPIED FRANCE

GENERALLEUTNANT ROBERT GRAF VON WALBURG—right-hand man to Rommel, who was at this very moment racing back from celebrating his wife's 50th birthday in Herrlingen to Army Group B Headquarters at La Roche Guyon—stood atop a giant shore battery with his *Wehrmacht* 7x50 Zeiss binoculars aimed at the roiling sea. As the first streaks of dawn's nautical twilight trickled across the Norman landscape of cliffs, dunes, and beaches, he hoped to catch a glimpse of the Allied flotilla of battleships, cruisers, supply ships, and small landing craft that might very well be heading towards the French coast. Only three hours earlier, the Allies had launched a massive airborne assault inland from the coast, which signified that the cross-Channel invasion had begun.

A part of him still couldn't believe that his son Erik had succeeded beyond his wildest dreams and discovered not only the enemy's order of battle for Fortress Europe, but their important double agent system. Now everything that the Allies had been doing to confuse Army Group B these past six months made complete sense. All OKW had to do was to use the new intelligence carefully and deliberately to turn the deception back onto the enemy for as long as possible. While ultimate victory may still be out of reach, an honorable peace would now most certainly be possible. But first, the enemy had to be driven back into the sea.

And yet, how could that happen when he and everyone else in the German Army had that buffoon armchair-general, Adolf Hitler, to contend with!

From Rommel and von Rundstedt both, he had already learned that the little Bohemian corporal had refused not one, but two requests to release Panzer Group West from Paris and the 1st Panzer Division from Pas de Calais to Normandy. Upon learning of the Allies' early-morning, inland airborne assault, Rundstedt had ordered the two reserve panzer divisions, the 12th SS Panzer and Panzer Lehr, to move immediately toward Caen to make them available for counterattack in Normandy. Walburg agreed with his two senior officers that the airborne landings appeared to be on such a massive scale that they could not be a mere deception maneuver and would have to be reinforced from the sea. The only place such large-scale landings could come in lower Normandy were on the Calvados and Cotentin coasts, and it was here, on the wide beaches north and south of Pointe du Hoc where they would need the critical reinforcements of Tigers, Panzers, Panthers, and StuG tanks to meet the expected massive Allied attack.

But the damned Führer—that maniac who would destroy an entire *Wehrmacht* division rather than give up an inch of ground—had forced Rundstedt to countermand the move-out order and recall the reserves. He had been sleeping—*my God sleeping!*—and General Jodl refused to wake him a third time. The two reserve divisions could not be committed until Hitler gave the order, and the last report was that he was still fast asleep like a hung-over grenadier.

Walburg couldn't believe the fate of his entire country rested on such an imbecile. My God, they needed the damned tanks now while there was still cloud cover and Allied planes were mostly grounded, not a day or two from now. By then it would be too late. Three hours earlier Allied paratroopers had landed all along the peninsula and they could not be a mere deception.

Precious time was being wasted.

The pewter-gray predawn light began to play across the water. Stepping down from the massive concrete bunker, he walked to the tip of the point, a sharp protrusion of interbedded, fractured limestone, sandstone, and marlstone that stood a hundred feet above the Channel. Looking through his binoculars, first north and then south from the sharp rocky point—towards what his Allied adversaries had codenamed Omaha and Utah beaches and were soon about to make legendary—he saw a coastline bristling with murderous firepower and defensive strongholds that he had played a major role in creating.

For the past six months, he and the Desert Fox had worked tirelessly to build the "Rommel Belt" all along the coast from Holland to the Loire, throwing up a total of 20,000 coastal fortifications, emplacing 500,000 foreshore obstacles, and laying 6.5 million mines to create a "zone of death." Peering up and down the coast, he gazed out upon countless batteries, mortars, machine-gun nests, thickets of barbed wire, land mines, antitank "hedgehogs" made from welded steel girders, concrete pyramid-shaped "dragons teeth" to slow down and channel tanks into "killing zones," and more than a million upright stakes in the fields beyond, known as "Rommel's Asparagus," to impede airborne landings. From bunkers, machine-gun nests, trenches, and gun emplacements, the German defenders would pour an inhuman wall of fire into the Allied attackers.

Studying the defenses, he took pride in having created one of the strongest positions on the Atlantic Wall. But even these well-fortified beaches would fall within hours of a full-scale amphibious attack without the powerful reserve tank divisions. What good was an inhuman "wall of fire" and "zone of death" when the Allies had all the advantage in airpower and seapower and a mentally unhinged tyrant refused to give his generals the panzers they needed to drive the invaders back into the sea?

He turned his binoculars again out into the Channel, searching for enemy ships and scout planes. To the west, the dark gray clouds and patches of clear sky blended with the slatey blue ocean like a Dutch oil on a canvas. Though the light was improving with every minute, it was still only 0530 hours and his visibility was limited even with binoculars. He stared at the white-capped rollers chugging towards the limey cliffs and sandy beaches.

He thought back to those simple summers on the Dutch coast and at the Broadmoor in America with his family before everything had changed. It haunted him to this day that he had allowed his family to be torn apart. How foolish he had been to let his wife and two sons trundle off to America following Hitler's rise to power. How cowardly he had been to allow his wife to have an affair with that damned Frenchman Renault just to spite him. Had he subconsciously wanted to drive her away? In the end, all he had done was throw away everything that was important to him—and now all that he was left with was a feeble, blood-drained facsimile of his once great Fatherland, a broken and beaten country led by a maniac who would slaughter all of his own people rather than do the honorable thing and surrender his armies to the Allies.

My God, he thought, *how badly I have failed in this life.*

Suddenly, the crash of a huge wave brought him back to the present. Was it his imagination or did he feel a vague presence, a change? No, he wasn't imagining things. His soldier's instinct told him something wasn't right. He focused his binoculars on the distant horizon again, scanning for the Allied armada that would—

Wait, what was that? He could have sworn he saw a flicker of movement on the hazy horizon. He scanned again, adjusting the focus and squinting into his field glasses.

The breath caught in his throat.

It was like a dream—or more appropriately a nightmare—suddenly and miraculously transformed into a tangible reality.

He checked the horizon again to make sure. He couldn't believe his eyes, and yet, what he saw was unmistakable.

Even in the diffuse predawn light, there was no doubt about it now.

Somehow, the moment he and everyone German soldier stationed on the Western Front had prepared for, and dreaded, for the past six months was actually happening: a fantastic armada—thousands upon thousands of ships—had crossed the Channel undetected and was about to impinge upon *Festung Europa.*

The Allied fleet was so big it looked like a floating city.

He briefly fingered the Iron Cross at his throat—he had won the same battle decoration as his son Wolfgang for his tank battle heroics in Tunisia—and loosened a button on his greatcoat, turned on a muddy boot heel, and started walking briskly towards the concrete observation bunker.

That was when the klaxon sounded and he heard the first shore battery open up.

He made a mad dash for the protection of the bunker. All along the coast shore guns began barking and thundering, the black splashes leaping from the sea in fountains of spray. By the time he had ducked into the bunker, a major with the 352nd Infantry Division in charge of the artillery forward observation post had already hailed Army Group B Headquarters. Walburg took the phone from him and was quickly routed through to Rundstedt, as Rommel had not yet arrived back from Herrlingen.

"Field Marshal, the invasion by sea has begun!"

"So the air assault was prelude to a seaborne invasion. I knew it!"

"It is no feint. There are thousands of ships. This is a large-scale attack, most likely from Saint-Mère Eglise all the way to Caen. Many, many ships. Our artillery is engaging them now!"

"How soon until the enemy hits the beaches?"

"Less than an hour!"

"We must cut them down at the beaches!"

"Yes, sir, and to do that we must have the panzer reserves! Our only chance is to drive them back into the sea and not allow them to secure a beachhead!"

"That is not your responsibility, General von Walburg! You are there as an observer!"

"But Field Marshal, without the panzers we have no hope at all!"

"You must leave that to me! Attend to the invasion front!"

"Damnit, man, we need those—"

He was cut off as a massive explosion rocked the bunker, followed by another and another, until the entire reinforced-concrete casemate was filled with an echoing wall of thunder from hundreds upon hundreds of naval guns opening up along a fifty-mile firing line.

"Field Marshal, Field Marshal!" he cried desperately, but the line was dead and Rundstedt was gone.

The bunker shook again and men jumped into battle positions. The Allied counterbattery bombardment had commenced with a roar so deafening that he couldn't even hear the sound of his own voice. He quickly stuffed wads of cotton into his ears to prevent the shattering of his eardrums, as men in muddy field gray dove to the concrete floor, covered their ears, and stuffed them with whatever they could find to protect themselves from the concussive blasts.

Raising his binoculars, he peered through the slit-opening facing the sea as the radio man called in ship coordinates. He could see the muzzle flashes from the battleships' 14-inch guns and the crimson parabolic arcs as the Allied shells soared towards the coast. Giant craters were being blasted out all along the chalky, grass-covered salient of Pointe du Hoc. Down on the beach and along the smaller bluffs, the smaller batteries, pillboxes, and machine-gun nests were also taking a terrific pounding.

The more protected bunker continued to reverberate from the terrifying explosions. The concussion ghosts rippled the men's *feldgrau* uniforms like an advancing hurricane. The offshore battleships and cruisers created a continuous wall of sound that was made even louder by the thundering shore batteries and the screaming and shouting of the men in the bunker. The reinforced-concrete of the Pointe casemates was supposed to be impossible to penetrate, but within minutes a series of direct hits from the 14-inch shells had ripped out huge chunks of concrete, wrenched away steel reinforcing rods, and rendered deaf and unconscious half of the troopers inside the bunker. The air turned acrid with the stench of fresh powder. A fine confetti of disintegrated wadding filtered down like Vesuvian ash. The rain of iron created fresh stress cracks in the concrete, tore out any and all objects that were screwed or clamped to the walls, and shattered light bulbs.

Soon Mustang and Spitfire spotter planes zoomed overhead. Now that it was light enough for spotter planes to direct fire, they swooped in aggressively for a closer look, pinpointing muzzle flashes coming from the bluffs as well as heavily reinforced forward observation posts and shore batteries. With the Allies' uncontested aerial supremacy, German soldiers recently had started joking that

American planes were gray, British planes black, and Luftwaffe planes invisible. With the spotter planes now in the battle, the cannonade from the sea became even more concentrated and lethal. The huge naval shells continued to blast out giant craters in Pointe du Hoc, tumbling great chunks of cliff into the sea, pulverizing the casemates of the observation posts and artillery strongpoints.

Soon, he saw the massive enemy flotilla in all of its terrifying glory. Peering through his binoculars, he could swear he saw more ships than sea. There were three huge battleships, countless destroyers and heavy cruisers, and myriad smaller vessels with frothy whitewater spilling over the gunwales. Furthest offshore were the battleships, cruisers, and bulky transports, and in front of them raced the destroyers and landing craft, heading towards shore in columns of Higgins boats, DUKWs, LCIs, and LCTs. The sheer size of the assault force—with battle ensigns snapping and wakes boiling white—was staggering. In that illuminating instant, *Generalleutnant* Robert Graf von Walburg knew that his son Erik's bold mission had ultimately failed in its objective. Germany was *kaput*.

And so was he.

He turned calmly on a booted heel, stepped out the door, and walked outside into the hailstorm of exploding artillery shells.

He knew it was all over and didn't want to live anymore. He had failed as a father, failed as an army commander, and in six months, his country would be in ruins.

What was the point of living in a world of nothingness and utter ruination with French peasants spitting and cursing at you and all of your material possessions seized from you and no one to love you and hold you when you grew old?

An artillery shell exploded twenty yards away and he tumbled onto the ground, his eardrums shattered and bleeding even through the cotton wadding.

He rose to his feet and staggered towards the jagged, craggy promontory. God, how he wished he could turn back his life and start all over again with his family. His beautiful boys, his wonderful wife, how had he let them all slip away? True, he had spent considerable time with Erik when Rommel had taken him onto his staff, and he had been granted a leave to be there in person for Wolfgang's Iron Cross ceremony. But those few precious moments were not enough. His relationship with his two sons had been nothing more than a superficial bond among fighting soldiers with a common enemy.

It was not the same as a family.

He reached the edge of the cliffs, the projecting knob of Pointe du Hoc. On both sides he saw pill boxes, antitank sites, *Nebelwerfer* rocket-launcher pits, and artillery positions being devoured by the enemy cannonade. He stuck out his arms, as he supposed Christ might have done when nailed to the cross, and waited for the shell with his name on it to devour him.

"Kill me now, God!" he shouted, his voice drowned out by the roar of artillery. "For I have failed myself, my family, and Germany! I no longer want to live! No, I no longer *deserve* to live!"

Within moments of his appeal to a higher power, his final wish was granted and he was blown into a thousand bloody bits. His final earthly thought was a mental image of him, his wife, and three sons strolling through the Tiergarten on a sunny summer day, slurping ice cream cones as squirrels chased one another playfully through the giant oak trees.

In that final moment, it had seemed to General Robert Graf von Walburg as if his life would last forever.

EPILOGUE

JUNE 6, 1947

ENGLISH CHANNEL OFF OMAHA BEACH AND POINTE DU HOC NORMANDY, FRANCE

WITH A FULL WIND IN THE SHEET, the sailboat glided across the water with ease two hundred yards off sandy Omaha Beach. Katherine reached out and gently touched Jack Morrison's hand gripping the tiller. Then she gave him a soft peck on the cheek. The war seemed a long time ago. But now, staring out at the legendary beach and craggy Pointe du Hoc where so many brave American and German soldiers had died, she felt the pain and suffering of that epic conflagration stir something deep inside her. Splotchy altocumulus clouds formed a heavenly backdrop to the former battleground, and higher up wispy cirrus floated across the light blue sky like stacked carvings of Thanksgiving turkey.

She was grateful that the war was over. But more than that, she was grateful to have a semblance of a family again.

She smiled appreciatively at her sons Erik and Wolfgang, sitting along the port railing of the twenty-one footer, drinking calvados and taking in the fat waves rolling up Omaha Beach while basking in the rarified Norman sunlight. Her boys were precious to her and she knew that they were lucky to be alive. They had been spared the death penalty three years earlier only because they had saved J. Edgar Hoover's life and had signed an official, joint U.S. and British government non-disclosure agreement stating that they would never in their lifetime disclose anything about the "wartime events" they had participated in from May 24 through June 6, 1944. To these events the OSS and British intelligence had given the name "Operation Cheyenne" with a nod to the climactic episode that took place atop Cheyenne Mountain. Katherine, too, had been forced to sign the legally binding agreement to ensure that her sons were not sent to the electric chair or hung from the gallows. The word from her boss Donovan inside the OSS was that Hoover had insisted upon the wartime documents being officially sealed and classified by the U.S. government until May 2015, seventy years after the German surrender. The iron-fisted FBI director was reportedly peeved at having been saved by a pair of, in his words, "murderous Nazi subversives" at the mountaintop radio tower and was the primary impetus behind the cover-up.

"Erik, Wolfgang, would you like another sandwich?"

"Thank you, Mother, but we have already had three each," replied Erik, who was, to her chagrin, skinny as a rail from the past two years of incarceration in a French labor camp for German POWs. He and Wolfgang had been released by the U.S. Army to France in the summer of 1945 after a year of solitary confinement in a U.S. military prison, and they had been set free from the labor camp in Alsace only last week. They had both lost forty pounds since being returned from America to Europe and subjected to the severity of their retributive French wards—who acted in deliberate violation of the Geneva Convention by starving German prisoners and forcing them to clear dangerous land mines by parading them through minefields.

"I know you are trying to fatten us up, Mother, but if we have any more we will get a stomach ache," said Wolfgang cheerfully.

She smiled ruefully at them; their cheeks were as sunken as the D-Day bomb craters on Pointe du Hoc and it made her both sad and angry at the French. Then again, she could hardly blame the nation that had given rise to the great Napoleon, Voltaire, and Marie Curie for taking out its vengeance after what that maniac Hitler and his Nazi henchmen had done to their beautiful country and its fine people. "All right, but let me know if you need anything else," she said to them.

"Don't worry we will, Mother."

"You do love to dote on those boys of yours," said Jack Morrison with a smile. "But if anyone deserves it, they do, after what they've been through."

"I'm still worried about them," she said. "They have aged so much and lost so much weight."

Morrison nodded sympathetically. "You should be thankful to have them back, Katherine. That damned war claimed the lives of more than sixty million people, including your son Max and your ex-husband Robert, and yet Wolfgang and Erik were fortunate enough to survive. And let's not forget how lucky you and I are. I thought we were goners back there on that mountain, and yet here we are sipping calvados and sailing a boat along the coast of Normandy."

She sighed heavily. "You're right. I should be grateful that I have them in my life. And you as well. That is cause for celebration."

He gave her a comforting hug and they fell into silence. Her sons had been among the nearly 750,000 German POWs that France had kept laboring in her cities and fields and clearing dangerous minefields for the past two years following the war. While de Gaulle's liberated nation was beginning to release selected German prisoners, it was only because of her OSS work on behalf of the French Resistance, and the relentless efforts of her husband Jack and his high-ranking military contacts in Occupied Germany, that she had been able to secure an early release for her two sons.

But at least now, she had them back.

"They're going to be fine," whispered Morrison to her. "We're all going to get back on our feet together."

A tear rolled down her cheek. "Thank you, Jack. I'm lucky to have you."

"No, I'm lucky to have you. No one can jitterbug like *my countess*."

"You're just trying to make me laugh."

He grinned. "Guilty as charged."

"The thing is all I ever wanted as a young girl was to have a lovely family."

"Well, you've got one again now. I'm not going anywhere, and neither are those fine lads of yours."

"They like you, you know."

"That's because we fought together—and against one another—in battle. Once that happens, even sworn enemies become fast friends."

"No, they really like you. It was their idea to come here to Normandy with us. They wanted to see the place where, for one day, the war could have gone either way."

"It was a damned close call. The Germans were fully alerted and should have been ready and waiting at Normandy. But luckily, Hitler was a fool and refused to send the panzers right away. If he had, the Allies would likely have been driven back into the sea and D-Day would have ended in a massacre. Then the Allies might have packed it in entirely. Or, at the very least, the war would have dragged on for years and millions more would have died."

"The whole world was very fortunate that things turned out as they did."

"Look, there it is, Mother!" cried Wolfgang, pointing to the knob of sea-battered marlstone projecting from the coastline. "That's Pointe du Hoc!"

"So this is the place where their father made his last stand," observed Morrison.

She nodded somberly. "They wanted to see it from the water. The way Robert died…well, it's quite a legend. Wolfgang and Erik heard the story from a German lieutenant and a sergeant they met at the French labor camp in Alsace. They say Robert singlehandedly fought off an entire company of Rangers that were scaling the cliffs with ropes. All he had was a pistol, a light machine gun, and a half dozen hand grenades. He forced them to go way around to the north there. He was wounded several times and finally killed by an exploding artillery shell. But not until after he had fought off nearly a hundred American Rangers for an hour."

"Do you believe the story?"

"It certainly sounds like Robert. But it's probably just a myth. Germans are good at myth-making."

"They're damned good at war-making too."

They laughed and then fell into silence. Staring up at the crumbly sea cliff and grassy, bomb-cratered hill beyond, she shook her head and sighed. "Poor Robert. But I suppose that's the way he always wanted to go. If you're a warrior, the best place to die is a battlefield, right?"

"No question about it. And like I said before, if Hitler had only listened to your husband and acted properly on your son Erik's intelligence, everything would have turned out differently. Hell, Germany may have been able to negotiate for peace on its own terms."

"I'm just glad it's all over," said Erik.

"Me too," said Wolfgang, squinting into the sun. "Now there are only the memories. One day, even the French will forgive us."

"It will probably take a generation or two, but I'll bet you're right," said Katherine into the brisk sea breeze. "But the most important thing is that you two are free to live your lives again."

"Yes, let's have a toast to freedom!" exclaimed Erik.

"Wait a second," said Wolfgang. "We're not really free, you know. How can we be when we can never tell anyone—not even our future children or grandchildren—about the two weeks during the war when we held the fate of the world in our hands and saved J. Edgar Hoover's life? If we utter a peep about what really happened and the U.S. or British governments catch wind of it, we could be thrown back in prison again."

"Oh, I wouldn't worry about it if I were you," said Katherine.

"And just why not?"

"Because no one would ever believe such a far-fetched tale anyway."

"That's true," said Erik, chuckling along with his brother as the seawater sprayed up at them. "Sometimes Wolfgang and I can't believe it actually happened ourselves."

"And besides," said Katherine, "the most important thing is that you're both still alive. That means a lot more to me. After all, I had to give birth to you two rapscallions. You don't know the meaning of pain until you've given birth to ten-pound baby boys."

"In that case, my lips are sealed," exclaimed Erik.

"Mine too," agreed Wolfgang.

They all laughed and tipped back their glasses of fine *Colleville-sur-Mer* apple brandy before refilling them again. Looking at her happy sons, Katherine felt tears of jubilation come to her eyes. She wanted to remember this day for the rest of her life: Erik and Wolfgang's smiling faces; the sunlight sparkling off the water; the cool ocean breeze; the waves sweeping majestically towards the sandy beaches and rocky cliffs; the bundles of seaweed floating past with little air-filled bulbs; the flocks of sea gulls flapping their wings across an endless Norman sky.

The wind changed to a southwesterly. Morrison let out the mainsail, as the one true seaman among them, Wolfgang, had shown him how to do minutes earlier. The sheet took the wind, and the little sloop jumped ahead like a pony nudged by a pair of spurs. As the boat settled into a gliding rhythm, she again looked up at the prominent cliff where her first husband had taken his last dying breath. Her sons were pointing at the prominence and jabbering excitedly, and she wondered what it was that fascinated them so about this place.

Was it because their father had died here, or because of the mythical importance of the battle, or because of the pivotal role that both of them had played in the events leading up to the invasion? Looking up at the rocky point, pockmarked with bomb craters like the surface of the moon, she realized that their fascination was probably driven by all three reasons.

They sailed on with only the feel of the Channel winds on their faces and the gentle flapping of the sheet. There was tranquility to the sea and sandy beach beyond. A tranquility that she knew hadn't been present three years ago during the Allied invasion.

She preferred Normandy in its present, peaceful state.

"I love you, Jack," she said quietly, nudging up close to him.

"I love you too," he said, smiling affectionately.

"I have a family again."

"Yes, you have a family again. A family that you can always count on. And a family that has one hell of a story to tell."

"Are you referring to Operation Cheyenne by chance?"

"Indeed I am."

"Are you suggesting that my sons and I don't actually honor the legally binding non-disclosure agreement the U.S. and British governments forced us to sign and tell the world a yarn that it will never believe?"

"You know perfectly well that your future grandkids and the whole goddamn world have got to hear that story, Katherine. It's too good even if it is unbelievable. That's all I'm saying."

"My, my, Colonel Morrison, I believe it is you who are the subversive one, not those two boys of mine."

He gave a guilty grin. "You just have to wait for a while to tell it is all."

"The official OSS records are sealed until 2015, seventy years after the war in Europe ended. I'll be long gone by that time."

"Oh, you and your boys don't need to wait that long."

"Well, how long do you think we should wait?"

"Just until that son of a bitch Hoover retires or dies. That should do the trick."

"Oh, you are a devil."

"Indeed I am. That's why I married a countess."

She leaned over and gave him a kiss. They beamed at one another. And then she peered up, one last time, at Pointe du Hoc. Looking up at the massive rocky face and remnants of the German fortifications beyond, she paid silent tribute to her once-beloved husband—the father of her three boys—and the other brave souls who had fought and perished on this hallowed swath of land and sea on June 6, 1944.

AUTHOR'S NOTE

Bodyguard of Deception was conceived and written by the author as a work of historical fiction. Although the novel takes place during World War Two and incorporates actual historical figures, events, and locales, the novel is ultimately a work of the imagination and entertainment and should be read as nothing more. The names, characters, places, government entities, armed forces, religious and political groups, corporations, and incidents, as portrayed in the novel, are products of the author's imagination, or are used fictitiously, and are not to be construed as real.

With that disclaimer up front, I find it both fun and useful to give readers a little peek behind the curtain to separate fact from fiction, and real-life figures from invented, or highly fictionalized, characters. More than fifty actual historical figures populate the pages of *Bodyguard of Deception*, and many of these characters figure prominently in the events depicted in the novel. For these actual living and breathing historical figures, I have tried to recreate them and their worlds with meticulous fidelity. Where possible, I have taken their actual wartime quotes, or large portions of their actual words from transcripts, documents, and other quoted materials. At the same time, however, the book's characters are part of my overall imaginative landscape and are, therefore, ultimately the fictitious creations of the author, reflecting my personal research interests and biases.

At the top of the political hierarchy that existed during the global conflagration known as the Second World War were such flawed luminaries as Roosevelt and Churchill, and such indisputable monsters as Hitler, Stalin, Tojo, Himmler, and Goebbels. All of these larger-than-life actors, both good and bad, appear in the novel in some fashion, reflecting the global nature of the conflict, which no person on earth should ever forget claimed the lives of more than sixty million human beings in a mere five years.

With regard to the roster of American military personnel and civilians, the real-life figures in the book include the following: General Dwight D. Eisenhower, Supreme Commander of D-Day and Allied Forces in Europe; U.S. Secretary of War Henry L. Stimson; Julius Amberg, special assistant to Stimson; General George S. Patton, a key component of the Overlord FUSAG deception; Brigadier General B.M Bryan, Assistant Provost Marshal General responsible for governing the U.S. internment camps for German, Austrian, Italian, and Japanese prisoners of war; and General William H. Shedd, commander of the U.S. Army's 7th Service Command that assisted in the interview and roundup of escaped German POWs in Colorado and neighboring states.

Director J. Edgar Hoover, who ran the FBI with an iron fist from 1924-1972, really did devote considerable manpower to chasing down Nazi spies and escaped

German POWs during the war. Hoover's real-life assistant was indeed FBI Assistant Director Clyde Tolson, his protégé, longtime companion, and second-in-command, played by actor Armie Hammer in the Clint Eastwood-directed film *J. Edgar*. The legendary FBI director really did butt heads with, and do everything in his power to outmaneuver, his Ivy League-educated nemesis William "Wild Bill" Donovan, the American spymaster who created the Office of Strategic Services, the precursor to the modern CIA.

Ernie Pyle was, of course, the legendary Pulitzer Prize-winning American journalist writing about the "dogface" soldiers from North Africa through the liberation of Paris, and later in the Pacific. There really was a Chef Stratta at the Broadmoor Hotel during the war, and he was said to have kept the hotel's guests and officers from Camp Carson sumptuously well-fed despite widespread rationing of war-time foodstuffs. German-American Charles Lindbergh and his German friend Viscount de Stroelbergh did, in fact, stay together at the legendary Broadmoor Hotel before the war. Legendary jazz musicians Woody Herman and Count Basie were indeed kicking out lively bebop when Hitler was attempting to take over Europe, but to the best of the author's knowledge, they never played the Broadmoor Hotel together at the same time. Walter Winchell really was a leading American newspaper and radio gossip commentator during the war, and the legendary comedian Jack Benny certainly made Americans laugh during this epic period. And, of course, Babe Ruth, W.C. Fields, James Cagney, Clark Gable, John Wayne, Marlene Dietrich, Dizzy Gillespie, and Ingrid Bergman not only lived through and entertained the world during these tumultuous times, but all of them contributed to the war effort in various ways. In fact, Clark Gable flew combat missions in Europe as an observer-gunner in B-17 Flying Fortresses, earning the Air Medal and Distinguished Flying Cross for his efforts. It was said that Adolf Hitler favored Gable above all other Hollywood actors, and during the war he reportedly offered a sizable reward to anyone who could capture and bring the man that had made Rhett Butler a household name to him unscathed.

The actual military and intelligence figures representing the German war machine brought to life in the novel include the legendary Field Marshal Erwin J.E. Rommel, the Desert Fox, who was essentially forced by Hitler and the Nazi regime to take a cyanide suicide pill on October 14, 1944 for his alleged complicity in the July 20 attempt on the Führer's life; the anti-Hitler Admiral Wilhelm Canaris, chief of the *Abwehr*, arrested in July 1944 for his involvement in the July 20 plot, later murdered by the Nazis after a fake trial in April 1945; Canaris's murderous SS successor, *Brigadeführer* Walther Schellenberg; Otto Kretschmer, the most successful German U-boat commander of the war; Field Marshal Gerd von Rundstedt; Generals Wilhelm Keitel and Alfred Jodl of the *Oberkommando der Wehrmacht* (Supreme High Command of the German Armed Forces), both deservedly hung at Nuremberg; Rudolph Diels, the dueling-scar-faced head of the Gestapo in 1933-1934; Friedrich-Adolf Krummacher, the head of the OKW Intelligence Branch; and SS *Obersturmbannführer* Heinz Linge, Hitler's personal valet. And though they weren't actual combatants, let's not forget Hitler's mistress, Eva Braun, and his Reich Injection Master, Dr. Theodor Morell; Axis wartime propaganda broadcasters Axis Sally (Mildred Gillars) and Lord Hah-

Hah (William Joyce); or Dr. Rudolph Fischer of the Swiss Legation, whose job it was to protect the rights of German POWs in the U.S.

But if there are numerous real-life American and German characters in *Bodyguard of Deception*, it is the British who steal the show. Let's face it, no one does espionage like the Brits (WWII spymaster Ian Lancaster Fleming and his iconic literary creation James Bond anyone?). With that in mind, most of His Majesty the King's characters in the novel were either actual Double Cross spymasters or major contributors to the deception during the critical days leading up to the D-Day assault on Hitler's *Festung Europa*. Most prominent among them was Scottish MI5 intelligence officer Thomas Argyll "Tar" Robertson, whom the astute reader will recognize that I have only superficially disguised as Lieutenant Colonel Timothy Abernathy MacGregor, or "Tam" MacGregor. The real-life Tar Robertson really did wear a Glengarry cap and McKenzie tartan trews of the Seaforth Highlanders, was the brains behind Double Cross, and was universally well-liked by those who knew and worked with him. This bloody Yank, yours truly the author, was so enthralled by the real-life Tar Robertson that I had to adopt him as my own. For those who prefer the original, I can only apologize for my selfish American literary transgression.

In addition to my fictionalized version of Tar Robertson, other key British military and intelligence figures that truly did inhabit this particular time and place in history include: the fearsome, monocle-wearing, and larger-than-life Colonel Robin "Tin Eye" Stephens, commandant of the infamous Camp 020 at London's Latchmere House, who worked closely with Tar Robertson and truly was a first-rate interrogator as well as a raging xeno- and homo-phobe; Tin-Eye's clever assistants at Camp 020, Captains Short and Goodacre, as well as Dr. Harold Deardon, the resident psychiatrist; Major Sir John C. Masterman, distinguished Oxford don and chairman of the Double Cross Committee that ran and controlled German double agents living in England; Sir Frederick Morgan, Deputy Chief of Staff at Supreme Headquarters Allied Expeditionary Force in London; Field Marshal Sir Alan Brooke, Chief of the Imperial Staff; Sir William Stephenson, head of British Security Coordination in New York City; the unscrupulous Claude Dansey, deputy chief of MI6; and, last but not least, Field Marshal Bernard Law Montgomery, victor over Rommel at El Alamein and commander of all Allied ground forces during Operation Overlord from the initial landings until after the Battle of Normandy.

Most of these Brits (and Scots) were directly involved in the Overlord deception and Double Cross, and played an important role in the ultimate Allied victory. And yes, so too did the turned Double Cross agents like Dusko Popov, code-named Tricycle. In real-life, J. Edgar Hoover didn't like the Yugoslavian playboy and highly valued asset of Tar Robertson's British Security Service. But, as history has conclusively demonstrated, J. Edgar didn't like a lot of people. Especially, his flamboyant American OSS rival Wild Bill Donovan and members of British Intelligence during the war.

SOURCES AND ACKNOWLEDGEMENTS

To develop the story line, characters, and scenes for *Bodyguard of Deception*, I consulted hundreds of archival materials, non-fiction books, magazine and newspaper articles, blogs, Web sites, and numerous individuals and visited most every real-world location in person. These principal locations included numerous physical settings in London, Northeast Scotland, and Normandy as well as in Colorado Springs, Royal Gorge, and other plains and mountain areas east and west, respectively, of Colorado Springs. All in all, there are too many resources and locations to name here. However, I would be remiss if I didn't give credit to the key historical references upon which *Bodyguard of Deception* is based, as well as the critical individuals who dramatically improved the quality of the manuscript from its initial to its final stage. Any technical mistakes in the historical facts underpinning the novel, typographical errors, or examples of overreach due to artistic license, however, are the fault of me and me alone.

As a history aficionado who has always loved stories of the American West and World War Two, I have long wanted to write a novel that incorporated both of my research passions. That became possible when, several years ago, I read Ben Mcintyre's *Double Cross: The True Story of the D-Day Spies* (2012) and *Agent Zigzag: A True Story of Nazi Espionage, Love, and Betrayal* (2007) along with Arnold Krammer's eye-opening *Nazi Prisoners of War in America* (1996) Between these three well-crafted books, I learned about Double Cross and its cast of memorable British-controlled spies, while simultaneously discovering that, between 1943 and 1945, nearly a half million German prisoners were held in 511 POW camps across the United States, many of them in the American West. POW internment camps like Camp Trinidad in Southern Colorado and Camp Papago Park in Phoenix, Arizona, were the scenes of exciting mass German escapes and FBI manhunts, forced POW labor to alleviate the drain of able-bodied workers fighting overseas, and internal battles and political murders between Nazi and anti-Nazi German prisoners.

It wasn't long after digesting these three great historical reads that I envisioned a WWII spy novel that would be uniquely set in both the European theatre and my home state of Colorado. What came to me in my overactive filmographer's head was a kind of *Das Boot* (The Boat) meets *Eye of the Needle* meets *The Great Escape* with a hint of Arthur Penn's classic *The Chase* as well as *The Fugitive* thrown in for good measure. But I wanted another important twist that deviated from most WWII books and movies: I wanted my lead German to be a sympathetic character even though he was fighting for Hitler's Nazi Germany.

In writing the novel, there were many excellent historical works in addition to those listed above from which I drew facts and inspiration. The interested reader is referred to the following additional sources. The list is especially useful for those who would like to know more about Double Cross, D-Day, German U-boats, and German POW camps in the U.S., as well as the real-life WWII-era characters in *Bodyguard of Deception.*

General WWII Military and Espionage: *An Army at Dawn: The War in North Africa, 1942–1943* (2002), *The Day of Battle: The War in Sicily and Italy, 1943–1944* (2007), and *The Guns at Last Light: The War in Western Europe, 1944–1945* (2013) by Rick Atkinson; *The Second World War (2005)* by John Keegan; *D-Day June 6, 1944: The Climactic Battle of World War II* (1994) by Stephen Ambrose; *Deceiving Hitler: Double Cross and Deception in World War II* (2008) by Terry Crowdy; *The Spies Who Never Were: The True Story of the Nazi Spies Who Were Actually Allied Double Agents* (2006) by Hervie Haufler; *Camp 020: MI5 and the Nazi Spies* (2000) by R. "Tin Eye" Stephens; *The Game of Foxes: The Untold Story of German Espionage in the United States and Great Britain during World War II* (1971) by Ladislas Farago; *Operation Mincemeat: How a Dead Man and a Bizarre Plan Fooled the Nazis and Assured an Allied Victory* (2010) by Ben Mcintyre; *The Deceivers: Allied Military Deception in the Second World War* (2007) by Thaddeus Holt; *The Double-Cross System in the War, 1939-1945* (1972) by J.C. Masterman; *We Have Ways of Making You Talk...World War II British Interrogation Tactics: A Historical Moral Study* (2010) by Patrick Doerr; *Hoodwinking Hitler: The Normandy Deception* (1993) by William B. Breuer; *Hitler's Spies: German Military Intelligence in World War II* (2000) by David Kahn; *Wild Bill Donovan: The Spymaster Who Created the OSS and Modern American Espionage* (2011) by Douglas Waller; and *In Time of War: Hitler's Terrorist Attack on America* (2005) by Pierce O'Donnell.

German POWs in America: *Prisoners of War at Camp Trinidad, Colorado, 1943-1946: Internment, Intimidation, Incompetence, and Country Club Living* (2007) by Kurt Landsberger; *A German Odyssey: The Journal of a German Prisoner of War* (1991) by Helmut Hörner and Alan Kent Powell; *An Historical Analysis of the Psychological Trauma Suffered by German Prisoners of War held in the United States during World War II* (2001) by Amy C. Hudnall; *The Faustball Tunnel: German POWs in America and their Great Escape* (2006) by John Hammond Moore; *Prisoners on the Plains: German POWs in America* (1993) by Glenn Thompson; *Lone Star Stalag: German Prisoners of War at Camp Hearne* (2004) by Michael R. Waters; *The Enemy Among Us: POWs in Missouri during World War II* (2003) by David Fieldler; *Behind Barbed Wire: German Prisoners of War in Minnesota during World War II* (1998) by Anita Buck; *Hitler's Last Soldier in America* (1985) by Georg Gaertner with Arnold Krammer; and *Stalag Wisconsin: Inside WWII Prisoner-of-War Camps* (2002) by Betty Cowley.

German U-boats: the classic non-fiction work of *Das Boot* (The Boat, 1976) by Lothar-Günther Buchheim, which provides U-boat maneuver and warfare terminology; and http://uboat.net/, which provides extensive coverage of prominent German naval figures and U-boat battles, including detailed military reports of specific engagements.

I would also personally like to thank the following for their support and assistance. First and foremost, I would like to thank my wife Christine, an exceptional and highly professional book editor, who painstakingly reviewed and copy-edited the novel.

Second, I would like to thank my former literary agent, Cherry Weiner of the Cherry Weiner Literary Agency, for thoroughly reviewing, vetting, and copy-editing the manuscript, and for making countless improvements to the finished novel before I chose to publish the novel independently.

Third, I would like to thank Stephen King's former editor, Patrick LoBrutto, and Quinn Fitzpatrick, former book critic for the *Rocky Mountain News*, for thoroughly copy-editing the various drafts of the novel and providing detailed reviews.

I would also like to thank Austin and Anne Marquis, Betsy and Steve Hall, Governor Roy Romer, Ambassador Marc Grossman, Fred Taylor, Mo Shafroth and Barr Hogan, Tim and Carey Romer, Peter and Lorrie Frautschi, John Welch, Deirdre Grant Mercurio, Rik Hall, Toni Conte Augusta Francis, Brigid Donnelly Hughes, Peter Brooke, John and Ellen Aisenbrey, Margot Patterson, Cathy and Jon Jenkins, Kay and Charlie Fial, Vincent Bilello, Elizabeth Gardner, Danny Bilello and Elena Diaz-Bilello, Link Nicoll, and the other book reviewers and professional contributors large and small who have given generously of their time over the years, as well as to those who have given me loyal support as I have ventured on this incredible odyssey of suspense novel writing.

Lastly, I want to thank anyone and everyone who bought this book and my loyal fans and supporters who helped promote this work. You know who you are and I salute you.

ABOUT BESTSELLING, AWARD-WINNING AUTHOR SAMUEL MARQUIS AND FORTHCOMING TITLES

Samuel Marquis is a bestselling, award-winning suspense author. He works by day as a VP–Principal Hydrogeologist with an environmental firm in Boulder, Colorado, and by night as a spinner of historical and modern suspense yarns. He holds a Master of Science degree in Geology, is a Registered Professional Geologist in eleven states, and is a recognized expert in groundwater contaminant hydrogeology, having served as a hydrogeologic expert witness in several class action litigation cases. He also has a deep and abiding interest in military history and intelligence, specifically related to the Golden Age of Piracy, Plains Indian Wars, World War II, and the current War on Terror.

His first two thrillers, *The Slush Pile Brigade* and *Blind Thrust: A Mass Murder Mystery*, were both #1 *Denver Post* bestsellers for fiction, and his first three novels received national book award recognition. *The Slush Pile Brigade* was an award-winning finalist in the mystery category of the Beverly Hills Book Awards. *Blind Thrust* was the winner of the Foreword Reviews' Book of the Year (HM) and the Next Generation Indie Book Awards and an award-winning finalist of the USA Best Book Awards and Beverly Hills Book Awards (thriller and suspense). His third novel, *The Coalition*, was the winner of the Beverly Hills Book Awards for a political thriller.

Ambassador Marc Grossman, former U.S. Under Secretary of State, proclaimed, "In his novels *Blind Thrust* and *Cluster of Lies*, Samuel Marquis vividly combines the excitement of the best modern techno-thrillers, an education in geology, and a clarifying reminder that the choices each of us make have a profound impact on our precious planet." Former Colorado Governor Roy Romer said, "*Blind Thrust* kept me up until 1 a.m. two nights in a row. I could not put it down. An intriguing mystery that intertwined geology, fracking, and places in Colorado that I know well. Great fun." Kirkus Reviews proclaimed *The Coalition* an "entertaining thriller" and declared that "Marquis has written a tight plot with genuine suspense." James Patterson said *The Coalition* had "a lot of good action and suspense" and compared the novel to *The Day After Tomorrow*, the classic thriller by Allan Folsom. Other book reviewers have compared Book #1 of Marquis's World War Two Trilogy, *Bodyguard of Deception*, to the spy novels of John le Carré, Daniel Silva, Ken Follett, and Alan Furst.

Below is the list of suspense novels that Samuel Marquis has published or will be publishing in the near future, along with the release dates of both previously published and forthcoming titles.

The Nick Lassiter Series
The Slush Pile Brigade – September 2015 – The #1 Denver Post Bestseller and Award-Winning Finalist Beverly Hills Book Awards
The Fourth Pularchek – 2017-2018

The Joe Higheagle Series
Blind Thrust – October 2015 – The #1 Denver Post Bestseller; Winner Foreword Reviews' Book of the Year (HM) and Next Generation Indie Book Awards; Award-Winning Finalist USA Best Book Awards, Beverly Hills Book Awards, and Next Generation Indie Book Awards
Cluster of Lies – September 2016

The World War Two Trilogy
Bodyguard of Deception – March 2016
Altar of Resistance – January 2017

Standalone Espionage Thriller Novels
The Coalition – January 2016 – Winner Beverly Hills Book Awards

Thank You for Your Support!

To Order Samuel Marquis Books and Contact Samuel:
Visit Samuel Marquis's website, join his mailing list, learn about his forthcoming suspense novels and book events, and order his books at www.samuelmarquisbooks.com. Please send all fan mail (including criticism) to samuelmarquisbooks@gmail.com.

29975770R00179

Made in the USA
Middletown, DE
24 December 2018